The Rack II

Stories Inspired by Vintage Horror Paperbacks

Joe R Lansdale   Jonathan Maberry   Alyssa Alessi

Poppy Z. Brite   Christa Carmen   Mike Deady

Jamie Flanagan   Maxwell I. Gold   Larry Hinkle   Ai Jiang

Todd Keisling   Jenny Kiefer   Kristin Kirby

John Langan   Eric LaRocca   Jonathan Lees

Jessica McHugh   Lee Murray   B. D. Prince

Michael Rowe   Mike Sullivan   Morgan Sylvia

Tamika Thompson   Jessi Ann York

Edited by
Tom Deady

Foreword by
Sadie Hartmann

GREYMORE ▮ PUBLISHING

Greymore Publishing
PO Box 341
Vail AZ 85641
www.greymorepublishing.com

This is a collected work of fiction. The characters and events in this book
are fictitious. Any similarity to real persons, living or dead, is coincidental.

Cover Artwork and Design © 2025 by Lynne Hansen
Interior Design © 2025 by Greymore Publishing

ISBN-13: 979-8-9989589-1-5 (Paperback edition)

Contents

Introduction   vii
Sadie Hartmann

THE RAREST OF TERRORS (ALL I
COULD SEE)   1
Maxwell I. Gold

THE LAFFIN' MAN   3
Poppy Z. Brite

THE MALL   17
Lee Murray

COMEBACK KID   35
Christa Carmen

THE GREEN   55
Michael Rowe

DAUGHTER OF DOGS   87
Jessi Ann York

HEAD HUNTER   109
B.D. Prince

AS THE CIRCUS LEAVES TOWN   125
Morgan Sylvia

THE CREAK ON THE ATTIC STAIRS   151
Tamika Thompson

BATS! BATS! BATS! (FUN FOR THE WHOLE
FAMILY)   169
Jonathan Maberry

BLACK THUMB   195
Larry Hinkle

MIDNIGHT RIDER   207
Mike Deady

THE LIGHT YOU FOLLOW CAN BURN   225
Jessica McHugh

THE WASH   255
Kristin Kirby

BEEPBEEPBEEPBEEP   275
Jenny Kiefer

WE HAVE (NEVER) BEEN HERE BEFORE   297
Jonathan Lees

RED GOD WAITING   311
Ai Jiang

A SERPENT'S THIRST   323
Alyssa Alessi

THE END OF THE JETTY   335
Mike Sullivan

SICKLE-SHAPED CLAW   345
Eric LaRocca

THE WOODHILL WET NURSE   359
Todd Keisling

THE CARTOGRAPHER OF BLADES AND
STARS, OF FLESH AND AGONY   379
John Langan

BISTRITZ   421
Jamie Flanagan

BY THE HAIR OF THE HEAD   435
Joe R. Lansdale

Afterword   453
Tom Deady

Tom Deady (Editor)   455
Also by Tom Deady   457

Introduction

Sadie Hartmann

suicide, death, dog, folklore, october
KNIFE attic haunted, ghosts, killer BLOOD
small town, family, urban legend,
nostalgia, summer, relationships, creepy,

coming-of-age, dead, **memories**,
the circus marriage cemeteries **"good for her"**
trauma **mall,** pet, pranks missing kids
FEAR childhood, domestic drama, magic
violence, kids, body grief, treasures,
circus magicians, oddities, home basement
Halloween, infidelity, horror, gun
couples, bats, road, cursed objects,
ritualistc **SUMMER** BOOGEYMAN CHURCH
sacrifice **intrusive thoughts, teens**
medical procedures creature-feature
serial killers maggots
vengeance car accident HOMETOWN

Spin Cycle

As soon as I walked inside the laundromat, I realized I forgot
my phone. I patted my pockets with my free hand one more
time, and sure enough, I definitely left it on the charger back
home.

I groaned. So much time to kill! No phone. No headphones. No escape.

The place was pretty empty. Fluorescent lights flickered overhead. The machines droned on like insects. But at least it was warm and there were some available seats. I filled up two big washing machines with laundry, set my beat-up old baskets on top of the machines, and put in the appropriate amount of change. I wandered past the detergent machine, past the bulletin board full of curling flyers. That's when I saw it: a sagging wire rack in the corner, pushed up against the wall like it didn't want to be noticed.

A hand-lettered sign above it read: **FREE BOOKS**.

And at first glance I could tell, every single one was horror. The rack was packed with well-worn paperbacks boasting classic, deliciously lurid '80s covers: shadowy silhouettes holding rusty tools and screaming faces, A young man mowing a lawn in front of what looked like a haunted house, a scary dummy sitting in someone's lap–eyes bugging out of its sockets, and the titles were just as tantalizing,

Sickle-Shaped Claw by Eric LaRocca

The Woodhill Wet Nurse by Todd Keisling

Midnight Rider by Mike Deady

The Hair of the Head by Joe R. Lansdale

Bats! Bats! Bats! (Fun for the Whole Family) by Jonathan Maberry

Others were quiet, subtle things.

The End of the Jetty by Mike Sullivan

Red God Waiting by Ai Jiang

The Creak on the Attic Stairs by Tamika Thompson

I started flipping through them. Reading the first lines. Feeling that strange thrill you only get when a story grabs you by the throat without warning.

One story was called, **Comeback Kid** by Christa Carmen.

Introduction

The cover used to be red, but it faded to a dusty rose. There was a girl on the cover with her arms in a "V" wearing a gymnast's leotard. The coaches watching her from a distance had menacing expressions on their faces.

Another had a cover scrawled in sharpie, no author name, just the words **THIS BOOK IS CURSED** written in all caps. The back was blank. I flipped to the title page which read, **The Cartographer of Blades and Stars, Of Flesh and Agony** by John Langan. John Langan, where had I heard that name before?

Daughter of Dogs by Jessi Ann York looked promising, a woman in army fatigues crouched down with her arms wrapped around a friendly-faced dog, but something in the tilt of her chin and the glint in her eyes unsettled me.

I kept pulling more off the rack. It was like they had been waiting for someone. Waiting for *me*. Each one with its own flavor of fear and yet, repeated words and phrases jumping out at me…

suicide, death, dog, folklore, October

KNIFE

Something in the attic, haunted, ghosts, killer **BLOOD** small town, family, urban legend, nostalgia, summer, family relationships, creepy, coming-of-age, dead, memories,

the circus

cemeteries

marriage "good for her"

trauma, mall, pet, pranks missing kids

FEAR, childhood, domestic drama, magic violence, kids, body grief, treasures, circus magicians, oddities, home basement Halloween, infidelity, horror, gun

Ritualistic sacrifice

couples, bats, road, cursed objects

SUMMER

BOOGEYMAN

CHURCH
intrusive thoughts, teens
medical procedures, creature-feature, serial killers, maggots, vengeance, car accident
HOMETOWN
By the time the dryer buzzed, I'd read more horror in one sitting than I had in months. These stories were raw, unfiltered, and pretty fucking scary! Urban legends, nightmare fuel, unforgettable.

The kind of stories you whisper because you're afraid someone might be listening. This anthology is a bit like that wire rack. A collection of tales you weren't supposed to find —but did. Some are short and arresting. Some are jagged. All of them have teeth.

I felt like a woman possessed and I found myself scratching some notes in the margins of each book:

Sickle-Shaped Claw by Eric LaRocca- oddities, world traveler, archeology, found objects and treasures, eccentric older men, interviews, memories, haunted, the fear of being forgotten

Head Hunter by B. D. Prince- Teacher/student relationships, married couples, Father's Day, intrusive thoughts, oddities, cursed artifacts, collector, folklore, wealthy people, trophies

Bats! Bats! Bats! (Fun for the Whole Family) by Jonathan Maberry- Small town, Halloween, bats, coming-of-age, teenage boys, family relationships, seeking joy in horror & Halloween, part of Maberry's connected universe of stories and novels, domestic abuse

By the Hair of the Head by Joe R. Lansdale- Lighthouses,

Introduction

writers, witches, magic and magicians, ventriloquism, grief, possession, cursed

The Rarest of Terrors by Maxwell I. Gold- Poetry

Comeback Kid by Christa Carmen- career athletes, gymnastics, coaching, psychological childhood trauma, Olympic training, competing, isolation, secrets & lies, revenge,"Good for her"

Red God Waiting by Ai Jiang- married couples, domestic drama, infidelity, gods and demons, ritualistic sacrifice, vengeance

Daughter of Dogs by Jessi Ann York- Tennessee, Welcome home, Vietnam, K-9 units, photography, feral woman, Women's Army Core, alcoholism

The End of the Jetty by Mike Sullivan- coming-of-age, young protagonist, East Coast/Atlantic Ocean, summer vibes, creature-feature

The Mall by Lee Murray- The Mall, McDonalds, marriage, domestic drama, parenting, infidelity, distracted, missing kid, creepy child, holy shit that was scary

The Laffin' Man by Poppy Z. Brite- The Mall, nostalgia, friendship, coming-of-age, novelty gifts, death, grief, October, Halloween season, HEAVY, suicide and homicide, death of a child, gun violence

The Creak on the Attic Stairs by Tamika Thompson- death in the family, autumn, gun violence, coming-of-age, family, ghosts, attics, death of a child, gangs

Bistritz by Jamie Flanagan- human experiments, Romania, body horror, medical procedures, surgery, morgue, art, artist, cold, melancholy

A Serpent's Thirst by Alyssa Alessi- Patriarchal, feminist, village, first blood, religious, horror/trauma, snakes, lust, monsters

Black Thumb by Larry Hinkle- gardening, death of a dog, grief over the loss of a pet, burial of a pet, Pet Sematary vibes

The Light You Follow Can Burn by Jessica McHugh- divorce, unrequited love, memories, emotional cruelty, pet death (cat), burning it (alive), dead baby, cult, sacrificial offerings

beepbeepbeepbeep by Jenny Kiefer- Family, new baby brother, siblings, digital toy, nostalgia, coming-of-age, child protagonist, creepy! A favorite story

Midnight Rider by Mike Deady- Halloween Night, friends, teenagers, pranks, ghosts, amusement park, October, Ray Bradbury, suicide, carnival, grief

As the Circus Leaves Town by Morgan Sylvia- Summer, teens, carnival, small towns, magicians, memories, big top, carnies, magic, blood, circus

We Have [Never] Been Here Before by Jonathan Lees- film, haunted house, family, road trip, vacation, dog, car accident, child death, Jesus, demon, killer, family, crucifix, death

The Green by Michael Rowe- Summer, small town, cemetery, coming-of-age, memories, nostalgia, blood, gossip,

Introduction

mothers, animal deaths, boyhood, church, dog, magic, neighbors, coming-of-age, folklore, dead body, cursed objects

The Wash by Kristin Kirby- Arizona, hometown, childhood home, nostalgia, death of a parent, memories, bicycle, local legend, urban legend, ghosts, serial killer, child killer, nightmares, teens

The Woodhill Wet Nurse by Todd Keisling- Kentucky, college-age, spring break, stepfather, chores, job, boogeyman, serial killer, small town, abandoned house, maggots, corpse, pranks, urban legend, creepy children

The Cartographer of Blades and Stars, Of Flesh and Agony by John Langan- serial killer, vengeance, vigilante justice, victims, abandoned mental hospital, teens, murder, animal cruelty/death, violent, graphic, bloody, sister, grief, knife

You forgot your phone.
The spin cycle has started.
You've got time for one. Maybe two.
Just don't stay too long after the lights flicker.
Things in places like this... they notice. And maybe, they'll never let you leave.
-Sadie Hartmann
July 28th, 2025

❧ ❧ ❧

Sadie Hartmann aka Mother Horror is the co-owner of the monthly horror fiction subscription company, Night Worms and the Bram Stoker Awards® winning author of 101 Horror Books to Read Before You're Murdered from Page Street Publishing. Her second book, Feral & Hysterical:

Sadie Hartmann

Mother Horror's Ultimate Reading Guide to Dark and
Disturbing Fiction will be released August 2025.
She lives in the PNW with her husband of 20+ years where
they stare at Mt Rainier, eat street tacos, and hang out with
their 3 kids.

The Rarest of Terrors
(All I Could See)
Maxwell I. Gold

The rarest of terrors
was all I could see,
and hear,
from claxon screams
trumpeting across vast infinites
and wild dreamscapes to pathetic campfires;
and humbled spaces in cold libraries.
All that I could see
were the vile phantoms,
ghosts of children,
polyester film-coated ghouls with videocassette-coffins
pulled by junkyard-possessed cars,
and old gods
beseeched by strange stories
who wandered through slaughterhouse canyons
beneath slumber-brittle songs of basement dungeons
in the darkest nights;
and the rarest of terrors
which clawed and skulked along forest beds,

while dead leaves crunched under boot and bone as chilled
cackles of Yazoo Witches snickered
at the moon nestled in the darkest alleyways of my heart and
brain, too frail to withstand
     another trek
        down Slay Hollow
where the eyes of an ancient lighthouse
never told the truth,
never offered a way home,
except a faint spectral twinkle luring me down
     Maltby's Stairs,
        one step closer toward
the rarest of terror
on the other side of a cracked,
Silver Bridge whose dim, haunting prophecy flapped
in the stars
 – a reminder of all I could see –
the rarest of terrors, yet to come.

❧ ❧ ❧

Maxwell I. Gold is a Jewish-American author and poet with
an extensive body of work comprising over 350 poems since
2017. His writings have earned a place alongside many
literary luminaries in the speculative fiction genre. His work
has appeared in numerous literary journals, magazines, and
anthologies. Maxwell's work has been recognized with
multiple nominations including the Eric Hoffer Award,
Pushcart Prize, and Bram Stoker Awards. Find him and his
work at www.thewellsoftheweird.com.

The Laffin' Man

Poppy Z. Brite

IF YOU DIDN'T GROW up in the 1970s, it's impossible to overstate the importance of the indoor shopping mall. Maybe not for everyone, but for me and my few nerdy friends. For one thing, it was the first place we were allowed to go on our own. Parents never imagined that there could be any danger inside those retail palace walls. That alone made for a heady experience, strolling through the place just like grownups. There was real magic there in the mall, if you could find it, and not all that magic was benign.

But I'm getting ahead of myself. For the most part, College Square Mall *was* a safe place for twelve-year-olds, safe from the perverts our parents imagined and the bigger, meaner kids we knew were out there. It was deliciously air-conditioned in the summer, and whether we had money or not, there was always something interesting to look at. Seventy-nine stores! Ten restaurants! For a while it was even rumored that they were going to run a small roller coaster through the place, or maybe install an ice-skating rink, though neither materialized.

I didn't need roller coasters or skating rinks. I was happy

just sifting through all the interesting stores with my best friend, Alan. We loved the Chinese shop full of golden statues and bright silks, the Record Bar where you could page through a big book of all the songs in the world hoping to find the one you'd heard on the radio, the hobby shop with its model train that ran the length of the store, the Spencer's where we received a crude sex education via black-light posters and novelty gifts whose purposes were unclear but intriguing. There was no food court per se – the ten restaurants were scattered around the mall – but there was a counter stand where you could get soft-serve ice cream and pizza by the slice. As far as we were concerned, we could have lived very happily there.

Alan was a skinny boy with vivid blue eyes. He seemed always to be moving, plotting. Even when he was perfectly still, you sensed that his skin crawled on his bones. You didn't just go to the mall with Alan; you went on a mission, hunting for God knows what. He might dare you to go fishing for pennies in the fountain (I didn't) or flip off the mean cashier at the drugstore (I didn't) or spend five minutes in the ladies' lingerie shop (I did, braving a serious stinkeye from the saleslady on duty). He claimed he had taught the mynah bird at the pet store to say "shitballs," though I never heard it do so.

My favorite place in the mall store was the Little Professor bookshop. Reading was my refuge from bullies, boredom, and my own parents' unhappiness, and I could spend hours lost among those shelves. Alan was smart, but he wasn't a big reader. His favorite store, the Tinder Box, was mostly dedicated to the purchase, storage, and consumption of tobacco. It's hard to believe now, but back then anyone over sixteen could buy a box of imported cigarettes and light up right there in the mall. The Tinder Box was smaller and darker than most of the other stores. The glass cases held row after row of cigars lined up like tiny mummies in their colorfully printed boxes. The names were deliciously exotic to us: Puros Indios, Macanudo, Padron. There were humidors, meerschaum pipes, leather tobacco pouches. The scent of the place was rich and brown and deeply *male* somehow. I didn't like the place much, but I liked that scent. Alan did too. It only occurred to me years later that perhaps it smelled like the father he no longer had.

What fascinated him most in this shop, though, had nothing to do with tobacco. The Tinder Box also carried a few gift items that were, again, stereotypically male: beer steins, pocket flasks, and the like. The oddest one, Alan's favorite, was the Laffin' Man.

I've since learned that these things were sold in novelty shops around the country during the 1970s. Maybe you've seen them at flea markets or on eBay. At the time, I thought they existed nowhere but the Tinder Box in College Square Mall, and were solely intended for horrifying me as much as they amused my best friend. The Laffin' Man was really nothing but a disembodied face made of some glossy brownish-pink stuff that wasn't quite wood and wasn't quite plastic, some substance that was wrinkled and shriveled like an apple-head doll. His nose and cheeks were drunkenly florid, his lips parted in a bucktoothed imbecile's grin. Wispy gray hair in what used to be called a Dutch boy cut straggled out from under an Alpine hat of green felt. He hung on the wall, and beneath his chin was a short necktie with a sticker that said PULL ME. When you pulled on the tie, the Laffin' Man came to life.

The first time it happened, I almost cried. We had wandered into the Tinder Box because it was there, just as we explored most of the seventy-nine shops sooner or later. I thought it looked like a dull place – we didn't smoke and were too young for the line of manly gifts – but Alan made a

5

beeline for the display wall where the Laffin' Man hung. I wrinkled my nose when I saw what he was looking at. "That's gross."

Alan grinned. "What do you think happens if I pull it?"

"I don't want to – "

He gave the tie a healthy yank. The Laffin' Man sprung to life, his tiny eyes blinking open and shut, his tongue wagging obscenely. From his mouth spilled brainless mechanical laughter: "Ah-ha-ha-ha-HAH-HAH-HAH. Ah-ha-ha-ha-HAAAAAAAAH."

I backed up without thinking and bumped into a stack of cigar boxes. The man who ran the store glanced over at us in irritation, but he was halfway through a paperback titled *Lusty Librarians* and kicking us out would have required some effort. "Look, everybody!" Alan crowed to nobody. "Matt Alston is having a spaz attack!"

"I'm not having a spaz attack," I said. "It's just gross, that's all." Privately I thought, *I will see that thing behind my eyelids tonight, after the lights are off.*

The Laffin' Man was displayed with an assortment of his equally awful compatriots, some of whom could spit a stream of water at you. There was a Laffin' Lady in a flow-ered kerchief, a Laffin' Leprechaun with a red scruff of beard, a one-eyed Laffin' Pirate, even a Laffin' Santa Claus that made me want to swear off Christmas. Alan pulled the ties of all the ones he could reach and stood there grinning as their wheezy laughter washed over us.

"I think they're great," he said. "If I had one, I guess I'd laugh all the time."

Although I didn't like the Laffin' Heads, I could see why Alan did. They appealed to his love of chaos and absurdity, and he found their ugliness endearing because he believed he was ugly too. He often said so, very casually, as if it were a simple fact with no emotional resonance. I never understood it. His blue eyes were fringed with long dark lashes, his grin lit up a room, his body was graceful even at that gawky age. I thought he was beautiful, though torture would not have dragged that fact out of me. I was vaguely aware that some boys liked other boys, but I knew it wasn't supposed to happen and I never thought of it in connection with myself.

Even so, we began visiting the Tinder Box whenever we were at the mall, and I began plotting to get Alan a Laffin' Head for his upcoming thirteenth birthday. It wouldn't be all that easy. We weren't poor kids, but we weren't rich either, and the basic Laffin' Man – no special accessories, no spitting – retailed for $29.95. That was two months' allowance for me, or six lawns mowed for the next-door neighbor who didn't always remember to pay me. I swore off candy and started keeping all my pocket change in a jar marked **L.M.**

One reason Alan and I spent so much time at the mall was that we didn't like hanging out at either of our houses. My parents seldom argued in front of me, but the atmosphere in our home was perpetually icy, both of them with evil words poised on their lips to say when I wasn't around. Alan's house … well, one day I knocked on his door, and when no one answered, I let myself in. The living room curtains were closed, the room dark and still. As my eyes adjusted to the dimness, I saw Alan's mother sitting on the sofa. She was the prettiest mother I'd ever met, with eyes as blue as Alan's, but since her husband's death in a car accident a year ago, lines of grief had etched themselves in her face. There was a wine bottle on the coffee table in front of her and an empty glass beside it, bleary with fingerprints. I hoped she was asleep. I made it halfway across the room before she said, "Hello, Matt."

My mouth was suddenly dry, but I managed to say, "Hi, Mrs. Malloy."

"Are you scared of me? Please don't be scared."

Her eyelids were heavy, but she didn't sound drunk. I guessed she was a pretty experienced drinker by now. "No ma'am," I said. "I'm sorry."

I wasn't sure what I was apologizing for, but she apparently took it as an expression of sympathy. "Sorry, sorry, sorry," she said. "Everyone says they're so so so sorry, and I know they are trying to be kind. They really *are* sorry for what happened to my husband. But then they get to go on with their lives, just as if ours hadn't been shattered."

I couldn't think of anything to say, so I kept my mouth shut. Two decades later, a partner would tell me this was one of my gifts.

"The other driver's insurance was very generous," she continued. "This house is paid for, Alan will go to any college he likes, and I'll never have to work again. So I sit here and I drink wine and I don't look out the window. And Matt, do you know what?"

Wordlessly, I shook my head.

"I wish I *could* work. I'd love to have something to do. But whenever I go out in public, I can't stop crying."

This was too much for me. I fled the shadowy room and ran down the hall to Alan's bedroom. When I opened the door, he looked up at me, startled, from where he sat at his desk drawing on a pad of paper. Our eyes met, and I knew *he* knew how his mother had just waylaid me. It seemed unkind to acknowledge this, though, so I just said, "What are you drawing?"

He smiled sheepishly and turned the pad around. Done in Ticonderoga pencil, a decent likeness of the Laffin' Man leered at me.

❧ ❧ ❧

In retrospect, one of the scariest parts of being a kid is that you don't have the life experience to know when an adult is being inappropriate with you. *Inappropriate* doesn't always mean sex stuff, either. My brief interaction with Mrs. Malloy wasn't sexual, but it made me feel awkward and stupid, as if I should have known the right things to say but had failed miserably.

Instead of putting me off the friendship, though, this drew me even closer to Alan. For me, it had just been a weird encounter at a friend's house. He had to live with those curtains closed against the daylight, that sorrowful voice in the dimness and the sour-sweet smell of wine. I didn't kid myself that I could save him, but I vowed to at least distract him as much as possible. That included the Laffin' Man, who now resided in a gift box in my closet. I had purchased him with a summer's worth of chores and abstinence from sweets. I didn't much like having him in my closet – my imagination detailed how he might awaken me in the middle of the night, wheezing that mechanical laughter into the silence of my bedroom – but Alan's birthday wasn't until Halloween. I finally took his batteries out and stowed them in my nightstand drawer.

We both started seventh grade that fall. It was much larger than our elementary school, with lots of kids keen to establish their place in the pecking order. When we met up after school one day, Alan had a black eye that hadn't been there that morning. "You fall off the monkey bars again?" I asked him.

"Nah. I called Todd Watkins a shit-for-brains."

"Todd Watkins *is* a shit-for-brains." He was also a nose tackle on the football team.

"Well, Matt, *you* know that and *I* know that, but somehow or other, I failed to make Todd see it that way."

Instead of walking home, we decided to take the bus to

College Square, where kids like Todd had little interest in hanging out. (This would change the following year with the addition of a video game arcade, but I had stopped going there by then.) We made our usual visit to the Tinder Box, where I was afraid I would somehow give away my birthday secret. I needn't have worried; even Alan's admiration of the Laffin' Man was half-hearted that day. I thought he was upset about his shiner, but when we rested on one of the benches by the fountain, I found out otherwise.

"I think my mom's sick," he said to his folded hands. "She takes all these pills and she sleeps most of the time. Last night she tried to make a roast and fell asleep while it was in the oven. I didn't even know anything was wrong until the smoke alarm went off."

"Did you call the fire department?"

"No. I saw the smoke coming out of the oven and turned it off. Had to open all the windows. She never even woke up."

"I guess she's really sad since … you know, your dad."

Alan turned to look at me. Under the mall's fluorescent lights, his complexion was very pale. "I'm sad too, Matt," he said. "I'm sad all the time. But I don't want to *die*, you know?"

I nodded, feeling lost in deep water.

"She seems like she wants to die. And then I don't know what I'd do."

I wished I could put my arms around him. There was no code of conduct that allowed two boys to touch, and for a moment the pain of this was razor-sharp and blinding. Instead, I offered the only thing I could think of: "Come over for dinner. See if you can spend the night." My parents might despise each other, but my mother had a good dinner on our table every evening. I hadn't yet come to understand that this was not a right but a privilege.

"I better not. I should make sure she's okay."

"We can go by your house first. Take the bus. You can check on her, then walk home with me."

Alan hesitated, then nodded. "All right. Yeah, I'd like that."

Alan's mother was relatively steady that afternoon, and gave Alan permission to sleep over at my house. The trappings of October were beginning to appear in our neighborhood, blaze-orange pumpkins on porches, paper ghosts in windows, cardboard skeletons on doors. We tramped through crunchy brown leaves in the gutter, found half-rotted wild persimmons on the ground and tossed them at each other. My mother had made a huge, cheesy lasagna with garlic bread, and we were allowed to eat our portions in front of the TV while she and my father dined silently at the table.

Our sleepovers usually involved staying up all night, or trying to. Tonight we were both tired and snuggled into our sleeping bags by eleven. We whispered back and forth in the dark for a while, then fell silent. I thought Alan was asleep until I heard a muffled sob. And then I discovered that there was a way for boys to touch each other.

Alan and I weren't sexual that night, but we were tender in a way that grown men seldom experience. It was enough just to wipe the tears from his face, to wrap my arms around him and pull his head into the crook of my shoulder. We held each other all night, sometimes dozing off, sometimes coming half-awake and pressing our foreheads together, almost exchanging dreams as we faded back to sleep. I am an old man now and have had many partners, many cherished relationships, but I've never spent a night more intimate than that one.

I always thought Alan was incredibly lucky to have been born on Halloween. He got presents, cake, *and* trick-or-treat candy. I gave him his gift after school that day. I couldn't find any wrapping paper at my house, so I'd wrapped it in the

Sunday funny pages to at least give the package some color. Though it was after three, Mrs. Molloy was asleep in her room.

"Do you want to wait and open it after your mom gets up?" I asked.

"Oh – no. No, she already gave me my presents this morning."

His cheeks colored a little, and his eyes wouldn't meet mine. I got the idea Alan's mother might have forgotten his birthday altogether. The thought made me want to cry. "Okay, open it now," I said hurriedly.

He ripped into it, and when the picture on the box came into view, his jaw dropped. "No way!" he shouted. "Matt! How did you manage to do this?"

"Oh, I sold some drugs around school. Heroin, cocaine, that kind of thing."

Alan was too enthralled by his gift to acknowledge my lame joke. He removed the box lid and carefully, almost reverently, lifted out his very own Laffin' Man.

"He's so cool," he breathed. "We gotta hang him up and try him out."

We searched out a hammer and a nail, and soon the Laffin' Man had taken pride of place on Alan's wall. "You should get the first pull," Alan said, nudging me.

"Nope. It's all yours."

He pulled the absurd little tie, and the Laffin' Man came to life, eyes blinking, tongue churning. "Ahhhh-HA-HA-HA-HA-HAAAAAH. Ahhhh-HO-HO-HO-hah-hee-hee."

I couldn't help taking a step backward, but Alan was laughing too. He threw his arms around me and planted a goofy, smacking kiss on my cheek. I saw genuine happiness in his face, and I was glad.

Then it was time to get into our costumes. Alan was a red devil, plastic pitchfork included, and I was a kind of robot-bug creature with antennae made of toilet paper rolls spray-painted silver. Though we hadn't discussed it, we both knew this would probably be our last year trick-or-treating. Some of our classmates had already declared it babyish. Tonight I didn't care; as we started out into the crisp, dark evening, every worry lifted from my shoulders.

There was magic afoot that Halloween night, the ordinary magic you take for granted as a child and spend the rest of your years wishing you could relive. Every porch was decked with fire-kindled jack-o'-lanterns, cardboard gravestones, even a few bloody corpses sprawled on hay bales or lurking under trees. The harvest moon was as large and as orange as you could hope for. The other trick-or-treaters were mostly younger than us and friendlier than our classmates. Everyone was generous with the candy. Alan kept poking me in the butt with his pitchfork, which to a couple of pre-adolescent boys was the height of hilarity. I think that must have been the last great night of my childhood.

The first terrible day of my adulthood came not long afterward.

It was a Saturday morning, and Alan and I were going to meet up and do something or other – ride bikes, I think. Some excuse to be together. I felt pretty good. The weekend was young, Thanksgiving was on the way, and after that, you could almost taste Christmas. No one answered my knock at Alan's door, but by now I was used to going on in anyway.

The living room was dim, the curtains drawn as usual. When I first saw Mrs. Malloy, I thought she was asleep on the couch again (*asleep* was what I said in my mind; it seemed kinder than *passed out*). I had to get several steps closer to her before I saw the blood on her face. She had lain on her left side and shot herself in the right temple. Her eyes were wide open, fixed on me. I felt accused by them somehow. Blood soaked the couch cushion and dripped onto the floor, cutting a vivid crimson path across the worn boards.

"Alan," I called. "Alan!"

Listening, I became aware of a noise farther into the house. If I hadn't been so shocked by the sight of Mrs. Malloy, I would have heard it sooner.

The Laffin' Man was laughing.

He went on and on doing it, as if someone were pulling his tie over and over again. I pelted down the hall and tore Alan's bedroom door open. Alan lay on his bed with his arms flung back above his head and his legs half-sprawled over the side. I was afraid to approach him, helpless not to.

Mrs. Malloy had shot him in the chest – twice, I think I heard later. She must have wanted to make sure he didn't suffer. Regardless of her intention, she had botched the job; Alan was still alive, blood pulsing from the wound, soaking his sheets. His eyes rolled toward me, marked my presence. His hand groped for mine.

"Ah-ha-ha-ha-ha-ha," he whispered. "Ah-ha-ha-ha-ha-ha."

I whirled away from him, toward the Laffin' Man on the wall. How I hated that face now! Its filthy tongue flapped, its piggy eyes blinked, and I seized it from the wall and flung it out the window. The window was closed, but I threw it hard enough to break the glass. That was what alerted a neighbor, and that was how they found the three of us – Mrs. Malloy dead, Alan dying, and me crouched in the corner hysterical, sobbing, "Make him shut up. Make him shut up."

❦ ❦ ❦

Mrs. Malloy had used a small-caliber pistol, and for a few hours the surgeons thought they might be able to save Alan. His body was too damaged, though, and he died early that evening. I didn't say anything when my parents told me. They thought I was being very mature about the whole thing. I heard them talking about it, and for once they didn't sound as if they were being forced to speak to each other under threat of durance vile. They never did end up divorcing, for whatever that's worth. Probably not much. Plenty of people stay together because it's too scary not to, or just too much trouble.

I don't know what happened to the Laffin' Man after I threw him out the window. Maybe the neighbor picked him up, or maybe the garbagemen got him. I never saw him again. For a long time I almost forgot about him, but as I age, the memories of my youth grow clearer. I went back to College Square Mall a few years ago, half wanting and half dreading to revisit the Tinder Box, but it was gone. So were most of the other stores. The malls are corpses now, sent to their graves by the convenience of online shopping.

What was the Laffin' Man? Did he truly hang there in that nightmare house just laughing and laughing away with no hand to pull his tie, laughing and laughing as my friend who had loved him lay dying? Was he the vessel for some dim and sadistic consciousness, brought to life by the unhappiness in that house? I don't know. I *do* know that I think of him on the long sleepless nights which seem to come more often now that I am old, and on the longest of those nights, I pray that I will never again hear him laughing.

Oh, please don't let me hear him laughing.

Please.

❧ ❧ ❧

Poppy Z. Brite is the longtime pen name of Billy Martin. Since beginning his career in the small-press magazine *The Horror Show* in 1985, he has published eight novels including *Lost Souls*, *Exquisite Corpse*, and the Liquor series, as well as several short story collections and assorted nonfiction work. Brite is also the editor of the erotic horror anthologies *Love in Vein* and *Love in Vein 2*. In addition to writing, he runs the online curio shop PZBaubles New Orleans, specializing in vintage Tarot cards, quirky jewelry, religious objects, and more. He lives in New Orleans with his husband, the artist Grey Cross, and their cats.

The Mall

Lee Murray

MY WIFE EXHALED, slow and deep. "Fine," she said.

Yeah, I didn't come down in the last shower of rain. The tone. The clipped ending. The speed of delivery. Quite obviously, it was not fine. Nothing was fine, no matter how many times I'd said I'm sorry.

The car keys jangling in her hand, Ruthann gave a weary shrug. "Whatever. Come, don't come. I don't care." She picked up her purse and slung it over her shoulder. As a writer and scholar of the human condition, I prided myself on being a keen observer of character, that and fourteen years of marriage had taught me a thing or two; her body language was way too snappy to be nonchalant. It didn't take a rocket scientist to work out that she cared very much.

"Course, we'll come," I said. "Won't we, buddy?" I ruffled our seven-year-old's mop of hair, making those unruly ginger curls even more unruly.

Matty twisted away from me, like I'd jabbed him with a hot poker. "Gerroff, Dad. I'm not a baby."

I whipped my hand back, as if *he* were the hot poker. "Sure. I know that."

17

Ruthann rolled her eyes. She took her old jacket off the hook, the light blue one, and helped Matty thread his good arm into the sleeve, rolling up the cuff to reveal his hand, then she buttoned the coat over his cast and sling. "There we go," she said cheerfully. She ruffled Matty's hair.

He didn't pull away.

I fixed on a smile. What else could I do? The responsible parent, she was making a point.

"It's a girl's coat," Matty whined.

"No one will know, buddy," I said. "It'll keep you warm. You can take it off once we get to the mall, okay?"

"Mom—"

"Dad will carry it for you," Ruthann said, forestalling any further grumbling.

While Ruthann locked up the house, I rushed out ahead of them, so I could help Matty into his booster seat. I lifted him in and buckled his seatbelt – taking care not to bump his injured arm – and felt a sharp rush of tenderness. I hadn't even wanted kids. That had been Ruthann's idea, but the moment Matty arrived, with those adorable dimples, the tiny tuft of hair, the way he killed me with his giggles, I couldn't help but love the little guy.

He was a great kid. The best.

And I was a shit dad. I didn't deserve him. The broken arm was my fault. I'd lost track of time, hadn't I, been on the phone to a coworker when I should have been picking him up from the school bus. He'd almost made it home too, only he'd been in a hurry to get away from the bus bullies – kids who think it's fun to torture a kid with ginger hair – and he'd slipped on a patch of ice and fallen awkwardly. I mean, there was a chance he might've fallen anyway, even if I had been there, although I didn't say that to Ruthann. As far as she was concerned, I was supposed to meet him, and I didn't, and now Matty had a broken arm. And then she'd found out which co-worker I'd been talking to, and all hell had broken loose.

The whole Carly-thing wasn't a big deal. I wasn't having an affair. I hadn't actually *done* anything. It was just a bit of casual flirting – a few naughty phone calls and some harmless office banter. Everyone did it, didn't they? But Ruthann didn't see it that way. Said it was crossing some line. We'd had a massive row about it, the night of the accident, hoarse and hissing and hateful, while Matty had slept in the next room.

So now Ruthann was the one driving us the eight blocks to the mall. Normally, having her drive didn't bother me – hey, I'm all for women's rights – but today being relegated to the passenger seat felt kinda shitty. It didn't help that Matty was kicking the back of my seat.

I clenched my fist around my seatbelt.

It was too quiet. I put on the car radio. The opening bars of "Snoopy's Christmas" blasted, the saccharine tune making my teeth ache. *Hell no.*

There was an ejected cassette in the tape deck. Without checking what it was – anything was better than "Snoopy's Christmas" – I punched it in and pressed play. The track played: Rick Springfield's "Jessie's Girl". It was like I couldn't cut a break. I bent to press fast forward, but at Ruthann's glancing glare, I pulled back.

Jesus. "Jessie's Girl" it is then.

Ruthann used to be more fun. These days, with her job and the house and everything, it seemed like she was tired all the time. I still loved her, but it wasn't the same. And now she was annoyed with me. Oh, I wasn't worried that she would leave me or anything. I knew she'd come around eventually and be her usual warm and willing self. My wife wasn't the quitting type. Plus, we had Matty to think about. I just had to ride it out. Mind my P's and Q's and wait for her to thaw.

The issue was, how long would that take?

We drove around the car park until we found a free spot.

"So," I said when we got inside. "What is there left to sort?"

Crouching to unbutton Matty's jacket, Ruthann pressed her lips together. "Only everything," she mumbled.

"Right." That was my fault, too. In the annual hospitality one-upmanship stakes, this year was our year, meaning my sister and her family were coming to stay for the holidays. I loved my sister, and Matty got on great with his cousins, but more than two days with my brother-in-law was a trial. Mike was a tech guy. Or he used to be. Not the smartest tool in the box as far as I could tell, but he'd gotten lucky a few years back, founding a start-up that had sold for a small fortune. Set him up for life, didn't it? Two houses mortgage free and more in shares and stock options. These days he consulted a few hours a week and carted his money around in a wheelbarrow. Even with Ruthann's nurse's salary, our income didn't come close. I was happy for my sister, but the offers of money – we only want to help – and the backhanded compliments – really, Ruthann, you sewed them yourself? – could be hard to swallow.

An ongoing reminder to Ruthann that she'd married a loser.

I took the jacket from her and draped it over my arm. "Any ideas?"

"Why do I have to have all the ideas? It's *your* sister."

"Maybe smellies?"

Ruthann sighed. "Didn't we get her smellies last year?"

"I don't know. Did we? It's just an idea."

"Okay." She clucked her tongue in a way that said it was not okay. "We can run into Bed & Bath. Get her some fancy bath salts. What about your niece and nephew?"

I shrugged. My sister's kids had everything. Last year,

they got a Nintendo game console, for fuck's sake. How was anyone supposed to top that? And on our budget? "Let's just go to Toys-R-Us and look around," I suggested.

"Choice. Toys-R-Us," Matty said, tugging at my sleeve. "They have the new Masters of the Universe action figures."

Ruthann raised her eyebrows at me. "Masters of the Universe?" she said. *"I didn't know that."*

As Matty raved about He-Man and Skeletor and Castle Grayskull, the two of us did the Jedi mind trick thing over his head. We'd been wracking our brains for something for him for Christmas and now we had an idea. It was the first time we'd been on the same page in a week.

"Maybe let your mom go," I said.

"But I wanna go."

"Why don't you and Dad go to McDonalds, instead?" Ruthann said, using the classic parents' bait and switch.

"Now there's an idea," I said, playing along. "I could murder a quarter pounder."

"Can I get a cheeseburger?" Matty asked.

"Sure," I said.

"And a strawberry sundae, too?"

"If you're good."

"Daaad," he wailed. "Pleeaase. I'll be good!"

"We'll see then, won't we?"

Ruthann stepped across and scanned the store locator map, using her finger to trace the quickest route. "I'll go to Bed & Bath on the way back. Meet at the playground in half an hour?" She tapped the spot.

I nodded. "Sounds good."

Before she hurried off, she threw me a smile. It was luke-warm, but it was a start.

"Come on then, buddy."

Matty and I battled through the throng of holiday shop-pers, past the giant central Christmas tree smothered in tinsel, towards the McDonalds restaurant at the south end of the mall. All the way kids screeched, and Christmas carols blared. It was deafening.

We were next to the playground, in the nexus between Sears, The Boston Store, and one of those new Victoria's Secret lingerie stores, when I had the brilliant idea to get something special for Ruthann for Christmas. That way she'd *have* to forgive me. The Boston Store would have a jewelry counter. I could run in and grab something now and the store would giftwrap it for me. Except I couldn't afford a diamond. On a subeditor's wages, I could barely stretch to a cubic zirconia. Could I pass one of those off as a diamond? Nah, that wasn't going to work. Ruthann did our family accounts; as soon as she saw the receipt, she'd know. So not jewelry then. Nothing from Sears, either. Nothing practical and lost-lasting. What I needed was something small and delicate. Intimate.

Like a sexy negligée.

I turned to look at the Victoria's Secret store, past its pink façade with the elegant black frilled edging to the tables piled high with silk and satin.

I grinned. Perfect.

I really shouldn't leave Matty alone, though… Then again, it would only be for a couple of minutes. Ruthann would never know. Besides, bras and bustiers were not the kind of gifts you shared with your kid – especially not when the gift was for his mother.

I checked out the playground. It wasn't much: meant for toddlers, there were some odd speed humps, a few beanbags, a tiny slide, and a couple of those funnel-things for climbing through, all on bright blue safety matting, with benches around the perimeter. Inside the plastic barriers, a handful of kids were careering about playing tag and shrieking at the top of their lungs, while shopped-out battle-weary adults, presumably their parents, clutched their shopping bags and watched from the sidelines. At the top of the yellow slide, a lone blonde-haired kid of around four stared at me from under a blue baseball cap. His eyes were a piercing blue, as if they'd been painted on. Like one of those old kewpie dolls. Catching my gaze, he cracked a cheeky grin, then pushed off down the slide.

I grabbed at the neck of Matty's sweatshirt. Yanked him to a stop. "Matty, wait here a moment, will you, while I get your mom a gift."

Turning to me, Matty pulled a face. "Here? But Dad, this playground is for *babies*."

"I know, buddy, but I want to get something in that store over there." I tipped my head towards Victoria's Secret. "You don't really want to go and look at a bunch of women's undies, do you? I promise won't be long." I bundled the jacket at him. "Just sit down here on one of these benches and watch the other kids for a bit. I'll be right back."

"But Dad—"

"I'll only be a few minutes. Then we'll go to McDonalds. I promise."

All at once, the boy with the blue baseball cap was there. Sidling over to Matty, he picked up Matty's good hand and gave it a pat. "You can be my friend," he said. "We can play on the slide." Under the rim of his cap, the boy lifted his eyes at me in what would've been a conspiratorial grin – that is, if he hadn't been only four.

Matty, on the other hand, gave me a look that was pure Ruthann.

"Go on," I told my son. "Go with your little friend, and later I'll get you that sundae you wanted. Just be careful, okay? Try not to bump your arm. I won't be long."

"Dad—"

"I'll be in this store here. I'll only be a minute."

I turned on my heel and strode into the store.

❦ ❦ ❦

Having an idea is only half the battle. Finding the right gift for Ruthann proved harder than I thought. While Bing Crosby crooned through the loudspeakers, I flicked through the racks of corsets and teddies, through stacks of French knickers and balconette bras, trying to work out what said sorry *and* sex, *and* was still in my budget. I wasn't having much success.

After a while, a shop girl approached me in a waft of floral perfume. "Maybe I can I help?" she said. In her twenties, she was supermodel material. I mean truly wow. Bubbly and effervescent, she was as tall and fluted as a champagne glass – even her name tag said Crystal.

"I'm looking for a gift for my wife," I told her.

"Well, you came to the right place. What did you have in mind? Something for every day, or is this for a special occasion?"

"Hmm. Good question," I said, and I flashed her a twinkling smile. "Let's just say, I'd love it if it were an everyday event." I dropped my voice, lingered on the words.

Her laughter tinkled through the store. 'Oooh, naughty."

"Maybe something for bedtime.?" I dipped my head in mock shyness, letting a lock of hair drop over my forehead. Ruthann once said it made me look like Robe Lowe in *Class*.

"You'll want a nightgown," Crystal said. "I know just the thing. They're over here."

"Of course. I'm in your hands…" I knew I shouldn't flirt, not after the blow-up over Carly, but I'd mentioned my wife, so it was fine. Crystal knew the score. Where was the harm?

As we passed the doors into the mall, I glanced out at the playground, catching a glimpse of the kid in the blue baseball cap, the big 'C' square in the center above the rim. He was playing with my son. I couldn't see Matty – he was obscured by two women chatting – but the jacket was still there on one of the benches. Everything was fine.

I turned and chased after Crystal.

Choosing the gift took maybe ten minutes. It didn't feel like long, anyway. Just the time it took to select the style and find the right size. (I guessed my wife was about Crystal's size, and she'd offered to model it.) Afterwards, we took the rose-gold satin nightgown (we'd settled on a size 12, D-cup) to the counter, where Crystal wrapped it in frothy cream tissue, and I filled out the check. It was a way more money than Ruthann and I usually spent on gifts for one another, but Crystal had convinced me that it was worth the investment.

She primped the ribbon and pushed the package across the counter. "We'll need your address and phone number on the back of the check, please. And some ID."

"Sure thing," I said, dolloping on the charm. I added my contact details. Showed her my driver's license. It was company policy, but you never knew, right?

I zipped the package into my jacket pocket. "You're a life saver, Crystal," I said. "Thanks ever so much."

"Of course, Mr.—" She flipped the check over. "…Moore. That's what I'm here for. I just hope your wife will be happy."

I grinned. Turning to leave, I lifted my arm in what I hoped was a causal wave and sauntered out the door. *Same, babe.*

The magic lasted all of ten paces.

Shit! My wife. I said I'd meet her in a half hour. I checked my watch. I'd been in the lingerie store a full twenty minutes, and I still had to take Matty to McDonalds. There might just be time, but only if Matty and I were quick.

Wait. Where the heck was Matty? I scanned the playground. He wasn't on the slide. Or slouched in a beanbag. I straddled the barrier and crouched to check inside those tunnel things, although how the heck he could be inside with a broken arm, God only knows. He had to be here some-where. He wouldn't just wander off, would he? I did a tour of the playground in case he was hiding from me on the other side of the plastic barriers. He might be annoyed with me, or maybe he was playing a game. You never knew with kids, did you?

"Matty!" I called. "Come on, buddy. Time to go."

I'd come full circle. Where on earth was he? The jacket was gone, too.

"Hey, have you seen a kid with his arm in a sling?" I asked a guy sitting on one of the benches. He'd been there before, hadn't he? He must've seen something.

The man shook his head. "Sorry."

Damn. I spun around, scanning the crowd, searching for that unruly mop of ginger hair. "Matty!!" I yelled over the piped music. "Let's go."

That's when I saw that the kid with the blue baseball cap was still there. He was watching me from one of the benches, peering out from under that damned cap.

I rushed over. "Hey kid, where did Matty go?"

"Matty?"

"My son. You were playing with him."

The kid smirked. "He wasn't very happy. You left him all by himself."

"I left him with you. I was only gone a minute." Why was I defending myself against a four-year-old?

Suddenly coy, the kid dropped his head. He threaded a finger into the last buttonhole of his shirt, and whispered, "Matty went away. A grown-up came and took him."

I almost died with relief. I knew it; Matty was a good kid. He would never just go off somewhere like that. He was with

Ruthann. He had to be. If Ruthann had finished her shopping early, she would have come to join us at McDonalds. Her route would have brought her right past the playground.

Fuck. She'd be even more pissed off now that I'd left Matty alone. Again.

"So a lady came, with red hair? Where did they go?"

He grinned. "Not a lady. A man."

My blood ran cold. Some guy took my kid? Panicked, I grasped the boy by the upper arm and pulled him towards me. "What man? What did he look like? Where did they go? Which way?"

"Hey!" One of the women broke away from her conversation and strode in my direction, her bosom wobbling. "Let him go," she roared. Everyone looked up. "You leave that child alone!"

I stepped back, horrified. I'd just assaulted a kid.

The boy rushed to stand behind her, his chubby arms wrapped around one of her legs and his cherub face peeking out the side.

The woman patted his head. "You okay, honey?"

Still clutching at her, the boy nodded.

"I… I just…" I mumbled.

What was happening here?

The woman put her hands on her hips. "You should leave before I call mall security."

Of course. Yes. Mall security. Good idea. But I had to talk to the boy first. He was the only one who knew where Matty was. The last one to see him. "Please," I urged. "I just need to talk to him. My son—"

"You're saying this is your boy?"

"No, no. That's not it. You don't understand. You see, I went—"

"But I do understand," the woman cut me off. "I understand that creeps like you don't get to terrorize someone

27

else's kid. What's wrong with you, anyway? Can't you see you're frightening him?"

For fuck's sake. The stupid cow! She was the one who couldn't see. The rim of the baseball cap was in the way, wasn't it? You only had to check out his face to know that kid wasn't the least bit frightened. It was a ploy. A pretense. There was something about him. Honestly, I'd swear the little fucker was laughing at me. Those blue eyes. It was like they were drilling into my skull.

Desperate, I tried to step around her. "Please. I just need to…"

The second woman bowled over and blocked the way, hiding the boy behind a cage of legs.

What was this? A coven?

"You heard my friend. Get lost, buddy."

I backed away. They watched me leave, following me with their eyes. I ducked around the corner, out of sight…

Out of sight…

My hand on the wall, I bent over and took some deep breaths.

Matty was gone.

Missing.

And from outside a Sears department store, just like poor Adam Walsh a few years back. The photo of Walsh in his t-ball uniform, the baseball cap, with his missing teeth and his big apple pie smile, burned in my brain. He'd been in all the papers, on all the networks. Like Matty, the boy been just seven years old when he'd been abducted from the Holly-wood Mall in Florida, prompting a statewide search.

Meanwhile, Adam Walsh's mother had been busy looking at lamps…

My hands went clammy, and my knees trembled. No, no, no. Matty couldn't be missing. Not like that. The blonde kid in the playground was wrong. Or just winding me up. There was something weird about him. All I needed to do was think like a seven-year-old. What would Matty do if he was bored?

I snapped my fingers. McDonalds. I promised him we'd go after I'd bought the gift for Ruthann. He must have figured he'd wait for me there.

I fought my way against the current of shoppers to McDonalds. It was lunchtime on a Saturday and just two weeks from Christmas, so the place was packed with families standing four and five deep at the counter in places.

I tried to remember what Matty had been wearing. Jeans and…his dinosaur sweatshirt? The Go-bots one? It didn't matter. No one had Matty's ginger hair. I chose the shortest line and elbowed my way through the crowd towards the front.

"Hey, you need to wait your turn like everyone else," someone griped.

Fuck that. I didn't have time to mess about in line. My kid was missing.

The pimply teen behind the counter yelled, "Next!"

I pushed in front. "Sorry. I'm not here to order. I'm looking for a ginger kid. Maybe you've seen him?"

"Yeah, I'm just here to take the orders, not look for people's kids."

"I'm sure you would have noticed him if he'd been here," I blurted, and I lifted my left arm, gesturing to it. "He had his arm in a sling."

The teenager shook his head. "Have you seen how many kids are here? Next customer!"

A burly man in a Packers shirt muscled forward, trying to shove me out of the way.

I turned to face the crowd, my back to the counter, and raised my arms. "Please," I shouted over hubbub. "I'm looking for my boy. Matty's seven. Red hair. He's got a broken arm. Has anyone seen him?"

Packer man turned to the woman beside him. "The guy's kid wandered off."

The woman shrugged. "He could be anywhere." Leaning across the man, she touched my arm and said: "Have you tried the toy store? Or maybe Santa's Grotto?"

The toy store! Of course. That had to be it. Matty will have gone to Toys-R-Us, looking for Ruthann. Maybe he got distracted by the toys. I'd probably get there and find him in the Masters of the Universe aisle, playing with the latest Skeletor.

"Great idea. Thank you," I said.

"I hope you find him," the woman called.

I didn't stop to reply. I raced back past the playground in case Matty had come back. He hadn't. The two women were still there, though. And the kid. They all stared at me as I went by. For fuck's sake. You'd think I was a serial killer or something.

Seeing them reminded me about mall security. Yes! I'd seen the mall office earlier. It was on the way to Santa's Grotto. I raced up and thumped on the door. Nothing. I tried the handle. Locked.

A man leaning against the wall, said, "They said they'd be back in ten minutes."

I didn't have ten minutes. "Right. Thanks," I said, and I sprinted on to Santa's Grotto.

The grotto was teeming with kids; none of them were Matty.

The Toy-R-Us box store was one of the mall's anchor retailers. The place was a license to print money. Even when they're on the bones of their bums, people always buy toys for their kids. My lungs burning, I dashed past the greeter and ran perpendicular to the aisles, looking along each one. When I got the end, I ran back the other way, in case Matty had been gazing at an end display.

Ran there and back again.

Matty wasn't in the aisles. I couldn't see Ruthann, either.

I accosted a staff member. "Where are the Masters of the Universe figures?" I huffed.

The girl blinked. "Aisle six?"

Except Matty wasn't in aisle six and nor was He-Man. The store had completely sold out. There was just a single olive-green Kobra Khan on the shelf. The snake-man screamed at me through its plastic packaging, its jaw stretched open in a silent howl.

By now, I was feeling sick. I ran out of the store, my eyes scanning every group. So many kids. None with ginger hair. How long had it been since I'd last seen Matty? They say first few hours are crucial in a kidnapping. *No, no, no.* That wasn't what this was.

I checked my watch. Thirty minutes and some. If she wasn't with Matty, Ruthann would be at the playground by now. Unless she'd been held up in Bed & Bath? I ran back through the mall, my trainers squeaking on the polished tiles, sweat pouring down my face.

The same guy was still leaning against the wall beside the mall office. I slowed, about to knock, but he shrugged and shook his head. They were still not back then? For heaven's sake. Where the hell was mall security when you needed them?

I kept running.

And I kept thinking about Adam Walsh.

The desperate search.

The impassioned pleas by the boy's parents.

The child's decomposing head found in a ditch days later.

Even now, Adam's body was still missing.

If I had breath to spare, I would have sobbed. Not my Matty. My baby. He had a broken arm. I had to find him.

I raced on, past the Christmas tree, and ducked into Bed & Bath. My wife wasn't there.

When I got to the playground, I pulled up. It was like a scene from the twilight zone: eerily quiet. Even the ring-a-ling of Christmas carols had faded into nothing. There were no adults on the benches. No Ruthann waiting patiently and definitely no Matty. Only the kid with the blue baseball cap remained, perched at the top of the slide, like he had been the first time I'd seen him.

I'd fucking had enough of this. I stalked over and looked him dead in the face. "Where is Matty? You said a man took him. Which way did they go?"

Wait! *There are no adults on the benches.* I narrowed my eyes. "What's your name? Who are you with, anyway? Where are your parents?"

The boy waved a hand towards Victoria's Secret. "My dad's in there. He said he won't be long. Just a couple of minutes. Afterwards, we're going to McDonalds. He promised."

The fuck. He was mocking me!

I leaned in close and hissed in his face. "What have you done to Matty, you little fuck?" Flecks of spittle landed on his cheek. The boy didn't even flinch.

"What have you done to Matty, you big fuck?" he hissed back, imitating my voice.

The sweat on my skin froze. It was so *adult.* So fucking creepy.

"I'm going to ask you one more time. Where. Is. Matty?" I snarled. It was all I could do not to rip the kid from limb to limb. But he was the only one who knew where Matty was.

"He needed to pee." A child's voice. "He went to the bathroom."

"What?"

The boy only smiled. Then he slid down the slide away from me.

Oh my god. Matty. Where were the bathrooms? The signs pointed to an alley beside Sears. I ran down the corridor and into the Men's Room. Checked the stalls on by one. The third stall was locked. I braved the splashes of urine and peeked under the door. Man-sized New Balance sneakers.

"Matty?" I called. "You in here?"

No answer.

"Matty!"

The last door in the row had been vandalized. Half off its hinges, it was covered in red graffiti. Something illegible and violent. My heart thundering, I pushed it open.

Stuffed behind the cistern was Ruthann's old blue jacket, the one Matty had been wearing.

Thank heavens. Matty had been here. This was proof.

But when I pulled the jacket clear, a strip of white fabric dropped on the floor. Matty's sling. I picked it up. Turned it over.

It was smeared with blood.

I raced back into the mall, my legs as heavy as plutonium. This time, the boy in the baseball cap wasn't at the playground. Instead, my wife was there, waiting on one of the benches. Leaping up, Ruthann rushed over, her arms loaded with shopping bags. "Where have you been? I've been looking all over. Sorry I was late back. I popped into Sears for a bag so I could hide Matty's present. You won't believe it, but I got the last He-Man in the store…" She slowed. Gasped. "Jim? What's going on? Where's Matty?"

"The police. We need to call the police." I handed her the bloodied sling.

Her eyes widened. "No." Crumpling to her knees, the shopping bags floating around her, Ruthann screeched. "Matty! Matty! Matty!"

As a scholar of the human condition and keen observer of character, I knew already that I'd lost them both.

In the distance, a blue baseball cap bobbed in the crowd.

❦ ❦ ❦

Lee Murray ONZM (Officer of the New Zealand Order of Merit) is a writer, editor, poet and screenwriter from Aotearoa New Zealand, a Shirley Jackson Award and five-time Bram Stoker Award® winner. A *USA Today* bestselling author with more than forty titles to her credit, including novels, collections, anthologies, nonfiction, poetry, and several books for children, Lee holds a New Zealand Prime Minister's Award for Literary Achievement in Fiction, and is an Honorary Literary Fellow of the New Zealand Society of Authors. Among her recent works are feature film *Grafted* (directed by Sasha Rainbow), horror anthology *This Way Lies Madness* (Flame Tree Press) co-edited with Dave Jeffery, and prose-poetry collection, NZSA Cuba Press Prize-winner *Fox Spirit on a Distant Cloud* (The Cuba Press). Read more at https://www.leemurray.info/

Comeback Kid

Christa Carmen

THE FIRST THING Nan notices about her new home away from home is the way the mineral smell of chalk mingles with the sharp tang of the pine forest. They told her this place would be nothing like the *other* home away from home at which she'd spent the last nine summers. That learning to coach elite-level gymnastics would be fundamentally different from training as an elite-level gymnast.

Already, she has a feeling they were wrong.

Nan surveys the empty gym, still surprised by the lack of longing she feels for being out on the equipment. She can remember sprinting down the runway and gripping the uneven bars in her hands. The way each bone in her toes would crack as she rose up onto them in preparation to mount the beam. What she cannot recall is so much as a flicker of joy as she saluted the judges after a near-perfect routine.

Nan checks her watch. Russell was supposed to meet her here at five. It's ten minutes past that now. She runs a hand over the well-worn leather of one of the beams, trying to ignore the sensation of being watched. An empty gym unnerves her, mostly because it is such an anomaly. But especially here, at this remote training camp in Maine, two miles from an access point to the Hundred Mile Wilderness section of the Appalachian Trail, the emptiness feels heavy and profound. Where was the creaking of equipment under the weight of tumbling bodies, the coaches barking out corrections, arms crossed and eyebrows furrowed? Nan jumps onto the beam to wait, telling herself she's being ridiculous. A couple of days from now, she'll be pining for some time to herself.

A light catches her eye through the window, a soft glow across the dark path coming from the building next door. As she's contemplating whether she's in the right place—*Is the first evening of training in the pit gym instead of the main one?*— Russell strolls in, red-white-and-blue-trimmed wind pants swishing, his high-top sneakers glowing like freshly fallen snow. Reflexively, some deep part of her curls in on itself, tightens, condenses, even as, just as reflexively, the corners of her mouth turn up in a smile.

"This wasn't too early to meet, was it?" Russell asks and rubs his moustache. It's just like him not to say hello, not to acknowledge that it'd been two months since she'd seen him, longer than they'd gone without seeing each other since she was six years old.

Nan yanks at the sleeves of her sweatshirt. "It's fine. The taxi dropped me at three, and I already unpacked."

"Great." He stares around the gym, nodding like she's said something he needs to acknowledge. She knew this would be uncomfortable, but the awkwardness is on another level. Not to mention the lingering disquiet.

Not because of Russell, per se. It's no secret among the gymnasts (but a massive secret from everyone else on the planet) that a large percentage of elite coaches are perverts and rapists. The sport's top admins are co-conspirators. And the national team doctor? Suffice it to say that Henry Broussard had never left an athlete better than he found her. Russell's abuse was never sexual. Psychological warfare is his modus operandi. Verbal attacks. Humiliation. Controlling his gymnasts' food, their weight. Emotional manipulation. Despite the nearness of these memories, the unease Nan feels has everything to do with this place, not Russell Walker. Its silence. Its mineral smell. Its isolation.

"So, um, what's the plan?" she asks. "There's some sort of initial training session I'm supposed to attend, right? How many others are getting certified to coach alongside me?"

"There're a few. They'll be here tomorrow."

How many? she wants to ask. *And what time tomorrow?* Why does he insist on these endless games? She's spent sixteen years playing them, had thought she was in for at least four more. But then the unthinkable happened, and everything changed.

Nan Youer's devastating mistake at the U.S. Olympic gymnastics trials five months prior was touted as the single most shocking moment of any qualifying event in any sport. Nan had been favored to win Olympic gold, to sweep the event finals, to lead the women's team to victory over Russia. To not have even made the team was unfathomable. Her picture was supposed to be on every breakfast table across America, smiling out from the side of a Wheaties box. Now she is a mere footnote in the record books of 1988. The other gymnasts, girls she counted as friends—her *only* friends—for the entirety of her childhood, wouldn't go near her after it happened, as if her failure was a contagious disease they didn't want to catch.

But what those girls didn't know is that when Nan missed catching her most difficult release move, plummeted to earth, and dropped below Tiffany Garrett on the leaderboard, she hadn't felt horror or sadness or disappointment.

Neither had she felt shock or grief or regret. She'd felt relief. Sweet, unmitigated relief. She'd been looking for an excuse to get out of the sport for a long, long time. Not making the Olympic team had granted her that freedom.

And so, a second seismic wave of shock swept the world when she'd announced her retirement before Team USA had even boarded the plane for Seoul. No one, however, was more bewildered than her longtime coach. In the never-ending parade of interviews he gave in the wake of her announcement, Russell, head of the women's national team and coach of no less than seven Olympic champions, twelve world champions, and six U.S. national champions, claimed that Nan was better than all those previous medal-winners combined. He railed that he would never recover from the "enormity of her desertion," and from her "selfish refusal to make a comeback." Nan had kept her head down and ignored the media circus, no small feat, since coverage of her retirement had drawn far more of the "crazies," as Russell called them, than news of her past successes ever had.

As for coaching, Nan doesn't consider traveling to the same competitions and spending time with the same people the best use of her newfound freedom, but not having to subject her body to the daily abuse, the backbreaking routines, the sprained ankles and bruised thighs, the blistered hands and unending mind-fuckery is enough, at least for now. Besides, she needs some way to make money in order to start a life of her own, and gymnastics is all that she knows.

Nan yanks her thoughts back to the present, where Russell is still standing, scuffing the toe of one white sneaker against the mat. "Sooo," Nan says, knowing that even by drawing out this one word she's risking his ire but forcing herself not to care, "should I head back to my cabin? Call it a night?" She yawns. "I am pretty beat from traveling."

"We've got conditioning," he replies bluntly, and the thing inside her curls tighter. It's the part of her that wears armor, weathers his attacks, that allows her to remain steadfast and soldier-like on the outside no matter how scared, tired, bored, lonely, or injured she is on the inside. That thing forms a little ball at her core and grows, pushing a voice that's been silent for too long up and out of her throat.

"Why do I need to condition if I'm no longer training?" She digs her fingernails into the beam, though she hates how the half-moons mar the leather. Something flares inside her, and she is pleasantly surprised to discover it is anger. Anger directed at Russell, anger she doesn't plan to swallow down. "Was bringing me here really about letting me coach, or is it another attempt to get me to not retire?" Her anger brightens to a brilliant yellow blaze. "Because I told you it's too late. I am done. Nothing you can say will make me change my mind."

"No one *brought* you here," a heavily accented voice says from behind her, and Nan suppresses a groan. Cherry Constantine walks across the mats in her ridiculous high heels, navy pantsuit, and enough hairspray for *three* assistant national team coaches. "You came here on your own. And we respect your decision, prăjitură. Though, it is such a shame." Cherry clucks her tongue. "You have dee best toe point in all dis country, yes? Romania too. Nowhere will we find toe point like yours again."

Nan resists the urge to roll her eyes, but cool relief floods in to douse her anger. "Okay, then," she says with a concilia-tory shrug, "we're on the same page: I'm here to learn to coach. And you two *aren't* here to convince me to make a comeback. Which brings me to my original question: why would I have to condition?"

"Because the pullups and ab exercises and cardio training that helped you as a gymnast will help you as a coach,"

Russell says. His tone has shot past impatient and gone straight to that dangerous monotone that means Nan should quit while she's ahead. Now there is neither anger nor relief but a swift, numbing chill.

Why has she come to this place with these people? She could have gotten a job waiting tables or cleaning houses. *Or, you big stubborn baby*, a voice in her head chastises, *you could call just* one *of the numbers in your little black notebook, and all your money problems will be solved.* Nan shakes this thought away. But why *has* she allowed herself to be sucked back into this world instead of making a clean break?

"Do you understand me?" Russell challenges. No matter that, by his logic, he and Cherry should be joining her in the impending workout.

Nan shrugs out of her sweatshirt, trudges to the uneven bars, and lets Russell lead her through an hour and twenty minutes of conditioning. Several times, as she jumps and pushes, strains and spins, she thinks she catches sight of the faint glow of lights from the gym next door, and once, she swears she hears the tinkle of piano music, the same opening chords over and over, as if someone is working the choreography kinks out of a new floor routine. She considers asking Russell if there's someone else here, a gymnast they weren't willing to leave at their main gym in Massachusetts while they came to Maine, a new prodigy—the new Nan, even?— but decides against it.

Finally, Russell is satisfied. Nan pulls on her sweatshirt and mumbles goodnight. Cherry locks up and walks with Russell in the direction of their ostentatious house. Nan walks in the other, to one of fourteen tiny cabins on the grounds. Again, she smells the sharp scent of pine and stale, powdery chalk, a combination that strikes her as natural and oddly misplaced, inexplicably worrisome.

She keeps an eye out for signs of life, signs of the gymnast she thought she heard across the path, but there is only a formidable moon high in the sky and stars far brighter than any she can ever recall seeing. When is the last time she looked at the stars as opposed to the glittering gold medals in her head, medals to please her coach, her parents, her country?

From now on, Nan promises herself, *I will look at the stars every night. To remind myself what really matters, what I've escaped from. I just need to get through this certification, to coach for long enough to make a bit of money, then I can set out under those stars for something greater.* It's a solid goal. An admirable dream. Better than yearning for Olympic podiums and the covers of cereal boxes, in Nan's humble opinion.

Back at the cabin, she showers, dresses in fresh sweats, and crawls into bed, but she lies awake, unable to sleep. The noises and lights from the other gym trouble her, as does the quiet of the forest, the distance between her tiny cabin and all the others. Russell said the rest of the trainees would arrive tomorrow. Is she the only one out here tonight besides Russell and Cherry? Besides the lone, mysterious gymnast she still isn't sure exists?

In her tossing and turning, Nan catches sight of her black notebook on the nightstand, and recalls the latest journalist to reach out. This one was from the *Times*, and he'd offered more money for an exclusive interview than all the others reporters combined. "The public needs to hear your story," he told her. "There's been enough comments from your teammates, your coaches. It's time for a Nan Youer's post-Olympic trials, post-*career*, tell-all."

She'd written his name and number in her notebook and promptly pushed him out of her mind. Nan writes all their names and numbers in her notebook, but she hasn't called a single one. She can't. How to explain her reasons for leaving without blowing the lid off the whole rancid pot of USA

Gymnastics? The exploitation and molestation. The assaults and starvation. Once, at Worlds, Cherry locked Nan in her hotel room and fed her nothing but raw vegetables through a crack in the door. At nationals in '85, Russell forced her to compete with a torn meniscus in each knee. To avoid having to be seen by the abhorrent Dr. Broussard, Nan had completed with far more—and far worse—injuries. Every gymnast knew to avoid Broussard if they could help it.

If Nan was shunned for her mistake at trials, she can't imagine the repercussions of going public with the truth. Still, lying in this cabin all alone, far from her family and civilization, navigating this new, uncertain dynamic with her former coaches, Nan is comforted by the long, neat list of phone numbers. *They're a lifeline to something*, she thinks, as the notes of the piano music she'd heard earlier play over and over in her head. *Protection*. Much like the other way she goes about making sure she's protected these days.

With this final thought, Nan allows herself to succumb to the silence. As the Hundred Mile Wilderness presses in from all around her, she drifts into a deep and dreamless sleep.

❧ ❧ ❧

Nan eats breakfast in her cabin, eyes glued to the windows, but spots no other coaches-in-training arriving, no cars at all. She arrives at the same gym as last night at ten minutes till eight. Russell shows up at ten minutes after the hour.

"Ready for conditioning?" It's not a question. A retort half-forms in her mouth, but all that's released is a resigned sigh.

Two hours of suicide sprints and plyometrics, and planks later, Nan is sweaty and exhausted. She is rethreading the elastic around her ponytail when a flash of movement draws her eye. It's from the window in the other gym. She squints, sees a blur of color trailed by a ponytail much like the one she's just secured. A gymnast, sprinting down a vault runway? It is hard to know for certain, for whoever it is has passed out of view.

"Where's Cherry?" Nan asks carefully.

"Reviewing applications for summer camp." Russell frowns. "Why?"

"I... " She knows she should say nothing but wants so desperately to break free from Russell's grasp, to step out of his long and suffocating shadow. "I saw someone practicing next door," she says, more careful still. "I thought maybe Cherry was holding a private session in the other gym?"

"Nonsense," Russell countered. "The only one here is you."

That tightening at her core. The chill, despite her sweatiness. "And why is that?" Her voice is small, but at least she's voiced her question. "I thought there were supposed to be others."

Russell purses his lips. He cocks his head. He seems to be considering whether he should comment further, and ultimately decides to go on. "There was supposed to be. But then we got to thinking, if all goes well, we shouldn't need anyone else besides you."

❦ ❦ ❦

It's noon on the third day. Nan picks at a salad in her cabin. She's been ruminating on Russell's words for the last twenty-four hours and has come no closer to convincing herself that all he meant was she was the only new coach Team USA required. She's submitted to three conditioning sessions a day, terrified that at any one of them now, she'll be thrown a leotard and told her retirement from gymnastics is over. She's decided that if this happens, she'll throw the leotard back, storm from the gym, and call for a taxi. Problem is, she doesn't know the location of a phone.

And she means to remedy that today.

Russell cancelled their afternoon session, told her to enjoy the break while he and Cherry attended to some matters pertaining to their gym in Massachusetts. Nan grabs a black sweatshirt and a small, rather heavy black fanny pack, into which she adds her notebook. She slips out into the overcast Maine day and heads back to the lodge where she picked up her salad an hour earlier.

All her meals have been prepared for her, so she, Cherry, and Russell can't be the only ones here. Knowing Russell, there's a dietician on the premises. Nan needs to be careful. She doesn't want anyone seeing her prowling around, and that applies to more than just her coaches.

She makes her way past the cabins, still on the lookout for signs of the other gymnast. She's continued to see evidence over the last two days, but nothing beyond glimpses of light and flashes of color from the other gym, along with the chords of piano music, a melancholic melody that drills into her brain. She shakes off the memory, fanny pack thumping into her hip. She breaks free from the copse of pines and creeps around the back of the building.

The lodge appears abandoned, but Nan peeks into the windows all the same. She sees an industrial kitchen, the remnants of the salad she'd been served for lunch, the long, sharp knife used to chop her grilled chicken. No dietician. No Russell. No Cherry. Nan walks to the door and lets herself inside.

It's cool and quiet in the lodge, and she wastes no time in looking for a phone. Nothing in the kitchen. She strides on silent feet to the front foyer. No phone here either. Nor is there one in the parlor, which Nan imagines is used in the same way as the parlor at the main national training camp in

Colorado: to assure parents who are leaving their daughters in Russell and Cherry's care that they'll be okay. That they'll be cherished not just for their skill and their potential but for the young women they'll grow to be. *Beyond* their final tumbling pass, their last stuck landing. That they'll be loved. That they'll be safe.

Nan abandons the parlor, continues exploring the first floor, then the second, and finds herself back in the foyer having found no phone, no hookup, no cable. It's as she's sneaking back to the kitchen, wondering how she'll manage to gain access to Cherry and Russel's house without them catching her, since that must be the location of the phone, that she sees the door to her left, shrouded in shadow. She missed it her first time through. She's opened the door, stepped onto the first stair, and pulled the door closed behind her before she can consider if this is a good idea.

The stairs don't creak under her careful feet. At the bottom, there's a light switch, but she doesn't flick it. Not yet. Not until she sees what is down here. A faint glow emanates from around the corner up ahead, the accompanying buzz of the fluorescents like the drone of a small swarm of flies. But the haze of light and the droning hum isn't what draws her attention. Not fully. It's the smell. Chalk. And pine.

And the pungent, metallic, unmistakable, dread-inducing scent of blood.

Nan creeps forward. Closer. Closer still. At last, she's at the corner. She grips the wall. Her fingers don't shake. The perks of two decades of learning to disconnect her internal anxiety from the external manifestation in her ligaments and muscles. With a deep, steady sigh, she leans forward and peers into the basement.

At the horror before her, Nan's first thought is to wonder how she got down the stairs and across the anteroom without discerning the sounds of another human. The man leans over a sink at the far corner of the basement, his back to her, engrossed by something beyond her field of vision. She knows it's Broussard before he even turns around. Knows it from his hunched stance, his balding head, the way the muscles in the sides of his jaw twitch as he licks his lips.

Good that she's recognized it's Broussard because she doesn't want to stare at the man any longer. She needs to take in the room. To make sense of what she's seeing. The basement has been converted into some sort of lab. Stainless steel tables. Grossing stations. Dissection carts and embalming sinks. All manner of surgical equipment. Clamps. A bone saw. A scalpel. The glass-walled refrigerator beyond the sink is filled with dozens, maybe hundreds, of bags of blood; its shelves are lined with body parts in jars. Severed limbs lie on beds of dry ice like cocktail shrimp.

It's the hum of the refrigerator. That's why I didn't hear there was someone down here. But more importantly, that's why Broussard doesn't hear me. Nan backs up a step, but not before she discerns that the sink in front of the doctor is filled with blood.

She turns on feet lighter than any that have soared above a balance beam. Without a breath, without a sound, she crosses the anteroom and flies up the stairs. She is out of the lodge and halfway back to her cabin before she forces herself to slow, worried that Russell or Cherry will appear and wonder why she's fleeing through the firs and the pines. She makes it the last two hundred feet without seeing anyone, slips into her cabin, and locks the door behind her.

Nan paces for what feels like an hour, eyeing her fanny pack each time she passes it on the table by the door. She can't call anyone. Can't go anywhere. Can't stop seeing the image of Dr. Broussard leaning over something in the sink. She doesn't understand. The girls always tried to stay away from the national team doctor lest he use his private exams to perform "spinal alignments," "muscle therapy," or whatever other bullshit euphemism-of-the-month Broussard used for the assaults he perpetrated against his victims. But torture? Murder? It seems insane.

Even if murder is too far-fetched, Nan can't conceive of anything good going on in that room. She wants to believe that someone would have noticed if gymnasts were going missing, that someone would have raised hell until the authorities stepped up, but deeply disturbing shit got swept under the rug in this organization every damn day. How easy would it be for a coach, a doctor, to tell a frantic mother her daughter had run off, that she'd been unable to deal with the pressure of her training? How easy for the missing ones to make way for new girls, full of hunger and talent? The elite gyms across the country had always been outfitted with revolving doors.

Nan's eyes flick to the cabin windows. If Broussard had seen her, wouldn't someone have come by now? As if in response, there's a pounding at the door. Nan freezes, but her heartrate doesn't rise. Her palms don't get sweaty. After a single deep breath, she retrieves her fanny pack, fastens it beneath her sweatshirt, and opens the door.

Russell looms before her in a red-white-and-blue track suit. He looks a little flustered but nothing out of the ordinary. Nan makes herself meet his eyes.

"You finish everything you had to do with Cherry?" she asks.

He nods. "We'll start the evening session a little early. It's going to be a long one."

Nan nods. "Okay." She grabs a water bottle and adds, perfectly casually, "How about we workout in the pit gym?"

Russell had already started down the path away from her cabin, but at this, his head jerks back to her, and he stares, silently, intently.

"We'll use the regular gym," he finally says. "Pit gym is under construction right now anyway."

On the walk over, trailing behind Russell, Nan considers her options. Russell doesn't seem aware of her self-guided tour of the lodge's basement, but she still has no idea where to find a phone. She could run, but how far would she get out here in the backwoods of Maine? One wrong turn and she's lost in the Hundred Mile Wilderness. No, she needs to play along, at least for now. She'll look for a phone tonight.

But as the conditioning session wears on, dread weighs on Nan's muscles as much as fatigue. Something isn't right. Russell is driving her hard, too hard, demanding more repetitions, more difficult sequences. His intensity is manic, his concentration an impenetrable brick wall. Nan fights to keep up, to not make him mad. She's struggling through another series of pull-up/V-ups when she sees a light flicker in the gym next door. It goes out, flickers on again, then stays on, a warm orangey glow that glimmers among the trees like a distant sunset.

"Again!" Russell shouts. "Faster this time."

She wants to protest, to ask about the other coaches, to complain this isn't what she signed up for. But she forces herself to complete the set and drops to the mat, shaking and sweating. The sounds of her catching her breath almost drowns out the pulse of piano music, a low trill that she feels in her chest more than she perceives with her ears. Russell is rubbing his moustache with one hand and gesturing toward the high bar with his other. Nan knows this hyper-focused, impatient expression as well as she knows her own face in the mirror.

"I have to use the bathroom," Nan says, cutting him off before he can speak.

A flush creeps up Russel's neck and across his cheeks, but before he can explode, Nan grabs her sweatshirt, along with the fanny pack atop it. "I have to deal with some, um, womanly issues."

Russel's cheeks redden further, but he waves his hand, indicating she should get as far away from him as possible. Nan knows this man, knew this was the only thing that would buy her a couple of minutes. She carries her things across the mats toward the locker room. But instead of turning into the dark space, she cuts right, jogs down a hallway, and lets herself out through the side exit. Along the path, fallen pine needles muffle the sound of her footsteps.

Nan straps the fanny pack around her waist and dons the sweatshirt. She enters the pit gym through the back. Lilting piano music reaches her ears.

Nan creeps down a short hallway, but stops before the end of it. Someone is clapping along with the piano chords, their rhythm keeping time like a metronome. Nan knows that clapping, feels it echoing in her bones.

Cherry, Nan thinks, just as the Romanian barks out, "Lighter! Daintier! And dee toes! Point dee fucking toes!" There's the telltale pounding of the spring floor as the unseen gymnast launches into a tumbling pass.

Nan takes a slow step forward. Then another. She's close enough to the wall to peer around it. The music crescendos. Nan grips the wall. She leans forward. Sees Cherry to the right of the floor, her kohl-rimmed eyes narrowed in concentration. Sees Dr. Broussard, his bony fingers tented in front of his body. Sees the gymnast, small and sleek, her body pirouetting around the floor mat. Faster. Faster. So fast, Nan can't tell what she's seeing. Something about the girl looks... wrong. Like she's both the most talented gymnast Nan's ever seen and bizarrely robotic. Her movements are too crisp, too exact. Even her leotard is odd, pieces of the crushed velvet fabric seeming to trail along her skin as if its edges are fringed and frayed.

The girl launches into her final tumbling pass. It's a full twisting double layout. But that's impossible. No one has ever performed that skill before. Nan's head spins at the thought of it. The girl moves like a top through the air, her form never breaking, never faltering.

But the moment the girl lands, something happens. Despite perfect form and exceptional height, the girl's body buckles. Her ankles give out. She collapses to the ground like a doll that's been thrown onstage from a balcony. Like every bit of energy, the spark of life, has gone out of her.

"Fucking dammit!" Cherry screeches. "Broussard! You said dis one's parts would hold!" The music ends, plunging the gym into silence. Cherry storms onto the floor in her towering heels, grabs the girl by the ankles, and hauls her off the mat.

The first unwanted twinge of fear presents itself; Nan stuffs it down.

"I do not understand," Cherry hisses at the doctor. Broussard bends and helps Cherry lift the girl from the mat. They move her onto an adjacent stainless steel table Nan hadn't noticed before. The gymnast twitches and jerks. Her eyes roll back in her head. A thin line of froth appears at her mouth. Nan stifles a gasp when she realizes the leotard isn't fringed...

The girl's head is connected to her neck by dark and jagged stitches.

Nan's gaze travels the length of the gymnast's body. Every point not obscured by crushed velvet is a tapestry of horror. Her flesh is pallid, bruised purple in places. Frankensteinian stitches hold shoulder to torso, hand to arm, ankle to lower leg. Despite these stitches, she is perfect. The perfect *gymnast*. Child-sized. Prepubescent. Thin and muscular and pretty and pert. *They created her*, she thinks. *Built her the way they've been trying to build the perfect gymnast for years.*

Broussard reaches for a small bucket she hadn't seen, dips

what almost looks like a paintbrush into its depths, then slathers the place between the girl's ankles and shins with a thick, whitish-green paste. The smell of chalk and pine is heady. Nan starts to bring her hand up to her nose. But before she can, a hand wraps itself around her neck.

"Woman issues, huh?" Russell growls. "You're going to be dealing with a lot more than woman issues in a minute." He drags her from the shadows of the hallway, out into the relative brightness of the gym, dodging her kicking legs and flailing arms.

"I wanted you in better shape before you underwent the procedure, but your meddling, coupled with Nadia's little setback tonight, means we'll have to do it now." He throws her to the ground. Nan pops up instantly, eyes darting between Cherry and Broussard.

"I told you we would never find toe point like yours again," Cherry says.

Nan steps back, bringing Russell into her line of vision with the other two. Broussard licks his lips. Russell rubs his moustache. Cherry scowls.

Nan slips one hand under her sweatshirt, digs into her fanny pack, and emerges with the gun.

It's small, an easy-to-wield Smith & Wesson. Nan knows exactly how to use it. Russell had been right; her retirement had drawn out more of the crazies than usual, and it made her feel better to have the gun. Safer. More in control of her fate.

"Thank you for drilling into me the importance of training and preparation," she says. Cherry opens her mouth, but Nan levels the gun at Cherry's midsection and squeezes the trigger. "Besides the obvious," she says, and jerks the gun in the direction of the monstrosity on the table, "that was for locking me in that hotel room in Australia and feeding me nothing but celery and carrots."

She turns. Russell is gaping at her, twin splotches of color in his cheeks.

"Nan," he says.

Nan doesn't let him finish. She's sick to death of hearing what he has to say. She lowers the gun and shoots first one knee, then, before he can collapse, she shoots the other. Russell joins Cherry in writhing agony on the ground. A few feet away, a chalk stand has been overturned. Their blood pools with the white powder to form a thick, scarlet paste.

"That was for making me compete with two torn meniscuses."

She turns her attention to Broussard, who is taking slow, cartoonish steps backward, as if he might simply escape while she reminisces about the past with her former coach. She points the gun at his crotch. "Tell me where the phone is," she orders.

Broussard grunts.

"*Tell me where the phone is,*" Nan says in the same voice that the doctor—that all three of them—used to use to demand things of her, of other gymnasts.

"The... it's in the lodge. There's a stairwell hidden at the back behind the kitchen."

"Thank you," Nan says. "That's very helpful." Still aiming at his crotch, she pulls the trigger. Broussard hits the mat like a rotted-out tree. He howls. Bright red blood shoots between his fingers. His face twists with pain. This display doesn't bring her pleasure, but she experiences a certain amount of satisfaction on behalf of her teammates.

"That's," she begins, unable to keep the disgust from her voice, "oh, who am I kidding? We all know what the fuck that was for." And with that, Nan turns and starts to walk away.

A noise stops her. Two, actually: an otherworldly humming and a low, short groan. Raising the gun, Nan turns back around.

The stitched-together gymnast is sitting up. She rubs the sutures at her neck, the place where Broussard spread the paste, which is now glowing with a soft, cool light. She reaches down and rubs the sutures at her legs and ankles next. It's *the paste* emitting the humming, and while Nan doesn't understand how this is possible, it is no less unbelievable than the girl sitting before her. From this lesser distance, the girl—Nadia, Russell had called her—appears both more macabre and more beautiful at once.

Nan is about to cover her ears against the noise when the humming stops as abruptly as it started. The stitched-together gymnast cocks her head as if suddenly aware of the groans coming from beneath her. She looks down, sees the mangled forms of the trio responsible for her state. Nan watches Nadia watch them, the pools of their blood seeping, spreading, growing into a glistening black lake. Sees her strange, bright face break open in a smile.

Nan lowers the gun. She goes to Nadia, helps her off the table. She puts an arm around her, and together, they leave the pit gym in their wake. Nan leads them purposefully in the direction of the lodge, the perfect, patchwork gymnast striding next to her, as lumbering as a monster. As graceful as a shadow.

She'll call an ambulance when she gets to the phone. She doesn't want Broussard or her coaches to die. Just wants them to answer for what they've done. She steals a glance at Nadia's feet, then her own. *For what they were going to do*. The hidden stairwell at the back of the kitchen is their destination. She should have known the phone would be hidden. Russell Walker and his games. All three of them and their obsessive guarding of secrets.

Nan feels for the notebook in her fanny pack, fans the pages and pages of phone numbers as she walks out into the night. She'll call the reporter from the *Times*. Give him a different kind of tell-all from what he was expecting. The sky is a cold, clear tapestry. As she walks, she remembers the promise she made to herself.

Look up, Nan. Don't forget to look up. Beside her, Nadia follows the trajectory of her gaze.

Above them, billions and billions of stars twinkle back.

❧ ❧ ❧

Christa Carmen lives in Rhode Island. She is the Bram Stoker Award-winning and two-time Shirley Jackson Award-nominated author of *The Daughters of Block Island*, *Beneath the Poet's House*, and the forthcoming *How to Fake a Haunting*, as well as the Indie Horror Book Award-winning *Something Borrowed, Something Blood-Soaked*, the Bram Stoker Award-nominated "Through the Looking Glass and Straight into Hell" (*Orphans of Bliss: Tales of Addiction Horror*), and co-editor of the Aurealis Award-nominated *We Are Providence* and the Australiasian Shadows Award-nominated and Ditmar Award-nominated *Monsters in the Mills*. She has a BA from the University of Pennsylvania, an MA from Boston College, and an MFA from the University of Southern Maine.

When she's not writing, she keeps chickens; uses a Ouija board to ghost-hug her dear, departed beagle; and sets out on adventures with her husband, daughter, and bloodhound–golden retriever mix. Most of her work comes from gazing upon the ghosts of the past or else into the dark corners of nature, those places where whorls of bark become owl eyes, and deer step through tunnels of hanging leaves and creeping briars only to disappear.

The Green

Michael Rowe

TWO THINGS MADE news in the town of Oldright's Cabbagetown neighborhood in the summer of 1969 when Terry Nulty was eight. Neil Armstrong and Buzz Aldrin became the first humans to walk on the lunar surface, and something in the grass near the Dromgoole family crypt in St. Brendan's Cemetery bit Mary Agnes O'Toole so badly that she needed fifteen stitches in her left hand.

From what Terry had heard—Mary Agnes was two grades ahead of him, so he had no first-hand knowledge, only what had filtered down through the usually unreliable schoolyard grapevine, and from listening to his mother gossip about it with her friends over coffee in the kitchen as Terry listened from the upstairs landing—Mary Agnes and two of her friends had been playing among the graves after church.

"Who lets a young girl play in a graveyard, especially in her Sunday best?" Maureen Nulty, Terry's mother, tut-tutted to her best friend, Frieda Woolwich, Cabbagetown's dowager gossip. "Can you imagine? But the O'Tooles were always such an odd lot. The sort you never see at church unless there was an occasion, or to be seen."

"Maureen, I'm shocked!" Mrs. Woolwich trilled, sounding not at all shocked. "That poor girl little. Her little friends dragged her out of that graveyard *drenched* in blood, screaming blue murder. Blessed little fool that she was, she was poking her hands around behind some of the really old tombs at the far end, almost to the edge Potter's Field scattering grounds. You know, the ones with grates and doors on them. I heard from Birdie Clemmons that by the time they got Mary Agnes to the emergency, she'd lost a pint of blood and was near to fainting. Running some sort of high fever, too, Birdie says."

From his perch above the kitchen, Terry heard the sound of his mother's coffee cup clicking against the saucer. He knew from experience that her brow was furrowed, and her lips pursed.

"Birdie would know for sure," his mother said sagely, though Terry knew Birdie Clemmons had just heard it second hand like everyone else. "She always has her ear to the ground." The coffee cup clinked against the saucer again. "Do they know what did it? Did little Mary Agnes see anything at all? A rat? A racoon? She'd have seen it if it were a fox or a coyote, of course. Couldn't have missed one of those. Could it have been a squirrel?"

"For the Lord's own sake, Maureen," Mrs. Woolwich scoffed. "A *squirrel*? Whatever did it darn near took her hand off, or so they say. A *squirrel* doesn't do that. The bite was small, I'll grant you that. More like a rat's bite, they say, but deep. Very, very deep. Poor Mary Agnes, bless her. It's a mystery, that's for sure. Birdie said that the doctors hadn't ever seen a bite like that. But if I were you, Maureen, I'd keep Terry away from there. You never know."

"Oh, to be sure. None of the children are allowed to play

there anymore anyway, says Father Malloy. Though why he'd even need to say that is beyond me. It's a resting place for the dead, not a playground."

There was a moment of silence, then Mrs. Woolwich said pointedly, "Especially not boys like Terry, Maureen. You know how he is. He needs to be playing with boys his own age, normal boys, doing normal boy things in the fresh air and sunlight, not moping around and playing with girls, or lurking around cemeteries, bless him."

Terry heard his mother sigh, and he felt a familiar twinge of something between rage, shame, and sadness flare in his chest, knowing what that sigh of hers meant—it carried the weight of his entire childhood with it. He suddenly wished he hadn't been listening at all.

"No," his mother said. "Especially not boys like Terry." She sighed again, more loudly this time. "Don't worry, Frieda. He's not allowed to play there either. And you're right, of course, he needs some real friends. A graveyard is no place for children anyway."

It was decided by the mothers of Cabbagetown that the St. Brendan's graveyard was henceforth off limits to their children. The grounds had been searched by animal control from perimeter to perimeter for any trace of whatever had injured Mary Agnes, but to no avail. There was a less assiduous search of the ravines bordering the cemetery which sloped down towards the railway tracks along the Oldright River, but nothing of note lived down there except racoons, a few coyotes, and the occasional scant rangale of grazing deer.

Of the lives of the vagrants who came and went in the ravines, and who occasionally camped under the Oldright Bridge before the police could drive them off, the town knew nothing and cared even less, so whatever fate they met, whether they lived or died, and how, was irrelevant as long as no one had to see it, and no one ever did.

From time to time, the bodies of animals—racoons, the odd coyote, even, sadly, every now and then, a dog or cat that had wandered off—were found, mangled in the ravines bordering the cemetery, but no one thought anything of it except that it was sad. But that was occasionally the price of living in a town that encroached on wildness, as Oldright did.

Still, the prohibition remained in place. No child ventured into the cemetery, and whatever lived among the graves and tombs of St. Brendan's was left undisturbed for almost three years, until the lush spring of 1972 when Terry opened the gates himself.

❦ ❦ ❦

Everyone in Oldright said Terry Nulty should have been born a girl.

They said it in different ways and with varied intentions and tones, but never to make him feel good, happy, loved, or included. At best, he felt their worry that something was amiss in what should have been a well-ordered *normal* boyhood, a boyhood in which what they saw as Terry's unnatural softness should play no part.

Boys, he was often told, in one way or another, were made for sports, for dirt, for scraped knees, for pirate adventure, for captured frogs and snakes

When Terry was six, Dora Burns from down the street had knocked on the door asking for donations for her church, which was raising money to buy picture Bibles for the heathen children of Congo, so they could avoid hellfire in the afterlife. Mrs. Burns didn't attend St. Brendan's. The church she attended, the Holiness Tabernacle, was just past the Oldright town line, in a warehouse from which guitar music and loud singing could be heard on

Wednesday nights as well as all day Sunday, and Sunday night too.

Maureen was reaching into her purse at the exact moment Terry crossed the living room with his colouring book and a fresh box of crayons, with Bodger, the family's arthritic Labrador, trotting behind him. Terry could see from the way his mother was sitting on the edge of the sofa with a fixed smile on her face that Mrs. Burns had pushed her way in, and Maureen Nulty was making the donation to get her out of the house before his father came home.

Mrs. Burns had turned to Terry and sized him up with her cold silver eyes as though she was seeing him for the very first time, even though she'd been living on the street since Terry was born. She asked him in a bright voice why *in heaven's name* he was inside drawing on such a beautiful day instead of playing in the park with the other boys.

Terry replied, "Because boys are rough and cruel."

He'd spoken plainly, with a child's intuitive clarity, and he'd meant exactly what he'd said. For one awful moment, Mrs. Burns' face twitched as she tried to control herself. Then she'd broken out into shrill, chirping laughter and clasped her hands to her breast as though Terry had said the funniest thing she'd ever heard.

"Boys are so rough and cruel!" Mrs. Burns squealed, mimicking Terry's voice in an ugly falsetto that made even his mother flinch. She turned to Terry's mother. "Mrs. Nulty, what's wrong with him? Is he a boy or a girl? You'd better watch out, or he'll be wearing your dresses before you know it. If you bring him down to the Holiness Tabernacle, we can say some prayers over him and drive that sodomite demon of effeminacy right out of his poor little body, and he can meet some wholesome Christian boys, too."

Maureen went white. Terry flushed bright scarlet. He knew, from the pitch of her laughter, that what was funny to

Mrs. Burns wasn't what he'd said about boys being rough and cruel. She was laughing at *him*.

He ran from the living room and locked himself in his bedroom, where he burst into tears. From downstairs, he'd heard his mother and Mrs. Burns shouting at each other, and then the front door slammed. Terry had never heard his mother shout at another adult besides his father before and he was shocked in spite of himself.

His mother had come up to his bedroom afterwards and told him she was sorry, and that Mrs. Burns was a very unhappy woman, and probably very lonely too.

"She's an old pan-face," Terry wept. "I hate her."

"That's not very nice, Terry," Maureen said, trying to suppress her smile at *pan-face.* "We shouldn't call people names."

"She called me names," he insisted. "She called me an 'effeminacy.' She watches me sometimes when I walk past her house with Bodger, and her face is really mean. She called me 'little sister' once, and not in a nice way. I don't think she likes me, and I never did anything to her."

"Terry," his mother said carefully. "I'd like you to avoid Mrs. Burns from now on. Cross the street when you pass her house. I don't think she's entirely well. When people are cruel like that for no reason, there's usually something wrong with them. She's very religious, too, which makes it worse."

Terry was momentarily puzzled. "But aren't we religious, Mom?"

Maureen sighed. "Not the way Mrs. Burns is, Terry. They're not like us. Catholics don't carry on in public like those people do."

That night, Terry was given a second helping of dessert. Afterwards, when he was in bed, he heard his mother on the telephone calling the other mothers of Oldright and telling them about Mrs. Burns' visit.

"I'm telling you, Mary Pat, she frightened me," Maureen confided to Mrs. Hannigan. "I just think we should all be very careful of her. I know Terry is…different. I'm not saying he's not. But boys grow out that. I'm telling you, no normal grown woman speaks to a stranger's child that way, in their own home. Yes…I agree. Yes, Please pass that along. I'm going to call Joyce next. If you could tell Anne, that would be terrific. I think we'd all be a lot safer without Dora Burns on our doorsteps, begging for money for God knows what. You too, pet. Goodnight."

Within the week, Dora Burns was socially dead in Oldright.

Then, in the early hours of the morning, a little more than a month later, the neighborhood was awakened to the sound of sirens and the flashing of police lights, and screams, outside the Burns' residence. When Terry's father went out in his bathrobe to investigate with the other fathers, one of them told him that Mrs. Burns had been led away in handcuffs. The details were mercifully obscure, but there was some talk of a bow and arrow, and her husband's dog, which she'd apparently always hated.

"Dear God," Maureen said when her husband came back in and told her. "We were living down the street from a monster."

"We don't know all the details yet, Maureen," Sean Nulty said. "There's bound to be a lot of gossip, and we should make sure we're not adding to it. I hope you knew what you were doing, calling all your friends about her, and cutting her dead. I hope that didn't push her…well, you know. Over the edge."

"You're right about the gossip" she replied, ignoring her husband's implication. Both of them knew full well that Oldright thrived on gossip, and this story would take on a life of its own with or without their participation. "But at least we don't have to worry about her frightening Terry anymore. And frankly, she frightened me as well. You know those Protestants are crazy, Sean. Especially the Baptists. And that woman's type of Baptist is the craziest of all."

The next day, with his wife still in police custody, Mr. Burns' cousins arrived with a small, rented cube van. Within half a day, they had loaded up his belongings, and Mr. Burns himself, and driven away from Oldright forever.

Over the course of the awful, humiliating year that followed, his parents had enrolled him in sports teams with other boys.

It was not lost on Terry that, in spite of their loving words to him the night after her visit, they believed that Mrs. Burns hadn't been entirely wrong about their son. In spite of how disturbed she clearly was, his parents believed Mrs. Burns had seen something in Terry that they themselves had been trying to ignore, but which everyone else could likely see as plain as day. The perfidy of that knowledge stabbed him like a needle.

Sean had signed his son up for baseball, for soccer, even for hockey that fall, but eventually even Terry's father had to admit his son's athletic talents—if he had any—must lay elsewhere. His parents left Terry more or less alone after that, which suited everyone concerned, especially Terry, because Terry had a secret.

His secret was that Mrs. Burns had been right—Terry should have been born a girl, and the first true betrayal he experienced in his life was his own body's betrayal of his soul.

❧ ❧ ❧

In church Terry heard Father Malloy extoll that everything was possible with God, even miracles.

He listened raptly as the priest described the process of transubstantiation, how the bread and wine became the literal body and blood of Christ, even as they retained their original outer appearance. When good Catholics died and ascended to heaven, they were granted new, unearthly bodies in the spirit, which sounded to Terry like magic from one of his books of Celtic folktales about changelings, and banshees, and witches, and fetches.

In truth, Terry had always felt full of magic, no matter how many people told him he was just an ordinary little boy and should act like one for a change.

Playing alone down by the Oldright river, he felt every season, as though the cycles of the earth were changing inside of him, not just around him. In winter, past curfew, when the dark came early and the evening skies turned as holy blue and orange as any stained-glass window at St. Brendan's, Terry whispered to the coming night, urging its progress, delighting in the stars that appeared above as he ran home in the dusk by the light of the streetlamps.

In the spring, he could swear he *felt*, not just saw or smelled, the earth waking up. In summer, he could not believe that any ordinary boy felt the sun touch his skin in quite the way he felt it touching his, like a private gift.

Standing on the sidewalk with that sun behind him, Terry wrapped his windbreaker around his waist and pressed his legs together, making a shadow that looked like he was wearing a skirt. He pined for long hair and pretended that his hair was merely cut pixie-short, and that it was by his choice, and temporary.

Terry wanted to ask Father Malloy if God would ever consider granting him the new body—the girl's body he should have always had—now, not later, not after death, but he already knew the answer he would receive, even without the all-too-familiar looks the priest already gave him, as though he knew Terry's secret too.

Still every night of his life, as far back as he could remember, Terry had gone to sleep with one prayer on his lips before falling asleep: *Please God, when I wake up, let me be a girl.*

And every morning when he woke up and looked down, it was just another morning that God hadn't listened.

❦ ❦ ❦

Sometimes after school, Terry stopped by Moira's Antiques on Parliament Street to explore the bric-a-brac that had once belonged to Oldright's "great ladies," as the proprietor, Mr. Francis, described them. Poking around the trays of dusty paste jewellery and cheap plastic cameos, Terry suspected that the ladies hadn't been all that grand, but he appreciated the fact that Mr. Francis always seemed happy to see him and let him stay as long as he wanted and never made him feel like a strange little sissy boy to be endured and patronized.

Mr. Francis, who had never been married, was the only adult in Terry's world with whom he felt completely comfortable and accepted. He felt *seen* by Mr. Francis, as though some unspoken commonality allowed Mr. Francis to look past the obstruction of his body and see what Terry actually was.

Terry had heard other adults refer to Mr. Francis slyly as a "confirmed bachelor," which sounded perfectly fine to Terry, though he sensed it wasn't meant kindly when they said it. Something about the tone, or the slant of the eyebrow, reminded Terry of how they looked when they were telling him to get outside in the fresh air and play sports.

That late spring afternoon in 1972, Terry found an

ancient fur coat on a grimy satin hanger at the back of the shop. The coat, probably a decent imitation mink forty years before, had seen better days. It was the most beautiful thing Terry had ever seen.

He must have sighed audibly enough for Mr. Francis to hear, because Mr. Francis' voice drifted back from behind the cash desk where he was reading a movie magazine with Elizabeth Taylor on the cover. "If you want to try it on, Terry, go ahead," Mr. Francis said kindly. "There's a mirror in the dressing room."

When Terry stepped back out onto the floor of the shop, enfolded in the coat, smiling shyly. Mr. Francis clapped delightedly. "Why Terry, you could be the very legend of the Lady of Dromgoole in that coat. You look like a film star." Mr. Francis laughed, but it was a gentle laugh. "You were born for glamour."

Terry tuned away from the mirror and faced Mr. Francis. "The Lady of Dromgoole? Who's the Lady of Dromgoole?"

"You know the Dromgoole family, the ones in the graveyard at St. Brendan's with the big tomb at the far, far end, by the hill to the ravines? It's a bit of a ruin now, but you've seen it, I'm sure."

"Maybe," Terry said, knowing full well that he hadn't seen it. "We don't really go there since...well, you know. Mary Agnes getting hurt. We're not allowed."

Mr. Francis nodded, then continued. "Some of the early settlers in Oldright fancied themselves a bit grand, though most were no better than anyone else," he said wryly. "Just take a walk in the graveyard at St. Brendan's and you can see for yourself. Those families building those tombs expected to be remembered as kings. They settled their families down for their eternal rest accordingly. The Dromgooles, for instance. My granny worked as a housemaid for old Mr. Dromgoole in the 1920s, when he owned the original mill.

She always said he fancied himself a lord of the manor type. He claimed he was descended from the old kings of Ireland, if you can imagine it. He liked having Irish people working for him too. It might have been because he believed in extending a helping hand, but it could just as well have been because he never stopped feeling like an outsider himself, no matter how rich he was."

"But who was the Lady of Dromgoole?" Terry interrupted. He didn't care about the town's social history, but this Lady, whoever she was, sounded like something out of a storybook. It had never in his life occurred to him that anything with even a tangential connection to legend, or magic, could even exist anywhere as hidebound and suffocating as Oldright. "Was she a real person?"

Mr. Francis said, "My granny told me she was a family legend of the Dromgooles. Some ancestress or other—supposedly a princess of some sort, a thousand years ago." From their 'royal' times, no doubt. He chuckled indulgently. "One night, when he was in his cups and Granny was working late in the kitchen, he told her the story of Lady of Dromgoole. The Lady apparently had some dealings with the Old Ones, with the mischief makers, and that she'd haunted the family ever since."

Terry's eyes were wide. "The mischief makers?"

"You know," Mr. Francis said. "The goblin folk. Mr. Dromgoole called them 'the Green.' Aren't your people Irish too, Terry? You should know these things already." He winked conspiratorially. "Anyway, according to old Dromgoole, this Lady made some sort of bargain with them, but she welched on it, so they cursed her, or blessed her, depending on the story. The spirits can be so very unforgiving." He laughed again. "Truth to be told, Terry, most of the Dromgoole family spirits came out of a whiskey bottle, my granny always said."

The Green

❦ ❦ ❦

The wrought iron gates of St. Brendan's Cemetery weren't locked. There had been no need to lock them—the twin edicts of the mothers of Cabbagetown and Father Malloy three years before had held faster than any lock. They yielded easily when Terry pushed them open, just wide enough for him to slip through and into the graveyard.

He looked around quickly to see if anyone had noticed him, but he was entirely alone in the vast silence. Beyond the gates lay the cobblestoned path leading down to hill where the edge of the cemetery grounds grew unkempt and abutted the crest of the ravines beyond.

It was only early spring in Oldright, but already the air throbbed with the humid promise of the hot summer to come. The green scent of lush grass, crab apple blossoms, honeysuckle, and heavy new leaves was almost suffocating in its sweetness.

Terry checked his watch. It was already five in the afternoon, and he was due home for dinner at six-thirty. There was just enough time for him to explore St. Brendan's and find the Dromgoole family crypt. His *need* to see the crypt, after listening to Mr. Francis' story of the Lady of Dromgoole, possessed him entirely, overriding even his knowledge of how angry his mother would be if she ever found out that he'd disobeyed her by coming here.

As he followed the path down the hill towards the edge of the cemetery, where the oldest graves lay, Terry noted the complete absence of any sound. No wind stirred the treetops, no birds fluttered in their branches. Even his footstrike was absorbed by the soft earth littered with rotted pine needles and wood chips left over from winter. The only thing Terry heard was his own breathing.

At the end of the cobblestones, the path gave way to and

overgrown dirt path and veered sharply to the right. The thick trees cleared, and Terry had a view of the ravines and the wooden bridge above the Oldright River. The placement of graves on either side of the path grew sparser, and the inscriptions on the ones that remained were worn down by a more than a century of violent weather, to the point where the inscriptions were illegible, save for an odd letter or the fragment of a date.

Then, abruptly, rising above a small pine grove perched atop the highest point of land before the sharp drop into the ravine below, Terry found what he was looking for.

The crypt was constructed entirely of dove grey and black marble and granite, except for a wrought iron grate at the base of the east wall, which faced the ravine and the river. All around the tomb, a thick profusion of purple and white flowers carpeted the ground. Two wide marble steps led to the front entrance with two pillars flanking an iron door which looked to have been soldered shut more than a century ago.

The tomb, on its promontory, asserted itself imperiously over the surrounding graves and smaller cenotaphs. Above the door, below the peaked ridge of the roof, the name DROMGOOLE was cut deep into the worn marble.

Terry thought of Mr. Francis' words about the Drom-gooles expecting to be remembered as kings. He thought of the entombed bodies in their coffins, sealed away from the light and from the world of the living. If indeed they truly were the descendants of the kings of Ireland, this cemetery, an ocean, indeed a world, away from their homeland, seemed to Terry a lonely and desolate place to rest.

A darting movement among the graveyard flowers imme-diately to Terry's left caught his eye, and he reflexively took a half-step backward.

It happened so quickly that when he looked down, the

flowers were still twitching slightly and the grass around them was flattened, as though something had just moved through it. But he saw nothing except that the shadows from the Dromgoole crypt were lengthening by imperceptible degrees as the sky began to warm to the peach hues of spring dusk. The clouds shifted in the sky, flooding the graveyard with momentary brilliance.

Something glittered on the ground near the edge of the first step to the tomb door. Terry walked over to the steps and picked the object up.

In his hand was a heavy gold coin, worn almost smooth on both sides. It was like no coin he'd ever seen. He rubbed it between his thumb and index finger, clearing away the dried mud that covered half of it. On one side of the coin was the outline of a man's face in profile. His head was wreathed in a laurel crown. He had seen those in portraits of Roman emperors in history books, and in drawings of Pontius Pilate in his *Illustrated Children's Bible*. The letters encircling the coin were hard to read, but Terry thought he could make out the word *Brittaniarum*, which meant nothing to him. On the other side of the coin, a man in armour wielding a sword sat astride a horse, trampling some sort of beast. The year engraved at the bottom was 1825.

Terry tucked the coin into his pocket and turned away Above, in the trees, he heard a branch snap and something like a hiss—short and sharp, like an animal that had been disturbed in its slumber and woken to show a mouthful of teeth.

Terry realized two things in quick succession, his body reacting before his mind: he was abruptly aware that he was suddenly chilled; that, and he had the clearest possible sense that he was not alone in the graveyard. Every fantasy of romantic legends, or magic, or mystical ladies was gone, replaced by an instinctive, pressing need to be away from that spot, away from what now felt like hundreds of pairs of unseen eyes studying him with awakened interest, away from a lonely, desolate spot where he'd been forbidden to be in the first place.

Terry looked towards the ravine. He knew that if he ducked down the hill behind the tomb, he'd be out of the cemetery and into the open space of the ravines in less time than it would take him to retrace his steps along the path through St. Brendan's to the entrance.

Another branch snapped, this time closer to the base of the tree directly behind him. He turned and hurried down the hill.

❦ ❦ ❦

Terry was halfway through ravine when he saw the old man standing alone on the edge of the Oldright Bridge, staring into the river. Because his head was down, he couldn't see his face, but Terry didn't recognize him, even from his clothes, which were ragged and filthy.

And then the man stepped to the edge of the bridge and jumped.

For an instant his body seemed to hang suspended in the air, bent forward as though he was bowing, then it plunged downward, head-first, his legs scissoring in the air as he fell. The man landed half in the water and half on a rocky break-water that rose up in the middle of the river just below the surface. A muffled *snap* carried across the water and Terry knew his neck had broken on impact.

Terry stared, struggling to take in what he had just seen. Then he began walking slowly toward the spot where the man's body had landed, picking up pace with every stride until he was running. He didn't see the hidden root until it tripped him sending him face-first into the dirt, twenty-five yards from where the current had already carried the man's body to the river's edge.

Raising himself on one arm, he could see the man's body was moving. For a moment, his relief that the man was still alive overwhelmed him, but Terry saw that the man's head lolled at an unnatural angle and his eyes were closed. He was quite dead. The man wasn't crawling up riverbank, he was being dragged.

Terry stood up and stared harder. What he'd first taken for riverside grass was alive and moving. It rippled and undulated around the man's prone body like a corona, propelling it laboriously up the ravine hill towards the cemetery.

Coming closer still, Terry knew that what he was seeing was impossible, and yet he was seeing it. Dozens—no, hundreds—of tiny bodies surrounded the dead man, each one lifting or pulling some part of the corpse. Those that weren't toiling skittered across the man's chest and face, lifting his eyelids like they were window shades, then letting the drop again. Still others pulled the man's filthy white hair and beard, as though testing it for durability before seizing it and joining the others in their labours, using the hair like a rigging sling until it pulled out of the dead man's scalp, and they gave up, returning to the work of hauling the body by its clothes.

When Terry tried to focus on their faces, his vision blurred and did not clear again until he'd looked away. When he looked back again, he could see everything—the ravine, the dead man, even the creatures who, by now, were making remarkable progress up the hill towards the outer edge of the Dromgoole plot, except for their faces.

Then, abruptly they stopped moving. Their heads, or indeed what Terry assumed were their heads, crested with a shock of something like hair, inclined in Terry's direction, and he knew they had seen him. He could feel their eyes on him, even if he could not see their faces, and he sensed infinite coldness there. The creatures stepped away from the body and began moving slowly, and with menace, towards the spot where he stood frozen.

And then, with the last bit of strength and courage he had left, Terry turned and ran, as fast as he'd ever run in his life, in the direction of the Oldright River, and home.

❧ ❧ ❧

Terry woke to a sound like scratching at his window, and then the unmistakable sound of the latch turning on the frame. He felt a gust of cold night air as the window swung open in the darkness of his bedroom.

He'd gone to bed in tears; his parents had not only *not* believed his story of the old tramp jumping off the bridge, but they had also accused him of making it up as a story about why he'd been late for dinner. When he tried to tell her about the rest of what he'd seen, his mother had been apoplectic.

"I don't want you going to Moira's Antiques anymore, Terry," she said. "Not ever. It's not healthy. I don't know what we're going to do about you, young man, but I've just about had it with your...your *dreaminess*. It's all fine and good to have an imagination, Terry, but yours is out of control. No more fairytales, no more spending hours in that place, playing with rubbish. You're too old for this sort of thing, and I want you to start acting like a normal boy. We'll talk to Father Malloy about it on Sunday after church, and I'm going to call that odd Mr. Francis tonight and tell him that you're grounded."

Terry had begged her not to call his friend Mr. Francis. He promised her that he'd tell Mr. Francis himself tomorrow, but Maureen Nulty had made up her mind. After dinner, she ignored him until it was his bedtime, and she'd dispatched him curtly.

He knew better than to try to tell her why he was afraid to be alone in his room that night, and he'd tried to stay awake as long as possible with the light on. But in the end, he'd fallen asleep, and one of his parents had turned it off.

And now there was suddenly movement all around him and he could hear what sounded like the patter of dozens of tiny feet against the hardwood floor. When something landed on his chest and scampered away, he barely stifled a scream. He needed light at that moment as much as he needed oxygen.

Terry fumbled for the switch of the lamp on his night-stand and flicked it on.

In the circle of light around his bed, thirty or forty of the creatures from the ravine sat staring at him, unmoving and unblinking. Some were perched on his dresser, still others on his desk. A cluster of them sat on the shelves of his book-cases, legs dangling as though they were sitting on bleachers in a sports stadium waiting for a game to begin.

He saw them in their entirety this time—their ivory faces, their almond-shaped eyes with the ruby-red irises, their red mouths full of tiny sharp white teeth that gleamed in the lamplight—without the shifting illusion of perspective he'd experienced in the ravine, when their faces had blurred and shifted whenever he'd tried to focus.

They're allowing me to see them this time, Terry thought in wonder. *Last time, they didn't want to be seen, so I couldn't see them. Now they want me to see them. It's magic. Real magic, not the pretend kind.*

One of the creatures jumped off his dresser. A shim-mering green fire trailed in its wake as it landed on Terry's bed. It pointed its finger at Terry and shook it slowly back and forth

"I'm sorry," Terry whispered. "I didn't know it was yours. I just found it on the ground. Please, take it back."

The creature opened it mouth and hissed, the same awful sound Terry had heard in the trees by the tomb when he first put the coin in his pocket, and Terry saw all of its sharp teeth at once. He closed his eyes and waited for whatever would come next.

When he opened his eyes, the creature was bending low over Terry's hand, as though scenting it. It looked up and stared solemnly into Terry's face, then bent down and breathed in deeply again. The red mouth curled into a smile, and it stroked Terry's finger with both its hands in a gesture that was somehow both loving and familiar.

"You can see me?" Terry asked in wonderment. "You know me already, don't you?

The others, one after another, leapt down from their various perches around the room, all trailing the brilliant green fire behind them until the room was lit with the emerald phosphorescence of their passage. They surrounded Terry on the bed, all of them staring, all of them touching, caressing his arms and legs, and gently touching his face.

Terry said the only words that came to mind. "Make me a girl," he whispered. "Make me the Lady of Dromgoole. Use your magic," he pleaded. "If God won't do it, will you?"

If anyone in Cabbagetown had passed the Nulty home on Hyacinth Street that night, they might have seen the eldritch green light flickering from the topmost window until just before dawn.

But no one passed, because everyone in Oldright was asleep in their beds where they belonged; indeed, where any decent, practical man or woman, unburdened by an excess of imagination, or dreams, belonged. And when the sun came up, the Nulty house was just a house again like all the others, one among many where nothing remarkable ever happened.

❧ ❧ ❧

Mr. Francis looked up from the behind the cash desk when Terry walked into the store the following afternoon, but he wasn't smiling. He sighed and folded the newspaper in his hands. To Terry, he suddenly looked very old, and very stern, like every other grownup.

"Terry." Mr. Francis' voice was chilly. "What brings you in here today young man?" He'd always welcomed Terry unequivocally in the past, without asking ever him what had brought him into the store. What had brought him into the store had always been self-evident to Terry, and Terry had always believed Mr. Francis had been happy to see him. And he'd never, ever called Terry *young man.* But today he had, and the expression on Mr. Francis' face stopped Terry cold.

"Mr. Francis," Terry said. "What's wrong?"

"Terry, your mother called me last night. At my *home*," he said with emphasis. "She said you told her some wild story about why you were late getting home. Something about green elves, or leprechauns, or some such thing. Something about dead bodies, too. Did you say those things?"

Terry stared blankly. "I told her the truth. I saw them. Yesterday," he said. "The goblin folk. They live in the Dromgoole family crypt. The ones *you* told me about. I *did* see an old man jump off the bridge. I *did* see them carry his body up the hill to the graveyard. Last night they visited me in my bedroom. It's all true. Don't you believe me? Why are you acting like this, Mr. Francis?"

"I do *not* believe you, Terry."

"I'm telling you the truth." Terry said flatly. "This is what happened."

"Terry, you could get me into a lot of trouble," Mr. Francis said. "I know you don't mean to, but here we are."

"Get *you* into trouble? How?"

"I'm an unmarried man, Terry, and I run this shop alone in this town. People talk. I've let you come in here for three years to play dress-up, and play with the jewellery, and to carry on. I've really enjoyed our talks. You've got a vivid imagination. But I think your mother is right. You're too old to be hanging around in an old antique store. You should be out in the fresh air, playing with—"

"Boys my own age," Terry finished dully. "Is that what you were going to say, Mr. Francis? That's what everyone says. But I don't like playing with boys my own age. I like playing by myself, and I like coming in here." He hesitated. "Besides, I don't think I really *am* a boy."

Mr. Francis stiffened his face assumed a rigid cast that Terry had never seen before. "Terry, you *are* a boy. Whatever you pretend to be when you dress up in women's clothes here, you're just an ordinary boy, like all the others. It's all make-believe. I'm telling this to you because we're friends. And you need to stop telling stories that aren't true. I feel guilty for letting you carry on like this for so long, but I—"

Terry reached into his pocket and slapped the gold coin on the cash desk in front of Mr. Francis, cutting him off. "If I made it all up, then what's this?"

Mr. Francis frowned and picked up the gold coin. He pulled open the drawer under the cash desk and took out a magnifying glass and held the coin up to the light.

"Where did you get this, Terry?"

"I found it on the steps of the Dromgoole tomb. Last night, they came to my room to take it back, but they let me keep it. I don't know why."

Mr. Francis turned it over in his hands and looked at it

again. "You say you just *found* this? Just lying around by a grave? In plain sight? I don't believe you, young man."

"Not just *any* grave," Terry said, ignoring the fact that Mr. Francis had not only just accused him of being a liar, but also called him *young man* for the second time. Beneath the deep hurt he was feeling at this latest betrayal by yet another an adult—this one a friend, at that—who refused to believe that he was telling the truth, a spark of genuine anger flickered. "I found it by the Dromgoole family crypt. I told you. I don't care if you believe me or not. I'm telling the truth."

"This is an 1825 George IV gold sovereign, Terry," Mr. Francis said stiffly. "It's very rare, and very valuable. Less than four hundred thousand were even minted, and very few of them survived being melted down and turned into gold bars after World War One. People don't just leave these lying around. Tell me the truth. Did you steal it? If you tell me the truth, maybe we can fix it. I want to help, but you need to be honest, now."

Terry's vision blurred. "I didn't steal it. I already told you where I found it. I told you about last night in my room, and you don't believe me. I've never lied to you, and I'm not lying now!"

Mr. Francis gazed at him thoughtfully for a moment, his face softening, then silently handed him a tissue. He waited for Terry to compose himself, then spoke gently.

"Terry, I'm sorry," he said. "I shouldn't have called you a liar. You're a good boy, and you've always been honest. But I think you're very, very confused about what's real and what isn't. Maybe some of that is my fault for letting you hang around here playing with all these old things. But let's just imagine for a minute that I believed everything—*everything*—your mother told me you said. Let's imagine that it's all true: you finding the coin out in the open, where you say you found it. The old man on the bridge no one knows, the little green people visiting you, and all the rest. Let's imagine that you really *are* touched by some sort of magic, and you can see things no one else can." He paused. "Is this really something you want to play with? Those old families, you know, they brought things over with them on those boats. They may have been poor, but they brought everything they had, the good and the bad. Who knows what else they brought? I don't believe in old stories. And like I said, old Mr. Dromgoole was a drunk. But here and now, this gold coin you say you found in the graveyard obviously belonged to someone, and sooner or later they're likely come after it. Or" he added, "if they let you keep it, I'd wonder what they wanted in return."

"Never mind," Terry said. He wiped his eyes with his fingers. "It doesn't matter. You don't believe me. No one does."

Mr. Francis took a deep breath. "I think it's probably best that you do as your mother says and stay away from the shop for a while, Terry. I'll be happy to see you here again sometime later, when you're a bit older. I'll even keep that old fur coat for you!" Mr. Francis laughed, but it was a brittle, artificial laugh. "Right now, though, you live in your imagination too much for a boy your age."

Terry was about to protest again, but he knew it would be pointless The friendship with Mr. Francis was over. To Mr. Francis, he was, now, nothing but *a boy your age*, and a strange, dishonest, overimaginative one at that. If Mr. Francis had ever seen him as a magic girl inside a cumbersome boy's body, as Terry had always imagined Mr. Francis did, he didn't now. The bitterness and disappointment and betrayal pulled him with the inexorable force of an undertow.

"Do you want to keep the coin?" Terry said dully. In that moment he was utterly past caring. He hated the coin. He hated Mr. Francis. And mostly he hated himself. "Maybe you can sell it? I don't want it. Here," he said, sliding the coin back across the cash desk. "You can have it."

Mr. Francis was silent for a moment. He leaned back in his chair without touching it the coin. "No thank you, Terry," he said. "I don't want it in the shop. In fact, I don't want it anywhere near me. It doesn't belong to either of us. Like I said, I don't believe in goblins, but I still don't want whoever it *does* belong to knocking on my door some night, looking to get it back."

🍃 🍃 🍃

The rain that had been threatening all afternoon was falling in sharp cold spikes by the time Terry reached St. Brendan's just after five o'clock. The iron gates were unlocked and ajar, and he slipped through the entrance with ease.

Terry had wept all the way from Moira's Antiques and his eyes felt as though he'd rubbed them with sand. The cemetery beyond the gates was a green and white blur as he made his way along the path into the old section.

He knew the way by heart this time, and he moved quickly, giving no thought to his sodden state, or how he would explain it to his parents when he got home. The sky had grown prodigiously dark, and the rain was coming down harder. A sharp crack of lightning split the sky, and the air was suffused with the metallic sweetness of ozone.

Terry briefly tried to remember the rule of lightning—hide under a tree or stand in open ground? —but by the time he heard the basso profundo peal of thunder that shook the trees, he realized he didn't know, and he didn't care. The rain felt good on his face, cooling his sore eyes, and that was enough.

And in the next flash of lighting, Terry realized he'd made better time to his destination than he'd thought.

Rain ran like vertical rivers from the sides of the Dromgoole crypt. Broad puddles like small ponds had appeared in the spots where the earth of the wide plot was naturally dimpled with indentations he'd not seen the day before. The mud had risen to meet the carpet of flowers and grass, and they floated in the pooled rainwater like spatterdock.

Resting on the ground, in the exact spot where he'd found the coin the previous day was what Terry first took to be a sodden bouquet. Stepping closer, he saw that it was an intricately woven flower crown of purple and white flowers, flattened by the rain.

Gingerly he reached down and picked it up. Then, he placed the wreath on his head. He was unsurprised to find that it fit perfectly, as though it had been made for him. He closed his eyes and smiled.

Of course it fits me perfectly, Terry thought. *Of course it was made for me. It's a crown fit for a princess. It's a crown fit for the Lady of Dromgoole.* And then, rapturously: *They see me, even if no one else does.*

"Thank you," Terry whispered to the rain. He felt all the anguish leave his body. "Thank you."

Terry didn't notice the slumped figure carrying the umbrella standing under the magnolia tree nearest to the tomb until it was illuminated by a particularly bright flash of lightning. At first, he didn't recognize her, but then she spoke.

"What are you doing here, you little freak?" Mrs. Burns said. She sounded genuinely curious, as though she'd spotted Terry at the cinema and was asking him if he enjoyed the show. Her eyes were very bright. "You dirty little accuser of the brethren. Why are you out prowling around graveyards?"

"Mrs. Burns?" Terry drew a sharp intake of breath. "What are *you* doing here?"

"What are you doing here?" she mimicked in the high falsetto Terry remembered so well from that afternoon in the living room two years and half years before. This time, to Terry, she sounded quite insane. Her clothes were muddy, and her gray hair hung in lank gray clumps around face. "What do you think? I followed you in here, you little fairy. You were off in your own world, like you always are. I've been following you all day." She pulled a knife out of her raincoat pocket. "You and I need to have a little talk about what you and your bitch of a mother did to me. You wrecked my marriage, and I had to go away."

Terry felt his bladder empty, sending a warm stream of piss down his leg. "I don't know what you mean, ma'am" he said. "I didn't do anything to you. You just…went away."

"I know you called the police when I had that fight with my husband. I know you were watching when the police took me away. I know you were laughing. I saw you from your bedroom window. You were laughing at me."

"I wasn't." He backed up slowly. "I was asleep. I never saw anything. Mrs. Burns, why are you out here in the rain?" He looked over at the Dromgoole crypt with growing dread, knowing, as this madwoman did not, that they weren't alone. "Mrs. Burns, it's not safe here. We need to get you away from here. You need to stop shouting at me and calm down."

"There's nobody out here," she said, ignoring him. "I could do anything to you I wanted, and no one would even know. You could even scream, and no one would hear you over the rain. You and your mother ruined my life. You made my husband leave me."

"Mrs. Burns, *please!*" Terry pleaded. "They can hear you. Please, we have to go."

She tested the blade with the ball of her thumb. "Then again, even if I didn't use this, no one would believe you. No one would believe that I was walking around with a knife. Even if, say, someone threw some poisoned hamburger over the fence for your dog and he ate it, no one would know who did it. Everyone knows you're a liar, Terry, as well as a pansy. Everyone knows you go to that queer's antique store on Parliament Street and try on *fur coats* and *dresses*. Did you really think he never told anyone? He's a gossip, like those men always are. He told *everyone*. We laughed about it in church, before I went away. You have no *idea* how much we laughed. And now, I'm going to tell everyone about you prancing and mincing around this graveyard wearing flowers in your hair."

"My mother was right" Terry whispered. "You're crazy." His rage, which had banked since his discovery of the gift of the flower crown, blazed white hot again. "If you won't let me help you, it's not my fault. You deserve it."

Beneath the rhythmic drumbeat of the rain striking the muddy ground, Terry heard a familiar susurration from the depths of the Dromgoole crypt, and from high above, in the trees surrounding the graves. He saw the grass around the tomb separate and shiver, spraying droplets of water into the low air. As he squinted down through the rain, trying to focus on what he was seeing, Terry caught a flash of tiny, familiar hands, tapered with pearlescent claws he knew were as cruelly sharp as razors, which disappeared again behind the grass, into the mud.

For her part, Mrs. Burns didn't appear to hear anything at all except the rain, and the sound of her own grating voice. She was waving the knife in broad circles now, no longer even looking at Terry, but calling him all the foulest words—

words that he'd heard plenty of times from older kids, but which felt like whiplashes coming from an adult, especially as awful an adult as Mrs. Burns.

Terry realized that whatever was going to happen was going to happen. He felt some pity, but he was also very tired of feeling betrayed.

The Green fell on Mrs. Burns like a storm, dropping from the branches of the trees and tangling in her hair. They leapt at her from the roof of the crypt and sank their teeth into the soft skin of her face, and she began shrieking, peal after guttural peal, as the blood began to flow and her face became a crimson mask of agony. When they swarmed up her legs, scampering across her body and burrowing their faces wherever they found exposed flesh, shredding her clothes where they didn't, her screams spiralled upward into a higher and higher pitch as more and more blood ran into the puddles of rainwater like a gruesome tributary.

She fell on her knees, trying to claw the creatures off her body, but they held fast and burrowed deeper, biting harder and with increasing ferocity. When she opened her mouth to scream, one last time, two of the creatures scuttled across her face and sank their teeth into her tongue.

Terry felt his gorge rise. He had a sudden ricochet of memory—his mother, describing what had happened to Mary Agnes O'Toole in 1969, when something had bitten her behind these graves. *Mary Agnes was lucky*, Terry thought, feeling a horror so intense it felt like ecstasy. *She got away.*

He wondered how many times a scene like this one had occurred at St. Brendan's in the century and a half since the Dromgoole family settled in Cabbagetown and unpacked their secret treasure from the old country.

Writhing on the ground, Mrs. Burns reached one arm weakly toward Terry in a final act of mute supplication. He stepped back and whispered, "I'm sorry." And then, her thrashing body went still, and her eyes closed.

Terry heard the sound of metal grinding upon metal. The iron door of the Dromgoole crypt, which Terry had thought sealed, stood open, pushed outward from the inside. The century-old darkness and all its secrets loomed beyond.

The Green began to drag her up the steps and through the door. The trail of blood was already being sluiced away by the rain, and even to Terry's inexpert eye he knew that all traces of it would be gone within an hour. And as for the rest of Mrs. Burns, Terry knew that his new friends had even less of a desire to be discovered than he himself did.

Correction—than *she herself* did. Terry would never again be *he*. From now on, she was the new Lady of Dromgoole. In time, everyone would know it, just as she and her new friends now did.

Terry saw a shimmer of green fire eddy towards her from the door of the tomb as it swung shut, sealing itself again as though it had never been opened.

One of the creatures landed on her outstretched hand, light as a butterfly. It stared at her adoringly with its wide red eyes. Terry reached into her pocket with her other hand and proffered the gold sovereign.

It touched the coin and stroked it. Then it shook its head slowly, even regretfully. The creature laid a finger to its lips in an unmistakable gesture of silent conspiracy. Then it was gone.

By the time Terry reached the gate of St. Brendan's the rain had stopped, and the sun had come out. The air was again redolent of lilac, crab apple blossoms and honeysuckle, and the soft, milky light was shot through with prisms of yellow and green from the rain.

Sunset was two hours away, but Terry still had to come up with a believable story to tell her mother about why she was late for dinner again. She wasn't worried, though, she'd think of something.

Looking behind her one last time, Terry saw the most perfect rainbow descending in an arc from the sky over the ravines, touching the tops of the trees above the promontory where the Dromgoole tomb stood.

She knew that if she stared at it, the rainbow would vanish, because the legends were true: the guardians of every treasure beneath the earth worth discovering were shy that way.

🍃 🍃 🍃

Michael Rowe was born in Ottawa, and has lived in Beirut, Havana, Geneva, and Paris. They are the Shirley Jackson Award-nominated author of three novels, *Wild Fell*, *October*, and *Enter, Night*, as well as an award-winning essayist and a former journalist. Rowe is the author of two books of essays, a book of interviews, and the editor of four anthologies of short fiction, as well as the recipient of the Lambda Literary Award, the Spectrum Award, the New York Publishing Triangle Award, and the New Millennium Writing Award. In 2022, they wrote the Introduction to *Rolling Stone* magazine photojournalist Nate Gowdy's monograph, *INSURRECTION*, which won the 2023 Paris Photography Prize. Michael Rowe lives in Toronto.

Daughter of Dogs

Jessi Ann York

"No, I don't give a damn about the stupid 'Nam vet coming home today." Sheron Underwood sits hunched on the snow-dusted porch steps. "I was in the sixth grade when we pulled out of that dumb fucking war." The now twenty-three-year-old woman takes a swig of her steaming hot toddy. "She should have graced us with her presence *then*, if she wanted my smiling face at her welcome parade. I'm stayin' home."

"But it's not just her." Aunt Underwood leans against the doorframe, her velvet-gloved fingers loading film into her Polaroid Sun 660 instant camera. "She's bringing the abandoned K-9 units she spent the last year going back to Vietnam to search for."

"Since when do you care bout 'Nam and canines?" Sheron huffs another swig of hot toddy.

The Polaroid Sun camera clicks as Aunt Underwood takes practice photos of her disgruntled niece sitting on the porch steps in front of her. Beyond the Underwood house, the Wartrace Creek sits eerily silent. The extreme chill from the month prior still has parts of the water frozen. The gray winter sky in this part of Tennessee is about as dismal and barren as Sheron Underwood.

"A woman traveling Vietnam all by herself." Grandma Underwood muses from her rocking chair, her puffs of breath spiraling like spirits into the frozen air. "With only a pack of dogs to keep her company."

The old lady's favorite felt hat, the one with the quartz wolf brooch, casts a devious shadow over her grinning face. Sheron has never seen her grandmother without it.

"She left Rob Maddon all by himself." Sheron spits off the porch steps into the snow. "The war ended, but that woman just *had* to keep serving. And then when she finally *does* unlist, she goes and makes a big show out of rescuing those mutts."

"Why are you so protective of that boss of yours over at the distillery?" Aunt Underwood frowns at the instant photos she's taken of her niece. "From what I can see, he treats you terribly."

"Rob's hard on me, *because* of his damn 'Nam vet wife." Sheron finishes her drink. "I have no interest in feedin' that woman's ego today."

"*I* want to feed the wild dog woman." Grandma Underwood rises out of her rocking chair. "Maybe she'll keep coming back to Wartrace, if we do."

"I've heard she's covered head to toe in traditional Vietnamese tattoos." Aunt Underwood sighs longingly.

"*Why* would that fool stain her body with ink from the country she lost to?" Sheron spits a second time into the snow.

"Why would she go back for the dogs?" Aunt Underwood shrugs.

"She *is* a dog." Grandma Underwood descends the porch steps. "A feral woman. Just like the three of us." The old lady now adjusts the quartz wolf brooch on the top of her head, as she looks down at Sheron. "We need to meet her."

It always caused a scene whenever the Underwood women left their home.

Especially when all three of them were together.

Grandma Underwood, as usual, insists on carrying her mason jar of salt. Today the glass container holds a green-eyed bullfrog dehydrating inside its center. The crowd gathered around the town square instantly backs away from her, even before they see the frog writhing within the jar. There are several rumors about the men who make the mistake of meeting up with the old woman at the Walking Horse Hotel in the town square, the most prominent one being that they were transformed into the salted amphibians that Grandma Underwood constantly sprinkled around the Underwood home.

Aunt Underwood, who never went anywhere without one of her cameras, was said to peer into the very core of your soul after she took your photograph. Parents make it a point to cover their children's faces, as the thirty-five-year-old single woman clicks away with her Polaroid Sun. Aunt Underwood exclusively dresses in velvet and furs, even when she isn't presenting at the art museums or galleries where her photography is hung.

And then there was Sheron Underwood, whose Momma was sucked up into a twister on the exact day the poor girl turned thirteen. The only power Sheron had presented thus far was being the most gloomy, unpleasant, and downright heinous presence in all of Wartrace, Tennessee. Which seemed a huge feat, until you realized the rural town's population was barely over five-hundred people. The gossip among the townsfolk is that the twenty-three-year-old girl was at the ripe age when the women in her family communed with Satan to get their powers.

This, of course, was all bullshit to Sheron.

Aunt and Grandma Underwood would *never* worship a *man* like *Satan.*

No, those two only prayed to the solid amethyst wolf altar they kept in the back of the house. And she was a *lady* wolf, from what Sheron had overheard of the women's late-night invocations. So it was no surprise to her that the other women in her family were spellbound by the stories of the feral dog woman who'd spent the last year wandering the distant jungles of Vietnam.

Sheron, on the other hand, wasn't impressed.

At least not yet.

Only when the Vietnam War vet's truck is discovered totally abandoned on the outskirts of town a whole hour later, does Sheron's interest pique.

"Apologies for the wait." Rob Maddon's face is redder than a rooster's comb when he returns with the group who discovered the truck. "My wife apparently wanted to walk the dog first after the drive from the airport, but I'm sure she'll be back soon."

"Dog?" Grandma Underwood scratches under her felt hat. "As in singular?"

"Well, the war did end over ten years ago." Aunt Underwood looks up from her camera. "Now that I'm thinking about it, most of the K-9 units would be awfully old now. Maybe our feral friend was only able to find one during her journey?"

"Then why would Rob make it sound like a whole damn kennel was coming home with her today?" Sheron's stone-colored eyes narrow on her boss.

All last month at George Dickel distillery, she'd been forced to listen non-stop about how the Maddon house was going to be overrun by a pack of slobbering dogs.

The question was, who'd been exaggerating?

Rob's wife or Rob?

So far, the woman in question had shown zero interest in appearing before the large crowd her husband had gathered for her. It didn't match the picture of the attention-seeking hero that he'd painted of her during her absence.

Aunt Underwood clicks a single photo at Rob Maddon's red face, then frowns deeply.

"Let's leave." She whispers to Grandma Underwood.

"Thirty more minutes." Sheron crosses her arms. "I want to see the kind of woman who keeps a crowd like this waitin' in the cold."

"Building this crowd wasn't her idea in the first place," Aunt Underwood says. "She's not coming, and he knows it."

❦ ❦ ❦

"I want you to quit your job at the distillery."

It's a day later, and Sheron Underwood is in her normal spot on the front porch steps, only this time Aunt Underwood is standing in front of her shivering.

"Because of one photo you took yesterday?" Sheron grunts after her standard sip of whiskey. "No."

"I know you enjoy your job, because your mom used to work it—"

"I *got* my job, *because* Momma used to work it." Sheron corrects her aunt with a snarl. "And I'm about to be promoted to manager. No, I ain't quittin'."

"You've been saying that for the past year. That man won't let you get promoted." Aunt Underwood squeezes her velvet camera harness. "Just like he won't let that poor wife of his get any peace. I've seen it. It's why she left for Vietnam in the first place. I want you far, far away from him."

"I'll do as I please." Sheron spits.

This entire conversation was fucking ridiculous to her. It

wasn't like Rob Maddon had purposely gathered all those townsfolk yesterday, just so he'd have an excuse to get mad at his shy wife when she hid from the crowd.

That would be absolutely insane–right?

"You're going to walk over to Maddon house this instance, tell him you're quitting—" Aunt Underwood pauses to smooth the creases of her velvet dress. "And then you're going to invite Miss Maddon over for dinner on your way out."

"The hell I am." Sheron rises to her feet, causing the entire porch to creak. Her body is dense from carrying grain bags and barrels every single day at the Dickel distillery.

"Your mom also got this angry whenever I confronted her about Rob." Aunt Underwood mutters at the snow.

"He's hard on us. So what?" Sheron knocks all the icicles off the porch railing with a single kick of her boot. "Tough love is just how men like him communicate. You wouldn't understand. Your pretty little skin is too thin for it."

"Is that truly what you believe?"

The two women blink. Grandma Underwood has somehow snuck up the gravel path to the house without making a single noise. Today the old lady has a red-gilled mudpuppy inside her mason jar.

"Believe what?" Sheron can't meet her grandma's wispy blue gaze directly.

"Tough love." Grandma Underwood holds up the mason jar to marvel at her mudpuppy's unnatural, hazel-colored irises. "You think it makes you stronger?"

"Sure." Sheron shoves her hands into her pockets. "Why not?"

"Stronger than your aunt?" Grandma Underwood continues smiling at the jar, as if it's more interesting than this conversation. "Who you are talking back to right now?"

"Look, *she* started it. I'm just—"

"Stronger than me?" The old lady glances up at Sheron with the same intrigued grin, as if her granddaughter is just another creek critter to collect.

Sheron doesn't get a chance to register the frequency of that comment. She's too distracted by the German Shepherd wobbling up the driveway. The closer the retired K-9 unit gets, the more white hairs become visible around its muzzle. If it weren't for these distinct age spots, the dog would be solid black.

"Which one of you is responsible?" Sheron grunts, as the German Shepherd helps itself to the porch step directly below her feet, its old ears drooping slightly.

Aunt Underwood doesn't bother responding. She's too busy whipping out her camera to snap a photo, before her niece can shoo the dog away.

"Such a fetching familiar." Grandma Underwood coos at the German Shepherd. "You'll have to ask Miss Maddon what her name is."

"Seriously, you two?" Sheron grits her teeth, as the older ladies gather to "ooh" and "ahh" at the photo Aunt Underwood took. "That Nam' vet's probably worried sick about her old fart of a mutt. It ain't funny."

"Oh, it's hilarious." Aunt Underwood gleams at the instant photo. "I've never seen more bizarre timing."

"Whatever." Sheron's face turns bright red, as the dog whimpers for the girl to pet her. "I'm taking the mongrel back before someone spots us from the road and gets the wrong idea. All we need is another rumor about you two sacrificing people's animals." Sheron pauses halfway down the steps, the dog merrily in tow behind her. "And I am *not* quittin' my job while I'm there."

"Invite Miss Maddon over for dinner instead." Aunt Underwood waves her niece off.

Sheron is barely halfway down the gravel driveway, when

she hears a distant voice calling for the dog. The Vietnam vet is two miles down Bugscuffle Road and hollering at the top of her lungs. The instant Sheron walks out onto the street with the solid black German Shepherd glued to her side, the war vet begins sprinting toward them. The woman looks about the same age as Aunt Underwood, and yet is somehow twice as thin and short. The tattoo-less, doll-like girl with silver-blonde hair does not match the image Sheron had in her head. At all. Maybe she really *was* a woman like the Underwoods, if the jungle hadn't swallowed her dainty body whole.

Sheron decides to say absolutely nothing, as the 'Nam vet drops to her knees in front of the German Shepherd. The Underwood woman would rather wait and see what the stranger willingly reveals about herself first.

"Oh, Kali." The woman pulls the dog's face into her own. "My heart."

Kali barks in confusion, as if her ancient K-9 nose can still register the cortisol and adrenaline sweating in beads off her 'Nam vet. The cataracts inside the dog's deep brown eyes practically melt into chocolate now that she's in the presence of her favorite human.

"I'm okay girl, you just scared me a little." The woman looks up at Sheron. "Kali is usually so well behaved, I swear. The fence at our house was left wide open, and she didn't know any better."

"Who left it open?" Sheron fights to keep her face expressionless.

There's a twitch inside her stomach. Something about seeing the war hero on her knees is simultaneously frustrating and exciting for the twenty-three-year-old. She can't decide if she wants to yell at the stranger to get up off the slushy road, or if she likes the feeling of being on top of her.

"What's your name?" The war vet remains on her knees. "My friends call me Maddon."

Sheron says nothing back. She's too busy digesting the fact that Maddon won't call Rob out for leaving the gate wide open, but she *will* claim his surname as if it's her own. It reminds Sheron of how her aunt and grandmother similarly go by "Underwood" to the rest of the town. If those women ever did have first names, Sheron and the rest of the town had long forgotten them. The same could be said whatever man their last name had come from.

"Underwood." Sheron offers her hand to Maddon.

The mix of frustration and excitement knotting inside Sheron's stomach only expands, as she nearly yanks Maddon into her chest. The war vet somehow weighs even less than she looks.

"Good lord, woman." Sheron steadies the shivering stranger by her shoulders. "When was the last time you *ate*?"

"I was on the move a lot last year. Picked up a parasite or two on the journey." Maddon quakes inside Sheron's grip. "But my word, *you're* more toned and thicker than the gaur meat I got those bugs from." She pauses, as if lightheaded. "I mean that as a compliment by the way."

"How else would I take it?" Sheron flashes her teeth.

Maddon grins back, sheepishly. Then winces.

Sheron assumes that Maddon is just pale and drained from fretting over Kali.

"How'd someone as delicate as you serve in the army for fourteen years?" Sheron says. She's intrigued by Maddon purposely not spilling the details on who she is or what she's accomplished.

"I was an intelligence specialist." Maddon reaches down to rub Kali's ears, instead of making eye contact with Sheron. It's clear she's uncomfortable talking about herself.

"What's that?" Sheron presses.

"I gathered, analyzed, and disseminated information." Maddon's sheepish grin only stretches. "Kind of like what you're doing right now."

"So you weren't Kali's actual handler?" Sheron doesn't bother hiding her curiosity anymore.

"I assisted in the planning and coordinating of missions." Maddon winces a second time. "Which usually involved sending K-9 units, like Kali, off to sniff for bombs and tunnels."

"So you went back to 'Nam to make amends for the mutts you put in danger?" Sheron said.

"Of course." Maddon frowns, her glassy eyes the same color as the shards of ice in the cedar trees above Bugscuffle Road. "Why else would I go back there?"

That was the exact moment Sheron claimed Maddon as her own. The traumatized woman didn't see herself as God's gift to earth at all, and Rob really had been projecting whatever narcissistic complex he had onto her. Which had Sheron *pissed* on her behalf.

"Why'd our dumbass military abandon the poor mutts in the first place?" Sheron says the next day, as the two women walk Kali beside the Wartrace Creek.

The dog's big, brown eyes are rounder than hedge apples, as she searches for the perfect stick to bring back to her war vet.

"They wanted to pull out fast, and the K-9 units were deemed as excess equipment." Maddon kneels to take the stick from Kali.

The ice on the river has begun to thaw, and the German Shepherd enjoys lapping at it in between rounds of fetch.

"Why'd you keep serving such God-awful people after all that?" Sheron asks a full week later, as Kali pulls even larger sticks from the melted edges of the creek.

Bits of sunlight break through the cedar trees, turning

their half-melted icicles the same watery blue as Maddon's gaze.

"I was in WAC, so I felt distanced from the branch of people who made those horrible decisions," Maddon says. "I only stayed for my team."

"What's WAC?" Sheron asks two weeks later.

"The Women's Army Corps," Maddon says, skipping a rock across what's left of the ice along the edges of the creek. "We were disbanded and integrated with the rest of the male troops in 1978." She then pauses to call for Kali, before the dog can go too deep into the water after the rock. "I really miss them."

"Are the male troops the reason you left?" Sheron asks a whole month later, when the creek is completely thawed and flowing again.

The clouds are gone, and only a crisp sky, as silver as Maddon's hair, remains.

The war vet says nothing, her focus on Kali's head staying above the creek.

Sheron playfully nudges the Nam' vet out of her trance.

Then flinches when Maddon instantly slaps her away.

The echo from Maddon's open palm against Sheron's face crackles like a whip across the frigid water.

"Sorry. I'm so sorry." Maddon backs away from the creek. "But you shouldn't touch people unless they give you permission to, Underwood."

Kali is at her comrade's side and snarling at Sheron. Whatever scents the dog's ancient nose are picking up from Maddon's body have the K-9 enraged.

"No, I'm sorry." Sheron rubs the spot where her temple is already starting to bruise. She can't help but think back now to how much the war vet had shivered the first time they shook hands.

"I—" Maddon can't finish, she's so embarrassed.

"*I'm* sorry." Sheron insists. "Tell me more about WAC?"

A second freeze rolls in that afternoon, and the creek turns back to solid ice.

❦ ❦ ❦

"I need you in my office, Underwood." Rob's face is its standard shade of rooster red.

"No." Sheron grunts. "Should've asked before I was halfway out the door. We'll talk in the mornin'."

"We'll talk now." Rob raises his voice, so that the other men in the distillery turn their heads. "It's about my wife."

"Oh, yeah?" Sheron does a half-turn in the doorway. "You get drunk and leave her dog gate wide open again?"

There are three things that prick at Rob in that moment.

The first is the Sheron's blatantly disrespectful tone.

The second is that it was *Maddon's* gate. Not his.

And the third was that Sheron was absolutely correct about him being drunk.

Again.

The searing silence that follows makes it clear Rob regrets calling attention to their dispute. He wasn't expecting the twenty-three-year-old to snap back. Normally Sheron obeyed him without question, but things had changed ever since Maddon's return.

"You need a ride home, Rob?" Sheron smirks in the doorway. "I can help Maddon find poor ol' Kali, if you've sipped too much of your own product again today."

"You spend any more time with that damn woman, and your head is gonna swell even larger than hers." Rob puffs his chest in front of the other men. "I don't want you 'round each other no more."

"Hey, you don't have to tell me twice." Sheron huffs, her gaze aimed toward the beams of sunlight that bleed between the cedar trees beyond the distillery's open doorway. "I haven't seen Maddon since she gave me this pretty little shiner on my temple almost a week ago. How's she doing?"

The next time Sheron glances back, Rob has his hand on her shoulder and is shoving her out the doorway. Sheron can only laugh in wonder, as he slams the distillery door closed behind them. The ice-coated parking practically hisses from the amount of hot air rolling off their inflated silhouettes.

"Why is she calling *your* name at night?" Rob shouts.

"Why is she *what now*?" Sheron isn't laughing anymore. "The fuck are you insinuating, Rob?"

"That *bruise* on your temple?" Rob jabs his finger at Sheron's face. "Do you two *dykes* think I'm stupid?"

That's the exact moment Sheron put in her two-week notice, with a direct punch to her boss's face.

Aunt Underwood, to her absolute delight, pulls up just in time to catch a glimpse of her niece wiping Rob's blood from her fist. She is cheering Sheron on, grinning ear to ear with pure delight, practically wrecking the family truck out of sheer excitement.

Until she snaps a photo with her Polaroid Sun.

"You know, you don't have to cave and show your belly so easily. I deserved that punch." Sheron remembers the last thing she said to Maddon beside the creek.

The memory burns and bites inside her stomach like whiskey.

"No one deserves to be punched." Maddon's ice-colored eyes had watered. "For any reason. Ever."

"Have *you* been punched?" Sheron's tone darkened. "Is that why you always act all submissive and stuff?" The twenty-three-year-old's knuckles popped. "Who punched you?"

"I'm not submissive." Maddon's face scrunched at Sheron's clenched fists. "I just don't like being aggressive, and I shouldn't have to act that way to get respect."

"Yeah." Sheron sighed, once she realized how loud her gruff voice was echoing off the creek. "You're right. I'm sorry."

"No, you're fine." Maddon kneeled to pet Kali. "I like spending time with you, Underwood."

"You do?" Sheron scoffed. "Even though *I'm* aggressive?"

"Not toward me, you're not." Maddon looked up from Kali, her face flushed. "I can show my stomach around you, and still feel safe."

Sheron said nothing, the creek somehow growing louder inside her ears.

🥄 🥄 🥄

"You said it's been an entire week since you've last seen Maddon?" Aunt Underwood chases up the porch steps after Sheron, once they're home. "You need to check on her. Tonight. Now."

"You heard what Rob said." Sheron's face is as red as the leftover smears of blood on her fists. "Whatever's going on in Maddon's bedroom is between her and husband. I ain't got no part in any name callin'."

"Lord, don't be such a bull." Aunt Underwood groans. "It perfectly normal if you two have feelings—"

"*Feelings?*" Sheron whips her head over her shoulder. "I ain't no fucking queer. Shit, I don't even like men. I'm *nothing*. No romantic feelings. For nobody. Ever."

"Sheron Underwood, that might damn well be the queerest thing I've ever heard." Aunt Underwood stomps her velvet boot against the porch, causing the mason jars lining the railing to clink. "And I can promise you, it will be the single biggest regret of your life, if you don't check on that poor woman tonight."

"Now, now, ladies." The front door creaks, as Grandma Underwood shuffles outside. "You're disruptin' the moon water."

"Please talk sense into her." Aunt Underwood flits past Sheron to show her camera to the family matriarch. "*Please*."

"I'm not making anyone do anything." Grandma Underwood hides her grin with a yawn, then nods toward the cold stars that twinkle beyond the porch. "What was it our Sheron said about tough love?"

❦ ❦ ❦

Two weeks later, Kali is in front of the Underwood home.

Only the dog's eyes are the color of ice instead of their usual brown.

Sheron Underwood hesitates to acknowledge the German Shepherd, her gut instantly twisting in on itself. Sheron's cup of hot toddy shakes inside her hands, but never reaches her lips.

"You're not going to say hello to your friend?" The brim of Grandma Underwood's felt hat just barely conceals her shit eating grin, as she rocks in her chair.

Sheron says nothing, her gaze locked on Kali's muzzle. The war dog's gray hairs have drastically spread up its entire face since the last time Sheron saw her. They're almost as silver as the flurries of snow chittering down from the sky. Aunt Underwood remains inside, the floorboards whimpering, as she paces back and forth behind the front door. The dog with ice-colored eyes doesn't pant or wag its tail. It merely sits and waits for Sheron to take them to the creek.

There is no one on the other line when Sheron tries to call the Maddon house. Only a pop and a shudder, as the phone cord practically unravels inside Sheron's white-knuckled fist.

"Can you take a picture of it?" Sheron asks later that night, when the dog still hasn't moved.

It's hard to tell whether or not the gray on its muzzle is spreading, or if the dog simply has remained still for so long that frost is now creeping across her in a silvery layer.

"I really don't think it would make you feel any better if I did," Aunt Underwood says, face down on the couch. "In all honesty, I know *I* don't want to look at that photo."

"Weren't you supposed to go job hunting today?" Grandma Underwood cleans her jars by the sink, now that the sun has gone down. "Your aunt has her photography. I have my salt circles. You'll need to find your own calling, now that your time at George Dickel has ended."

Sheron says nothing. The twenty-three-year-old hasn't so much as blinked at her grandmother ever since the dog with ice-colored eyes first showed up that morning.

"You can't hide inside this house forever, Sheron." Grandma Underwood's expression remains hidden, as she washes her jars by the sink. "I'm sure she won't bite."

"I don't understand." Sheron mutters between clenched teeth. "Maddon didn't do nothin'."

"Yes, my dear." There's a clink as Grandma Underwood places her final mason jar into the drying rack. "And neither did you."

"Then why is the fucking dog outside?" Sheron snaps.

"Like I said," Grandma Underwood turns away from the sink. "Your aunt has her photography. I have my salt circles. And you had your walks by the creek with that feral woman and her dog." Grandma Underwood's smile is as sterile as the searing white moonlight outside. "Time to move onto the next thing, sweet girl."

❦ ❦ ❦

"Can you promise me something?" Sheron remembers the order she'd given Kali the first night they met.

The memory is as loud and cold as Tennessee creek water inside Sheron's head. Kali had panted and slobbered at Sheron's feet, while Maddon fixed the latch to the dog gate behind them.

"You keep that poor woman as close as possible to you." Sheron backed away, as the dog tried to lean into her hand. "*Especially* when she's at home with Rob."

Kali whimpered, confused by Sheron's refusal to pet her, despite the intense eye contact.

"I need to know Maddon has someone who's always next to her inside that house," Sheron said. "Okay?"

At the sound of Maddon's name, Kali stopped panting. Then perked her old ears, as much as she could manage, beyond their natural droop.

For a fraction of a second, Sheron felt herself fall into the ancient K-9 unit's foggy brown eyes. The intensity of her favorite person's name inside her hot ears. Frost teething at the splits inside worn paws that once traveled across red, blistering rice fields. Rattling cages and brittle chicken bones. Shrapnel and smoke. Loyalty and longing. Hiding and running. Screaming. Then silence.

"Kali."

Both Sheron and the dog turned their heads at the exact same time. It had vibrated through the two of them, the sheer joy of the sound of that name, now amplified tenfold by Sheron's order, as if it were the first time Maddon had called out to Kali in the jungles of Vietnam, echoing again and again. River to river. Ashes to dust. One lost dog to another.

"Come here, sweet girl."

Sheron watched the German Shepherd run toward her war vet, knowing with full confidence that the two would never be separated.

🐾 🐾 🐾

"You secretly wanted the feral woman to stop by our house that first day." Grandma Underwood stands next to Sheron by the window. "Didn't you?"

A full night and day has passed, but the dog still waits for Sheron in the front yard.

"Maybe I was curious after the weird show Rob put on in the town square." Sheron glances over her shoulder. "What's your point?"

"If you wanted to know why no one at the Maddon house is answering your calls." The floor creaks as Grandma Underwood shifts her weight. "You could."

Outside, the dog with ice-colored eyes moves even more silently than the frozen creek beyond the Underwood home, its entire body now as silver as the blistering stars in the midnight sky.

"No, not that direction." Sheron's breath fans out around her in moonlight like a noose. "We need to go to your house."

The dog stares back at Sheron without blinking, its hunched shoulders still pointed toward the creek.

"After we go to your house, I promise I'll take you on a walk beside the—"

Before Sheron can finish, the dog with ice-colored eyes has jerked its head toward the direction of the Maddon home, as if it somehow knows the futility of those words.

Sheron doesn't bother to knock when they reach the

Maddon home. The door is ajar anyways, and there are claw marks surrounding the knob on the other side.

Rob Maddon is, of course, passed out on the couch, with seven empty bottles of George Dickel surrounding him. Sheron can only assume the stupid man was so wasted, he couldn't stop Kali from clawing open the front door to escape. Shattered picture frames glitter on the floor. Dents puncture in fissures across the walls. Splatters of dried blood clot in the carpet.

Maddon is nowhere to be found, but Sheron knows better than to call out for her.

She's known since the first second she saw the dog with ice-colored eyes.

Sheron recognizes the rotting smell drifting through the house, and follows it toward the basement door, which is also ajar and covered with claw marks. A glass of George Dickel is shattered beneath its hinge, as if Rob had made the mistake of opening the door too soon for Kali.

"Two weeks." Sheron says to the dog. "I didn't check on you both for two whole weeks."

The trail of shattered glass and dried blood continues down the steps and into the shadows of the basement. Sheron can't bring herself to turn on the light, the smell is so strong.

She can picture it all inside her head. The fight that carried over when Rob came home to Maddon with a bloody nose. His drunk fists beating into her, because he couldn't get to Sheron. Kali trying and failing to stop him, because the poor dog was too old. A hard thud at the foot of the stairs, followed by the desperate scamper of paws. Soft whimpers. The door locking shut. Two weeks without food. Meaty, red stench of a freshly pummeled corpse.

"It's okay, Kali." Sheron's voice is as numb as her fingers. "I know Maddon wouldn't have wanted you to starve down there with her." Sheron's eyes have adjusted to the dark now, and she can faintly see the outline of the gnawed remains.

The dog with ice-colored eyes seems utterly disinterested in what's left of her bones. Observing Sheron's reaction to them is much more important. She gingerly sinks her teeth into the twenty-three-year-old's jacket, then leads them both down into the darkness.

Sheron complies, even when the dog pulls her directly on top of the bones. Just as the first sob is about to leave the twenty-three-year-old's constricted chest, there is a stir from upstairs.

Rob Maddon cusses, as his feet touch the floor and immediately meet broken glass. He is still so utterly wasted, Sheron welcomes herself inside his wet brain before he can. He is, after all, a dog in his own crude way. Without knowing why, the drunk wanders toward the basement, where Sheron's sobs remain lodged inside her burning chest. He stumbles toward the open door, fumbles for the light switch. Then nearly tumbles, when he sees Sheron and Maddon hunched at the foot of the stairs surrounded by a circle of gore and bones.

"Fall," Sheron orders, with tears in her eyes and sparks between her clenched teeth.

The command is twice as strong as the one she gave Kali.

Sheron now steps out of the way, as the drunk piece of shit collapses down the stairs and pierces his head into the ribs and rot below.

Rob Maddon twitches, his mouth gaped in silence.

"Eat." Sheron turns toward the dog with ice-colored eyes. "Consume the fucking fool who did this to you."

The dog reveals its teeth–almost as if grinning.

Then sinks her fangs directly into Sheron's arm.

It's one clean bite. One solid pound of flesh that dances across the tip of Maddon and Kali's tongue, as they bolt out of the house and into the spiraling snow. A single, permanent scar that Sheron will carry for the rest of her lonely life. Because while the war vet and her K-9 unit would be bound together for all eternity—Sheron Underwood would certainly be alone.

"Ah, yes." Grandma Underwood smiles, when the twenty-three-year-old stumbles up the porch steps an hour later with a chunk of her forearm missing. "Tough love."

❧ ❧ ❧

Jessi Ann York's debut novel, TALONS AND NIGHTSHADE, is forthcoming March 2027 from Wednesday Books, an imprint of Macmillan. You can also find her short stories at several professional rate horror markets, including PseudoPod, Vastarien, Cemetery Gates Media, Love Letters to Poe, and more. Her first two stories, "Phases of the Shadow" and "Women of the Mere," were mentioned as standouts in the Summation section of The Best Horror of the Year Vol. 13, and her last two published stories, "Dimorphism" and "Mother of the Wind," were also mentioned in Best Horror of the Year Vol. 16.
Her creative work is represented by Elizabeth Copps, the founding agent of Copps Literary Services.

Head Hunter

B.D. Prince

CHANDLER PRATT STOOD on the mansion's porch surveying the two-story Tuscan columns. It seemed absurd to call the massive entryway a porch. There must be something more aristocratic sounding. Facade? Veranda?

The mansion wasn't his... yet. But not being born into the right family didn't mean he couldn't adopt one. He glanced at his corpulent wife clutching a gift bag and adjusting her dress which strained at the seams. Chandler sighed. Diana was all Hilton and no Paris.

He'd met Diana during her junior year of college while he was casting a production of Seven Brides for Seven Brothers. She hadn't exactly caught his eye but her last name definitely caught his ear. Everyone in town knew the name Nathan Cromwell, seeing that he owned half of it. Once Chandler discovered her daddy issues and how starved she was for affection, the rest was academic.

The university frowned on teachers dating their students so they kept their affair secret until after graduation. Despite her father's disapproval, Chandler got the last laugh when they eloped to Vegas.

Diana pressed the doorbell. Stately chimes echoed off the marble vestibule inside. She waited patiently despite still having a key. The awkward formality puzzled Chandler. She glanced back at him and smiled apologetically.

He wiped sweat from the back of his neck. Despite putting his long hair up into a "man bun," the humidity made his pores yearn for air-conditioning. He suspected his father-in-law took pleasure in making him wait, like a king reluctantly granting permission to approach the throne.

"We don't have to stay long, do we?" Chandler asked.

"It's only one day a year."

"That's what you said about his birthday. And Thanksgiving, and Christmas..."

The massive front door finally opened revealing a balding, gangly butler clad in formal attire.

"Miss Diana."

"That's *Mrs. Pratt*, there, Jeeves," Chandler said.

Diana entered and flashed a smile. "Thanks, Carl."

Chandler brushed past the butler into the grandiose foyer, their footfalls echoing off the marble floor. Surveying his future home, Chandler admired the grand staircase and vaulted ceiling with its glittering crystal chandelier.

"Please let Father know we've arrived, will you Carl?"

"Yes, ma'am."

Chandler strutted into the library and helped himself to the bar. He poured himself a glass of 20-year-old, single-malt Scotch, relishing its sweet almond finish and hint of smoke.

Surveying the floor-to-ceiling bookshelves, Chandler wondered how many the old man had actually read.

"Chandler, darling, do try and be civil today. It is Father's Day, after all."

"Me? Your father is the instigator."

"At least *try* to be cordial? For me?"

Chandler returned for a refill. Civil? With the man who

never missed an opportunity to emasculate him? She had a point, though. It wouldn't be wise to get written out of the old man's will.

Mr. Cromwell strode into the library. "Diana! To what do I owe the—"

Chandler snuck up behind the patriarch and shouted, "HAPPY FATHER'S DAY!"

Mr. Cromwell startled and clutched his chest. He turned slowly, face twisted in pain. The old man opened his mouth to speak but instead, his eyes rolled back in his head and he dropped dead on the floor...

At least that's what Chandler hoped would happen. Instead, his father-in-law hunched his shoulders and turned with a scowl.

"What are you trying to do, boy, give me a coronary?"

Chandler smiled.

Cromwell nodded at the glass in Chandler's hand. "I see you found the Scotch."

Chandler raised his glass in a toast. "You do have discriminating taste, Mr. Cromwell."

Cromwell muttered, "Wish I could say the same for my daughter."

"Happy Father's Day," Diana said, giving her father a peck on the cheek.

He wiped his cheek. "No need to get all slobbery about it."

Diana reached into her gift bag and produced a small, black felt box. "I got you something."

"You shouldn't have."

"I wanted to. Go ahead, open it up."

Cromwell opened the box revealing a gold tie clip. "Guess you can't have too many of these."

"It's a Cartier." Diana beamed. "And it belonged to John D. Rockefeller!"

Cromwell gave the tie clip a second look and grunted.

Diana's smile faded and her gaze fell to the floor.

Chandler cleared his throat.

"Oh, I almost forgot. Chandler has something for you, too. It's a poem!"

"A haiku, to be exact."

"Chandler wrote it himself."

Cromwell's brow furrowed. "He wrote me a *poem?*"

"A haiku," Chandler repeated.

"Well, hot diggity damn. Ain't this my lucky day."

Chandler threw up his hands.

"Father, don't be so rude. Chandler put a lot of time and thought into this." She turned to her husband. "Go ahead, honey."

Chandler struck a Shakespearean pose and gazed into the distance as he recited.

"Eternal winter
Gold apple rusts on the limb
As the hourglass bleeds."

Diana applauded. "Isn't that beautiful?"

Cromwell looked bewildered. "That's it?"

"Haiku is a very concise, structured form of poetry," Chandler explained.

The old man smirked. "Guess I shouldn't be surprised all I'd get from a socialist is empty rhetoric."

Diana sighed. "Oh, Father, you're incorrigible." She shot Chandler an apologetic look. "And no, that's not all Chandler got you. Here."

She pulled a cigar box out of the gift bag and thrust it at her father.

"They're Cuban," Chandler said with pride. "Philosophy professor at the university owed me a favor."

"You got me commie cigars?"

Chandler sighed.

"Ah... I'm just busting your balls, boy," Cromwell said. "Commies *are*_good for *two* things: vodka and cigars."

Cromwell ran a cigar under his nose. Was that a slight nod of approval? That'd be a first. Cromwell retrieved a cutter from behind the bar, guillotined the cigar's tip, and offered it to Chandler.

Trimming another, Cromwell placed the Cuban between his lips and gestured toward an ornate crystal table lighter.

Chandler retrieved the lighter and handed it to his father-in-law. Instead of taking it, he just glared. Chandler grudgingly obliged and lit the old man's cigar.

Cromwell puffed the Cuban then exhaled a cloud of smoke toward Chandler. Again, the slight nod, and this time, a thinly-veiled smirk.

Chandler smiled and counted, Three... Two... One...

BLAM!

Cromwell's cigar exploded, taking most of his face with it. A crimson spray speckled Chandler's face. Flesh shrapnel rained down around him, tobacco shards flittering through the air. A tooth skittered across the floor bouncing off Chandler's shoe.

The explosion left a scorched hole in the middle of Cromwell's face. His front teeth were gone, lips shredded, nose obliterated. Both eyes dangled by their optic nerves. The shredded butt of the cigar lolled on his blackened tongue.

Chandler grinned blissfully, contemplating his newfound fortune.

"Well, aren't you gonna join me?" Cromwell asked, breaking Chandler's reverie.

His smile faded beholding his father-in-law's intact scowl. Chandler sniffed the cigar. It smelled like an antique leather book excavated from someone's barn.

Lighting his own cigar, Chandler took a deep drag,

wishing it were cannabis. He stifled a cough drawing a grin from Cromwell.

The butler entered the library. "Begging your pardon, sir. The manager of Arcane Antiques and Curiosities is on the line. Your item is ready. Shall I see if they'll deliver it Monday?"

"Monday?" Cromwell barked. "Why the hell not today?"

"Apparently, they don't deliver on Sundays."

"Horseshit! You know how much I've spent there over the years?"

Chandler asked, "Is that the antique shop on Fourth and Main?"

The butler answered, "Indeed."

"I could pick it up," Chandler said, sensing his chance to escape.

"That's so sweet!" Diana cooed. "Isn't that sweet, Father?"

Cromwell cast a sideways glance at Chandler and grunted.

"What do you say, Father?" Diana asked.

Cromwell nodded at the butler.

"Very good, sir. I'll let them know."

❦ ❦ ❦

Chandler finished the skinny chai latte he'd purchased en route before entering *Arcane Antiques and Curiosities*. A bell dinged overhead. The air was redolent with the scent of leather, foxed books, and furniture polish.

"Feel free to look around," a man shouted from behind an antique cash register. "Let me know if you have any questions."

Chandler waved dismissively.

It didn't take long to discover that this was no typical antique store. Unlike most that were little more than glorified thrift stores, Arcane Antiques and Curiosities contained an eclectic assortment of rare and unusual items, many accompanied by stately provenance. Diana undoubtedly procured the Rockefeller tie clip here.

Chandler strolled past a vintage suit of armor and a complete skeleton, undoubtedly real. Cabinets displayed fine bone china; blood-red ruby glass; and the eerie green glow of uranium glass.

The quaint shop featured other oddities like vintage medical and embalming tools, a creepy ventriloquist dummy, and peculiar taxidermy including a quartet of taxidermied frogs, each playing a different musical instrument.

The further he ventured, the stranger and more exotic the items became. Near the back, he found a two-headed calf and an elephant-foot trashcan. Were these things even legal?

On the rear wall hung a variety of hand-carved tribal masks and primitive jungle weapons, each deadlier than the last.

One barbaric weapon stood out from the others. Its primitive forged head featured a keenly honed hatchet blade on the front and a lethal spike on the back. He could only imagine the sort of damage this weapon could inflict.

"Careful, it's rather sharp," said the balding, rail-thin man in the dapper suit, startling Chandler. "It may be a primitive weapon, but I assure you it's no less deadly."

Chandler carefully returned the weapon to its rack.

"Igorot headhunting axe," the man said. "Barbaric, yet sophisticated in its efficiency. Much like the Igorot warriors."

"Igorot..." The name sounded familiar to Chandler.

"It means 'mountain people' in Tagalog."

Chandler rubbed his chin. "Filipino?"

"Indeed. Most people don't know that the Igorot headhunters helped the U.S. forces defend the Philippines against the Japanese during World War Two."

"Is that right?"

"General Douglas MacArthur himself said, when it came to hand-to-hand combat, he'd never seen their equal." With a gleam in his eye he added, "So you could hardly blame the General for turning a blind eye when the tribesmen wanted to... keep a trophy or two."

Chandler raised an eyebrow.

"I see you have an appreciation for the... exotic," the proprietor said.

Chandler smiled. "I do have rather eclectic taste."

"Where are my manners? I'm Phineas Taylor, owner and curator of this fine establishment."

"Chandler Pratt. Pleasure to meet you." The curator took Chandler's hand in a cold, bony-fingered embrace.

"If I might be so bold," Phineas said, "might I suggest something that may appeal to your rather... sophisticated palate?"

"Why, please do," Chandler said, delighted the refined gentleman recognized his discriminating taste.

"I shall return." Phineas bowed slightly and stepped away.

Chandler stared at a menacing tribal mask bearing an angry baboon-like visage. Its wooden snarl sported lengthy, flesh-ripping fangs.

The hair on the back of his neck bristled. Were those jungle drums pounding in the distance? Or just his heart pounding in his chest?

"I think you may find this of interest." The man's voice made Chandler jump.

The shop owner presented a mysterious wooden box hewn from a single piece of timber. Its dull, black exterior seemingly absorbed the light around it. The wood appeared charred as if passed through the fire to harden or perhaps from someone's failed attempt to destroy it. Chandler stared at the eye carved in the lid, mesmerized by it... until it blinked.

He gasped and recoiled.

"I suspect you will find this enchanted treasure to your liking," Phineas said, raising an eyebrow.

The primitive hinges creaked as he raised the lid. The owner reached into the box's shadowy depths. It seemed to swallow his fingers. "I procured this specimen in the Kalinga Province from an Igorot tribal chief."

Phineas pulled his hand from the box, clutching the hair of a shrunken human head! A wooden skewer pierced the nasal column. From the hair on its furrowed brow and eyelashes, to its stitched, puckered lips, this was obviously no mere sideshow gaffe. Butterflies stirred in his stomach: part nausea, part exhilaration.

"Taking a head was a rite of passage into manhood for many tribes," the owner began. "The severed, shrunken head, or tsantsa, was also used in harvest rituals to ensure a bountiful yield."

Phineas held the shrunken head out to Chandler.

He recoiled.

"It won't hurt you," the owner said with a grin. Then his countenance darkened. "Unless, of course..."

Chandler leaned in. "Unless..."

"Unless you remove the shackles that bind the spirit."

A chill crawled up Chandler's spine.

"You see, headhunters sewed the mouths shut to prevent the spirit from escaping and wreaking vengeance on its killer."

Chandler studied the face with morbid curiosity. "Why sew the eyes shut?"

"Igorot tradition held that the first person the tsantsa laid eyes upon was presumed to be their killer."

Chandler's eyes lit up, ideas whirling in his head.

Observing Chandler's reaction, Phineas asked, "May I wrap it up for you then, sir?"

Chandler suddenly remembered what he'd come for. "I'm actually here to pick up an item for a Mr. Nathan Cromwell."

"Why didn't you say so?" the owner smiled. "Mr. Cromwell is one of our best customers! Shall I charge them both to Mr. Cromwell's account?"

Chandler grinned. "Indeed."

* * *

The antique shop owner loaded a large, thin, rectangular object wrapped in brown paper into the back of Chandler's wife's Range Rover. A rare painting, perhaps?

Chandler set the tsantsa box on the passenger seat, then drove off. Gradually, a low monastic hum vibrated throughout the vehicle. Was it coming from the road or the box? He shuddered.

A sinister plan formulated in his mind as he drove. Spotting a hardware store up ahead, he pulled in and parked discretely in back.

Chandler wandered the aisles collecting duct tape, a ball of twine, and a hunting knife. As he set the items on the counter, the clerk eyeballed him suspiciously. Chandler quickly added a pack of gum, as if fresh breath made him look less like someone plotting a murder.

* * *

Back in his car, Chandler tore off three strips of duct tape and stuck them to the dash. He threaded and tied a length of twine to the end of each strip.

Inhaling deeply, he retrieved the shrunken head from its

box, again struck by its hideous appearance. Its charcoal-blackened face scowled back at him.

With trembling hands, Chandler meticulously snipped the stitches from each eye, carefully sealing them with the duct tape as he went. With each cut, he flinched, terrified its eye would spring open and the tsantsa's spirit would identify him as its killer.

The air inside the car was stifling. Sweat ran into his eye, stinging. He frantically blinked it away.

Last came the mouth. Its lips looked and felt like charred grubworms. His stomach churned. Chandler snipped the first mouth stitch, quickly covering it with tape. He held his breath, dreading the avenging spirit's escape.

With every stitch he removed, the chance of freeing the spirit increased. Why were there so many?

He slid the knife blade under one of the final stitches when a car horn blasted. Chandler's hand jerked, slicing the tsantsa's lip. His heart nearly leaped from his chest. He hurriedly taped the mouth shut.

In the rearview mirror, he spotted a vehicle waiting for his spot. Let them wait.

Chandler peeled the corner of the tape from the tsantsa's mouth revealing the final two stitches. A black, viscous fluid oozed from the cut lip.

The horn blasted again, making him jump. He'd come too far for some impatient idiot to pressure him into making a fatal mistake.

He inched the trembling knife toward the shrunken head then stopped to steady his hand. Chandler tried a breathing exercise his therapist had taught him. Deep breath in through the nose, slow exhale out.

He tried again. Inhale... Snip. Tape. Exhale. One more. Inhale. Thread the quivering knife point under the final stitch and... *HONK*!

Chandler jerked, slashing through the remaining stitch and stabbing the knife blade into his thigh. He screamed and yanked it out, blood staining his pant leg.

HONK! HOOONK!

Chandler swung open the Rover's door and charged toward the honking asshole, unaware he still clutched the knife.

The BMW driver slammed it into reverse, squealing the tires. So much for discretion.

Chandler parked the Range Rover in front of his father-in-law's mansion. While the butler hefted Cromwell's item inside, Chandler secreted the tsantsa box behind his back.

He followed Carl into the library, where Diana relaxed on the couch and Cromwell reclined in a leather, high-back chair, scotch in one hand and cigar in the other.

"You're back!" Diana said then frowned. "What happened to your leg?"

"It's nothing."

Cromwell seemed surprised that Chandler managed to complete the errand.

"Where would you like this, sir?" the butler asked.

"Let me see it first."

Carl delivered the large rectangular package to his boss.

"Did you get a new painting, Father?" Diana asked.

Cromwell handed his glass to Carl. "Fetch me a refill, would you?"

"Yes, sir."

"And go easy on the soda."

While the others were distracted, Chandler pulled out the tsantsa box. His palms were so sweaty he almost dropped it.

His heart pounded. Chandler was so vested in his father-in-law's demise that he hadn't considered whether the story about avenging spirits was true. But he'd come too far to back down now.

The box's lid creaked as it opened. Reaching inside, Chandler pulled the hideous shrunken head out by its hair. Twine dangled from the duct tape sealing the eyes and mouth. He'd knotted the three strands together, enabling him to remove all the duct tape with a single pull. He set the box down.

Cromwell tore open the package revealing an ornate, gold frame.

Diana leaned forward on the couch. "Oh, father, that frame is gorgeous!"

Chandler held the shrunken head out in front of him, grasped the lengths of twine, and yanked.

Cromwell finished unwrapping his new treasure. Chandler expected to see a portrait but instead was greeted by the tsantsa's reflection.

The shrunken head came alive. Its eyelids sprung open and its brow furrowed. The tsantsa's eyes burned red with fury.

Its mouth creaked open releasing a deep, reverberating groan. The bottles on the bar clinked together. Books tumbled off shelves.

Diana cowered as the whole room quaked, the guttural noise filling the library.

Cromwell used the mirror as a shield while keeping it from shattering on the floor.

A smoky black mist poured from the tsantsa's mouth.

Exhilarated yet terrified, Chandler kept the shrunken head at arm's length, his pulse racing.

The acrid smoke coalesced into the shape of a tribal warrior. A primitive headhunting axe appeared in the warrior's hand.

Chandler grinned. The old man's fortune would soon be his!

The warrior took one step toward Cromwell then did an about-face. His eyes locked with Chandler's. What was it doing? The avenging spirit was supposed to kill the first person it gazed upon!

Then it hit him.

The mirror... the first thing it must've seen was *his* reflection!

The warrior advanced.

Chandler backpedaled.

Diana screamed.

He held the tsantsa before him like a crucifix warding off a vampire.

The primitive creature swung the axe.

Chandler's severed hand thumped off the hardwood floor.

The shrunken head rolled toward Diana, eliciting another scream.

Chandler leaped back as the blade sliced through his shirt. Checking his abdomen, his face paled as a red line appeared.

Then widened.

He tried to hold his midsection together with his remaining hand, but it was futile. Shiny red ropes of intestines unspooled from his body, splattering onto the floor.

He dropped to his knees, gawking up at the avenging warrior spirit come to life. Unable to form words, Chandler pleaded with his eyes.

The axe rose to the sky before arcing down and decapitating him.

Its mission of vengeance complete, the tsantsa's spirit disintegrated into a puff of black smoke.

Head Hunter

❧ ❧ ❧

Nathan Cromwell sat at the desk in his study, reading the financial section of the newspaper. A knock came at the door.

"Come."

The door opened and Carl entered carrying a parcel wrapped in brown paper and tied with string.

"Delivery, sir."

Cromwell gave a nod and the butler entered, placing the package on his desk.

"Anything else I can do for you, sir?"

"That will be all, Carl."

"Very good, sir."

The butler left, closing the door behind him.

Cromwell grinned as he read the label - *Arcane Antiques and Curiosities*.

Cromwell retrieved an ornate letter opener from the desk drawer. Slicing open the package revealed an intricately carved, black wooden box. He rubbed his age-spotted hands together then opened the lid.

Beneath the excelsior packing, he discovered a twist of brown hair.

Grasping Chandler's man bun, he raised his shrunken head. Although a third of the size of the original, it was unmistakably his son-in-law's head.

Cromwell admired his trophy a moment before returning Chandler's head to the box and placing his newest tsantsa on the shelf with the others.

❧ ❧ ❧

B.D. Prince was raised in Michigan before moving to California in his twenties to pursue screenwriting and a tan.

B.D. Prince

The dark fiction and comedy writer credits these proclivities to growing up near a cemetery and being endowed with a freakishly long funny bone.

Prince got his start writing humorous greeting cards and penning one-liners for Joan Rivers. Now an award-winning author and screenwriter, Prince won the 2024 Imadjinn Award for the novel "28 Years Haunted." Having published numerous short stories, his recent novella collection, "Eye for an Eye," and his upcoming short story collection (Sept. 2025), B.D. Prince is currently writing a new horror novel and developing projects for film and television.

Facebook: /bryan.prince.52

Instagram, X, and Tiktok: @clownprinceb

Member HWA

As The Circus Leaves Town

Morgan Sylvia

I

I AM eighteen when I find out what they are.

What I am.

It's one of those midsummer days when you can almost feel the wheel of the year turn, kind of like our Ferris wheel. The sky is blue, for once, or at least blue-ish. The rains had finally returned that summer, tamping the dust down a bit. A light breeze clears the ever-present stench of sulfur and rot, but does little to ease the sweltering heat.

That was the first year that we—*Countess Dawson's Cirque Of Mystical Wonders*—returned to Pacer's Grove since before the drought. We usually moved clockwise around the territories, but that year our path became more of a zigzag. By the time we finished our stint in Chicago and got through the Midwest shantytowns, the west was burning again. We went northeast for the summer. Of course, no matter where we went, it was always Isis, pointed our way. Gordy, the Rubber Man, said she threw runesticks. Mama Zizi once told me she tosses darts at her map. Fran, the contortionist, said she read tea leaves.

Turns out it was a much darker magic, brought us back to that place.

The old timers say there's something unique about every spot on Earth. Its position, its magnetism, its climate, its history, its architecture, its food, *something*. I rarely paid attention. That isn't to say I never noticed the ever-changing landscapes we journeyed through, especially now that the dust was settling and color was returning to the world. Like other travelers, we mark our way by unique ruins. The mountain of melted tires outside of Detroit. The glass plains near Reno. Mount Rushmore. Some of those landmarks serve as seasonal markers. I associate the broken arch in St. Louis with fall, as we always cross the Mississippi at the end of summer.

Even nomads fall into cycles.

Not that we really cared about time. Our convoy traversed miles and moments and years, but it never mattered to me where we were. The places we played always blurred together in my mind, each melding seamlessly into the next. Pacer's Grove was no different: a small cluster of businesses flanking a small square or main street.

Except that it was familiar.

It shouldn't have been. All I ever recalled of my childhood are fragmented, kaleidoscopic snapshots of carnival life. Theo, the sword swallower, holding a razor-sharp blade above his open mouth. Radu, making fire dance across his chest. Isis, captivating crowds with her illusions and mindreading skills. The endless lines of people outside of Mama Zizi's tent, waiting for her to tell their fortune. The smells of fried food and popcorn wafting in the sticky summer air beneath string lights, mingling with the roar of the Big Top crowds. The sideshow. The midway. The poppers. The rides. These things made up my world. My earliest memories are of napping in Mama Zizi's cart, watching the dusty sunbeams that slipped past the heavy purple velvet curtains. There is nothing before that.

Or at least, there wasn't.

I don't notice anything unusual at first. Larry, Ezra and I have gone into town on a supply and errand run ahead of opening day. We follow the downtown wagon, which will drive around with an exhibit of oddities to attract crowds. Larry's truck bounces to a stop before the general store, then sputters into silence as he kills the engine. I slide out after Ezra, only to immediately regret not bringing a parasol. I raise a hand to shield my eyes from the blinding sunlight as I look around, the heat of the pavement blazing through my thin shoes. Barefoot kids in patched clothes run back and forth through the dusty street, their shouts hanging in the sweltering heat.

"Think maybe they have sugar?" Ezra muses. "I'd like a sweet tea."

"First things first." Larry pulls a poster board out of the back of the truck. "Gotta draw the crowd before you can work 'em."

"These are getting pretty beat," Ezra takes out the biggest one, which depicts Isis with her crystal ball under a caption that reads *Isis, Mistress Of Dark Magic*. "Should see if they have paint here."

I pull another posterboard out of the back. *Maxiumus the Magus: World Famous Magician*, the caption reads. *Wizardry And Wonder!*

My face stares out of the fourth. *Katarina, Wind Dancer. Watch Her Soar On The Flying Trapeze.* Dust and wind have dulled the colors, scratched the paint, chipped away the gleam in my eyes. I'm alone in the depiction. Ezra refused to be on any poster board. I knew better than to ask why. It's one of the rules of carnie life: Never ask about life before the carnival.

Ezra picks a fleck of peeling crimson paint away, leaving a hole in my lip. "We need to add new tricks. The Shooting Star and Gazelle are old news. I think we should add the Quad."

"They won't know what a quad is," I tell him. "Any more than they know the Tkatchev Somersault Full Twist or the Crane Jump."

He doesn't try to hide the reproach in his voice. "Then they won't know if you miss it. *Again.*"

I've only recently joined the shadow carnival, and even more recently the aerial ballet. I had always wanted to be a bally girl, as we were known. When I was young, I had been tasked with small chores: cleaning, polishing shoes, running messages, helping the candy butchers. Later, I took tickets. For extra money—cherry pie, as it was called—I sold pot and tobacco out of an usherette tray I'd made from one of Mama Zizi's old posterboards.

And then, one day, I was no longer a child.

I remember the day I was summoned into Isis' tent. I stood there nervously, looking into her eyes, which were always like dark suns. "It's time for you to join the shadow carnival," she said, tapping a gleaming nail on her vanity. "You must learn a performance skill. Unless you *want* to be a candy butcher and sell garbage. I understand Mama Zizi showed you some of her tricks before she passed."

I should have known it was coming. The daytime events were mostly kid-oriented. The games were lighter, and the emphasis was on food and fun. The night dreamers wove a different spell. Once the sun set, the carnival took on a darker nature. The stilt walkers painted their faces to look like demons, and the fire dancers captivated crowds with their pyromancy and their skimpy, sequined outfits. The main stage moved from clown shows to burlesque, and the magic shows got rather saucy.

"She did," I told her. "But I'm no good at telling fortunes. I want to be a bally girl."

Isis raised a perfect brow. "Fine. But train with the other acts, too. You can't rely on any one thing to get you through. And we need some more versatile performers. We have enough aerialists for now."

That said, she sent me out into the night, into the swirling crowds and the scents and sounds that made up my—our—world.

I spent the better part of a year being sawed in half and put back together on Magus' stage. I delved into acrobatics, gymnastics, contortion, balancing, and juggling. I learned various sideshow classics: the Cyr wheel, the Danish pole, lassos. I tried out knife throwing and teeterboard, ran various booths and prize wheels. I taught myself to walk on stilts, learned to glide across hot coals and nails. I learned to dance with fire, tried my hand at painting faces. Nothing really fit.

Then an opening in the aerial ballet had sealed my fate. I'd immediately taken to the skies, realizing right away that I'd found my place. Every night now, I am dressed in illusion and sent to dance in the air far above the cheering crowds.

But here, on the dusty pavement of a dusty town, I'm just another face in the crowd.

The sun is burning my skin. Ezra notices my arm reddening and scowls. This is not out of concern for me, but because if my skin peels, he'll have trouble catching me in midair.

I pull the threadbare shawl over my arms, despite the heat.

Thunder rolls in the distance, reminding us not to dally. Ezra and I move like a well-oiled machine, setting out the easels and poster boards, our movements as precisely timed as they are when we're in the sky, soaring like birds above the crowds. Well, perhaps not *that* precise. But we know what we have to do. I need thread, beeswax, candles, corn starch, and lipstick. Ezra will hit the hardware store for nails, rope, and other necessities while Larry deals with the food orders and handles the bribes and other legalities.

I spot the apothecary sign down the block, and start walking in that direction.

I don't get far. In fact, I don't even make it past the mercantile. I am passing the small alley on the other side of the building when the memory hits out of nowhere.

I stand in the same small alley, facing the same (now overgrown) lot, the same (now collapsing) empty house. There has been an incident. A happening, of some sort. A crowd gathers around and above me. They murmur excitedly to one another, their voices an agitated blend of shock and concern. I hear growling nearby. Someone is restraining a snarling dog.

A blonde woman wearing a faded cowboy hat kneels before me. She takes my face in her hands and moves my head from side to side, checking for wounds. Her skin is reddened from the bite of toxic winds. My gaze fixates on a crusty yellow scab on her nose as she lifts my arm. Following her gaze, I see that my hand is torn open and bleeding. My blood falls to the thirsty ground in thick crimson droplets. The withered earth sucks them up, and the beads vanish into the dust like the cities in the west.

The woman looks angry. "Never approach a dog with puppies," she snaps. "You're lucky that's all she did. She could have torn your face off."

"Better just hope that dog isn't rabid," someone says.

"My Jonah got rabies," another person puts in. "Took his mind

before it took his body. Grew a terrible fear of air and water at the end."

"Maybe the dog took my Missy," another woman says. Her voice cracks with grief. "And the others."

"And Sean Carmichael?" Another says. "No dog did that."

"Stop with the monster talk," the woman kneeling before me mutters. "The worst monsters are human. Think you'd have learned that by now."

I am swooped into the air, into the comfort of familiar arms. I cling to the woman, bury my face in her neck. As she starts to walk away, I look back over her shoulder. I'm watching the puppies, but then someone steps out of the shadows, dark gaze fixated on me. The memory is clear enough that I recognize her face.

Isis.

Fear rises through me, and I cling tighter.

The memory stops there, a single drop of water where there should be a river.

❧ ❧ ❧

Larry and Ezra notice that I've stopped moving. They cover the distance between us in a few strides.

"EEAll eeokeeay?" Ezra asks. People are walking past us, so he speaks in the secret language we use around the normies. The key is simple but effective: just add an extra 'ee' before vowels. It sounds alien to the unsuspecting, but we have no trouble deciphering it. *All ok?*

I look around, scanning every detail of the dingy town. "What's this place called again?"

"Pacer's Grove."

"Pacer's Grove." I try the words out on my tongue. They don't seem familiar.

Larry spits a wad of tobacco onto the dry ground. "Why?"

As I turn to face him, the sun comes out from behind a

cloud, bathing everything in gold. I squint, tears streaming against the light. "I've been here before."

Ezra frowns. "You told me they found you in the south."

Squinting isn't enough: I put a hand to my forehead to block the rays. "That's what Mama Zizi always said."

"Mama Zizi also said there used to be giant lizards here," Ezra mutters. He looks up at the sky. "Bigger than buildings. Bigger than the Big Top. Fairy tales."

He shouldn't be looking at the sun, I think. *It will burn his eyes like it did Mama's, the year before she died.* "I remember this place," I insist.

"So what?" Larry gives me a cold look. "What do I keep telling you? You're one of us. Doesn't matter where you were before."

Larry loves to talk about the glitz and glamour of carnie life. I'd grown up listening to his diatribes about how we were the equalizers, the bringers of dreams. *You don't choose this life, child,* he likes to say. *It chooses you. Where else will you see a banker in line next to the plumber who fixes his sink? Where do you see the son of the doctor screaming on a ride beside the carpet bagger that shines his shoes? We bring dreams into the world. People come here and forget the shit out there. They forget the pain, the suffering. They become something. And they become community. That's beautiful, innit? We transform them. We do!*

Usually, I find his musings inspiring. Today, they rub me the wrong way. I look him dead in the eye. "Is this where Mama found me?"

Larry scowls. "You think I remember where we find every stray we pick up?"

"You know where *you* came from," I snap.

Ezra shoots me a warning look. I am treading on sacred ground, and I know it.

Larry's expression hardens. Coldness comes over him like frost over a window. And just like that, the mood is on him again. He'll stalk the crowds tonight with that gleam in his eye. Many of those who walk past our ticket gate will leave with both lighter moods and lighter wallets. Later, he will count his dollars and coins in the cook house. Not that it matters. He'll spend the entire take on booze and women at whatever watering hole we pass next.

"Cool it," Ezra hisses. "What's wrong with you?"

A family wanders up to the poster boards, and our conversation is cut short. We move into performance mode, transform ourselves into our stage personas, rope them in. *Packing the house,* as the saying goes. When we have paper, we hand out fliers in the town. In some places, we send a wagon ahead to attract crowds. Today, there is just us.

We sell them dreams, which they pay for in blood and gold.

My thoughts spin, topsy-turvy, as we finish our errands and load the goods into the back of the truck. I look back towards the alley before I climb into the sweltering cab, willing another memory to appear. None do.

We ride back in silence.

Our current site is just a few miles off the pothole-laden main road, on an old high school football field. They've just finished putting the Big Top up when we return, and are setting out the bleacher seats. The smaller tents and booths are popping up in their customary places around it. Clown Alley once more stands between the Big Top and the back yard, the off-limits area. This is all carefully orchestrated, a choreography perfected over countless miles and seasons. The layout is always the same: we only change it when geography forces us to. We tear our world down every week, only to pull it out of the crates and boxes and recreate it again somewhere else. One day there is an empty parking lot or field, and the next there is an entire realm of brightly-colored tents and booths and banner lines, as though we'd dreamt it into existence. I suppose we do. The transformation never ceases to thrill me.

It isn't a glamorous life. We all have multiple jobs. It can be dusty and sweaty and crowded, and some days the endless sea of dusty faces flashing past in hopeless desperation gets overwhelming. You don't have to look too close to see the glitz and glamour is an illusion. The paint on our signs is chipped and fading, the flags on our bannerline are thread-bare, and our tents and outfits have been patched more times than any of us can count. But maybe Larry is right. You put it all together, and it becomes something.

I go to the Big Top and check out our platforms, test the Spanish web, run through a few tricks on my own. At dusk, I grab a bite from the cook house, then go to join some of the other performers at a campfire. Magus is practicing his new bit. He stands on a rock, gesturing about. I can tell by the glitter in his eyes that he's had too much to drink. Rosa, one of the fire eaters, practices her pirouette. Radu walks behind her, his skin giving off sparks. Someone starts playing a calliope, and I am once more comfortable in my world of dreams.

Or I would be, save the growing sense of unease rising in my soul.

Magus leans forward, his eyes glittering in the night. He pulls a rose out of my hair, gives it to me. "Why so glum, little dove?"

I hand the rose back to Magus. "Do you know where Mama Zizi found me?"

Ranu answers for him. "Wasn't Mama Zizi found you," he says. "It was Isis."

I freeze, turn to stare at him. I want to question him, but he melts back into the night with Rosa.

Magus turns the rose into a bat. "A wizard once said that all the world is a stage," he muses. "But we are the stage, and the world moves around *us*. Does it really matter whether you entered stage right or stage left?"

I sit back, listening, as the conversation takes a decidedly philosophical turn. Magus likes to ponder the mysteries of the universe on nights like this, even as he devises new ways to dramatize them. Over the years, I've learned nearly all of the typical carnie tricks: the weighted games, the sleight of hand, the clever apparatuses. But I've never been able to figure out how Isis withstood the voltage from her globe, or why Ranu's skin sometimes gives off sparks, or why some acts in the shadow carnival accept blood instead of coin.

Magus releases the bat, lets it fly away. I look up, notice how dark the sky is. Only then do I realize what night it is.

The new moon.

Time to pay the piper.

I leave the others to their chitchat, make my way down the deserted midway to Isis' tent. Her wagon has already been pulled out into its stage configuration. Faded signs and flags proclaim her power. *Mistress of the Mystic Realms*, some say. *Watch Her Dance With Death.* Tomorrow, this area will be packed with crowds of people seeking answers, trying to catch a glimpse of the beyond, hoping to get some sense of purpose, perhaps, or one last communication from a loved one. But right now there is no one around. I approach alone.

I slip inside the tent, looking around at the familiar trappings. The crystal ball. The Pickled Punk: a fetus in a jar. The skull of a two-headed cow. Crystals and statues and all sorts of oddities. A set of books on her shelf catches my eye. They are fancy tomes, printed with matching gold text and elegant filigree. The first is titled *Kephn, Katsue, And The Sleeper In The*

Mound. The second is *The Draugr And Other Revenants.* There's something familiar about them, but I can't put my finger on what. I am sure that there was once a third, but I have no idea how I know that.

"Katarina," a silken voice says behind me. "I trust you are well."

I jump and turn as Isis steps forward from the shadows.

Where did I come from? I want to ask. *Did you find me? Did Mama lie?*

The words stick in my mouth. Her strange aura settles over me like a blanket.

The silver dagger sits on the table, waiting. I feel again the strange buzz in my thoughts as I pierce a vein and let the crimson liquid into the goblet. I look at the scar on my hand as I do so, wondering how I never noticed the fang imprints before.

Isis watches quietly, her eyes glittering in shadow. A moment later, she peers at the ruby liquid, swirls it around her good crystal goblet, sniffs. "You need more iron, little bird," she says. "Try to get some steak from one of the grease houses."

I never know what she does with the blood. Part of her magic, I assume. I open my mouth to ask, and then I am back outside again, under the stars. I've no recollection of the time that passed between, but it must be late. There is no one around, and the sky is paling in the east. Even the pie car, where we get our food, is shuttered and empty. I wander the empty paths, make my way to the makeshift barns, where moveable fences corral the horses, cats, and elephants. I love to watch them, but they want nothing to do with me. They always shrink from my presence, no matter how quietly I speak or what treats I offer. Once I opened all the cages and stood there, waiting for them to run to freedom.

None did.

As The Circus Leaves Town

The tiger roars a warning at me as I pass her cage. I turn to face the north, toward Pacers Grove.

Something in that direction calls me like a lodestone. For the first time in years, I allow myself to wonder where I came from.

❦ ❦ ❦

I wake early, nestled into the quilts on the daybed in the only home I've ever known: the cart that was once Mama Zizi's. There are still pieces of her around. Her diaries. Her antique cast iron cookware. Her quilts. Mostly it is Ezra's things, scattered about. He is gone: he usually slips out with the dawn. I open the cart door, step out into the bright gold sunlight and look around, eyes streaming.

Opening mornings are always special. There is always a building anticipation of what the night's crowd and performance will be like. We use this time to rehearse, limber up, fix our costumes. Already the performers are stretching, working on routines, tweaking their choreography. I don't like rehearsals as much as the others do. I prefer the live shows. I sometimes feel as though I am not real until there is a crowd to cheer for me, to gasp and clap as I sail through the air.

Still the calling burns through my thoughts.

This time a voice rises with it. *Come to me.*

I find Ezra at the cook house tent, getting breakfast. "I need you to drive me into town."

He raises an eyebrow. "If this is about whatever you remembered yesterday, best leave it alone. We need to work on the Quad."

I just look at him. "I'm going with or without you. If you don't drive me, I'm taking the Gilley wagon."

He scowls, shovels the last of his powdered eggs into his

mouth, fills a thermos with coffee, and grabs his bag. We start walking toward the back parking lot. One of the elephants screams as we get into the truck, trumpeting her rage into the sky.

The cracked tar road brings us into town and then beyond it. We pass block after block of crumbling ruins. Most have been picked clean. The few that are occupied are fortified for defense, hidden behind makeshift fences, walls, and gates. Later, their owners will gasp and gape and laugh at our performances. But I don't care about that now.

Before long, the town gives way to scraggly woods. I scan the arid landscape, looking for something familiar. Nothing rings a bell. I'm about to give up and tell Ezra to turn around when we round a bend and a roofline comes into view above a tangle of trees.

I sit up straight, goosebumps prickling over my skin. "There!"

Ezra slams on the brakes, and I almost careen into the cracked windshield. He turns down the driveway. Scraggy trees scrape the window, scratching what remains of the seafoam-blue paint. The truck hasn't even fully stopped when I get out.

The house is an old, three story Victorian farmhouse, the type they built long before the fall. The paint was once a sickly peach-pink, the color of pale flesh. Not healthy flesh; the skin of a fading elder. Dust and poison winds are slowly wearing the hues away, turning the wood beneath to weatherworn grey. A massive oak towers over the porch. The roof sags, as though the house's spine has buckled. Most of the windows are cracked or broken. Shapes and shadows lurk in its darkened interior. The place is completely silent: no birds or bugs break the stillness.

Every hair on my body stands on end.

As The Circus Leaves Town

A voice rises through my thoughts, dry and lifeless as Midwest soil. *Welcome home.*

And just like that, the floodgates open.

🕮 🕮 🕮

I stand in the same spot, staring up at the same house with the same hideous peach paint. There are two boys with me. Memory offers their names. The taller one, the blond, is Dave. The shorter, olive-skinned one is Jonesy.

My brothers.

"I don't know," Jonesy says. "Pretty sure this is the place Kevin was talking about, the spot where they found those bodies. Probably picked clean anyway."

I am fidgeting with anticipation. "There's goods inside," I announce. I rub the bandage on my hand, where the wound is still healing. "I know. I can feel it."

Dave points to the house. "Look. Someone's been inside recently. That plastic over the windows isn't shredded. No way it got through winter."

"Doesn't look like there's anyone there now," Jonesy says.

I start walking forward. "Let's go!"

We creep up the worn steps. The door opens easily. Too easily, perhaps. We look up and around, scanning for booby traps, then enter hesitantly. The shadows inside are thick and silent and full of secrets. To my right, a set of wooden stairs ascends into darkness. I can't see much at first. Then Dave steps forward, opening thick curtains. We all stare around, dumbfounded.

"Jackpot," Jonesy murmurs.

Whoever lives—or lived—was some sort of collector. Every room in the place is stuffed, floor to ceiling, with, well, everything. Many of the items seemed tied to the occult. We find shrunken heads, crystals, jars of feather and bone, oils and incense and bottles of bones and dust. Dave shakes a small glass globe that contains a small snowscape. A plastic creature I vaguely recognize as a polar bear sits on a plastic sled, chubby and happy as a fake plastic blizzard swirls around it.

One room holds nothing but books. I flip through several tomes about ghosts and mystics. Several are focused on strange monsters. The Lamia, the Upir, the Vrykolakak, the Vourdalak. They don't seem all that different than the cannibals in the New York ruins, but I am fascinated anyway.

"Ain't got all day, Katie," Dave says.

I reluctantly put the books down. We work like mice, scratching though the dusty rooms. We are good scavengers, able to quickly determine what the tinkers would buy and what they wouldn't. Our pile of picks grows.

Eventually, Dave, glances out the window. "Sun's going down. We should get going." He looks around. "Where's Jonesy?"

I shrug and yell for him. "Jonesy!"

No reply.

We call him several times, then go room to room, eventually ending up on the second floor. We find him in the last bedroom. He is just standing there, staring into an ornate mirror cabinet, which is chained shut and painted with strange runes and symbols.

"Jonesy?" Dave steps forward.

He ignores us.

"What are you doing?" I ask.

He doesn't look at us. "Pieces broken," he mutters. "Pieces missing. They knew the red thirst would never fade. The blood is the life why should we be denied the crimson gold. The error was in the third gate, the key was the secondary arm of-"

"Come on," Dave says, grabbing his arm.

Jonesy turns to us. His eyes have turned black.

From somewhere far below comes a sound that I can only describe as an inhuman howl.

Fear washes over me like a wave, igniting every survival instinct inside me. I turn to Dave. His face is white with horror.

"Get out of here!" Dave shouts. He turns and runs, hauling a dazed Jonesy behind him. I follow on their heels, slamming the door shut behind me. Panic races up and down my spine.

As we bolt down the hall, I hear the creak of the bedroom door I'd just shut opening again. Fueled by sheer terror, I try to move faster by jumping some of the stairs.

Bad idea.

The creak of wood beneath my feet turns to a splintering CRACK! as the rotting wood gives way. I freeze in place. Dave stops and turns, reaching out for me. I grab his hand, but it is too late. The stairs collapse beneath me. Instead of being hauled to safety, I pull him down with me. We fall into cold, black nothingness.

There is nothing after that, until the carnival.

The memory sears my thoughts, but no others follow. I blink, stunned, and stagger back, trying to process the recollection. Looking at the house, I feel again that terrifying drop as I plunged through the air, and I realize what drove me to the trapeze.

It was never the crowds or techniques I sought to master as an aerialist, but my own fear.

"That's where I fell first," I murmur. "I didn't know how to land yet."

Ezra frowns. "You really think you know this place?"

I ignore him and move forward. My heart pounds in my chest as I step onto the porch and open the door.

The air inside feels thick and hushed. The foyer and stairs are exactly as I recall, except for the gaping hole where the steps collapsed beneath me. The pile of goods we left behind is scattered about, having clearly been ransacked several times. I spot the broken globe Dave played with on the floor. It's cracked now, the liquid spilled out and dried, the plastic bear half-melted I wander to the room with the books, find the missing third volume to Isis' set. *The Lore Of The Blood Gods.*

I put the book in my bag, along with a few others I recall leafing through, and then move to the stairs and look down into the shadows.

I'm not sure if I see or imagine the gleam of bone in the dust below.

"What are we doing here, Katarina?" Ezra grumbles.

"Blood," I murmur. "The blood is life."

Ezra's eyes cloud, and I see something I'm not used to. Fear. In the sky, he spins and twists dauntlessly, without a thought of falling, as natural in the air as a bird. So do I. But he is compelled by adoration. He lives for the roar of the crowd, the thunder of applause.

Something darker drives me.

"We should go," he says, grabbing my arm. I brush his hand away, and move back to the stairs, eyeing the hole and the landing above.

He knows what I'm going to do before I do it. "No, don't—"

I vault easily over the gash, using the handrail as a guide. At the top, I turn and look down at Ezra, holding out a hand.

He shakes his head. "I'm not going up there. We're going to miss the opening." He starts muttering about show times.

I'm not listening. I'm staring at a few framed photographs on the stairway wall. I don't recall seeing them before. But then, it wouldn't have meant anything if I had.

In the first photo, Mama, Isis, Radu, and Magus stand before a Ferris wheel. *Our* Ferris wheel. I can tell by the vivid colors that the photo was taken in the old world. The people in the background look happy and healthy, plump and well-fed In another picture, Mama and Isis stand on the front porch of this house.

In that photo, the massive tree that now stands beside the porch is just a sapling.

I glance out the window. "Ezra? How old you think that tree is?"

He looks puzzled. "Couple hundred years?"

A sick feeling twists through my stomach.

Come to me, the voice whispers.

A strange calm comes over me. I find my way down the hall to the room where we found Jonesy, and slowly open the door.

It's all a blur after that.

Ezra eventually comes after me, drags me away. I remember little of this. I don't really return to myself until later, when he brings me dinner from the pie car. He tells me that I was speaking in tongues, that I refused to leave without the mirror box, which I wrapped in thick dusty drapes.

My thoughts run crimson.

Everything is wrong with my performance that night. We are sold out—a straw house, as they say, meaning that the place is so full we've spread straw down to form makeshift seats. But I just can't get into the zone, can't meld my mind into the crowd as I usually do. I miss trick after trick. Someone even boos me. That's never happened before.

We signal to Carmine, the ringleader, to end our first set early. He shoots us a withering glare before announcing the elephants. It's very frowned upon to cut a show short—giving them a John Robinson, as they call it—especially before a packed house, but it's better than giving a disappointing performance.

Between sets I pace circles in the staging area, which is at the edge of Clown Alley. Painted faces leer at me in silence. Nightmares claw their way through my thoughts.

The second performance is no better. Ezra snaps and hisses between tricks. My skin burns, as though I am on fire.

I'd never pondered much about what I'd lost. The ruins we rode past every week made the question seem irrelevant. Two thirds of the world was gone, they said. But that night I scour the faces in the crowd. Twice I spot women who look like the blonde in my memory. I gasp and choke for breath in the air.

"What is wrong with you?" Ezra hisses through the smile plastered on his face after I nearly miss a catch. I ignore the question, try to find my pace. But I only fumble again.

And then, during the finale, I deliberately miss his outstretched hand. Instead of landing the catch, I sink like a stone through the air. Like I did that day.

The last thing I notice as I fall away from him is that his eyes have gone black.

Then I hit the net, and the third memory is unlocked.

❦ ❦ ❦

There is no time to scream as I plummet into darkness below. It's not a long drop; a split second later, the impact of the fall sends shock waves through my entire body. My head hits something hard, and pain explodes in my shoulder. My thoughts break apart, kaleidoscopic. Dave is even less fortunate. I hear a crash and the snap of bone when he hits, and then I hear him scream,

I lose consciousness, and there is just blackness.

I don't know how much time passes before I open my eyes. Fading daylight filters through the hole in the stairs. Everything else is pitch black. Terror blankets my senses, scattering my thoughts. I gingerly try to move my limbs and neck. A searing pain tells me my arm is broken. I look at it, see the bone jutting through my flesh. Fear rises through me like a wave. Something crawls over my leg.

A low moan rises through the stagnant air. I turn my head the other way and see Dave. He's impaled on something. A piece of wood protrudes from his chest. His breaths are wet and labored. He's covered in blood.

So much blood.

Something moves above me. I see a silhouette in the light coming through the hole in the stairs. It's Jonesy. "Jonesy!" I call. "Get help! Go get Momma! Dave's hurt!"

He doesn't move.

"Jonesy!" I struggle to my feet.

"The red thirst," he mutters. "They should have tried a different snake."

I frown. "What? We need help!"

Dave makes a gurgling sound.

Jonesy just stands there. I realize he isn't looking at me. He's staring up at something at the top of the stairs.

Something I can't see.

That something suddenly shoots through the air. I catch a glimpse of it as it crosses over the hole, but it's moving too fast for me to really get a good look. It moves with impossible speed, knocking Jonesy out of my view. Jonesy gives off one ear-splitting scream.

And then his voice is cut off, and there is just a slurping sound.

I try to scream, but a wave of dizziness overtakes me and I fall back into darkness.

I wake confused and terrified, my heart thudding in my chest. I look up at the gash in the stairs, and realize dimly that I'm trapped in a cellar, alone, with no visible way out. My thoughts are slow, awkward. I can't figure out where I am or how I got there.

Then I hear a sucking sound. I turn my head, see a pale form crouching over Dave's bloody corpse. It turns to me, opens a mouth filled with rows of razor sharp teeth, and emits an ear-splitting shriek. Then its eyes fix on mine.

I fall under its spell, and a strange calm comes over me. "The red thirst," I murmur.

The thing changes, morphing into a beautiful woman.

"What do you know," Isis asks, tilting her head. "of the red thirst?"

She crawls toward me, black eyes gleaming.

As I see this, I also see the other being hovering in the shadows. It is nothing but a head, with trailing organs below its neck. Its skin is a sickly greenish color, and its eyes are blood red. Two rows of razor fangs fill its mouth. Its horrific visage is not improved by sharp, pointy ears, which resemble like those of a bat. It floats in midair, entrails dangling in shadow.

"I know what you are," I say, recalling what I read in the book. "Kephn. Created by dark magic."

Isis moves closer. A cool hand strokes my forehead. "Fate has saved you twice. Perhaps you will hunt for me one day, little bird."

Another figure moves out of the darkness. "Perhaps," Mama Zizi says. "When she's grown."

They speak in a tongue I don't understand. The kephn doesn't seem to notice or care. It is entirely focused on its next meal. It hovers in the air, then floats toward Dave's body. I turn my face away as it begins to feed, but I cannot block out the sounds of slurping and crunching.

There is the rustle of movement. I see a white face hovering over mine. A moment later something warm and wet drips into my mouth.

Isis' blood is rich and salty.

II

I spend the next few days reading. On closing night, I wait until the carnival is shutting down to unwrap the mirror box. I feel around the side of the mirror, find a small depression, then unlatch the box and open the compartment.

The kephn's head is withered and rotted now, but it moves as soon as I open the box. It sits atop its own innards, bound in silver chains. The box is stuffed with herbs: mustard, Hawthorne, vervain, garlic. I understand by now that these things and the runes on the box contain it, that they are all that contain it. Looking at the runes, I recognize Mama Zizi's handwriting, her favorite silver ink.

The thing's eyes snap open, blood red. "Drink," it gasps.

"She left you," I murmur.

"Horrible," the thing says. "They all left me. Ssso cruel. I'm so thirsty."

"You suffer." I tilt my head. "Poor thing. The red thirst."

Crimson eyes snap into focus. "Yessss. Release me."

"There is a price to pay for your freedom." I hold up Mama's diary. "I know where the rest of you is. If you betray me, I'll burn it. If you obey, I'll let you have the rest of your corpse back."

I'm lying, but it isn't smart enough to know that.

It does not take us long to come to terms.

I do not have a fancy knife and goblet, as Isis does, so I have to saw through his neck with one of Ezra's pocket knives. After I have drunk the thick, vile sludge, I gingerly unwrap the chains and take the head out. Intestines smear filth on my costume. I don't care.

Sharp fangs pierce my neck and I, too, am transformed, binding myself to blood and obliteration, transcendence and decay.

With a demonic cackle, the thing floats into the night to descend and gorge upon the departing audience. Distant screams mark the spot where the kephn has gone.

The screams sound like music to me now. I am almost sorry when they finally fall silent.

I wander out with the dawn, find Isis in her tent, staked through the lung. The glamours and lies that have blinded me for years fall away.

"I remember everything," I tell her. "I remember enchanting the crowds, pointing out victims for Magus. I remember luring men into your tent, slipping out into the night as you appeared."

The blood.

The blood.

The blood.

They called her *Vrykolakas* in the old world.

"How long?" I ask. "How long has it been since I fell through those stairs into your lair?"

"A century. Perhaps two. You slept through most of those years." She gasps for air. "It was Mama's lair, first. She found us. Bound us to her with magic."

I, too, have fallen out of time.

"Was it her idea to join the circus?" I ask.

Isis nods and gasps. "We hunt best on the move."

The kephn approaches, entrails floating over the earth.

Isis looks at the floating head. "I warned her not to try creating one of them. But she insisted. She said she knew her fate." She looks at me with blood black eyes. "As do you."

"It wasn't fate, saved me from you the first time," I tell her. "It was a dog."

She manages a wheezing laugh. "That dog didn't save you. It only interrupted me. You still came to me when I called." She turns her head to the hovering revenant. "You know how dangerous this thing is? It will leave mountains of corpses. We hunt discretely. It just kills for fun. You never should have released it."

"You never should have killed my brothers," I tell her.

148

As The Circus Leaves Town

Then I drive the silver dagger through her eye.

We leave town a fortnight later. In the interim, I've taken over Isis' spot, and added a new attraction: The Mirror Of Dreams. People stream in to see it. No one seems to notice that they leave with black, empty eyes, or that most have a new wound or bite mark. By the time we haul out, the baker is mindlessly stirring an empty bowl.

The last thing I do before riding away is burn the house to the ground. Then the carts and trucks move on, and I find myself again fascinated by watching the gold dust floating past the thick, velvet curtains. Ezra sits beside me, his eyes black and lifeless. The show must go on.

❦ ❦ ❦

Morgan Sylvia is a metalhead, an Aquarius, a coffee addict, and a work in progress. A former obituarist, she is now a full-time freelance writer. She is the author of two novels, Abode, which was recommended by the Library Journal, and Dawn: Book 1 of the Aris Trilogy; two novellas; and four poetry collections. Her work has been published in dozens of places, including Pseudopod, Wicked Witches, Northern Frights, Haunted House Short Stories, Endless Apocalypse, Under Her Skin, In The Cold, Cold Ground, and The Final Summons. Her second poetry collection, As The Seas Turn Red, was nominated for an Elgin Award twice. Her latest release is The Withering Hours: Dark Folk Horror. She was one of the writers for the award-winning audio drama Undertow: Blood Forest, as well as its follow-up Undertow: The Pulse. Sylvia belongs to several writers' groups: the HWA, the SFWA, the New England Horror Writers, Horror Writers of Maine, and Tuesday Mayhem Society. She lives in Maine with two tuxie cats, two evil goldfish, the cutest rescue dog ever, an overgrown rose garden, and a pet banshee. Forthcoming works include The Bloodgold Queen: Book 2 of The Aris Trilogy; The Zhur Lord: Book 3 of The Aris Trilogy; and an as-yet unnamed horror novel. Follow her at morgansylvia.net

The Creak on the Attic Stairs

Tamika Thompson

WHEN I WAS ELEVEN, my favorite uncle died unexpectedly the second week of October, but his funeral didn't happen until November. I didn't have enough life experience to know that multiple weeks with no burial was a sign that something had been amiss about his demise.

By the time the limousine pulled away from the cemetery, the grass had shriveled up and a frost had formed over it. Autumn in Detroit was as cold as someplace else's winter, and the numbness in my fingers and toes matched what I felt inside.

At the repast, my fifteen-year-old cousin Shareefa whispered to me, "You know how Uncle Luke died, don't you?" She talked with her hands to show off the French manicure on her acrylic nails.

Uncle Luke was my mother's brother, and since I had no father in my life, Uncle Luke filled that role. He took me to ballet practice and sat front row beside my mother at all my recitals. He was two years her senior, and no one mistook him for her husband because the family resemblance was so strong it was obvious he was her brother. Uncle Luke was the younger twin of my other uncle, whom everyone called Juke. I had no idea how or why they'd turned John into "Juke," but I sensed the reason wasn't good. Luke and Juke were identical, but I could tell them apart by the tiny mole Uncle Luke had just below his left eye.

There were other differences as well. Uncle Luke had a genuine smile with wide honest, green eyes that burst from his face like sun rays. He laughed easily and was slow to anger. Even when he chastised me for getting lippy with my mother, he'd deliver that message with a smile. "Manners, baby girl," he'd say. "Manners." And that was all it took to get me back on track because when Uncle Luke locked eyes with me, the rest of the world fell away.

Uncle Juke's eyes were equally green, but his facial expressions, the set of his mouth, even the tip of his head reminded me of a hawk. He was snippy when angry, and he also never came around as much. When he did, he was preoccupied, and once said to my mother, "Does your child always yammer on non-stop like this?"

Shareefa continued, "You never wondered how he died? You can be so naïve."

Between bites of food, I answered my cousin. "Mommy said Uncle Luke got sick."

Shareefa shook her head forcefully. The beads at the ends of her braids clapped together.

"Just gullible. If somebody told you the sky was purple, you'd be like, 'okay.'"

"He didn't get sick?" I swallowed. The macaroni thick in my throat, like I'd choke.

"At 30? He got sick and died at 30? Maybe if he was 70."

"People get sick and die from things all the time." I raised my voice. Gripped my fork tightly. "Cancer. Heart attack.

Pneumonia. Stroke." I scooped more mac and cheese into my mouth. I hadn't really felt like eating since I'd found out he was gone, but something about seeing his casket lowered into the ground gave me a resignation I hadn't had earlier in the week.

"Not sick, dumb-dumb. Shot."

"Shot?" I imagined the polished guns my uncles set on the counters whenever they entered my grandmother's home. Pistols were a familiar object. I'd never touched one, but I'd seen plenty up close. They were much different from the rifles in the cartoons I watched after school, with Elmer Fudd shooting at Bugs Bunny with a long shotgun. The weapons my uncles carried were smaller, fit neatly in their palms.

"Yeah. Shot. Killed."

When I was six, my mother explained mortality to me, but I didn't truly learn of death's finality until she told me I would never play hopscotch, share strawberry and grape Nerds, nor Moonwalk with Uncle Luke again. I'd miss the Moonwalk the most because Uncle Luke cranked up Michael Jackson's *Billie Jean* and slid across the living room with Shareefa and me. As big and lanky as my cousin and I had gotten, Uncle Luke still found ways to be the fun uncle. He'd tell us how to behave like ladies and to leave the boys alone and keep our "noses in them schoolbooks." He was adamant that he wanted us to establish ourselves in careers before marrying and having kids. "I don't want you two to need no man for nothing."

When they told me he'd died, I'd imagined him withering away in a hospital bed like movie characters. Not dying like the gang members on my street, bullet-riddled and lying in a pool of their own blood.

"Caught it through the eye." Shareefa touched the left side

of her face with the front of one of those nails, which curved and resembled claws. She could be so blunt. I sometimes hated her. "That's why his casket was closed."

I *had* wondered why I couldn't see him at the funeral. As much as I disliked my cousin in that moment, I knew she wasn't lying. Shareefa and her five-year-old brother Sean lived between the homes of my grandmother and my estranged aunt in Philadelphia, which gave Shareefa a worldly quality that I was in awe of. Her information was always too much, too abrasive, and delivered at the wrong time, but that girl was also the truth. I'd never known her to exaggerate, and she knew how special Uncle Luke was to me and wouldn't lie about that.

The macaroni and cheese slid from my plate and landed on the floor with a wet plop. Sean shouted, "She just made a mess all over Grandmother's carpet!"

When my mother and Uncle Juke's bloodshot eyes met mine, I yelled, "You lied!" and stormed into the bathroom. The space was bitterly cold and the lights dimmer than usual, but I was too hurt to notice.

❦ ❦ ❦

My Grandmother's house was on the east side of Detroit, not far from the river. It was two bedrooms downstairs with a third in the loft. One bathroom for the entire house with three exits—to the main floor, to the attic, and to the backyard.

When Uncle Luke had been alive and visiting town, he stayed upstairs. He had homes all over the place—one overlooking New York's Central Park, another in Toronto, and a third in Hollywood, with a pool and palm trees. He'd bring me souvenirs from his other homes, and promised me that

I'd visit them one day. Once, he'd even given me an eighteen-carat gold necklace with a heart pendant that my mother told me was too expensive for me to wear around town. "Only for special occasions."

Whenever he was upstairs and I had to use the bathroom, I'd lock the door so he wouldn't accidentally come down. That was his idea. He'd say, "Girls need their privacy. You always have to watch yourself. Be safe."

I didn't know what he meant, but I made sure all the doors were locked when I was inside just like he'd taught me.

And upon finishing, if I forgot to unlatch the one leading to the attic as I headed off to play with my cousins in the family room, he'd rap on the door with our secret knock—*Bum. Bum. Bum. Bum. Bum. Boom. Boom.* I'd giggle all the way back to the bathroom. And I'd throw open the latch and wait for him to emerge from the dark stairwell and say, "You locked me in. What do you think this is, prison?"

So, after storming off, with my mother and Uncle Juke closing in, I locked myself in that bathroom. Then I latched the door to the attic, and the one to the backyard. I sat on the toilet, lid down, and slid my shoes back and forth against the tile floor, the soles squeaking, the noise causing a distraction from the information swirling in my head.

Shot.

Which meant a bullet had pierced him.

What had been going through his mind then? He must have been terrified. In so much pain.

My mother and Uncle Juke called to me through the door. Uncle Juke sounded angry, likely because I'd called them liars and the word "lie" was verboten in our family.

My mother choked down a sob. "Baby. I can explain."

"Leave me alone," I snapped. "You didn't tell me the truth about Uncle Luke, and I'll be mad at you forever."

They quieted down. My grandmother said, "Leave her be. She's just hurting."

I ran through everything Shareefa had said. Who would shoot Uncle Luke? He literally was the sweetest man on the planet. He had a string of ladies who fought one another over him, but each one melted any time he spoke to them. And I couldn't imagine him getting into an argument with anyone. He was the one who'd always tell me to "be gentle."

Was he robbed? Was it accidental? There was a lot of shooting in my neighborhood. Guns would sometimes go off without anyone really meaning it. I'd lost my childhood play-mate Grace to a stray bullet. Maybe that had happened to Uncle Luke?

"Talk to me, Uncle Luke," I whispered.

An unexplained breeze moved through the tiled space, brushing my shins and lifting my curls. Footsteps descended the attic stairs behind the locked door. Slowly clomping, as if the person wore heavy boots. I stopped crying. Held my breath. No one was supposed to be up there in Uncle Luke's room.

I stomped over to the door, ready to fuss out whomever was there. Gearing up to say, *You better not be up there stealing Uncle Luke's stuff,* I reached for the latch. But before my finger retracted the gold metal rod, there was a knock from the other side of the door—*Bum. Bum. Bum. Bum. Bum. Boom. Boom.*

❧ ❧ ❧

Uncle Juke was the one who kicked in the bathroom door when everyone heard me scream non-stop for a full minute. He pulled me in for a hug but I bucked, pushed him away, and ran out back.

"The hell's wrong with her?" Uncle Juke started up, but my mother said, "Let her leave."

In the backyard, I sat on the swing, comforted that Uncle Luke's black Cadillac was blocking everyone's view of me from the kitchen. Even from the grave, he was protecting me still.

What I'd heard had been undeniable. That had been Uncle Luke's knock. That had been Uncle Luke. And it wasn't as if the sound against the wood itself had made me scream, rather the emptiness of the stairwell when I'd finally opened that door. Uncle Luke's smell was in there, the way his aftershave gave hints of mint. The warmth of his presence was there too, and when I reached my hand into the darkness, his scarf brushed against my skin.

Outside, the screen door opened and snapped back on its frame. Uncle Juke emerged from the house and shuffled over, hands in his pockets, his jacket collar high to guard against the chill. I was used to the cold because my school principal, Sister Margaret, insisted we go out for recess unless it was raining, but Uncle Juke shivered, tucked his elbows into his sides, and sniffled. His nose was red.

Uncle Juke sat on the swing to my right, and his lanky, noodle-like legs flopped off the seat. His polished leather shoes caught the pale sunlight.

"What did your mannish cousin tell you?"

I didn't want to talk. Especially not to him because he and Uncle Luke had the same voice. Juke and Luke used to be inseparable. They had a language of facial expressions decipherable solely to them. They giggled for long periods and only they knew why. I timed one of their laughter fits at fifteen minutes straight. The guffaws often annoyed my mother. But as time passed, and they worked more closely together in whatever job they had—it seemed to go from waste management to construction to ownership of a car wash chain depending on which of them was talking—the chuckles between them weren't as frequent. And in recent years, whenever they laughed together and Luke looked away, Juke's face would dissolve into an evil glare. That was probably the real reason I didn't like him.

"Girl, you better answer your uncle when I'm talking to you." Uncle Juke's words sliced through my memories.

"Shareefa said Uncle Luke was shot." The swing's chain squeaked as I rocked back and forth slightly, trying to calm my racing heart.

"And you didn't know that already." It was a statement, not a question. Of all the events that day, this realization seemed to hit Uncle Juke the hardest. "Didn't you ever wonder why it took so long to have his funeral?"

I shook my head. Tears spilled from my chin and landed on my dress' Bertha collar. I needed a sweater after all and was thankful when he pulled one from inside his coat and draped it around my shoulders.

"Shareefa's telling the truth. Luke was killed, and the police had to figure out who did it."

"Did they?"

"Nope. Still investigating. So, it took them a while to give us his body."

"Did you?"

Uncle Juke paused for a long time and stared at me through squinted eyes. The vein on his left temple throbbed. "Did I what?"

"Figure out who did it?"

"Oh." He relaxed his shoulders and loosened his grip on

the swing's chain. "If I did, I'd be out looking for him." His jaw clenched. "Why'd you scream?"

"I don't know." I never confided in anyone other than Uncle Luke. Not even my mother. Not even Shareefa.

"You sounded real scared."

I shivered, and not from the cold.

"What aren't you telling me? I mean, I know I'm not your favorite uncle," he chuckled, "but you can tell me things."

"Do you believe in ghosts?"

He cleared his throat. Uncle Luke used to relish these kinds of open-ended discussions. But Uncle Juke looked like he regretted suggesting I could tell him things. "I believe the information we have about life is so incomplete that we can't be closed off to any possibility."

"Do you or don't you, Uncle Juke?"

"Mind your tone, girl."

"Never mind."

"Now, don't go giving me no never minds. I guess I do believe in ghosts. Is that what made you scream?"

I glanced toward the top of the house, remembering how Uncle Luke would wave to me from that attic window and hold up his index finger to signal he'd be down in one minute.

"He's up there." I pointed to the dark and muted space, sensing Uncle Luke's spirit staring down at us. "Wearing the same clothes he did that last day."

The feel of that scarf brushing my hand in the stairwell popped in my mind. Without being able to see it, I knew it was the lambswool one my mother had bought for Uncle Luke. I'd picked it out. Standing in line at J.C. Penney, she'd told me how as kids Uncle Luke had taught her to fish and how it was wonderful for her to watch him teach me as well. "Be brave, baby girl," he'd told me when I reeled in my first bass. She and I reminisced as I picked out an extra soft scarf in Navy.

"What you talking about?" Uncle Juke's voice was steady, but pink crept up his neck and onto his cheeks.

"He has something to say, and I'm gonna find out what that is." That last day, when Uncle Luke headed out, I'd read the weather report, put the lambswool scarf around his neck, and said, "Stay warm." We embraced, and that was the last time I saw him alive.

"Something to say like what?" Uncle Juke checked the attic window then brought his gaze back to me on that swing next to him. He squinted. "Stay outta that attic. Ya hear?"

When I didn't answer, he rose, stuffed his hands back in his pockets, and crossed the yard to the house.

"And make sure you come in and apologize to your mom." His voice trailed off as he sped up, rushing away from me like I'd offended him. "My sister doesn't need any more stress right now."

He not only let that screen door slam against the frame, but he also closed the wooden door behind it. I imagined a gust of wind following him inside because seconds later, at the attic window, the lace curtain trembled, as if disturbed by a hand.

❦ ❦ ❦

That night, when the last piece of glazed ham had been eaten, the final glass of wine consumed, and the guests had all filed out to their cars and away from Grandmother's house, we settled down for bed.

No one seemed to have packed clothes for us to spend the night, but my mom and Uncle Juke were too exhausted and tipsy by nightfall to get behind a wheel. So, Uncle Juke slept on the living room couch near the front door, my mother in the guest room next to Grandmother's, and my cousins and I in sleeping bags in the den at the rear of the home, which I was happy about because I was away from the grown-ups and near the kitchen and bathroom.

In the darkness, I whispered to Shareefa about Uncle Luke. Her younger brother Sean had long past fallen asleep.

"Why can't they find the killer?" I pestered.

"Nobody talks to the police. And they don't have the murder weapon."

"What kind was it?"

"I heard it was a .38 but was nowhere to be found."

"Where did it happen?"

Silence from her.

"Did you hear me?"

"I heard."

"Where did it—"

"You really want to know?"

"Yes."

"They don't know where it happened, but his body was found in the river."

Tears stung my eyes. I let that thought sink in, of my uncle's body floating to the surface and someone finding his remains. I couldn't imagine anyone hurting him that way.

"Who did it?"

"Already told you, police don't know."

"But who do *you* think did it?"

Long pause. Shareefa never lied, but she sometimes buried the truth in silence.

"Our uncles aren't who you think they are, little cousin." She sounded disappointed. The same way she spoke whenever I borrowed her starter jacket or hot pink jellies without permission.

"What do you mean?"

"Ever notice they always carry guns?"

"Yes."

"You never thought that odd?"

"Everybody has guns. Mommy. Grandmother. Even Sister Margaret."

"Everybody *owns* guns. But who actually *carries* guns?"

I thought long and hard. "The police."

"Our uncles aren't police."

"You saying someone was after Uncle Luke?"

"*Someone* wanted him dead."

"Is Uncle Juke in danger too?"

"That's all I'm gonna say about that."

I hated it when older folks didn't tell me things. What did they really think I was going to do with the information? I had no power and no one to gossip to.

"Do you believe in ghosts, Shareefa?"

"Everyone that goes to church believes in ghosts. We literally pray to the holy ghost."

"I think Uncle Luke's ghost is here."

Silence again.

"Shareefa."

"What?"

"What aren't you telling me?"

"Grandmother said the day he was killed he still came home."

"What? What did she mean?"

"She said she was in the bed asleep, and she heard the key turn in the back door, the way it always did when he was in town and staying in the attic. She heard his footsteps enter the house, go to the refrigerator, open it, and get some food. But she said it was strange, because he usually announced himself when he entered and that time he didn't. So, she called out, "Luke?" and he answered, "Yes, Mother." And she called out, "All right, Good night, baby," and he'd answered, "Good night. Love you." And she heard his footsteps cross the kitchen, go into the bathroom, and up the stairs to the attic. She heard him move across the floor up there and that was that. She went to sleep."

"And?" My heart pounded. The sleeping bag made me sweat.

"His body had been found that morning, but she heard him come home that night. And the next day, when she waited for him at breakfast with a heap of bacon and an omelet, he never came down the stairs. And she called up to him again, but that time he didn't answer. And she went up there, and he wasn't there, and the bed hadn't been slept in."

"I heard him too." My voice quivered.

"He spoke to you?"

"No, but he did our secret knock, and I know it was him. I know he's up there."

"Well, if he is, I hope he goes away because I'm scared of ghosts, and I don't even want to talk about this anymore."

With that, Shareefa turned in for the night. I couldn't sleep right away. When I did, I had nightmares of my uncle up there in the attic, bloated and filled with bullet holes and river water.

I tossed and turned through the night. How was I supposed to live the rest of my life with this grief? Love didn't seem worth the pain of the loss, and the permanent separation made me angry I'd ever loved Uncle Luke to begin with.

I'd consumed too much cola at dinner and had to pee every couple of hours. The third time I was up, the clock on the bookshelf said 3:43am. I tiptoed past my copies of Baldwin, Angelou, and Walker, careful not to wake the snoring grownups, who would chastise me for my pop-drinking.

The toilet seat was colder than it'd been the two previous

times. Each trip before, I'd gone in without hearing any steps on the stairs or knocks on the door, and I grew more confident that the sounds from earlier in the day had been my imagination.

I washed my hands in the basin and thought I heard the creak on the attic stairs. I snapped off the water and listened.

No sound.

I held my breath as I dried my hands on the towel. Footsteps clomped rapidly and noisily down the stairs. This time I wouldn't scream. And as much as I wanted to, I didn't run off or scurry back to my warm sleeping bag. That secret knock started up— *Bum. Bum. Bum. Bum. Bum. Boom. Boom*— this time followed by whispers from the other side of the door.

🍂 🍂 🍂

The stairwell to the attic smelled like a cedar closet. The steps were wooden and original to the 1930s build. There were sixteen of them, I knew, because that's how Uncle Luke had taught me to count as a toddler—holding my hand as we descended.

The darkness in that narrow space was all-encompassing. My eyes ached as they attempted to dilate, and wet tears formed at the edges. I would have seen the same amount of nothingness if I'd closed my eyes.

"Uncle Luke?" I whispered, hoping his kind voice would guide me to what he wanted. If he had something to say, I had to know what it was, but I was also afraid that hearing him in the black void would make me scream again.

The air was stale, dry, warmer than it had been in the bathroom moments before, stifling and stuffy like a room that had been cut off from the rest of the house, shut up and avoided because it held memories instead of life.

One of the steps above me creaked, sending a jolt through me. My foot searched for the second step. My fingertips found the chilled wooden stairwell walls, and it occurred to me that it could have been a living person at the top, luring me up. I imagined a gangster with a pistol, a murderer with an ax, a slasher with a butcher knife. Those scared me more than my dead Uncle Luke. At least I knew he wouldn't harm me. But what if it wasn't him?

On the third step, I found the light switch. Three bulbs affixed to the ceiling snapped on. I squinted against the sudden brightness and found no one at the top of the stairs. I continued up. In the attic, the couch squeaked.

I eyed it. No one was there. But the footsteps were undeniable. The sound crossed the room and went to a rear closet, where my uncle's clothes and suitcases rested. The door clicked and moaned open. The light in there was already on, and on the shelf lay a lump of fabric. My eyes struggled to focus. It was the scarf my mother and I had gotten Uncle Luke for Christmas. The one I'd helped her pick out at the department store, the one I'd put on him that final time I'd seen him alive. The one that had caressed my fingers earlier in the day.

I moved forward and rose on my toes to reach it. My palm closed around the fabric. Something solid was inside. I gasped. I used both hands to pull it down, excited that I'd found the thing Uncle Luke wanted to show me. Was it more jewelry? Another book? A new treasure from his travels he hadn't had the opportunity to give me? But when I opened it, my fingers thick with excitement and nerves, a loud pop exploded, a piercing pain ripped through my forehead, and everything went black.

❧ ❧ ❧

The sun was out when I woke. My body felt light. Warm. Like I was dreaming and couldn't wake. Voices were everywhere. Frantic. Loud. Near. Far. I opened my eyes. My mother was wailing, with my grandmother and Uncle Juke holding her up. Police swarmed the attic. I rose to standing. Uncle Juke stared over his shoulder at the closet. And when I fully took in the scene around me, I screamed too.

My own lifeless body lay in a bag, with blood covering my head, chest and arms. A pool of it coated the floor, spilling between the wooden planks. The gun I'd found was now wrapped in plastic. An officer carried it down the stairs. They zipped my body in that black sack and removed my remains as well. But my mother and grandmother stayed, even as the house grew silent, even as, out the window, the neighborhood din became a whisper, even as the sun plunged to the earth. By evening, they were the only ones home.

Time sped up and slowed. My nights bled into days. I was lost, confused, angry, heartbroken. I'd never return to school, perform another ballet recital, hug my mother before bed, giggle at a movie with Shareefa and Sean, bake cookies after church with my grandmother, soar through the sky on the backyard swings. I lived outside of days, hours, minutes. I longed for clocks and schedules as much as I ached for my mother.

Then one day, the phone rang.

My grandmother answered, the tangled cord snaking down her forearm. Investigators had identified the gun that claimed my life as the same one that had killed Uncle Luke.

"The same?" My grandmother searched my mother's face. "Impossible."

All evidence now pointed to my Uncle Juke as Uncle Luke's shooter, the officer added. They'd already taken him into custody.

Grandmother dropped the receiver and fell to her knees. My mother held her. I yearned to embrace them. I envied their ability to speak face to face, to touch, and to wipe away the other's tears.

"I told Juke and Luke their iniquity would catch up to them," my grandmother whispered through sobs. "Told them about these streets. That if they lived by the sword…I just never thought they'd actually die by the sword."

And cut down my life in the process.

I now believe it wasn't Uncle Luke's spirit that led me to the loaded gun. Nor was it his ghost that returned that night after he was killed. I know my grandmother heard Uncle Juke arriving to hide that murder weapon, my uncles' similar voices throwing her off of the switch. But who had lured me up the stairs? Sometimes, I wonder whether the pistol itself did the leading. Firearms are like gods. They can remove people from the earth and rip them cleanly from the confines of time and space. So, couldn't a gun, with its capacity to take lives, build states, and start wars, also wield supernatural power?

❦ ❦ ❦

Years passed.

I remain in the attic.

I pace to stay calm. The creak on the attic stairs is from me now. One night, my footsteps must have gone on too long, because my grandmother opened the door at the bottom of the stairwell and shouted, "I rebuke you, Satan!"

Now, I witness my loved ones from the attic window or by eavesdropping through the vents. I spend my days reading books from the shelf, writing in notebooks, on slips of paper, on walls, hoping my message will one day appear to the living and they'll know I still have sentience even if my existence no longer holds meaning. I get a kick out of watching my cousins glance up at the attic as their mom, no longer estranged, drives them away from the house. I wave to them. Their faces grow concerned when the lace curtain trembles, as if disturbed by a hand.

❦ ❦ ❦

Tamika Thompson is an author of award-winning horror and suspense. Her debut gothic novel is *The Curse of Hester Gardens*, (Erewhon / Kensington, 2026).

Bats! Bats! Bats! (Fun for the Whole Family)

Jonathan Maberry

I

THE HANDBILL READ *BATS! Bats! Bats! (Fun for the Whole Family)!!!*

Cool artwork, too. All aflutter with bats.

Lots of them. Cartoony but pretty accurate. There were Fruit bats, Indiana bats, Big Brown bats, Silver-haired bats, California Myotis, Lesser Long-nosed bats, Eastern Red bats, Van Gelder's bats, Long-legged Myotis, Hawaiian Hoary bats, Honduran White bats, Townsend's Big-eared bats, Giant Golden-crowned Flying Foxes, Western Small-footed bats, Rafinesque's Big-eared bats, Hammer-headed bats, and…

Well, lots of bats.

Anatomically correct, though stylized to make the advertisement attractive and fun. The paper was a pale Halloween orange and the lettering black with white edging so the words popped. The bats were color-appropriate.

There were no vampire bats, though.

Tommy Pussett thought that was weird.

Not weird in any nefarious way—nefarious being on last Tuesday's *Word-a-Day* calendar page—but a missed opportunity. After all this was Pine Deep, the town that celebrated Halloween year-round. Except for December, when Santa and Rudolf were given some face-time. The rest of the year the town leaned into its reputation as the "most haunted town in America," according to a Life Magazine article from the '60s. It was the late 2020s now and the reputation hadn't worn off at all. Rather the reverse, with the high school football team switching from *The Trojans* (never a popular name except for local wags) to *The Scarecrows.* The failing Lincoln Drive-in was rebranded as the *Dead-End Drive-In* and only showed horror films. Tommy particularly liked the ones with a lot of girls somehow falling out of their clothes. His favorite was Brinke Stevens, a slender brunette who looked a lot like Tommy's eighth-grade English teacher. Mrs. Barnhardt, though, never fell out of even a single stitch of clothing.

Point is that Pine Deep was Halloween central. Round the clock and 'round the calendar. Pumpkins and corn mazes and hayrides and scarecrows. It was like that all through town. The town square had a statue of the Headless Horseman even though the Washington Irving story was set in Westchester County, New York and not Eastern Pennsylvania. To be fair, the other local statues of the Wolfman—1941 version—the Frankenstein Monster, and the Hunchback of Notre Dame were never set in Pine Deep, either.

The whole town was filled with people who loved Halloween. Not specifically the holiday, but the tourist dollars. Nearly everyone profited from tourism. Half of the cars Tommy's dad worked on at Shanahan's Garage were visitor breakdowns.

So, the bats were in keeping with the spirit of the town... almost.

No damn vampire bats.

That bothered Tommy. It was a missed step that made no real sense. They could have had *only* vampire bats in the advertisement and left all of the exotics out.

That's how Tommy would have done it.

Tommy was something of an expert on Halloween. At thirteen, he was positive there was no one else in the whole world who knew more about that holiday, up to and including John Carpenter and the entire cast of the movie.

That said…the flyer was intriguing.

Bats! Bats! Bats!

Fun for the whole family, it said.

"Yeah," said Tommy under his breath. "Sure."

It was worth a try.

II

Tommy's family did not want to go to see the bats.

He made his pitch, and it was a good one. Any normal family would have been reaching for their coats. His family wasn't normal.

Mom rarely went anywhere she couldn't grab a drink in fewer than ten steps. Dad was always working, which was good because when he was home he seemed to enjoy getting mad, and when he was mad he broke things. The TV once. Bunch of crockery. Tommy's older brother Kip's drumsticks *and* the snare. Tommy's ribs. Crow's nose. More than once. Mom's heart.

Kip didn't want to go see bats because Kip was mad at the world and all he wanted to do was bang on his drums or jerk off in the upper bunk when he thought Tommy was asleep. Kip had a bunch of magazines tucked inside a slit he'd cut in his mattress. The women in them looked like they drank at the same kind of bars Mom drank at, but had been doing it longer. They all looked kind of sad. Kip didn't seem to care.

As for Bethy, she was half-ass interested, but only in the fruit bats and flying foxes. She called them sky-puppies. But the idea of going to a whole show about bats creeped her out.

That left Aunt Lu, who was Gran's older sister.

Gran was two years in her grave, having failed only once to miss the end post on Songbird Bridge. She always drove fast and there were six or eight long scratches on the left side of her thirty-year-old Ford pickup for near-misses. She even used to brag about how she struck sparks from the post but never slowed a bit. Then there was that one time when she forgot to swerve at the right moment. Eighty-miles an hour and no seat-belt. They scraped her off the gravel verge where she'd slid thirty-one feet-four-inches. Tommy knew that because it was in all the papers. He went down to the bridge every day for two weeks to look at the gravel that was still stained. Then that storm washed it all into history's drainage ditch.

Lu was still around, though, but she had the dementia. Didn't know who she was half the time and didn't know who Tommy was the rest of the time. That sucked because he could remember her when she was okay. When she was funny and had a sharp tongue that could even put Dad in his place. Only person who ever could. She also used to love bats and could name any species she ever saw.

Past tense.

Now she sat in her room talking to people only she could see, going through the motions of taking cigarettes out of her pack, scraping a Lucifer match on the chair leg, taking a deep drag and exhaling up at the ceiling fan. Except there was no pack of cigarettes, no matches, and the ceiling fan hadn't worked in seven months. In a way, though, it was fascinating to watch.

Bats! Bats! Bats! (Fun for the Whole Family)

That was home for Tommy. Not a lot of fun. He wasn't sure there was a lot of love. The word was thrown around a lot and would flutter over the dinner table or around the Christmas tree. Flutter like, well, bats. Nice but bitey, too.

He knew that he was hardly the only kid from a tough family. Not the only one at school, not the only one in his neighborhood, not even the only one on his street. Times were tough, as they'd always been tough. Life was hard, as it had always been hard. And who ever lived a life without pain? No one that Tommy knew, that was for sure.

Joy for him was in monster movies and spooky novels and horror comics. Fun, for Tommy, was something out in the shadows or under the bed. Or scratching at his bedroom window on a windy autumn night. The rest of the family had different ways to make each day work. He didn't think bats were any part of that.

So, with the 'fun for the whole family' thing dead at the starting gate, Tommy called his friends.

III

Ricky Devlin was the closest thing Tommy had to a best friend. Ricky was the only kid in school Tommy could think of who didn't try to make an obscene joke about the Pusset family name. No Tommy Pussy or Tommy Pussygrabber bullshit. Just like Tommy was the only one around who didn't make Ricky *Devil* or Deviled Ham jokes.

Partly it was mutual respect. Partly it was a shared weariness for jokes that weren't funny. Not even the first time someone made them. Sure, other kids laughed, but then again some kids laughed at stupid stuff all the time. Tommy figured it was a measure of intelligence to laugh at good jokes and not at dumb ones. And maybe a meter for empathy

—another word-a-day goodie—to not laugh at a joke meant to hurt someone's feelings.

Tommy spent a lot of his alone time philosophizing on such things.

Ricky answered on the fourth ring, right before the call would go to voicemail. It was always the fourth ring for him. Someday Tommy would ask why.

""Sup?"

"'Sup," said Tommy. "You doing homework?"

"Nah. Finished that during detention. It was just some math stuff. I don't care about math."

Tommy *did* care about math because he sucked at it. As for detention, Ricky had his own favorite seat. His thing was talking back to teachers. He loved doing it and didn't mind the penalties.

"You see the signs about the thing?" asked Tommy.

"The bats? Sure."

Tommy never had to be too explicit with Ricky. The kid was probably a borderline sociopath, but he was sharp as a knife.

"You wanna go?"

"Dude."

It was said in the way that meant both *are you fucking serious?* and *What time?*

Tommy consulted the handbill. "Opens at seven."

"Crap, it'll be dark by then," said Ricky. "And you know my mom."

Ricky lived with his mom. Just the two of them. His dad and Ricky's older sister both died a few years ago. Dad from cancer because he smoked three packs a day and worked as a brake specialist, and brakes on all the older cars were lined with asbestos. Krissy got sick from Covid and just wasted away. Weird for someone so young. Ricky's mom was hard-core anti-vax, and actually blamed people who *had* been vaccinated for shedding spike proteins that Krissy caught. Or something like that. Tommy had never paid close attention to Mrs. Devlin's rants.

"You can say you're sleeping over here," suggested Tommy.

"Maybe." Ricky was silent for a moment. "If I'm not outside the Crow's Nest by quarter of then I can't make it."

IV

Ricky was there at quarter of.

He was inside the Crow's Nest, buying comics from Jose Gomez, the guy who'd bought the store from Malcolm Crow after Crow ran for chief of police. Half the store was always about Halloween, and the rest was split between whatever holiday was about to happen, racks of model kits and puzzles, and a really good selection of comics. Tommy was a Marvel guy all day, but Ricky was into DC and Dark Horse. He was leafing through a *Hellboy* comic when Tommy came in.

"'Sup?" Ricky.

"'Sup?" said Tommy.

"'Sup?" said Jose, who sat on a high stool behind the counter reading a Lisa Kastner werewolf novel. Tommy had already read that one. Viking werewolves. Very cool.

The store owner peered at them over the top of the paperback. "I bet I can guess where you two are going."

They looked at him. "We're just hanging," said Tommy.

"Like hell. You're going to see Mr. Attercop's show."

They both said, "Who…?"

"Attercop."

Nothing.

"The bat guy," said Jose.

"Oh," said Tommy.

"That's who's running the show?" asked Ricky.

"Yeah. I went to a preview last night."

Tommy stiffened. "There was a preview?"

"Last night, yeah," said Jose.

"And you went?"

"Sure. I went with a few of the others on this row."

That *row* was a two-block stretch of Main Street with some of the oldest and best known of the Halloween-centric shops. The Crow's Nest, Connie's Creepy Cookies, The Halloween All Year Costume Shop, Scarecrow's Antiques, The Haunted Book Shoppe, and others. None were run by the original owners, but the new generation of retailers had been in place since before Tommy was born.

In Pine Deep, everything was marked in time by *Before the Trouble* and *After the Trouble*. The 'Trouble' was the *other* reason Pine Deep was famous. This was a lot different than the place being known for its ghosts. The trouble was that terrible thing that happened in the middle 2000s when a bunch of White Nationalist bikers dumped a shit-ton of LSD into the town's drinking water and everyone freaked out. Not just tripping balls, but going totally nuts. People somehow got it into their heads that all the tourists coming to town for the huge Halloween parade and festival were vampires and werewolves and whatnot. It wasn't just that they were scared—this was farm country. Everyone owned a gun. There were a lot of deaths. A whole lot. The Trouble still stood as the worst incident of domestic terrorism in U.S. history.

Funny thing was that the conspiracy theory crowd online told a different story. In their version, there really *were* vampires and werewolves and ghosts abroad, and it was the monsters who did the killing. A local report, Willard Fowler

Newton, wrote a bestselling nonfiction book, *Ghost Road Blues: The REAL Pine Deep Story*, and that made the national press. Then some Hollywood types came in and made a movie out of it called *Hell Night.* The movie was shown at midnight every Friday and Saturday at the Dead-End Drive-in. Every weekend around the calendar.

Tommy didn't believe there had been real vampires in Pine Deep. He was weird and he loved Halloween, but that was a bridge too far for him. Ricky kind of *did*. And Tommy's Aunt Lu absolutely believed it, and people said she didn't have dementia so much as she'd been driven out of her mind by things she'd seen.

There were a lot of those kind of stories in Pine Deep.

"How was it?" asked Ricky. "All those bats, I mean?"

"Oh, it was really great," said Jose. "I learned a lot."

"Learned?" asked Tommy. "I thought it was a show."

"Not a show. Not really."

"What then?"

"More like a mix of zoo, museum, and a nature documentary," said Jose. "But with a cool light show and some surprises."

"What kind of surprises?" asked Ricky and Tommy at the same time.

Jose looked at them for a long moment, and then smiled. "Oh, I wouldn't want to spoil the fun."

"Awww, come *on.*"

Jose shook his head. "But I *will* show you something cool."

"Show us what?" asked Ricky.

"You'll have to promise not to tell anyone, okay?"

Tommy frowned. "Why not?"

Jose winked, still grinning. "Because it's not exactly *legal*," he said. "But it's really cool."

Tommy glanced at Ricky.

"I'm in," said Ricky. "Promise not to say anything."

"Yeah, I guess," Tommy said.

"No," said Jose, "you have to promise. No half-assing it."

"I promise," said Tommy in that sing-song way people do when someone else is dragging it out.

"Swear it," Jose said.

"I swear," said Ricky.

"Swear like you mean it. Swear on your mom."

Ricky shrugged. "I swear on my mom that I won't tell anyone."

They both looked at Tommy. He sighed as heavily as Atlas bearing the troubled heavens on his shoulders.

"Okay, okay, I swear on my mom."

Jose hopped off his chair, hurried over and locked the front door and put up the *Back in Five Minutes* sign. Then he grinned even harder and waved for them to follow as he headed to the back room. Ricky and Tommy shrugged and followed.

There was a thick pumpkin-orange curtain hanging between the store and a short hallway that led to Jose's apartment. He fished a key out of his pocket and unlocked his door and stepped in.

"Come on in, guys. This is really cool."

The room was hung with evening shadows and all the blinds were down, but Jose clicked on a standing lamp. The glow revealed a bird cage on an occasional table near the kitchen entrance. The cage was one of those boxwood affairs meant to resemble a Victorian cottage. There was, however, no bird inside. Instead, hanging from a little swing-bar was a bat.

A real live bat.

The boys hurried over, their faces glowing with delight.

"That is sooooo frickin' cool," cried Ricky.

"It's awesome," agreed Tommy.

The animal had short, black hair with a contrasting

reddish-brown mantle, and the tapered snout of a small dog. It was large for a bat, but still small, clearly weighing less than two pounds. It yawned and stretched and its wings swept out to a yard's width before folding back against its soft body.

"It's a fruit bat," declared Ricky.

"It's a black flying fox," corrected Tommy. He turned to look at Jose. "I thought it was illegal to have bats as pets."

"Hence the 'can you keep a secret'," said the store owner.

The boys bent and peered at the animal. It hung by clawed feet and looked adorable. Tommy knew this was exactly what his sister called a sky-puppy, and the nickname was obvious. It really did look like a small dog—a chihuahua, but mellower—with huge, liquid eyes.

Ricky began to slide a finger between the bars of the cage, then hesitated. "Wait, do fruit bats bite?"

Jose's smile had not flickered a bit since he invited them back to his apartment. "Why don't you stick that finger all the way in and find out?"

Ricky looked like he was considering it, but Tommy touched his arm. "Don't."

"Why not? It's not like it's a vampire bat."

"No, but bats carry a lot of diseases."

"*Fruit* bats?"

"Flying fox, and yes. Rabies and a bunch of other stuff."

"Not if he doesn't bite me."

Jose's smile finally flickered, just a little. "You know how they treat rabies, don't you? They take these long-ass needles and jab them all the way into your stomach. Hurts like hell."

Tommy almost spoke up, almost said that doctors didn't really do that, and real rabies injections didn't hurt that much, but he kept silent. The truth was that he didn't like the idea of a bat being kept in a cage. From what he'd read, they couldn't be domesticated, and captivity was no good for

179

something used to the wild. Also, the bat—though big for its kind—was still small and probably scared. Poking at it wouldn't make it feel good.

"Not worth trying," he finally said.

Ricky—who had not actually been all that committed to the action—withdrew his finger and then pulled his cell and looked at it. "The place is opening up any minute."

"Well," said Jose, "you two better haul ass. You don't want to miss the fun."

"Okay," said Tommy, "but how did you get a bat? Do they sell them?"

The smile returned. Bigger than before. Almost a Joker smile. "Oh, you'll see. I don't want to spoil the fun."

They smiled back and left. Jose walked them out. When they were half a block down the street, Tommy looked back and saw Jose still standing there. He thought, just for a moment, he saw something move inside the store, in the back. Someone wearing a black suit. Then Jose turned off the store lights.

V

There was a line outside of place.

The *Bats! Bats! Bats!* event was held in a medium-large store that used to be a resale outlet for gently used durable medical equipment. There were adjustable beds, portable commodes, wheelchairs, lift-chairs, walkers, electric scooters, oxygen concentrators, and other stuff Tommy hoped never to see in use or—worse—*have* to use.

The outside of the store was cool. The big picture windows no longer showed smiling old folks on stair chairs or leaning on bathroom safety bars. Instead, the windows were painted a deep black and flocks of bats fluttered in rippling waves the entire width of the building. All of the bats mentioned on the handbill were there. Still no vampire bats, which both confounded and annoyed him.

Ricky noticed that, too. They were twenty-third in line for tickets and he nudged Tommy with an elbow. "No vampire bats."

"Yeah."

"That's weird."

"Yeah."

"Hope they have some inside."

"Me too."

"I mean," said Ricky, "they better. Otherwise this could be lame."

Tommy nodded. The couple in front of them, Jonas Hiller and his girlfriend from college, turned around and agreed with him.

The four of them got into a discussion about bats, mostly in movies, and you don't talk about movie bats without talking about vampires. The general consensus was that the old-school puppet bats—marionettes, really—were better than CGI bats because at least puppets were real. It was not a logical argument, but they all agreed on it. Then, by the time they were near the ticket booth, the girl—it turned out her name was Aliénor and she was an exchange student from France and looked a little like Scarlett Johansson, which made Tommy uncomfortable in several ways—said that her aunt had bat houses all around her property in Provence.

"What kind of bats?" asked Tommy.

"Big ones," said Aliénor. "*Grande chauve-souris noctule.*"

"That's Greater Noctule bat," said Jonas, clearly proud that his major in French was good for more than meeting extremely hot exchange-students.

"They eat insects," Aliénor explained. "My aunt loves them, but from—how do you say—*l'amour de loin..*?"

"Love from afar," supplied Jonas smugly.

"Yeah," said Tommy, who was developing a deep understanding of that concept.

They talked more about her aunt's bats and then they were at the booth. Jonas, feeling expansive because he was with the most beautiful girl in the crowd, bought all four tickets. Ricky and Tommy thanked him a dozen times.

They went in through a door opened by a short man wearing a porkpie hat. He tore their tickets, returned the stubs, and asked each of them the same question, "You sure you want to go in there?"

He'd said it so many times it was automatic and uninflected. They each gave the obvious answer and went into the domain of the bats.

VI

There were indeed bats, bats, bats.

They were all over the place inside.

There were big glass tanks decorated with haunted houses, creepy old trees, graveyards, and ruined castles, and bats hung from every possible horizontal structure. There were bird cages of all sizes, with at least one and often as many as six or seven bats inside. There were bats painted on the walls, each done with such exquisite precision that it looked like real bats somehow stopped in time. There were huge flatscreens showing clips of bats in the wild, and others showing scenes from every conceivable version of *Dracula, Carmilla, Count Yorga, Dark Shadows,* and others. There were rubber and plastic model bats hung from the ceiling on fishing line. And there were bats painted on the floor, each of them glowing with luminescent paint.

Lots of bats.

All you could ever want.

Except still no vampire bats.

The lights, dim as they were inside, flickered and the canned music did a three beat—*da-da-daaaah*. Everyone turned to a spotlight that snapped down from an overhead pot light. A man stood there who had not seemed to even be in the room a moment ago. Tommy appreciated the trickery. Nice.

The man was tall and as thin as a rake-handle, with tiny hips flaring out to dramatically wide shoulders. He wore a tuxedo and Bela Lugosi-style opera cloak. His face was cartoonishly pale and the make-up job around his eyes made them appear red and glaring. Ricky leaned close to Tommy and whispered, "That is sooo cool."

"Yeah."

The man glared around the room, making a show of it, leaning dangerously close to those nearest him and spooking them back a little. Then he smiled and he had really huge fangs. Good ones, too. They didn't look plastic and Tommy wondered if they were caps. In the neighborhood in town called the Fringe, there were a lot of the punk and Goth crowd who were into all kinds of body modification. Some had fangs just like these, and Tommy knew that for a few of them these were permanent caps. That was weird to him, because how did they eat and how did they not bite their own lower lips? To him that question remained as unanswered as how the twenty-year old waitress, Patsy, who lived next door wiped her nose with all the studs and rings she had in nostrils and through her septril and septum. People, he decided, were weird.

The pale man spoke in a heavily accented voice. A deep voice, but the accent didn't sound legit. It was like one of those fake vaguely European accents some actors use in bad spy films.

He said, "Welcome one and all to Mr. Attercop's Horrifyingly Haunted House of Chiroptera. And I am your host and humble servant, Silas Attercop. I welcome all who come here freely and of their own will."

With that he performed a deep, sweeping bow.

"So…," said Attercop, straightening. "Has anyone seen any *bats* around here?"

It got the expected laugh, and then a chorus of screams as thousands of bats suddenly flew into the room. People jumped and swatted the air and ducked and shouted.

Then the laughter began.

One person at first, and then more and more as the crowd slowly realized the bats were a holographic light show. Intangible but convincing.

Tommy, Ricky, Jonas, and Aliénor had all backed into a corner, with Aliénor being the one who shoved everyone to safety. As soon as the trick became apparent, Jonas stepped and tried to be the man of the moment, proclaiming loudly that he didn't believe it all for a moment.

Ricky leaned close to Tommy again and murmured, "Pussy."

He wasn't making a joke about Tommy's last name.

Then everyone had a good laugh, and Mr. Attercop smiled and the moment became *his*. He waved his arms to gather the attention back to him.

"Bats are important," he said. "So important. They are ecologically vital. Without these *insectivorous*, insects like mosquitoes and flies and spiders would breed out of control. They are the best at pest control. Hmmm…we should send a bunch of them to Washington."

Everyone laughed. There was no part of the country, on either side of the political line, where a statement like that wouldn't hit hard in the funny-bone.

Attercop drank in the laughter and it was clear to Tommy that the man knew he'd just won his audience. The one-two punch of light show and truism did the trick. It impressed

Tommy the way a good standup comic does—working the crowd through emotional reaction and thought manipulation in order to get them to buy into the routine and therefore have a better time. The coach of the debate team at school told them all about what he called *benign manipulation.* Knowing that made Tommy feel like he was on the inside track of this gig. Like he and Attercop would understand one another.

"Bats are all natural conservationists," said Attercop. "They never take more than they need. They never wipe out a population of prey. They have always found a way to balance appetite with restraint."

Using video clips on the monitors, sound effects from hidden speakers, more holograms, and a good delivery, Attercop educated the crowd on all the wonders of bats. Not only the fact that any bat colony ate huge amounts of insects every night, but also the economics of reducing out-of-pocket pest control and fewer trips to the hospital or the morgue from diseases spread by insect vectors. Since Pine Deep was a small town in a huge swatch of farm country, there was a note about how farmers saved billions in pesticide costs and prevention of crop damage. He talked about those species of bats that acted as pollinators for fruit and vegetable crops. They also spread seeds through their droppings, which helped reforest burned out sections of the woods.

Attercop spoke at length, and instead of a lecture being boring, there was a compelling and almost hypnotic quality to his voice and delivery. He *owned* the crowd and they hung on every word, every projected image, and every new special effects treat.

And *finally* at the end of the talk, Attercop talked about bats in folklore and in pop culture. Dracula played heavily in that part of the story, and the host shared a very cool bit of trivia that Tommy knew but no one else did—the word *Nosferatu* did not, as Bram Stoker's novel insisted, mean 'undead.' It was an old Romanian word based on an older Greek word, *nosphoros,* which meant 'disease-bearing.' Or, as he phrased it, "Plague carrier."

He then plunged into an exploration of bats in fiction and film, which eventually took him to the topic of vampiric transformations.

"It is what people always claimed," he said, "that vampires could take on the aspect of wolves, and dark birds, and rats, and…of course…bats."

There was some applause for that. But one of the other college kids in the class had to be an asshole and go on a rant about how could an adult vampire—man *or* woman—turn into a vampire bat that weighed only a few ounces. But Attercop was ready for that, which proved to Tommy that he had received that kind of pushback before.

Attercop said, "A vampire is an illusionist. They do not actually *become* bats or wolves or anything else. Just as mermaids used illusions—glamours, to use the proper term —to take on the appearance of an alluring beauty, vampires take on the aspect of whichever animal suits their needs. Actually, nothing in folklore suggests there was any limit to the things they could become."

He then took a stroll along the path of explaining the vampire's strengths and weaknesses. Abnormal strength and speed, resistance to many kinds of injuries, unnaturally long lives…but also their aversion to the cross, to holy objects of any deeply-believed faith, how they could not enter any home unless brought in by invitation or other means, and how their aversion to garlic came about because garlic is a blood purifier.

Then his diatribe made a shift as he began talking about the dangers of GMO farming, and how *real* farms—he leaned on that word because this was good old American semi-redneck God-fearing farm country, god damn it—didn't buy into corporate greed. Attercop's lecture was all about how *real* farmers used *natural* methods to grow *honest* crops so *true Americans* could eat the fruits of *our modern Eden.*

That got a genuine and earnest round of applause.

Somewhere between that part of the talk and when the theme music from Francis Ford Coppola's *Dracula* began playing to usher out the crowd, a pitch was made about everyone doing their part to *help the bats help us.* Tommy was as caught up in it as Ricky, Jonas, Aliénor, and the rest of the packed house were.

It was strange, because Tommy didn't actually remember leaving, but he blinked and there they all were out on the pavement. He stared down at what he held. What they all held.

Little boxwood cages made to look like Victorian mansions. Each with a living bat inside.

Not vampire bats, but definitely bats.

Tommy felt something in his shirt pocket. He set down his cage and removed a piece of paper he didn't recall putting there. Once he opened it, the paper proved to be a certificate of ownership designed to look like formal adoption papers.

He said, "What the heck…?"

On the back of each of their certificates was information on the species of bat they had, some care and feeding instructions, and a lot of verbiage echoing what Attercop told them about how important—how *critical*—bats were for rebuilding the strong core of the American farm. It was written very well and compelling to read.

Aliénor and Jonas laughed with delight. Ricky grinned even bigger than Jose had. The whole crowd was delighted. Even the pedantic college kid and his friends. The members of the audience shared secret smiles as if they were all now key members in the battle against big corporations who wanted to use genetic manipulation to feed bad food to the public while lining their pockets with money that should go to honest Americans.

Tommy was completely apolitical and he hated the summer jobs he got working on one of the local farms. He didn't like to get his hands dirty, not even in good old American soil.

And yet, he picked up his lightweight cage and looked at the flying fox inside.

"Bethy's going to lose her mind," he announced happily. It made him feel a glow of fondness for his sister. For his older brother, Mom, and Aunt Lu. Dad, well...that would have been asking a lot.

They walked home, laughing, telling each other about what they had all just seen. Aliénor was the first to name her bat. She called her *Ma Petite Sirène.* My little mermaid, chosen —Tommy reckoned—because of what Attercop said about mermaids and glamours and all that.

She and Jonas peeled off to head down the crooked lane toward the college dorms. Ricky and Tommy walked down Main past the Crow's Nest. The door was closed and locked and the *Back in Five Minutes* still in the windows though the lights were on. They knocked, wanting to share their experiences with another member of the secret society of bat owners, but Jose didn't answer.

At the corner, Ricky went his way and Tommy watched him go. He felt odd and a little detached from things, but told himself it was just that the evening was strange, but fun. He looked down at his fruit bat, who looked up with intense little brown eyes.

"How about I call you Vampy?" Tommy suggested.

The fruit bat licked its muzzle.

Tommy took him home.

VII

He went in through the kitchen door because the lights at the back end of the house were out. He opened the door quietly and cocked his head to listen. Dad was in the living room yelling at some sports team. Aunt Lu was in there with him, nodding at whatever conversation was going on in her head.

Tommy went up the back stairs and crept past his Mom's room. All he saw was the red glow as she took a drag on a cigarette. He caught one snatch of a quiet conversation.

"...downstairs," she whispered. "I can get out later if he passes out. If not, then tomorrow...?"

Tommy could have deciphered what he heard, but he didn't want to break his own heart.

Kip was using tap-pads to learn a drum routine. There was a frenzied tappity-tap-tap-tappity that did not sound very musical. Angry, frustrated, rage-filled, sure. But not like the backbeat of any song he ever wanted to hear.

Bethy was asleep. Tommy cracked her door and peered in at her. There were dried tears on her cheeks and fresh bruise on the side of her mouth. Dad must have come home in a mood.

"Fuck my life," he said softly and closed her door.

He took the bat up to the attic and hung her on a hook he screwed into a ceiling joist. When he fished out the care instructions, a tiny key fell out. He hadn't noticed it earlier.

Tommy held it and considered. There were windows at both ends of the attic, and he went and opened them. He could smell cow manure on the breeze that came from the direction of the farms. A few little late-season flies came in and buzzed around the attic droplight.

"You don't want to be in a cage, do you, Vampy?"

The bat just looked at him.

"Bet you're hungry."

Those eyes seemed so big and moist and full of meaning.

Downstairs Dad started yelling. He did that. He'd get mad at something, take it out on whoever was in smacking range, grab a bunch of beers, watch some sports, brood, and then get mad all over again. When he got loud like this, he began looking for someone to blame, to vent on.

Tommy didn't want it to be him. Not again. He didn't want it to be Kip or Bethy, either. Or Mom. Or Aunt Lu.

The bat fluttered as if uncomfortable in her cage.

Tommy looked at her for a very long time. In the darkness of the attic, he played back the entire night. Mr. Attercop's lecture was there in his thoughts. Every single word.

One part of that lecture echoed in Tommy's head.

A vampire is an illusionist. They do not actually become bats or wolves or anything else. Just as mermaids used illusions—glamours, to use the proper term—to take on the appearance of an alluring beauty, vampires take on the aspect of whichever animal suits their needs. Actually, nothing in folklore suggests there was any limit to the things they could become.

At least an hour passed before he thought he understood what Attercop meant. Really meant.

It scared him. Of course it did.

It made him sad.

Of course it did that, too.

He looked at the bat.

His heart fluttered in his chest.

He opened his hand and looked at the little key. He could hear Mr. Attercop speaking in his head.

"*Vampires cannot enter a home unless invited,*" he'd said. Or words to that effect. And then advising everyone to bring their new pets home. Was that enough of an invitation? Tommy chewed his lower lip.

"Just tell me that it'll be okay," he said. "Promise me it won't hurt."

The bat blinked its watery eyes. That seemed like an answer.

Tommy slid the key into the lock, paused to take a deep breath, held it for as long as he could, then turned his wrist. The tiny lock clicked and the door swung open.

The bat dropped to the bottom of the cage and then crawled up the side to the open door. It perched there for a while, looking at him.

"Bethy, Kip, and Aunt Lu have been hurt a lot," said Tommy. "Mom, too, I guess. I mean, who likes being hit? Who likes being someone that someone else wants to hit? And knows he can and get away with it? Who wants to be in that kind of life?"

The bat was watching so carefully.

"So," said Tommy, "I think I get it. You and the handbills and that show. I get it. Maybe it's mean, but there's all kind of levels of mean." He gestured to the rest of the house beneath the attic floor. "All kinds of mean everywhere you look."

He thought he said, 'everywhere you look,' but his mind played it back. What he actually said was 'everywhere *I* look.'

Which is when he knew that he was right. About everything. About the town. About the bats. All of it.

He looked at the bat.

"Can you make it stop?"

The bat's head bobbed. Was that a nod or just a twitch? He didn't know.

"Dad's in the living room," said Tommy. "Aunt Lu, too. Everybody else is in their rooms."

He felt something on his face and wiped it away. His fingers glistened with tears. "I'll

just wait here."

The bat studied him for a long, long time.

Then it flapped its wings and flew past him. Tommy didn't turn to watch. But he heard something land heavily on the top step of the ladder. And slow, separate, definite steps as something—someone—climbed down into the house.

Tommy sat there in the dark.

And waited.

❧ ❧ ❧

Jonathan Maberry is a NYTimes bestselling author, 5-time Bram Stoker Award-winner, 4-time Scribe Award winner, Inkpot Award winner, and comic book writer. His science-fiction vampire apocalypse books, *V-Wars* was a Netflix original series starring Ian Somerhalder (*Lost, Vampire Diaries*). His *Joe Ledger* thrillers are in development for TV by Chad Stahelski, director of the *John Wick* movies; and his YA zombie series, *Rot & Ruin* is being developed for film by Alcon Entertainment. Jonathan writes in multiple genres, including horror, sci-fi, epic fantasy, mystery, and thriller. He is best known for his *Joe Ledger* weird science thrillers; the *Rot & Ruin* series of post-apocalyptic adventures; the *NecroTek* series of deep space cosmic horror, and *Mars One*, a science fiction novel about the first families settling on Mars. His other works include *Bewilderness* (an Audible original serialized portal sci-fi/horror), the *Pine Deep* novels (supernatural horror), the NY Times bestselling novelization of *The Wolfman; Kagen The Damned* (dark epic fantasy), and others. He has edited more than two dozen SpecFic anthologies including three *X-Files* books, *Aliens: Bug Hunt, Alien vs Predator: Ultimate Prey, Don't Turn out the Lights* (the official tribute to *Scary Stories to Tell in the Dark*), and others. His comic book work includes *Black Panther: DoomWar, Captain America, Punisher, Wolverine, The Avengers,*

Bats! Bats! Bats! (Fun for the Whole Family)

Marvel Zombies Return, Pandemica, Bad Blood, Godzilla vs Cthulhu, and many others. He has also written in the licensed worlds including *Hellboy, John Carter of Mars, The Wizard of Oz, Winnie the Pooh, Sherlock Holmes, C.H.U.D., True Blood, World of Warcraft, Diablo IV, Planet of the Apes,* and others. He is the editor of Weird Tales Magazine and the president of the International Association of Media Tie-in Writers.

Black Thumb

Larry Hinkle

My wife has a green thumb. Seriously, whatever she plants, grows. And it doesn't just grow—it *grows*. Once she took a piece of lettuce off my burger, rolled it around in her hands, then stuck it in the dirt. The next day, there's a new lettuce plant growing in the garden.

Me, on the other hand, well, I got the opposite of a green thumb, whatever that is. A black thumb, maybe? Yeah, that sounds about right. Any plant I touch dies. Hell, I swear sometimes all I have to do is just look at a plant to kill it. That hamburger lettuce she grew? Don't know if it's because it had cow blood on it or what, but it never tasted right to me. Too bitter, and the texture was more like raw meat. Mia insisted it was fine, although I never saw her eat any of it after that first bite. She couldn't bring herself to pull it up, though, so I touched it when she wasn't looking. It was dead the next day. Told her our dog Sunnie must have peed on it.

That could've happened, too. Sunnie had cancer at the time. We tried every treatment the vet recommended, and a lot of things she didn't. So for a while there, Sunnie's pee was pretty toxic. I was just glad she could still make it outside on her own most times. She beat the cancer, but nobody beats Father Time, and she died two days ago, peacefully, in her sleep.

She was fifteen, so it wasn't unexpected, but it still hurt like hell. Mia's the one who found her. I came home from work, and she was sitting in the corner of the living room, cradling our baby girl in her lap. She said it had just happened, but judging how red and puffy her eyes were, I worried she may have been sitting like that for hours.

I thought back to the day Mia had brought Sunnie home. Said she'd seen her wandering the Piggly Wiggly parking lot, chasing crows away from some French fries someone had dropped. She'd thrown a pack of Gaines-Burgers in her cart —*the canned dog food... without the can*, like they say in the ads. Thought she'd break up a few of them for the dog so it'd have a proper meal for once. But when she got outside, the poor thing was gone. She was too embarrassed to go back inside to return them, so she joked later that she was gonna try to mix them in with my sloppy joes sometime. Anyway, you can imagine her surprise when she opened the Pinto's hatch to put the groceries away and heard this frantic *click-click-click* running toward her. She turned in time to see Sunnie jump into the back of the car, climb over the second row, and plop down in the seat. One look at Sunnie's bright blue eyes and Mia was in love. Sunnie was part Australian Sheperd, and part something a lot bigger. And while I know Aussies are a smart breed, there was an intelligence in Sunnie's eyes that made me suspect she'd planned the entire thing.

From that day on, Mia and Sunnie were inseparable. They were quite a sight together, too. Mia might have weighed a teeny bit more, but when Sunnie stood on her hind legs, they were practically the same height.

I handed Mia a box of tissues, then sat down on the floor next to her. "I'm sorry, honey."

She nodded and wiped her eyes.

"What do you wanna do?" I asked.

We'd talked about burying Sunnie in the backyard, but I wanted to make sure she was still okay with it. Talking about it in the abstract's one thing, but now we were talking about it in the real. "I want to bury her out back," she said, "under her favorite tree." Sunnie just loves napping out there in the afternoon.

Sorry, loved.

Truth is, there wasn't a spot in the backyard that Sunnie *hadn't* loved napping in. Not long after we got her, Mia found her napping in the middle of the vegetable garden. That was the only time I'd ever seen Mia get mad at her. That garden was her pride and joy. You remember I told you about her green thumb? There wasn't anything that woman couldn't grow. We had every fruit and vegetable you could think of, including some you'd never expect to find in West Virginia. We had so much we were always giving it away to friends, family, coworkers, the local food bank. Town paper even came out and did a story on Mia one year. Slow news week in a small town, I guess.

I told her to go sit under the tree and I'd get everything ready. I grabbed the shovel out of the garage, then put Sunnie's favorite blanket on the ground next to Mia. Finally, I went back inside for Sunnie. I put her body down so that her head rested in Mia's lap. She just stroked her fur and sang the Sunnie song while I dug.

You are my Sunnie, my only Sunnie,
You make me happy when skies are grey.
You'll never know, dear, how much I love you,
Please don't take my Sunnie away.

I tried to keep it together, for Mia's sake, but I didn't do a very good job. At one point, after wiping tears and snot from my face, my hands slipped on the handle, opening a gash across my palm. I had to stop for a minute while Mia tore a small strip off Sunnie's blanket and wrapped my hand with it. We held each other for a few moments, and then I resumed digging.

I dug deeper than I probably needed to, but I didn't want to have to dig twice. Like I said, Sunnie wasn't a small dog. She weighed a touch over eighty pounds her last trip to the vet. And that was *after* she'd beat the cancer. Plus, I didn't want any of the local wildlife digging her up.

When it was done, I wrapped Sunnie in her blanket and laid her down at the bottom of the grave. I asked Mia if she wanted to say anything. She didn't, but asked if she could help me fill it in. I thought it might help with closure, so I handed her the shovel. She threw a few shovelfuls in, then gave it back to me.

After I finished filling in the hole, Mia knelt down and gently worked the earth, crumbling the bigger clumps like she would when tending her garden. I knelt beside her and helped smooth out the loose dirt, which was damp from our tears. She held my hand for a moment and squeezed. I flinched and pulled away, but not before a few drops of blood fell into the dirt.

I tamped the earth to discourage the critters from digging, then told Mia I was going inside to clean my cut and take a shower. Don't know if she heard me or not. Hell, I don't know if she even knew I was there at that point. I cried in the shower until it ran out of hot water. When I came back downstairs, the sun had set. Mia was still sitting out under the tree.

I brought her back inside and made us some dinner. We shared our favorite Sunnie stories over a couple bottles of wine and went to bed.

Mia usually lets me sleep in on Saturdays, so I wasn't surprised to find her side of the bed empty when I finally woke up. As I brushed my teeth, I heard her talking to someone downstairs. It was one-sided, so I figured she must be on the phone with her mom, or maybe the vet.

When I walked into the kitchen, I almost slipped on some wet dirt in front of the sink. It wasn't just there, though. There was mud and grass all over the linoleum. It looked like someone had tracked it in from out back.

There were paw prints in the dirt.

I followed them to the family room. Mia was on the floor, Sunnie in her lap, tail thumping.

My heart jumped, then sank. *Had we buried Sunnie alive?*

Mia wiped the tears from her eyes and apologized for not waking me up. She'd just wanted to spend some alone time with Sunnie. That was okay, I told her. I loved Sunnie, but she was always more Mia's dog than mine. You know how dogs pick their person.

Sunnie was covered in dirt and grass and vines. There were still bits of fabric in her teeth from where she'd chewed her way out of her blanket. I felt horrible. How could we have been so wrong?

I brushed the dirt and grass from her fur and tried to pull the vines off. They wouldn't come loose. Must be tangled in there, I thought, so I started picking at one of them. That's when I realized the vine was poking into Sunnie's flesh. There was no blood, but all the vines were like that. Stuck deep inside her.

As I watched, something wriggled underneath her skin, near one of the vines. And that's when it hit me. The vines were actually coming *out* of Sunnie. Sour bile filled my mouth, and I backpedaled so fast I knocked over a chair.

Sunnie looked up at me. Something in her eyes wasn't right. The intelligent, caring soul I'd always seen there was gone. Her eyes were vacant now. Dead. Even the blue was a duller shade.

"Hey, hey, it's okay," Mia said, trying to reassure me. "It's still Sunnie. Come here, pet her, you'll see." She reached up and grabbed my hand, pulling me down next to her. I tentatively scratched Sunnie behind her ear, in the special spot she'd always liked. She leaned her head into my hand like she'd always done, letting me know she liked it and telling me to pet her more. I relaxed a little. Maybe it would be okay.

Then Sunnie licked me.

Her tongue was cold. *Ice* cold. And rough, almost like a cat's tongue. Except it *wasn't* like a cat's tongue, because there were things moving underneath the pink flesh that gave it that texture. I watched in horror as a thin line wriggled toward the tip of her tongue, saw it push outward to the point I thought it would burst through her skin, before it retreated back into her mouth.

I shoved Sunnie's head away and ran into the kitchen. I barely made it to the sink before I threw up last night's dinner. The watery vomit was dark red from the wine, making the sink look like a slaughterhouse trough.

I'll admit I freaked out a little. Probably yelled a bit more than I should have. But Mia couldn't understand why I was so upset. She was eerily calm, as if she'd expected this to happen. When I told her something was wrong with Sunnie, that this wasn't right, she wouldn't hear it. Said she couldn't believe I'd even care about something like that. Wasn't it enough that she was back with us?

Sunnie didn't like the arguing, and started to growl, a low, menacing noise from deep in her chest. I'd never heard her make a noise like that before. It wasn't natural. Sunnie was a big dog, but she was just the sweetest thing. I'd never seen her hurt anything. Squirrels could run right up to her in the backyard, and she'd just wag her tail and smile. But *this* thing in Mia's lap, while it may have looked like Sunnie, it wasn't *our* Sunnie.

Mia tried to calm her down, but something in that dog was wrong. She attacked Mia, biting down on her arm so hard I heard the bone snap. I tried to pull her off, but Sunnie was strong. Much too strong.

I ran into the kitchen and grabbed a cast-iron skillet from the dish rack. When I got back in the family room, Sunnie was tearing into Mia's throat, sending ribbons of blood and drool flying as she shook Mia like a rag doll. I screamed and swung the skillet as hard as I could, smashing Sunnie on the side of the head. She went down and slid a few feet across the hardwood floor, but was back up before I could help Mia.

I swung at her again, but missed. My momentum spun me around, and Sunnie latched onto my forearm before I could swing the pan again. I punched her in the head with my free hand, but she wouldn't let go.

I rammed her body against the wall as hard as I could, but it only made her teeth dig in deeper. The impact knocked the pan from my hand. Blood was spraying from my arm now, and I slipped and fell on my ass.

Sunnie still wouldn't let go of me. My free hand slid through the blood pooling on the floor, reaching for something, *anything* to hit her with. I managed to grab the pan and swung wildly at her head. This time I connected, and I felt her bite loosen.

I hit her again with the pan.

And again.

And again.

Finally, she went limp.

I crawled into the kitchen and wrapped a dish towel around my arm, which immediately soaked through with blood. I grabbed three more from the drawer and pressed them to the wound, then wrapped plastic wrap around the towels as tightly as I could. It hurt like hell, and I thought I was going to pass out, but finally the bleeding slowed down.

I stumbled back into the family room.

Mia was gone.

But there was a trail of blood smeared across the floor.

So much blood.

I followed it to the patio door, then out into the backyard. Somehow, Mia had crawled out to the tree, where she'd tumbled into Sunnie's grave. When I got there, she was on her knees, one hand pressed up against the ragged tear in her throat while she desperately tried to cover herself in dirt with the other.

I reached down and tried to pull her out of the grave with my one good hand. She pushed me away.

"I have to stop the bleeding!" I cried.

"NO! It's too late for that!" She kept pulling more dirt into the grave.

I reached back down to grab her, but her arm was too slick from the blood, and I lost my grip.

"You have to let me bury myself." Her breathing had grown erratic. She gurgled her words and smiled at me, her teeth red with blood. "It's the only way," she pleaded, pulling another handful of dirt onto herself. The flow of blood from her neck had slowed. So had her movements. She managed to pull one more fistful of dirt into the hole, and then her body went limp.

I jumped down into the hole and threw her arm over my shoulder to lift her out. She twitched once, twice, and then went still.

Mia was gone.

I collapsed, Mia's lifeless body draped over me. I don't know how long I sat there in the grave with her, wishing it were me who'd died, but I knew what I had to do.

The grave wasn't long enough for Mia to lie flat across

the bottom, and it was too short for her to sit against the side without her head sticking up. I tried bending her forward, but she wouldn't stay down. Her body would flop to one side, and a shoulder would poke up out of the grave. Worse, every time I pushed her, thick dark blood oozed out of her mangled throat.

I couldn't bring myself to smash her down. Couldn't take a chance on breaking something. So I ended up lying her on her back and bending her knees up, like she was doing sit-ups. I wanted to curl up in there with her and die, but I knew I didn't have much time, so I folded her arms across her chest and climbed out of the grave.

The arm Sunnie had mangled hung useless at my side. She must have cut a muscle, because I couldn't move my fingers. With my good arm, I used the blade of the shovel to push as much dirt into the hole as I could. When I couldn't hold the shovel any longer, I dropped to my knees and scooped the dirt until I'd completely covered Mia's body.

I made sure to leave it plenty loose for her, though.

Then I sat down against the tree. And waited.

That was yesterday afternoon. It's morning now.

I've had time to think about what happened. *How* it happened, with the two of us burying Sunnie together. All I know is it had to have been Mia's green thumb that brought Sunnie back, and my black thumb that brought her back *wrong*.

I can only pray that Mia pulled enough dirt onto herself before she died.

Before I buried her the rest of the way.

We'll find out soon enough. Because about five minutes ago, the dirt started moving.

As I watched, a small shoot tentatively poked its way out of the ground. Its leaf unfurled and turned toward the sun, soaking in the morning rays.

The fingers of Mia's left hand just pushed their way out of the grave. Her nails are filthy, the undersides packed with dirt. Her wedding ring is gone. It must have come off as she dug herself free.

Now her right hand is out. A thin tendril extends from the tip of her middle finger and twists around, as if it's sniffing the air.

Her head pushes up next. Pale white vines snake through her hair, like a greenhouse Medusa.

She opens her eyes.

They're Mia's eyes, but they're not.

She sees me, smiles, and licks the dirt from her blood-stained lips.

They're Mia's lips, but God help me, it's not Mia who's smiling at me.

❦ ❦ ❦

Larry Hinkle is still the least famous author you've never heard of. A copywriter living with his wife and two doggos in Rockville, Maryland, when he's not writing stories that scare people into peeing their pants, he writes ads that scare people into buying adult diapers, so they're not caught peeing their pants.

His cosmic horror novella, The Eris Ridge Trail, was released to great reviews in March 2025, while his debut collection, The Space Between, was published in February 2024. His stories have also appeared in The Rack: Stories Inspired by Vintage Horror Paperbacks; October Screams: A Halloween Anthology; and multiple times on The NoSleep Podcast, among others.

He's an active member of the HWA (his short stories made

the preliminary Stoker ballot in 2020 and 2022); a graduate of Fright Club and Crystal Lake's Author's Journey short story and novella programs; an HWA mentee; and a survivor of the Borderlands Writers Bootcamp.

Stop by and visit him at thatscarylarry.com or stalk him on the socials at @thatscarylarry.

Midnight Rider

Mike Deady

Very late on Halloween night, Andy and Madison waited in line for the last Ferris Wheel ride of the season at Adventure Lake Park.

"I can't believe you were able to get tickets for the Midnight Ride," Madison said.

"It wasn't easy," Andy replied. "After this ride the park closes until spring, so everybody wants to be on it. But the *really* hard part was convincing my dad to let me borrow the car."

The line started moving.

"Hey, it's not midnight yet," Madison said.

"Legally, the park has to shut down at midnight. They get everybody seated earlier than that and start the ride. At exactly midnight the ride stops, and then they unload everybody. They've been doing this for years, and they have it all timed out perfectly."

The passengers ahead of them were seated. Andy and Madison shuffled to the front of the line. The ride attendant waved them onto an orange gondola car at the bottom platform.

"Good, we don't have to climb any steps," Madison said. "Hey, it's number thirteen! Cool."

She stepped into the car, hesitated, chose the right side, and slid across the plastic bench seat. Andy followed. They were pressed together, not unpleasantly.

The attendant gave a signal to the operator. The Ferris Wheel rotated ninety degrees and stopped. The last batch of passengers boarded below. And at last, the Midnight Ride began.

As the Wheel crested its first revolution, Andy said, "Look! We can see my father's car from up here."

"Damn it! We should have sat on the other side, facing the lake instead of the parking lot." Madison craned her neck around, trying to see the lake, but they had already descended too far.

Andy stood up. "We can always move to the other side."

"No! You're not supposed to do that!" She grabbed him and pulled him back down onto the seat, pressing against him even closer than before.

"Are you cold?" Andy asked hopefully.

"Freezing!"

He put his arm around her. At the apex of each revolution, they both looked over their shoulders for a glimpse of the lake on the other side of the grounds. They could see the entire park laid out below them. All the other rides had shut down, and a steady stream of people was heading for the exits.

The Ferris Wheel started slowing down. *It must be midnight already*, Andy thought. He realized they were stopping at the very top of the Wheel and would remain there until the passengers at the bottom were unloaded. *It's now or never*, he thought, and leaned in to kiss Madison.

She screamed.

Andy jerked his head back. "What the hell, Maddie?"

She pointed a trembling finger. Andy turned and looked.

A woman was sitting on the other bench seat in their gondola car.

❦ ❦ ❦

"And then she just disappeared!" Madison was still shaking.

James Walker, the park administrator, looked over his desk at the two teenagers who had been brought to his office after the park closed. He was tired and in no mood for Halloween pranks.

"What do you mean, disappeared? Are you telling me this woman climbed out of a Ferris Wheel pod a hundred feet in the air? After somehow climbing into it?"

"No, she just disappeared!" Her voice rose. "I already told you! When the ride stopped at the top, she just appeared out of nowhere. Then as soon as the ride started back down again, she just…vanished!" She looked at Andy for confirmation. He nodded.

Walker took a deep breath and slowly let it out. He decided to play along for the moment. "Okay, calm down. What did this woman look like?"

Andy finally spoke. "She was pretty old, maybe in her forties. Salt-and-pepper hair. Black coat, black jeans, black sneakers, black fingernail polish. You know, all done up for Halloween. Pretty good-looking for her age."

Madison glared at him, her distress momentarily forgotten. "You sure noticed a lot about her in a short time."

Walker stood up, suddenly interested. "Do you remember anything else about her?"

"No," Andy said. "Just that she looked scared, confused, like a little kid who's lost."

Madison started sobbing uncontrollably.

Walker stepped around his desk and pulled Andy aside.

"You could see she was wearing black fingernail polish? Wasn't it dark up there?"

"The moon was pretty bright. I know what I saw."

A moan from Madison interrupted them.

"You'd better get her home," Walker said. "Is she always like this?"

"I don't know. This was our first date." Andy glanced over at the nearly hysterical girl. "Probably our last."

After taking down the teenagers' contact information, Walker let them leave. He turned to Darryl Groves, Chief of Security for the park, who had been standing in the corner listening since bringing the two teenagers to Walker's office.

"What do you think?" he asked Groves.

"What do you mean, what do I think? It's obviously bull-shit. A Halloween prank."

"That's what I thought at first. But when they described the woman they saw..."

"What are you talking about? There was no woman. Nobody climbed in or out of a Ferris Wheel pod that high. Even if it were possible, no one else saw her."

"Weren't you listening? The kids both said she didn't climb out."

Groves smirked. "So, she flew out? Yeah, that's more believable."

"No, she didn't fly either. She appeared and disappeared like the kids said."

"Oh, come on, James. You're not saying you believe they saw a ghost?"

"You just started working here this season. Even so, I'm surprised you haven't heard..."

"Heard what, for Christ's sake?"

"Last Halloween, a woman named Judy Kelleher died on the Midnight Ride. Just dropped dead. Sudden brain aneurysm. Nothing her husband Martin could do, poor bastard. They were stopped at the top of the Ferris Wheel when it happened. In the same car, number thirteen. The kids' description of the woman matches."

"Jesus, how did I not know about this? Pretty creepy… But maybe the kids knew all this and used it."

"I don't think so. Even if they found a picture of her online, they couldn't possibly have known how she was dressed that night, right down to the fingernail polish. Those kids saw something. They were genuinely freaked out."

"Yeah, but think about it, James. If the Kelleher woman's spirit was haunting the Ferris Wheel, why were there no sightings all season until tonight?"

"I have an idea about that. Perhaps those old beliefs about the barrier between the living and the dead being thinner on Halloween are true."

"But it was Halloween all day and there were no other sightings."

Walker frowned. "You're right." He snapped his fingers. "I've got it! Halloween stands for All Hallows' Eve. The day before All Hallows' Day, or All Saints' Day. *That's* when the veil is supposed to be thinner, not Halloween. And All Hallows' Day started at midnight. I'm sure that's it."

"Uh-huh. So, let me ask you this: it's well after midnight now, still All Hallows' Day, so why isn't this spirit still sitting in the Ferris Wheel?"

Walker pondered this for a moment, then threw up his hands. "I don't have all the answers. I realize it sounds crazy, but I still think the kids were telling the truth."

Frustrated, Groves made one last attempt to get through to Walker. "Every teenager in the world has a cell phone. They record and post everything! It's a reflex. If there was really something up there, they would have whipped out their phones and captured it."

"Not if they were too shocked and frightened to even think of it."

"You've got an answer for everything." Groves could not believe the normally no-nonsense Walker would fall for such a tale. "I still have my doubts. Regardless, what are we going to do about it?"

"Nothing. As far as I know, the only ones who know about tonight's incident are me, you, the ride operator, the ride attendant, and the two kids. Let's just keep the whole thing quiet. I don't want a bunch of ghost hunters or other idiots breaking into my park during the off season. And I sure as hell don't want this getting back to Martin Kelleher. He lives here in town, you know."

"That's the first sensible thing you've said all night. Can you be sure the operator and attendant will keep their mouths shut?"

Walker nodded. "Yes. They were the same ones running the ride last year when Mrs. Kelleher died, so I know we can trust them."

"What about the two kids?"

"I don't think they'll be a problem. If they say anything, who'll believe them? It'll just seem like a Halloween prank. Without cell phone evidence, it never happened. Plus, they live a few towns over, across the state line. I think we're okay."

"Then it's settled." Groves moved to the door. "I've got to make my rounds. Happy frigging Halloween."

❦ ❦ ❦

The world turned. The seasons changed. Another autumn rolled around.

On a Friday evening in early October, Martin Kelleher's phone rang.

"Hello?"

"This is James Walker. From Adventure Lake Park. I'm not sure if you remember me?"

"Of course. What can I do for you?"

"I'd like to talk to you about something, but not over the phone. Can we meet for a drink at the Ninety Nine?"

"You mean right now?" Marty hadn't eaten supper yet, but he figured he could grab something at the restaurant. "I suppose so. But what's this all about?"

"I'll tell you when I see you."

Marty put on his coat and walked the three blocks from his house to the Ninety Nine. He entered and looked around. Walker, a redhead with thinning hair and a goatee, was easily recognizable. He was seated at the bar with a glass of wine.

They shook hands.

"Thanks for coming, Mr. Kelleher."

"Marty." He ordered a tall draft beer. "Now what's this all about?"

After a lengthy pause, Walker spoke. He related the events of the previous Halloween, leaving nothing out except the teenagers' names.

Marty noticed he had finished his beer while listening to Walker's incredible tale, and he ordered another. Prior to Judy's death, he would have dismissed a story like Walker's out of hand. Now he was surprised by his own desperate willingness to accept it.

"You honestly believe this?"

"Yes, I do, Mr. Kelleher. Marty."

"Why are you telling me this now? You said you had decided to keep it hushed up, especially from me."

"Things have changed. My wife is not in the best of health. I've taken early retirement and left the park. We're moving to Florida. I felt you deserved to hear the truth before I go. Straight from the horse's mouth, so to speak."

They shook hands again and Walker left.

Marty sat at the bar, trying to process what he had just heard. The next thing he was aware of was the bartender shouting last call. Stunned, he looked at his phone. He had been drinking beer all night on autopilot.

After walking home, Marty sat on the sofa and thought some more about Walker's story. Could it really be true? Could Judy's spirit be on that Ferris Wheel? Could he see her again, if only for a few moments? He tried to suppress his excitement and to use his analytical skills, dulled by the several mugs of beer he had consumed.

Judy had died in his arms two Halloweens ago at the top of the Ferris Wheel at midnight. The following Halloween, last year, the two kids had seen her spirit at the top of the Ferris Wheel at midnight, in the same gondola car. She had not been seen in any other car. It would seem her spirit was linked to that car, her place of death.

Marty believed Walker's theory that the barrier between the living and the dead was thinnest on All Saints' Day, which started at midnight on Halloween. But he was as puzzled as Walker as to why Judy's spirit was not seen the rest of All Saints' Day, when park employees were still onsite securing the facility for the season. There had to be a reasonable explanation, but it was late, and he was too tired and buzzed to think straight.

Marty turned to a framed photo of Judy on the end table next to the sofa. "Good night, Judy," he said to her, as he did every night. "I miss you so much." He got up and went to bed.

❧ ❧ ❧

Marty woke early with a pounding head and half-remembered alcohol-fueled dreams about skyscrapers and low-flying aircraft. He had forgotten to eat last night after hearing Walker's story, and his stomach was upset. He sat on the sofa with a mug of strong coffee, going over the whole thing again, trying to figure out what he was missing. It was just out of reach. After a while, the previous night's alcohol and lack of sleep caught up with him and he dozed, thoughts swirling around and around like a… *Ferris Wheel turning... propeller spinning... gondola car... airplane... skyscraper...*

Marty jolted awake. *That's it!*

He got off the sofa and started pacing. He had remembered an old John Christopher short story he had read years ago in some anthology. The plot, as best as he could remember, concerned a man who died violently in a biplane during World War I. His wife was so convinced that his vengeful spirit was trapped at the same altitude he had died that she never traveled in an airplane again. Fifty years later, she moved into the penthouse of a brand-new high-rise building, which was high enough for the husband to get her.

Marty thought he had the last piece of the puzzle.

Judy's spirit was trapped at the elevation she had died, the very top of the Ferris Wheel. That was why she disappeared when the car started descending.

Unlike the short story, her spirit was also linked to the specific place she had died. That was why she was never seen in any other car, even when stopped at the top.

Also, unlike the short story, her spirit could only be seen on All Hallows' Day. Because she had died then? Or could anyone's spirit be seen then under the right circumstances? Marty didn't know.

He tried to imagine what such an existence would be like. Appearing for a brief midnight moment at the top of the Ferris Wheel once a year, different people appearing across from her each time, pointing at her and screaming. The years flashing by like a strobe. The loneliness and confusion.

He believed he now had the answer to why Judy's spirit

wasn't seen the rest of All Hallows' Day. It was simply because after the Midnight Ride, there were no more rides, and the Wheel was parked with Judy's car somewhere other than at the top. He suspected that if the Wheel had been rotated any time on All Hallows' Day to get her car on top, she would have been there. Was it possible to arrange for that to happen this year? God, to be able to see her, be with her, for a whole day instead of just a few minutes!

Excited, he wondered if Walker would do this for him. He picked up his phone, but then he remembered Walker was no longer in charge of the park. He slammed it down in frustration. He briefly considered calling the new administrators, but he feared they would call the cookie truck to take him away in a straitjacket, and he could not blame them. It looked like his reunion with Judy would be limited to a short time at midnight. Still, it was better than nothing.

It was *everything*.

He needed to start planning. First thing, he would have to obtain a ticket for the Midnight Ride. No, *two* tickets, to ensure he was alone in the gondola car. Tickets were highly sought-after and hard to get, but Marty had managed to get them two years ago. No matter what it took, he would procure them this year too. If he had to, he would spend every penny he had for one more second with Judy. Next, he wanted to visit the park just to determine exactly how much time he would have with her.

Marty turned to the photo of Judy on the end table. "I'm going to be there next time you appear, Judy. God, I can't wait to see you again."

❦ ❦ ❦

The following weekend, Marty drove across town. He took the turnoff located just after the huge sign:

ADVENTURE LAKE PARK
NEW ENGLAND'S FUNNEST AMUSEMENT PARK

Marty had always wondered if funnest was even a word. He supposed if they called it the biggest or the best they could be sued. It was no Six Flags, but it was a good-sized park built on one side of the lake.

Even though it was still more than two weeks until Halloween, the parking lot was packed. He parked and made the long walk to the park entrance, the Ferris Wheel looming over the fence on his left. He passed under a garish sign:

SKAREFEST AND OKTOBERFEST
OCTOBER 1 THROUGH OCTOBER 31

He paid his admission, went through a security check-point, and entered the park. He had not been back since Judy's death, and he stopped for a moment and took a deep breath. He turned left, toward the Ferris Wheel. He found an empty park bench and sat down.

Marty studied the Ferris Wheel. There were twenty numbered gondola cars. Cars one through five were painted green, six through ten gold, eleven through fifteen orange, and sixteen through twenty silver. The four color groups represented the four seasons. He and Judy had ridden on the middle car in the orange group, number thirteen, the same one the kids had ridden last year.

Marty swallowed and forced himself to look at that car. The place where his wife had died. A place that held so much pain and sorrow for him. But now a place that represented hope, too.

Marty watched carefully as each ride was loaded and unloaded. The Ferris Wheel was stopped for each color group, always starting with the green cars, for at least two minutes while the previous ride's passengers disembarked, and a new batch was herded on. Once that color group was loaded, the Wheel rotated ninety degrees and stopped for the next, until all four groups were loaded. The middle car in each group was always the bottom car. Once the silver group was loaded, the ride started and always lasted four-and-a-quarter revolutions, at which point the unloading and loading process repeated.

Marty watched for a long time. Each ride was exactly the same. When the four-and-a-quarter revolutions were completed, the middle orange car was always stopped at the very top of the Ferris Wheel just like it had been on that terrible night almost two years ago. And it was always stopped for at least two full minutes.

Marty got up and spent the rest of the afternoon wandering around the park. He grabbed a slice of pizza from one of the park's many food stalls and sat on a bench near the lake. He longingly eyed the beer tent, but he never drank when he had to drive. He pulled out a worn paperback, Ray Bradbury's *Something Wicked This Way Comes.*

He read until it started getting dark. He returned to the Ferris Wheel and sat on the same bench as earlier. The multi-colored lights along the spokes of the Wheel were now turned on. Judy had always said they made it look like a giant glittering spider web. Marty smiled at the memory and resumed studying the Wheel, just in case there were any changes to its operation after dark. He watched and timed several rides and saw no differences from earlier. Satisfied, he rose and left the park.

* * *

Marty woke up on Halloween morning and looked at the clock. Plenty of time.

Out of nowhere, he felt a vague uneasiness. Was he having doubts now that the day was here? Was it all just delusional wishful thinking? Would she really be there?

He showered, shaved, dressed, and got ready to leave. He doublechecked that he had not forgotten anything, that he had his precious tickets for the Midnight Ride safely tucked away. He tenderly touched the photo of Judy on the end table and walked out the door.

He got into his car and started it up. When the radio came on, Marty immediately recognized the opening lines of "Somewhere Between Heaven and Earth" by Cidny Bullens.

Marty knew the song well. He had played the album on which it appeared over and over in the months following Judy's death. The song—really, the entire album—was a mother's elegy to a lost daughter, but it could apply to any lost loved one. The album's mood of overwhelming grief and loss had resonated with Marty.

He had never heard it played on the radio before. It had to be a sign. The song ended on a wishful note of being reunited, and Marty's anxiety evaporated. He pulled out of his driveway.

He arrived at the park as soon as it opened. He was deter-mined to recreate the last time he had been there with Judy two years ago as best as he could.

He took the lake cruise. The boat passed by houses on the other side of the lake that he and Judy had always wished they could afford. Now he was glad they had never bought one. To be able to see the place where Judy had died every time he looked out a window would have been unbearable.

After the cruise, he ate at the Oktoberfest-themed restau-rant. For dessert, he got an ice cream and strolled over to the bandstand. Marty was pleased to see the same Alice Cooper tribute band that had performed two years ago. As the Alice Cooper lookalike was led offstage in a straitjacket, Marty wondered again if he should be in one himself for what he was doing.

When it got dark, he watched the fireworks show over the lake. Marty remembered the joy on Judy's face as she had watched the colors exploding. She had never lost her sense of child-like wonder for fireworks, for parades, for Halloween, for amusement park rides. Especially the roller coaster. She would laugh ecstatically, while he held on to the bar with white knuckles, eyes closed, counting the seconds until the ride ended.

The feeling of unease flared up again. Marty turned away from the fireworks display and found the beer tent. He quickly downed two mugs of German pilsner, wishing something stronger were sold. But the beer calmed him and loosened the tightness in his chest.

The fireworks ended, and the crowd started dispersing. It was almost time for the Midnight Ride.

Marty hurried across the midway, through the thinning crowd and the costumed park employees. He arrived at the Ferris Wheel slightly out of breath. *Don't have a heart attack now*, he warned himself. He showed his tickets, got in line, and waited.

Finally, the penultimate ride slowed and stopped. The green group riders got off and were replaced by the first batch of Midnight Ride passengers. The Wheel rotated ninety degrees and the process repeated for the gold group.

The Wheel rotated again and stopped for the orange group. Marty waited impatiently for the previous passengers to disembark. He dashed onto the bottom car, ignoring the ride attendant's signal to go up the steps to a different car. The attendant rolled his eyes but did not stop him. He remembered that he and Judy had sat on the left side so they could see the lake, so he slid into the right side. When the other four cars were filled, the Wheel rotated one last time to unload and re-load the silver group. And then, a few minutes before midnight, the ride started.

Each revolution was an agony of anticipation. Would she really be there at the end? What seemed like a lifetime later, the Ferris Wheel finished its fourth revolution. His car slowed to a stop at the very top. His phone alarm beeped. It was exactly midnight.

And there she was.

"Judy…" The grief that had weighed him down since her death suddenly lifted. She was really here!

Judy looked across the gondola car at Marty. Her face lit up with recognition and relief. She reached for him.

Unsure if touching each other might destroy the fragile link between their worlds, he moved back out of her reach. He saw the hurt and confusion in her eyes.

"Don't worry," he said. "In less than two minutes, we'll be together forever."

After Marty returned from his visit to the park earlier in the month, he realized that seeing Judy for a mere two minutes would not be enough. He would be in agony until the next year rolled around. And what if something happened during the year? The park could replace the gondola cars with new ones. It could go out of business. He could simply be unable to get tickets. No, he could not take the chance of being separated from Judy forever.

He spent days online researching the best way to kill himself in less than two minutes. Preferably less than a minute, a minute-and-a-half at worst, just to provide a safety margin.

A bullet to the right spot in the head would do the trick, destroying the brain instantly. But Marty did not own a gun. He could probably acquire one, but he worried he would not be able to get it through park security.

Marty turned to fast-acting poisons and drugs.

The obvious choice was cyanide. He had seen dozens of movies where the captured spy would bite down on a cyanide capsule, dying almost instantly. However, in real life, cyanide could take several long, agonizing minutes to work. Marty was not concerned about the pain, just the time.

He moved on. Potassium Chloride, the lethal injection drug. Propofol, the drug that had killed Michael Jackson. Arsenic. Strychnine.

Same thing. They could all take much too long to work.

He found fentanyl. It looked promising. He read several articles about how dangerous it was, how many people had overdosed accidentally. But again, it was not dependably fast enough.

Frustrated, he followed a link to another article.

And there it was.

A drug used to sedate elephants and other large animals. Extremely small doses were fatal to humans. Injecting, swallowing, inhaling, even getting it in the eyes could stop the heart and lungs in seconds, or worst case usually within a minute or so. This was the one. It was called carfentanil.

After the long, frustrating search for the right drug, Marty was concerned that he would have an even harder time obtaining it. He needn't have worried. It turned out to be laughably easy and relatively inexpensive. He would have been appalled had he not been so elated. Once he obtained it, he filled a plastic baggie with enough of the powder to kill himself several times over.

🍂 🍂 🍂

He held up that bag and showed it to Judy. He had handled it with extreme care up to this point. He had even labeled it so as not to endanger whoever found his body at the end of the ride.

"Trust me," he said. "It's the only way. I have to die here and now at the same elevation as you did, or we risk being separated forever."

Judy looked from the bag to Marty. Her expression changed from confusion to comprehension. Then she smiled, a smile full of love for him and belief in him.

He smiled back. "I love you, Judy. Here I come."

Marty put the bag up to his face. He let the powder fall into his eyes, his mouth, his nose. He inhaled as much of the powder as he could deeply into his lungs.

The Ferris Wheel lurched and slowly started descending.

Judy disappeared.

No, Marty tried to scream, *it's too soon!* But already he had no breath left. His heart seized. He could not move.

A clarity came over him in his dying moment. He suddenly understood what had gone wrong, and what had been nagging at him all day: this being the final ride of the night, the passengers would be getting off, but no new ones getting on.

Taking far less time than two minutes.

He was going to die with the Midnight Ride in motion, mere feet below the elevation Judy had died. But it might as well have been a million miles. He would be separated from her forever. And she from him.

All because of his own catastrophic blunder.

The shock would have been enough to stop his heart, had it still been beating.

❦ ❦ ❦

Mike Deady

Mike Deady's work has appeared in More Than a Monster, Wicked Sick, That Is So Wrong, and Totally Tubular Terrors. He is a member of the Horror Writers Association, the New England Horror Writers, and the Boston Horror Society. He is a lifelong resident of Massachusetts. After retiring from a forty-two-year career in engineering, he started writing horror fiction at the urging of his brother, Bram Stoker Award-winning author Tom Deady.

The Light You Follow Can Burn

Jessica McHugh

HOPE WAS the red velvet bow that welcomed him home. Rage was the divorce contract it adorned.

Adam's wife had decorated the stack of papers like ending their twenty-four-year marriage was some sort of gift. The real gift would've been shredding the contract, for everything to go back to normal, he and Meg living in the house where they'd raised three beautiful children. Even if their kids didn't care for him very much, or respect him very much, or acknowledge his presence in the slightest. Being a family man was the best part of his life. He knew everyone in the neighborhood. He chaperoned field trips. He threw surprise birthday parties at roller rinks. It wasn't perfect—it was downright infuriating at times—but twenty-four years still wasn't enough.

Meg entered as if riding a bluster of wind, her jacket peeled open, her curls wild as onion grass.

"Adam? Oh, there you are. Sorry for the mess. I've been slacking on getting boxes out of here. Ramona's birthday really took it out of me." Setting two large paper bags on the table, she sighed, then embarked on the impossible task of

225

calming her hair. No matter how she petted and tucked, the renegade tendrils continued to vex her.

But oh, how they delighted him. She wasted so much time trying to fix something he always treasured, and she'd get so angry when he told her she looked beautiful when her curls had a mind of their own. She was fierce and untamed. Like Medusa. A Gorgon Queen.

He had the bad sense to say it aloud once, and boy, did she let him have it. He never took it back though. It was true, his wife was a powerful creature, unmatched in ferocity and flair, and still a mystery after all these years. But he did regret his stubbornness, because her resulting annoyance wasted even more time.

Time she'd promised him.

"The house looks fine. Where is Ramona anyway?"

"The mall."

"Of course. Where else?" He chuckled, but the red bow cut it short. It looked different. Was it getting bigger? Had she distracted him with her feral ringlets and replaced it with a more ostentatious ribbon?

A foamy gray "M" bubbled off his bottom lip, but he sucked it back before it fell. There was no point calling her out. What did the last word matter glancing off her back as she walked out the door?

She rifled through a box on the counter and cheered when she found a corkscrew. Holding it aloft like a sacred sword, she chirped, "Red or white?"

He pulled a bottle of red from one of the bags and tilted it toward her.

With her nose crinkled, she said, "Let's open a white too." Handing over the corkscrew, she turned to the cupboard. "Whoops, looks like I forgot to pack a few glasses."

"Those are mine."

She tilted the bottom of a cobalt glass at him, and he

sneered at the small masking tape label marked: "MEG." In fact, all except two of the remaining glasses were marked: "MEG." She'd been writing her name on their belongings for nearly a year, long before she told him she put the house on the market.

The night he noticed it happening, she was celebrating the sale of a new large-scale art piece by dancing around the house to Fleetwood Mac and spilling more champagne than she drank. When the record ended, Adam hopped up to flip it for her and caught her staring at the porcelain Nativity on the bookshelf.

She hated it. Adam did too, truth be told, but it was all his father left him in the will. Not money. Not his mother's wedding ring. Not even a photo album. A stark white nativity of unglazed porcelain was all he had to give. And it wasn't just for Christmas, his father explained. Jesus wasn't just for Christmas. Jesus was always with them. Especially with Meg, who her father-in-law knew wasn't a Christian.

Plucking the ivory savior from the manger, Meg slid a pen from her pocket, and Adam watched in confusion as she wrote on the bottom of the attached bassinet.

He didn't say anything—he'd just make it awkward and ruin her night—and not wanting to worsen her hangover the next day, he didn't ask her then either. The further the event disappeared into the past, the weirder it seemed to broach it. So, he didn't. Instead, he quietly overturned every object in the house.

Coasters: MEG. A snow globe from the Denver Airport: MEG. Salt and pepper shakers: MEG.

"What?" She looked at him over the rim of her wine glass.

"Nothing. I'm just—" He lifted the red wine waiting for him beside the contract. The same color as the bow. Tipping the glass to her, he said, "Thank you for coming. I didn't know if you'd hold up this part of the deal."

"You held up yours, I'm holding up mine."

The wine tasted bitter. "Maybe it's more accurate to say I didn't think you'd *have to* hold it up. I thought maybe...after all these years...we'd toss out the deal altogether."

She blinked coldly, then smiled with counterfeit warmth. "This is our last night, Adam. Do you want to spend our last night rehashing something we've been over a thousand times?"

"No. I want my wife back. My house. My family."

She finished her wine and sniffed his glass curiously. "May I?" She eased it from his hand and sipped. "Pretty good." Handing it back, she exhaled a sympathetic sigh. "Your family isn't going anywhere, sweetheart. Nothing is going to change all that much."

"You can't say that." He set down the glass too forcefully, and they both jumped. He didn't crack it—thank goodness, now that he knew it was hers—but he apologized anyway. "You can't say 'nothing will change,' and tack on 'all that much.' I don't want anything to change."

"I know. But that was the agreement."

"Why? I'm struggling to remember why."

"It's our last night, Adam."

"I know. I'm sorry." He rubbed his forehead. "I just don't understand why this is happening."

"You don't need to." She wrapped her arms around his neck. "Would you like to start with one of your rooms?"

A sob slipped out of him so unexpectedly, he had to withdraw from her embrace and turn his back before snot flooded down his chin. He sounded like a runt abandoned by its litter when he mewled, "Yes."

"Which one?"

"The den. The first Christmas." He wiped his face, downed his wine, and the red bow grew bigger in his periphery.

Pillars of boxes flanked Adam and Meg Faraday as they strolled through their dining room for the last time. They'd had the house built new in 1963, and as of their third and final child's eighteenth birthday in 1987, it was up for sale. Nearly every seat had been removed. The only tables were cheap collapsibles. Meg's art was the only remaining decor, but she'd taken the time to label that too. Her name shone pancreatic cancer pink on Post-Its stuck to homemade wreaths and braided bundles of flowers and herbs, behind macrame and within cyclonic wooden sculptures. It was especially cruel, because he would've liked to keep just one. She didn't need to label them. Or anything. He knew what was hers. All of it, even him, even if she resented it, he was hers to save or destroy, as much as it made him feel like a monster or a weakling, or like there was no light between, he loved her so goddamn much. When talk of the contract resumed on Ramona's seventeenth birthday, he never thought they'd be here, spending their last night in the house, with him still begging for scraps of her.

They added the den in '73, the construction of which entranced their young daughters. The uprooting, the noise. Mira, Bella, and Ramona stood on the precipice of new gulfs, where their screams disappeared within machinery din. Massive claws and shovels refashioned the earth around their home, unveiling a new world in their backyard. For Ramona, the youngest, it was real magic at work. Especially the building of the fireplace. From nothing, from an empty piece of slumped yard, a fire would begin, a fire would climb, a fire would devour. As would Christmas, in its way. But never so deliciously as the first one in the den, kindled by his little girl.

Flames crackled in the fireplace as Adam entered, and Meg stood from the hearth. How did she light it so quick?

Her rich brown curls bounced against her cheeks when

she turned. "Are you kidding? It took forever. Any clothes Santa got me are out of style now." She congratulated Ramona on lighting the logs and directed her to play with her sisters.

The girls tumbled jubilantly past, roaring as they explored the limits of the new den with jungle-gym theatricality, as only children could, enlivened by the scent of pine.

They were so big, even then. Even when they were toddlers, Adam felt like his daughters towered over him. With their baby dolls and stuffed bears and complex worlds within shoeboxes, they taught him one of the fundamental differences between young girls and boys. Boys played with guns and swords and detonated imaginary explosives to level entire cities because they thought dominance came from intimidation and destruction. But little girls didn't destroy things. Or rather, they didn't *only* destroy things. They *moved* them—to edges of cliffs, or the middle of highways. Little girls dominated quietly, with control. Then they watched in wonder, as the things they moved destroyed themselves.

Meg gathered the girls in front of the tree for a family photo. For a moment, he couldn't tell the difference between them. They all looked like Meg at her most adorably frazzled. Wendy Darling wrangling a cluster of Lost Boys who emulated her every move.

"Say cheese..."

Their teeth remained firmly clenched—their lips didn't even quiver—but they enunciated the word like it purred from a speaker box in their throats.

Meg took the picture and gave them leave to continue running around the room. Slipping her arm around her husband's waist, she leaned her head on his shoulder to gaze at the tree.

"It's so beautiful, Adam." She stroked his velvety cheek. "You're so beautiful."

Mira and Bella moaned, "Ewww…" in unison, while Ramona leapt onto the hearth and twirled in place. So much pride in one tiny body.

"Is that why you chose this Christmas?" Meg asked. "Her first fire?"

"Yes, but not only. There were lots of firsts that day. The first Christmas in the new den, Mira's first telescope, Bella's first time making cookies on her own."

Meg unwound herself from him. The memory had already started to drain from her, returning silver to the coils throughout her hair. "It was also the first death in our family."

"What? Who?"

Her head flopped to one side. "Oreo. My God, Adam, how could you forget?"

"Oreo? No. No, that wasn't--"

The fireplace roared behind Meg, and the entire room flared orange. Then came the smell. Not like the cookies or cinnamon rolls they baked that morning, or even the ham slow-roasting for an early supper.

"She was so old, so sick."

It was a meaty smell, but with a sour tang, even caustic, like a year's worth of antacid bubbling in a stomach too desiccated to absorb it.

"We told the girls she'd be cremated when she died. We explained it to them." Meg filled her glass with red wine that time and took a substantial gulp. "They thought she was dead. They thought they were helping."

A sticky squeal poured from the cat's mouth as the flames devoured its meager body, and the medicine they'd been pumping into her day after day foamed out of her yawning carcass.

"They even had a jar ready."

The girls watched the cremation like three rosy-cheeked

angels, their eyes alight with clemency as the last of the cat's air whistled loose. When Meg dismissed them, the fire died quickly, as if they'd taken all the oxygen from the room. She carefully scooped up some ashes, twisted the lid on the jar, and shoved it into Adam's trembling hands.

"What was your favorite present this year?" she asked as he raised tear-filled eyes to her.

Was it the power sander? No, that was the year before. And the camcorder was still five years off. What had he gotten besides a jar of cat ashes that year?

"I don't remember."

"Well, Bella's cookies were good anyway." She poked his chest. "Better than yours ever were. Baking was never your forte."

"I could learn."

"I'm sure you could."

"I could take a class. They have all kinds at the rec center."

"I hope you do." She transferred one of the wreaths from the wall to the tree.

"There was a reason I loved this day," he said, staring at the jar. "I just can't remember..."

She patted his arm. "Maybe one of my rooms will be better."

"Not unless we're dissolving this stupid contract in it."

She huffed. "You didn't think it was stupid twenty-four years ago."

"I was a kid twenty-four years ago."

She blinked. "And now?"

The jar became a wine glass she filled with scarlet slosh. He gulped his sorrow to prep his throat for the wine, but it still burned all the way down.

"You can skip all this, you know. I'd love to show you my latest art piece before you go, but...we don't have to go through any more rooms if you don't want."

He sipped the wine with both hands, like the girls used to drink grape juice after naps. Hungrily, messily. When it was empty, he thrust it at her just the same, silently requesting more. "No. This is my time. I was promised this time."

"And I'm happy to give it to you. I love you, Adam. So do the kids. We'll always love you. I want this to be as painless as possible for all of us."

"Then give me another turn. I forgot about Oreo. I need a better day."

The Christmas tree dimmed, and the yellowed light of the basement hallway bloomed overhead. It flickered a few times until Adam tapped it with his nail. When it was steady, he caught a whiff of something salty, like a coastal breeze wafting down the stairs behind him. A strange glisten cavorted on the steps, too, like sun on silverware, but Meg redirected his focus to Mira's bedroom door at the end of the hall.

It floated open as they approached, and Adam entered hoping for his eldest daughter's room bathed in a cheerful blush. Maybe in the 70s when she was a precocious preteen ballerina, or the early 80s when he volunteered to sit behind her at the movies so her massive hairdo wouldn't obstruct a stranger's view.

But the room was empty, save for the rosebud border crowning her walls. It was faded now, torn and sagging, but in a few places, the original color was as crisp as the first day. Crisper, even, and brighter. It glowed with unnatural light, and darkness clenched its fist on the rest of the room. Everything was insignificant compared to the border, the one she chose with him, hung with him, celebrated with him.

A shadow shifted to his right, but it couldn't have been Meg. She wasn't even in the room. Where was she? Still in the hall? It danced around him, lithe with subtle mockery. It could've been any of his daughters; they all moved like that.

Slower when they were little, which surprised him. But maybe they hadn't learned how to use their speed yet, their power and grace. It took practice for them to move around him as they did now, like he was barely there. He was an old pair of tap shoes. He was a letter from the *Who's Who of American High School Students* stuffed in a drawer. He was something to look back on fondly, but not something to carry forward into a new life. At that moment, he felt strangely akin to the border: past its welcome, old and embarrassing, something people tolerated until it was rolled up on a shelf like a dead worm.

"Bless you, Father..."

"Mira?"

He whirled around to see Meg in the doorway, brighter than the border.

"Who's Mira?" she asked, and his head bobbled in confusion.

"I...I don't know."

She pouted. "You're not cheating on me, are you?"

"Never. You're the only girl for me."

She grinned, a secret in her belly, a secret in her soul.

The rosebud border peeled with each step Meg took into the room. So did the paint, the plaster, and the carpets. The house unmade itself around them as they embraced, their bodies precariously balanced on the wooden beams of the unfinished floor. When their lips disconnected, she tossed back her hair and warbled, "Yes."

His brow crinkled. "Yes?"

"Yes, I'll marry you, silly."

The proposal. He'd nearly forgotten. Not the first, not even the third. He wasn't ready all those times, she said; he wasn't giving the contract the gravity it deserved. And maybe he still wasn't, but something about standing in their house's skeleton changed her answer.

He whooped in celebration and lifted her into the air. She cried out in excitement—and slight terror at the balancing act—clinging to him as he peppered her face with kisses.

"We could do this all over again," he said. "Get divorced. Get remarried. What do you say?"

Meg lifted her chin, her face as pink as Mira's rosebuds. Then it crumpled, and she shook her head, crushing a hopeful question into a life sentence. Devastated by her silence, he backed away, knocking over a stack of boxes that busted open like a dandelion releasing its seeds.

Family photos from summer vacations slid to the floor, though Adam was missing from most of them. He stood alone in front of monuments and welcome centers, his face shining between neckties and shoelaces that entwined the pictures.

"Hey, I've been looking for this." He pulled a blue tie from the box, and a handful of red yarn accented with wooden beads followed, knotted up in the silk.

"Why?" She pinched the label on which she'd written her name. "It's mine."

The beachy scent struck him again, and light flashed across corridor wall. "What *is* that?"

Meg giggled as she walked ahead, beckoning him to follow. But they didn't see the door to the kitchen when they reached the bottom of the basement steps. They weren't in the basement anymore. At the staircase leading to the second floor, Adam beheld the banister adorned in Meg's wreaths. Old ones and new ones, with satchels that smelled of lavender and sea salt hanging between, swinging ever so slightly as Meg started up the stairs.

"When did you put these up?"

Across the walls, braided stalks of seaweed and rosa rugosa grew with each step, covering the spaces where the family photos once hung.

"I wanted the house to look nice. Not all these boxes."

"I like the boxes. As long as they're here, they can still be unpacked." He gazed upon the living room, which spilled into the den. Or…it used to. But it stopped sharply now, as if they'd never had the addition. It ceased to be, and the ceasing was spreading. He pointed at it, the great black rot of his life. And his wife laughed in delight.

On the landing between the pair of staircases connecting the first and second floor, Meg stood with her back curved like the schooner's sail in the straw macrame on the wall. Her hand undulated, and the sails ballooned. The ship rocked so hard in the knotted sea, Adam felt the clashing waves in his bones, pulling and pushing him off balance. He grabbed the banister, dizzied by the sudden tilt, and reached for her hand. She pulled him from the stairs, but she wasn't there when he landed.

He was alone on the beach, as he often was as a child, but this time, the sea smelled like mercy. Salt air settled on his skin, filling the cracks between twisted flesh and giving the rough texture the appearance of a smooth white shell. As he admired the temporary reprieve from reality, the kids playing in the surf fled at his approach.

Of course they would. Why shouldn't a new, soft wave flee a jagged beach?

He just hoped the waves wouldn't shy from him when he needed them most.

"Please," he said, his toes licked by the warm surf. "Swallow me like an innocent. Blindly, impartially, uncondi-tionally, swallow me like a seed you never expect to bloom. To spill, maybe, but never bloom. God or fungus or nothing at all, however I break, whatever oozes out, let me be forgiven. For once in my life, please, let me be pure."

The waves deposited a heavy blanket of crystalline sand on his feet, and he closed his eyes, listening to the roar calling him home. It might've, quite quickly, if not for the sound of laughter from the bar on the edge of the boardwalk, where the rocky sand turned soft. He glanced over, immediately stung by a sharp glisten. Sun on silverware, probably, but it looked larger than that, more substantial. Like a star had fallen from the sky and needed a stiff drink after the journey. He wondered what stars liked to drink.

He'd only had one sip of alcohol his entire life. He hated it because of what it did to his dad, but the laughter and light coming from that bar didn't remind him of Dad. It was happy. And if not, it was a damn good fake. Maybe he could fake it too, for just one drink, to prove his father was the villain. Not the alcohol, not the fire, not even the war. Just him. It was his last day anyway. Why not prove Dad wrong on the way out?

He withdrew his feet from the hungry surf and faced the bar, where the airy laughter sounded like a dare. Not like one of Dad's though. This was new. Kind. Playful. Experimental. As complicated as walking in the sea with pockets full of stones.

Shedding the dead weight, he ambled toward the Lucky Seal, a teal and cream-colored shack adorned with oil paintings that didn't hold up well in the swelter and salt. But maybe that was part of their charm. They changed all the time, different for everyone, at every visit, like a memory itself, an inconstant portrait melting in the heat of the moment.

A man in a white shirt tossed a rag over his shoulder and leaned on the bar.

"Can I help you?"

He pulled his sleeves over his hands. "A drink. A beer."

"What kind?"

Something sparkled in his periphery. The star! What was the star drinking?

The woman at the other end of the bar absentmindedly fiddled with her silver cigarette case, flashing him with light every few seconds. She glanced over, and his skin bristled deliciously as curls fell across her face. She shook them off and swigged her bottle of Bud.

He said, "Budweiser, please," and the bartender popped open a bottle.

It sat for several minutes before Adam talked himself into wrapping his fingers around it, both vessels glistening with cold sweat.

He lifted it slowly, keenly aware of how the air in the room changed. He felt like everyone was staring at him but looking in the salt-stained mirror behind the bar, his disfigured face was the only one lifted from its beverage. No one was staring. No one cared enough to stare.

Why was that worse?

"Is it skunked?" The woman a few seats down tapped her empty bottle on the bar and batted her eyes.

"Oh. You're talking to me?"

She laughed. The same laugh he'd heard from the beach, like a windchime made of seashells.

"You're not drinking, so I asked if your beer was skunked."

"I don't know what that means."

She laughed again, and the bartender waved away the accusation. "The beer's fine."

"Then why doesn't he want to drink it?"

"Beats me."

"It wouldn't be the first time you sold a bad bottle."

Adam lifted his beer. "No, no, it's fine, really. See?" He tipped it back too far, and beer spilled down his chin, his neck, the dress shirt he intended to die in. He reeked of it. Reeked of Dad.

The woman was beside him before he could hide his face, but she didn't shy away when she dabbed it with a napkin.

"Sorry." She giggled. "I feel like that was my fault."

He took the napkin from her and turned away. "No, it was mine. Don't worry about it." With his face dried, he took another sip and made a yummy sound that made her chuckle as she twirled her cigarette case.

Despite his insecurity, he lifted his eyes, and noticing his focus, she clinked her bottle against his.

"What's your name?" she asked.

"Adam."

She sipped her beer and wiped a drop from her puckered lips. "The first man."

"Ha. Right. Certainly not the last," he said, and she giggled.

"I hope not. It's nice to meet you, Adam. Sorry to bother you."

"You didn't," he said, wrapping his fingers around the damp bottle. "You couldn't," slipped out louder than he wanted, and she cocked her head.

He was sure she heard the self-loathing in his voice, and now she pitied him. He should've cut his losses a minute back. Stopped talking, finished his drink, and left to finish what he came to do.

Silver flashed, and the cigarette case opened. He didn't see her remove a cigarette; it was just suddenly between her lips, and so was he.

He flinched when she struck a match and held his breath until she waved it out. People looked so ugly when they smoked, their lips pursed and puckered, like baby monkeys rejected by their mothers, desperate for the next best thing. The hunger of it hollowing their cheeks, the relief pouring out like exhaust from his father's Oldsmobile. But her face glowed when she inhaled, and smoke wreathed it in soft silver ringlets as if giving him a hazy glimpse into her future, older, grayer, but just as vivacious. He'd never seen anyone look so beautiful killing themself. Maybe he'd never been so beautiful as the day he killed himself too.

A fist of smoke smacked him across the face, and he realized she had moved to the seat beside him.

She exhaled at the ceiling and twiddled the cigarette. "You don't mind, do you?"

His eyes teared, his stomach turned, but he shook his head.

"Do you live nearby?" She twirled her finger around a tendril that fell into her eyes. There was something mesmerizing about the cyclonic way her hand moved. The entrapping way it moved.

"Yes. Do you?"

"I do."

"Did you grow up here?"

"No," she said. "Well, in the state, yes." She tapped a finger against her bottle. "Are you married?"

The bartender stopped cleaning a glass to stare at them, and Adam shook his head.

"How about you?"

"No. It's..." She knocked a cube of ash off her cigarette, her nose crinkled in frustration. "It's tricky where I come from. You can't marry just anyone you like. There are rules."

He blinked in confusion. "I thought you were from Massachusetts."

"Technically. But I didn't grow up on the mainland." As she fiddled with her keychain, a configuration of complex knots crafted from yarn and wooden beads, she nodded at the bartender for another beer, then smiled at Adam. "You are having another, aren't you?

One drink. That's all it was supposed to be. One drink to know what his father had chosen over him.

The bartender lit someone else's cigarette, but Adam didn't flinch that time. He was paralyzed, back at the house on Arthur Avenue, trapped in his smoke-filled room, listening to his mother's screams. His door was too hot to open. The window was painted shut, and for all his effort, he only scratched the glass. He yelled for his father's help, but it didn't do Mom any good, so he gave up quickly to conserve oxygen. Unsure if it would work, he emptied his nighttime cup of water onto his blanket, wrapped himself up, and crawled under his bed until the nightmare was over. Nearly three decades later, he was still waiting.

"I guess…one more couldn't hurt," he said.

Meg draped her hand over his, and the dull ache melted into bliss, the sea's mercy in a woman's touch. Below her silky skin, his hand appeared just as smooth, just as normal. Flawless. Vigorous.

When she leaned into the bartender's flame, the glow on her face bled onto Adam's, and he saw them both smoldering in the mirror behind the tiers of liquor bottles and stemware. She swayed into him, and he watched her focus move from their reflection to him, the real him, the handsome and unblemished him in the mirror.

His heart raced, and he pushed back from the bar so fast he nearly toppled out of his chair.

"Are you okay?"

Yes, I just need to use the—"

He glanced at the bartender, who pointed to a small hallway to the left. The moment Adam disconnected from the bar, his joy collapsed inward, like an invisible fist crushing a paper ball. He felt defeated, unwanted. But he also felt finished.

Ruin and relief.

Turning back, he outstretched his fingers to the bar and

watched in astonished terror as his hand softened to the kind a celestial woman like Meg deserved.

"False alarm," he said, returning to his seat. "I'm sorry. You were talking about where you grew up."

She pinched the knots in her keychain and sighed musically. "It's a beautiful place. A little behind the times, traditional, even superstitious, but they mean well. *We* mean well. Family is extremely important to us."

"To me too," he said. "Or at least, I want it to be."

"Are you close to your family?"

He shook his head. "My mother died when I was ten, and my dad..." His stomach roiled. Sometimes he thought his skin still smelled like fire. The nauseatingly sweet scent of meat cooking. His meat, his mother's. But not Dad's. The smoke had barely kissed his body when firemen broke down the door and rescued his son from under the burning bed, the floor so hot, he stuck to it like a rasher of bacon. Even though cancer was doing a number on him now, it didn't feel cruel enough for what he deserved. Adam hated him, yet he still sent a birthday card every year, because...he was family.

"I want that so badly. I want a family that cares for each other no matter what. And I want to be the kind of man who leads in kindness, who sacrifices everything for his family. I want to be the kind of family man that can undo all the trauma that came before."

She smiled, her eyes glimmering with...were those tears?

"That's beautiful," she said. "And it explains why no one's snatched you up yet. You're selective."

"I don't think that's the reason," he said, sipping the new bottle of beer. It tasted better than the first. Less offensive. Nearly satisfying. "So where are you from exactly?"

She clacked the beads on her keychain. "Have you ever heard of Onder Island?"

His eyes widened and he straightened in his seat. "Really? I've never met anyone from Onder Island before. Is that crazy? We're not even that far apart. What? Twenty-two miles?"

"More. But it can feel shorter. You catch the right head-wind..." She swallowed her beer in delight. "But no, that's not crazy. I don't know many mainlanders either."

"I hate to break it to you, but if you live on the mainland, you're a mainlander."

All mirth fled her face. "No, I'm not."

He raised his hands with a chuckle. "Sorry, I meant no offense."

Her cheeks flushed, and she dropped her gaze. "Anyway, dating is tough because I don't think it's fair to lead someone on if they aren't willing to accept what it means. What marriage means."

"What does it mean?"

She released her final drag longest of all, like the exhalation would filter every toxin from her. Maybe someday it would. Looking at her, she was saving breath just like him. And one day, when she was free, when they were both free, they'd finally experience the full capacity of their lungs. They'd breathe deep, be purified.

"There's an expiration date," she said. "Not on the love, not on the family unit, but at some point, in my culture, the marriage needs to end. When you get married, you sign a contract that states you'll divorce after the last child turns eighteen."

"Wait, how many years is that?"

"It depends on how many children you have."

"And the couples that can't have children?"

She sipped her beer. "Hasn't happened, far as I know."

"Would you really do that? You'd fall in love and get

married and then just divorce him when the youngest kid is out of the house?"

"It wouldn't be my first choice," she said. "But if it was the *only* choice, wouldn't you?"

One hand lifted her beer, the other her cigarette. God, she was beautiful. So beautiful he could ignore the drinking, even the smoking. He could sew every red flag into every red carpet she demanded. As he watched her consume the vices he'd loathed all his life, he realized he was smiling...and nodding.

"Yes," he said. "I would."

She wiped her mouth and clinked her bottle against his. "It might be worth discussing sometime. If you were..." She blushed. "I'm sorry, that was stupid. Never mind."

"No, no, tell me..." It was at that point he realized he hadn't asked her name.

"It's Meg," she said, unprompted.

He sighed her name back at her, and she sucked it up like nicotine.

"Did you know this would happen the whole time?" he asked, and her youthful blush darkened, even creased a bit.

"No," she replied. "But you did."

"No, I didn't." He shook his head angrily. He smacked the bar, and the bartender jumped. But Meg didn't move a muscle. "No! I didn't know it was real. How could I know?"

"Because I told you, sweetheart. You signed away your deniability, and you were happy to do it. You would've done it *that night* if I'd let you. If you recall, I dissuaded you from that."

"Yes."

"I wanted you to have time to digest."

"I know."

"I loved you already."

Tears ran down his cheeks, and he collapsed forward,

burying his face in his hands. "This isn't fair. No, it isn't just unfair. It's crazy, Meg!" He grabbed her hands and pulled her close, nearly pulling her off the stool. "We're really going to throw everything away because of some island cult you haven't even seen in years?!"

The bartender loudly set a baseball bat on the bar. "Hands off the lady, kid."

"She's my wife!"

"Not for much longer by the sound of it."

He released her with a sob, and the bartender retreated into the shadows.

"I'm sorry this is so painful, Adam. It's no picnic for me either."

"Yes, it is!" he wailed. "Because you're a fucking swarm of ants, Meg! That's all you've ever been. You sniffed me out. You feasted on me."

She glanced at her watch. "Ramona will be home soon. We need to hurry."

"I don't care. Let her see. Then you'll have to explain why you're divorcing her father, and you'll realize how insane this is."

"The girls already know, Adam."

He jumped out of his seat. "No, that's impossible. They never said anything."

"Of course not. They're women of Onder Island. They don't owe you anything."

"They've never even been there!"

She sighed. "Oh Adam..." Pulling his hands to her lips, she spoke hot against his fingers. Each story about a fake girls' trip or a bogus college tour felt like a fresh abrasion, like a kid falling off his sled, skinning his flesh on the ice, hands then knees then face. An open sore and its instant de-escalation. Ruin and relief.

That's what she was, wasn't she? Ruin and relief, a union

he agreed to with his very soul, whatever a soul was. God, he didn't even know what a soul was. What had he given her? What did he have left for himself?

He pulled free. "I want my last room."

She reached out again, and a sorrowful rage bubbled up in him so intensely he felt compelled to bite her fingers. No, not bite. Gnaw. Shred. He wanted to latch on and shake them like a dog snapping a pheasant's neck. Instead, he turned his lips to her palm and inhaled, tasting her in myriad ways throughout time. Salt and beer and smoke. Blood and baby shit and Pepto-Bismol. Cabernet and chocolate and a hand-made blanket buried in wet earth.

"Where do you want to go, my love?"

"The dining room. No specific day. I want them all. Holiday meals and breakfast-for-dinners, the girls' first solid food and every goddamn birthday cake. Shameless binges and fad diets, the eagerness, the suspicion, the outright refusal. If you're going to feast on me, I deserve to eat first."

Aroma told a story words never could. She gave him everything he wanted, all at once and forever, like a painting layered over and over, never losing the original details, just building on top of them, using them to create new versions of the people he loved, flitting around him through time. They grew, and he shrank. They helped Meg with dinner and set the table. They danced around her, practiced audition monologues and learned their multiplication tables. He hadn't just sat there while they feasted on the marrow of life, had he? He'd cooked too. Or if he hadn't, he certainly sepa-rated scallion greens from whites. He zested lemons and mixed sauces. He tasted experimental combinations and made yummy noises to encourage their culinary evolution. He hadn't just sat there. He contributed. He feasted.

Within the blurry inertia of the kitchen, Meg paused and

held out a spoon full of a pale orangey sauce. He suckled it and warmed at the expression that bloomed on her face. On Mira's, on Bella's, on Ramona's. He didn't realize they were standing in front of him until they exclaimed, "Happy Birthday, Daddy!"

The fear of being absent while his family cooked around him drained like grease into a disposable pan. They set the cake on the table, which remained consistent while the cake changed colors and tiers and the quantity of candles. Meg changed too. Her belly swelled and slimmed while joy and grief clashed in the battle for her expression. When time slowed, joy appeared to be the winner. He held up a finger doused in blue icing, and she licked with a happy hum as she stroked her baby bump.

Then she froze, and her smile cannonballed like suicide. The hand on her belly tightened to a claw, and Adam's blood ran cold.

"No," he whispered. "Not this day."

She crumpled to the floor, screaming, and he fell beside her. "Meg! What's wrong? The baby—"

"Mommy?" Mira and Bella huddled beside her. Even when Adam ordered them to leave the room, they didn't move. The six-year-old cradled her head. The four-year-old hummed softly.

Staring up at Adam, Meg wept. "I'm not ready."

"Stay right there. I'm calling 9-1-1." His hands shook, knocking the phone from the cradle. Reeling it up by the cord, he dialed and waited for it to ring, but all he heard was the soft breath of the sea.

"I'm not ready."

"It's okay, Meg. We're going to get you help." He desperately tapped the cradle hook. "What's wrong with this thing?"

A baby cried, and he dropped the phone. She was holding

the infant in her arms, weeping, while the girls marveled over the wriggling thing.

"Oh my God. How did you—just hold on, Meg. Let me get a blanket."

"I'm not ready."

"I know, just hold on."

She covered the baby's face with one hand. "I'm not ready."

"Meg, what are you—No, Meg, no!"

She squeezed hard, and the baby stopped crying, stopped wriggling, and the girls cooed in fascination.

Adam screamed and scooped the child from her arms. "No! No! What did you do?!" He touched its collapsed cheek, its purple chest, its tiny fists. "God in Heaven, Meg, what did you do to our baby?"

"I gave her to Onder," she said. "For you."

"What? No, I didn't want this!"

"You didn't want more time?"

He couldn't breathe. The infant was so heavy it dragged him to the floor, but once his knees hit the linoleum, the dead weight dissipated, like the newborn itself, disintegrating in his arms, turning to ash that swelled into the air. In that moment, his breath returned, and he inhaled every atom of his child. In it went, like a bad habit taking root, searing down his throat and into his lungs. He tried to cough it up, but it wouldn't budge. It settled. It colonized. It filled him with all the scars he thought he left in the bar on the shore, where the coastal mouth opened up to Onder Island like a broken tooth floating in the sea.

"What's wrong?" Meg asked as she bent over him, a wrathful willow. "I thought you wanted to eat first."

He coughed and beat his chest, but the dark sludge that poured out wasn't ash. It was earth. The same earth in which he knelt now, in the garden behind the house, where they buried the baby.

"What are we doing here?" he whimpered. "This isn't a room."

"Isn't it?" Meg said, kneeling.

She ran her fingers over the flowerbed, and it responded with blissful vibration.

But for him, it writhed. It seethed.

"This where I put them," she whispered. "All the ones I killed so you could be a family man for just a little longer. Doesn't that make you feel special? Doesn't that make you feel loved? The *most* loved?"

As he backed away, weeping, moaning, his hands crossed over his mouth to catch the vomit threatening to rise, she pressed her hand to the damp earth and hummed an island song.

"Please believe me, Adam, I take far less pleasure in this than most of my forebears. Some of them didn't even like men. But they married men for Onder. They had children for Onder. And yes, so did I. But I did those things for us first. Because I have true affection for you. Since the day we met. It's why I allowed so many before Ramona to die."

He trembled, sniffling, mucus pouring down his lips. "How many?"

Caressing his soft, wet face, she said, "I don't want to cause you any pain you haven't already agreed to in triplicate. But I chose you many times over. My love for you is a crowded grave."

He collapsed into her arms, and she stroked his hair.

"I remember you. Such a sad little boy. Afraid of his own skin."

"I don't want to go back," he wept.

"Never, my love." She gathered his face in her hands and

249

gazed into his eyes. "When waves crash upon the beach, they are not the same waves that go back to the sea. Because there is no going back. There is no going forward. There is only transformation."

"I'm so tired, Meg. I don't want to do this anymore."

"You don't have to, sweetheart." She kissed his forehead. "It's time for bed anyway."

He was still covered in soil when he opened his eyes, but the flowerbed had changed into the queen-sized bed he shared with his wife of twenty-four years. The headboard and footboard were gone, replaced by twisted branches knotted with yarn and beadwork. Crystals dangled from painted limbs, and macrame spiderwebs canopied the sculpture, creating shadows that danced across the Faradays' bedroom walls. They disappeared for only a moment when headlights flooded the room, snapping Adam out of his sorrowful trance.

"The girls." He sat up on his knees, only then realizing the sculpture closed him in on all sides. He grabbed at the branches, realizing they were wet. So was the macrame. The crystals dripped. The beadwork glistened.

"Meg…" He reached through the wooden cage. "What's happening?"

"It's my latest piece. *Onder Curral.*"

"What are you talking about?!"

"We all make one, but…" She pressed her lips to his hand, then held it to her cheek. "…never with such love as this."

The front door opened, and Ramona, Mira, and Bella's buoyant voices filled the house.

"Mom?"

"Up here, girls!"

Adam screamed and shook the branches. "No, Meg! Don't do this!"

His daughters entered the bedroom on a burst of song.

They embraced their mother. They set down their shopping bags. As their father shouted and smashed his body against the sculpture, they told her all about the outfits they bought, the outfits they nearly bought, the outfits they planned to buy, and oh yes, they had picked up an extra book of matches as requested.

Sandwiching their sweet faces in her hands, she grinned. "Happy Onder Curral, my darlings."

"Ramona, look at me, sweetheart." Adam reached out to his youngest daughter, teary-eyed. "Honey, you have to help me."

She approached curiously, touched the damp sculpture, and sniffed her fingers. "It's…briny." Looking to her mother, she chirped, "It'll burn?"

As Meg giggled an affirmation to her precious child, Adam shrank to a cold lump at the center of the bed. There, textured by shadow, his hands appeared thatched in scars. Trembling, he touched his face and felt the disfigurement of his youth returned.

"No…please, Meg, not this."

She approached slowly, her daughters at her side. "I love you, Adam."

"It's not real! It's a cult! Girls, girls, listen to me." He stared out the crevices at his children. "Your mother is sick. She comes from a sick place that put a lot of crazy ideas in her head. You have to believe me. You don't have to do this. Help me, please."

Mira stepped forward and bowed her head. "Onder bless you, Father."

"No!"

"Onder bless you, Father," Bella trilled.

"No, please." He choked on his words. "Mira…Bella… Ramona, my sweet Ramona, you don't want to do this."

His youngest daughter struck a match and giggled at the

sulfurous wisp that tickled her nose. "Onder bless you, Father."

"Wait. Wait!" He thrust his gnarled hand through the cage. "I didn't sign it. I didn't sign the divorce papers. You need my signature."

Twining her fingers with his, Meg said, "What did you think the red velvet bow was covering?"

All at once, he softened. He still trembled, but his arm wasn't a fearful dagger stabbing the air anymore. He was an oil bladder hemorrhaging fluid, bulging and flattening as it emptied, a burst of ruin, a burst of relief, until he deflated onto the bed.

He didn't scream again. But he didn't conserve his oxygen either. He gave it to them. And why not? It was theirs anyway, all this time, the way he belonged to Meg, he belonged to his children. Blanketed in his wife's briny art, he watched his youngest daughter strike a match and revel in the glow. As she lit the Onder Curral, Mira and Bella hung wreaths decorated with their father's picture, his best neckties, even a porcelain baby Jesus. They were part of the offering now, just like he was. But he wasn't afraid of the blaze. It was everything he'd ever wanted. Cult fable or not, he'd wanted to be this kind of man all his life. A man who stood on the brink of darkness and chose to follow the light. To her. To his children. To the soft skin of happiness.

A family man sacrifices everything.

❦ ❦ ❦

Jessica McHugh is a 3x Bram Stoker Award-nominated poet, a multi-genre novelist, & an internationally produced playwright who spends her days surrounded by artistic inspiration at a Maryland tattoo shop. She's had thirty-two books published in sixteen years, including her Elgin Award-nominated blackout poetry collection, "The Quiet Ways I Destroy You," her sci-fi bizarro romp, "The Green Kangaroos," and her cross-generational horror series, "The Gardening Guidebooks Trilogy."

Explore the growing worlds of Jessica McHugh at McHughniverse.com.

The Wash

Kristin Kirby

As SHE STEERED her car onto the off ramp to Copper Mesa, Arizona, Jenn thought she'd feel something more than just mild curiosity. She hadn't been back to her small hometown in eighteen years, and now driving along the main street, seeing some familiar places, noting other places gone or replaced, should have been more emotional for her.

Even pulling into the driveway of her childhood home brought only idle thoughts that the adobe looked faded, that the prickly pear cactus in the front yard was scraggly and needed care.

It was the wash that brought emotions trickling back.

Stepping out of the car, Jenn could just glimpse the arroyo winding its way behind all the houses in her neighborhood. Everyone called it a wash, a usually dry stream bed that during the monsoon season of summer sometimes filled with rain—and sometimes flooded if the rains were particularly heavy and long lasting. As kids, Jenn and her friends rode their bikes all around the wash, built forts among the palo verde and mesquite trees, played tag and kick the can until sunset. As teens, Jenn and her friends partied in the wash, drank beer and listened to music and made out, blanketed by the brilliant desert stars until all hours of the night.

These memories made Jenn smile wistfully as she unloaded luggage from the car and made her way into the house that was now hers.

News of her mother's passing hadn't been a surprise—she'd been increasingly ill with heart disease for years. Jenn had kept in contact via email and phone calls, but she and her mother had been mostly estranged since Jenn was a teenager. Since the day Jenn had been shipped off to an aunt in Seattle. With so much awfulness happening in Copper Mesa around that time, Jenn had been happy to go.

Over the next few days, packing up boxes of her mother's clothes and dusty knickknacks and ferrying them to Goodwill, Jenn was too busy to think very much about the wash, only catching glimpses of it through the back picture window as she went from room to room. When she did take a break in the evenings, sipping a glass of wine, she found herself standing at the window looking out at the blanket of stars and the wash below. But the wistful memories had started to recede, and something insidious was creeping in to fill the space.

These memories were full of fear, and dread, and violence. They made Jenn shudder and close the blinds.

On the third night in her old home, Jenn dropped into bed feeling a sense of accomplishment at getting most things packed up or gotten rid of. She had decided to put the house on the market as is—it needed some work, but the bones were solid—and going back to her life in Seattle. Copper Mesa didn't feel like home to her anymore, and that was fine. She could truly move on.

Maybe it was the second glass of wine, but as exhausted

as Jenn was, she had a hard time falling asleep. And when fitful sleep did finally come, the feeling of dread she'd been trying to keep at bay burst into her dreams. *Riding her bike on the familiar trail through the wash, the summer day overcast with impending monsoon rain, and the glimpse of the creepy old man with the walking stick as she rode past where he was hiding in the scrub.*

Jenn turned over restlessly in sleep.

All the kids knew who the old man was: Albert Ray Price, but they called him Sticky. He hung out in the wash drinking cheap liquor, had built a crude lean-to of branches where he slept many nights, a small, tattered Arizona state flag hanging limply from the top. Price could have been 50 or 70, it was hard to tell. His teeth were tobacco-stained, and a few were missing. The walking stick he always used was a tree branch, as tall as he was, and he took it with him everywhere, leaning on it as he made his way along the wash or a downtown street toward the nearest bar. One of his feet was twisted inward as a result of a car accident, and the shuffle of ill-fitting old shoes combined with the thunk of the stick with every other step made for distinctive sounds of his approach.

Jenn could hear the sounds in her dream, the thunk, shuffle-shuffle, thunk, shuffle-shuffle.

Riding her bike that day in the wash, looking for her friends from the neighborhood—mostly Luis, who she thought was cute—and keeping an eye on the gray clouds, because her mother was always worried she'd get caught in a flash flood if it started to rain. And only just glimpsing Sticky Price with his walking stick emerge from the scrub and thrust the stick into the spokes of her back bike wheel, stopping the bike up short, causing Jenn to tumble over the handlebars onto the dusty ground, stunned. Price grabbing her ankles and dragging her, screaming, into his lean-to.

Screaming, and nobody heard her. Because Price had waited until he was sure there was no one else around.

Jenn shot up in bed, hands flailing in front of her, even before she opened her eyes. When she did come fully awake, she sighed at the familiar defensive gesture she'd been waking from nightmares with since she was thirteen years old.

The next morning, groggy, Jenn made her coffee stronger than usual and sat at the kitchen table sifting through old photos. There were a few of her and Luis, with his ever-smiling face and the shock of black hair hanging over one eye, and of Hector, Luis's older brother, and Hector's friend, Mark. The older boys sometimes let Jenn and Luis hang out with them, especially when they were in the wash looking for lizards or jumping their bikes over ramps they'd made of old wood planks.

As dusk approached and Jenn had gotten back from a last run to Goodwill, she stood at the picture window and looked out at the wash. She'd noticed a couple of teenagers down there earlier, sitting on a log and smoking, but they were gone now. There'd been talk by the town council in the mid-1980s of constructing a cinder block wall along the edge of the wash that would span the backyards of all the homes along Jenn's street. It was thought the wall would block access to the wash for bikes and generally discourage the neighborhood kids from playing there. One kid had been bitten by a rattlesnake; another had broken his leg.

No mention of the two preteen girls who had been raped and murdered in '82 and '83, respectively, their bodies left on the rocks that built up and stabilized the wash on either side. There were a number of suspects, including Albert Ray Price, but not enough evidence, and methods of testing DNA weren't as efficient back then. Anyway, Price died later in the summer of '83. And there were no more murders.

Now, in 2005, the budget for a wall, let alone any impetus for its construction, was years gone. In this new era of videogames and the internet, kids didn't ride their bikes much down in the wash, and teens didn't party there as much.

Jenn restlessly turned away from the window and considered the bare walls and piles of boxes that had been her world for several days. She needed fresh air.

She went out onto the front patio and took some deep breaths. Clouds covered much of the sky, and Jenn wouldn't see her brilliant stars tonight. In fact, it had rained earlier and the streets were still wet. It was July, and monsoon season, and rain had been forecasted off and on for the next week.

Stepping over puddles, Jenn headed down her street toward the center of town. As she walked along, streetlights flickered on, amber and hazy. The moon shone briefly, then was covered by clouds.

As Jenn turned onto the main street, she noted a few places—the bank, the clothing consignment shop—were already closed. The corner grocer was open, but no cars were in the parking lot. There was no one out walking as she was. One car passed her and then turned a corner and was gone. The night was quiet. There were just the sounds of Jenn's breathing and her sneakers on the damp pavement.

She passed a vacant lot, mostly sand but with some sparse scrub. And there was a sound, like other shoes swishing on pavement.

And then a soft thunk.

Jenn stopped and turned to look. The street behind her was bathed in hazy light, the shadows between streetlamps dark. No one was there.

Jenn put a hand to her chest, feeling the jackhammer beat

of her heart. She took deep breaths and started walking again.

Another thunk. Then a shuffle. Behind her.

Jenn paused but didn't turn around. And she heard it again: thunk, shuffle-shuffle, thunk, shuffle-shuffle.

Of course it was her imagination, her nerves jumpy because of her dream the night before, because she was back in Copper Mesa, and there were bad memories.

Thunk, shuffle. Shuffle.

But Jenn turned around again anyway, because she knew who was behind her.

In the shadows between streetlights hunched a figure, just a silhouette. He had stopped walking when she did, and now he gripped a walking stick with both hands, waiting. Then the clouds parted, and the moon shone on Albert Ray Price, but as hazy as the light from the streetlamps, and mostly see-through.

"Because he isn't real," Jenn found herself whispering.

Price seemed to respond to the sound of her voice, straightening a little. He raised and lowered his walking stick, giving it two quick thunks on the pavement, and grinned at Jenn through yellow teeth.

"You fucker," Jenn said.

His image alternated between wavery and one-dimensional one moment, more solid the next, shadows from the moving clouds above contributing to Jenn's hallucinatory experience. She felt sure she was going to throw up. She turned and scanned the downtown buildings for anything open, and saw lights on at the Copper Cantina bar.

One thing she knew about Sticky Price was that he didn't move too fast—one of the reasons she eventually got away from him when she was thirteen. But when you were a ghost, obviously the laws of physics were different. Maybe he could be on her in an instant in that dark, deserted street.

So Jenn took off at a run toward the Copper Cantina. She didn't dare look back. She heard her own shoes thudding on the pavement as she listened, panicked, for his.

When she made it inside the bar, gasping, Jenn clung to the door handle for a moment, liking how solid and comforting it was. The place was bathed in dim lights and smelled of beer and pub food. Jenn had left town when she was seventeen and had never been inside. It was as sleepy as the rest of the town on a Tuesday, with only the bartender and a few customers.

As Jenn wandered dazedly toward the bar, she was startled to recognize the bartender cleaning shot glasses was Luis, the same shock of hair hanging over one eye but now streaked in gray. The last time she'd seen him had been her disastrous visit during his first month in college.

Walking through the campus square looking for Luis's dorm room, excited because she was going to surprise him, she'd had an argument with her mother about driving up to the college to see him, her mother calling her a tramp. She wasn't a tramp; she and Luis hadn't even had sex. Seeing a guy sitting on a bench in the square who looked like Luis but his back was to her, Jenn about to call his name. Then noticing he wasn't alone, noticing the blonde girl leaning close to him as he kissed her and played with her hair. It was Luis, turning to see Jenn, guilt making his shoulders sag. Jenn turning away, trudging back to her car in the parking lot.

Jenn sat at the bar and watched a stunned look of recognition wash over Luis's face.

"Hi," was all he could get out at first.

Then Luis reached out his hands, and Jenn gripped them. Her hands must have been freezing, probably still shaking, and Luis's gaze drifted to the bar's windows, and Jenn knew who he was looking for.

"He followed me," she said.

Luis studied her stricken face, turned to the bottles of liquor behind him, and poured her a shot of strong whisky.

"Is he out there?" she asked, after she downed the shot.

"No."

He poured her another shot, and she nursed this one. And it was suddenly like they were back in high school, and they were in sync, and it was easy.

"This town seems just as dead as it was back then," Jenn said. "No pun intended."

They shared a smile.

"It closes up around 8:30." Luis squeezed her hands again. "I'm sorry about your mom," he said.

"Thanks."

"And I'm sorry . . . about it all."

Jenn took a deep breath and let it out. "It was a bad few years all around. Since it happened. The wash."

Luis nodded. "Come and say hi to Hector," he said.

He led her to a gray-haired man drinking beer at a table in the corner. It was Luis's older brother, looking older than he should. Jenn thought maybe they all looked older than they should.

"Hi, Hector," she said, and he gave Jenn a hug.

They ended up sitting around the table talking even after closing, Luis locking the doors of the empty bar at 10 p.m. Jenn learned that Mark, Hector's best friend, had committed suicide some years before.

"He couldn't take it anymore," Hector said, his eyes wet.

Hector had started drinking most days and into the nights. Luis made sure it was at the bar where he could keep an eye on his brother. But he couldn't get Hector to stop, not with therapy, not with AA.

"But nobody knows what we done," Hector said. "Not some therapist or the cops or nobody."

Jenn was dismayed to hear Luis had quit college before

the end of his first year. He came back to Copper Mesa and took a bartending course.

"You would have made a great vet," Jenn told him.

"He takes care of all the strays in town," Hector said with a grin. "Including me."

And then they ran out of chat, and Jenn's gaze went to the windows, half-expecting Price's craggy face to be there, his yellow breath fogging up the glass. But there was only the night, and the rain.

Raining hard for days during the July monsoons, and the wash filling with water. And Luis and Hector and Mark hatching their plan: they'd trap Sticky Price in the wash, trap him and let him drown for what he did to Jenn earlier that summer. Going to his lean-to made of mesquite branches and scrub, not finding him. And Jenn shouting in the rain and wind, let's just go, let's get out of here before the wash fills up. The water was already past their ankles. Then Price showing up and yelling at them to get away from his place, waving his walking stick, threatening them. Mark and Hector grabbing the old man and pushing him into the lean-to, punching and kicking him to make him stay in there. Tying the sleeves of Price's shirt to the mesquite branches as he lay dazed. Jenn and Luis and Hector and Mark splashing through water to the bank of the wash and climbing the slippery rocks. Luis hesitating, he and Jenn locking eyes and both thinking the same thing: they couldn't leave someone to die, not even Albert Ray Price. Sliding back down the rocks as Hector and Mark yelled at them, barely hearing as the wind whipped rain against them. The water swirled around their knees now, and Luis tried to untie Price's sleeves, tried to get the shirt off him, but the old man swore at him and struggled and tried to bite him. The force of the water getting stronger, almost pulling Jenn and Luis under, and they had to give up and help each other back up the bank to solid ground, all four teens watching as the water rose higher and Albert Ray Price never emerged from his lean-to.

"He was evil," Hector said, twisting open another beer. "He was a child sex killer."

Luis stared down at the table. "But did he deserve to die like that? To drown?"

"Damn straight he did, any way it went down. What he did to Jenn, a thirteen-year-old girl, was enough. But he murdered two other kids. And the cops never did anything."

Jenn was hesitant to ask. "Did . . . Mark kill himself because of the guilt of what we did?"

Hector gave a sigh. "No. Sticky Price's ghost made his life hell. He made all our lives hell, but Mark finally couldn't take it."

"He's been haunting you all these years?"

"Our dreams mostly," Luis murmured. "But not always."

"I thought it was just me with the nightmares. All through high school."

Hector shook his head. "I hear that walking stick, and his kind of scuffling walk, ya know? In my dreams. But sometimes coming out of the Cantina at night, I see him on the street. Standing there looking at me." Hector took a long drink of beer. "This helps," he added, holding up the bottle.

Luis said, "He's been around more, and more corporeal, in the past few days."

Jenn looked at both of them. "That's when I got here—a few days ago."

Hector pushed his last beer bottle away. "You're stirring him up, sister. And something that evil, it stays strong if it's fed. We're feeding the evil, I guess, just by living here. And Jenn, you're like its energy drink."

It was late when they all left the Cantina. There was no sign of Price as they walked to Luis's car. Luis and Jenn dropped off Hector at his apartment, Luis waiting until he saw Hector get inside his door. Then he drove Jenn home. He walked into the house with her and looked through all the rooms to make sure they were empty.

"This is bringing back so many memories," Jenn told him. They were in the kitchen, leaning against the counter, side by side.

"Good ones, I hope."

"Mostly good."

Luis looked thoughtful. "Do you think Hector's right? Price was so evil that his spirit stays here getting juiced on our energy, because of what we did to him? He's getting his revenge?"

"Maybe. But something's keeping him connected to this town. I mean, why didn't he haunt me in Seattle? Why does his ghost stay here and haunt you three?"

"We're the ones who came up with the plan, Mark, Hector, and me. We're the ones who killed him."

"I wish I'd just gone to the police. Or at least told my mother what he did." Jenn's hands curled into fists on the counter. "I was scared. I was ashamed."

Luis put a gentle arm around her. "You were a kid dealing with something horrific and incomprehensible."

Jenn said, "We should have all gone to the police."

"Instead of murdering a man? Yeah, we should have." He lowered his head to look into her eyes. "But am I sorry he died? Not one bit."

At her front door, Jenn said, "If evil is that strong, we just have to be stronger, right? We have to fight it."

"I'm down for that," Luis said. "Will you be okay? Should I stay here tonight?"

Jenn gazed into his eyes, feeling like the years had never passed. "It's too tempting," she finally murmured.

He grinned. "I'm glad you're feeling it too." He headed down the walk to his car. "Call if you need me, okay?"

"I will."

Before she crawled into bed, Jenn made sure all the doors and windows were locked, all the shades were drawn, all the lights were on. She didn't know if that would stop Price from coming into her house. But she suspected he could only really haunt the wash or the streets of Copper Mesa, his usual hangouts when he was alive. Or dreams, of course.

The next day she met Luis and Hector for lunch at a local diner. Hector was quiet and hung over and said he hadn't slept well.

"Price? In your dreams?" Jenn asked. She had thankfully been so exhausted she didn't remember dreaming.

Hector nodded blearily.

"What you've all been dealing with. And then I come to town and make things worse." Jenn put a hand on Hector's arm. "I'm so sorry."

Hector shook his head. "You don't have to say that. I'm glad you're here." He picked at his fried egg with a fork. "I been thinking about this a while, and looking things up on the internet," he said, "and I got a theory. Why is Sticky tied to this town? Why's he been hanging around all this time?"

"That's what I was wondering," Jenn said. "What did you come up with?"

"Because something's keeping him tied here. Ghosts can get, like, anchored to a place."

"So how do you get rid of a ghost that's anchored to a place?" Luis asked.

Hector tapped his temple with a grin. "You take away the anchor, and they go to the light or some shit. They go away."

After lunch, Luis introduced Jenn to a local real estate guy he knew. The guy looked all through Jenn's mother's house and took photos, then said he'd call Jenn in the next day or two to set up the sale.

Later, as the sun set, Jenn and Luis stood in the backyard looking out over the wash. Clouds threatened to move in, but right now the sun was a low orange ball on the horizon. Their hands touched and then twined.

Jenn noticed the two teens from the day before were back, sitting on a mesquite log in the wash, smoking a joint. She pointed them out to Luis.

"They kinda look like us at that age," he said.

Jenn smiled. "Are you married?" she asked him.

"Divorced. You?"

"Same." A pause. "Kids?"

"No. You?"

"No." A pause. Jenn said, "I was broken for a long time. But the past few years have been a little better."

Luis was about to reply when screams came from the wash. The two teens were standing now, backing away in a hurry, pointing. Luis took off at a run, Jenn right behind him. They slipped a little on the rocks, wet from the recent rain.

The teens whirled, scared all over again, as Jenn and Luis came running over.

"What is it?" Luis asked, gasping for breath.

The bottoms of their jeans were wet from wading in puddles. The girl was holding her jacket tight to herself, shivering. The boy, shaggy haired, pointed to a cluster of mesquite and scrub.

"There was an old man there, spying on us. He came after us with a big stick. He looked like he was yelling but he didn't make a sound."

The girl held up her arm. On the sleeve of her jacket was a wet, dirty handprint. "He grabbed me! He wasn't there one minute, and then he was, and then he wasn't."

Jenn and Luis caught each other's eye.

Realizing she sounded just like her mother, Jenn said, "You both go home now, and stay out of the wash. It's not safe."

They watched the teens clamber up the bank and head to a car parked nearby.

Luis looked troubled. "He must be getting stronger if he's going after other people."

Rain started softly, but soon began pelting them in big drops. Jenn and Luis climbed out of the wash and went inside Jenn's house. As she made them tea, Jenn's gaze drifted to the picture window. Luis asked her if she was okay.

"Just thinking. What Hector said today makes total sense. If we can figure out what ties Price to this town, what his anchor is, and somehow get rid of it, he'll leave, right? We'll be free of him. This shit will be ended."

It was three o'clock in the morning when Jenn sat up in bed, Luis asleep beside her, with an idea about what Price's anchor might be. She sat a while longer, listening to the steady rain outside, before snuggling back down in the blankets, seeking the warmth of Luis's body.

The day dawned gray, still raining, and Jenn and Luis drank coffee and looked out the picture window at the wash. They could see rivulets of water running along the bottom of the stream bed.

Luis borrowed a razor and shaved while Jenn told him her plan.

"If I told you it's too dangerous, would you not do it?" he asked her.

"Nope."

"Then let's do it."

"Should we ask Hector to help us?"

Luis shook his head. "He's not in the best shape to be running around the wash, especially if it's flooding."

Jenn agreed. They ate a hot breakfast and drank hot coffee and slid on rain jackets. At the door, Luis kissed Jenn long and tenderly.

"For luck," he said.

The Wash

As they walked down the rocks lining the wash, they kept an eye out for Price's ghost. Thunder rumbled overhead. The rain was heavy, making the rocks and the sand in between that much more slippery and treacherous. At the bottom, they trudged carefully through ankle-deep water toward the piled branches and scrub where the two teens said they'd seen the old man.

Jenn felt kind of dizzy with fear. If she turned a corner and was suddenly face to face with Price, she wondered if she could hold her ground. He was a ghost, and supposedly they couldn't hurt you, right? But he had grabbed the girl's jacket so hard he'd left a handprint. He was strong.

Jenn told herself over and over that she was stronger.

Luis slipped in the watery sand, and Jenn reached out to steady him.

"Thanks," he said. Both of their faces were wet, their hair dripping.

Then they were at the spot where the teens had encountered Price. In the light of day, Jenn recognized the dirty remnant of an Arizona flag, just an orange and blue scrap, still tied to a branch. This was what was left of Price's lean-to, mostly destroyed and having floated downstream from its original location in 1983. Now it was clumps of scrub clinging to mesquite branches, severely weathered from years in the desert elements.

Jenn could tell from Luis's grim expression that he recognized the lean-to as well. He kept swiveling his head, looking around for any signs of Price.

"Be careful," he said, as Jenn hunched down and peered into the cavelike opening of the scrub and branches.

As she crawled inside, the day was suddenly gone and darkness enveloped her. Rain dripped steadily through gaps in the brush. She didn't think she was normally claustrophobic, but Jenn was almost hyperventilating as she crawled in deeper. She pulled a little flashlight from her pocket to run its beam back and forth along the inside of the lean-to. She was thankful it was made to withstand water, at least for a while.

The flashlight's beam revealed the tangled branches, the spiky scrub, the gaps that only reflected the rain outside. Everything was wet and dripping. Jenn honestly thought this was a futile, stupid idea after all.

And then she saw it. Price's walking stick, lodged in the branches, weathered and twisted after twenty-two years in the desert, twenty-two years trapped in the wash after the police had carried Albert Ray Price's body away and didn't bother with an investigation.

Price was never without this walking stick when he was alive. He used it to help him walk, to threaten people, to attack them.

To knock them off their bikes.

After death, he was never without the stick, even if it was as spectral as he was.

But this was the real one. And she hoped it was Price's anchor, what kept him tied to this world. Get rid of the walking stick, get rid of Price. Jenn was hoping to set it on fire, but the stick was soaked with rain, and she'd have to think of an alternate plan.

As Jenn grasped the end of the walking stick in her shaking hands, feeling revulsion at touching it, she felt something else too. Hands sliding across her ankles.

Recognizing the grip, she gasped and kicked at the hands, twisting to look down and seeing nothing, then just hands, ghostly hands made of dripping rain. Then she wrenched her body to the side, freeing her ankles, to look up and see Price's leering face inches from her. She screamed.

Now she felt his hands on hers, trying to pry her fingers from the walking stick, but she kept yanking at it, to free it from where it had been stuck so long, almost melded into the rest of the branches. His fingers scratched at hers, and she elbowed what she thought might be his neck, had he been alive and not a ghost. But he felt real, though a bit spongy, and she heard him grunt with effort. She remembered those grunts from when he was on top of her, when she was thirteen and so scared and in pain she couldn't move, couldn't scream, could only hold her breath and hope to survive.

But she refused to hold her breath now, and she screamed again, in rage, rain dripping into her mouth and eyes, as she elbowed Price's spongy face and neck, wrenching at the stick, and now Price was groping her, hands on her breasts and throat and crotch—

They were both lying in water now. The wash was filling up. Jenn tried to ignore the waves of nausea at Price's hands all over her, quell the flashes of memory from that day twenty-two years before when the same hands had violated a little girl and shattered so many years of her life. She clenched her teeth and kept jerking the stick back and forth to try to dislodge it.

Giving a final pull, Jenn heard a crack as she wrenched the stick free. It was bent a third of the way from the top. She saw Price's rheumy eyes widen in dismay.

Jenn gripped the two sides of the stick at the bend and brought it down on her knee, snapping the stick in two. Price snarled, and Jenn felt his bite on her arm even through her jacket. She slammed the two sticks on his ghostly but solid enough head of wispy hair. He opened his mouth to shout soundlessly, letting go of the bite.

"Jenn!" Luis from outside in the wash. "The lean-to's giving way!"

Jenn felt rushing water, noted the spindly branches shift and start moving with the tide. Something must have collapsed upstream, and this was now a flash flood.

"I'll hold it as long as I can!" Luis shouted.

Jenn felt the lean-to stop shifting, but she knew she had to hurry. She let go of the shorter piece of the stick, watched it swirl away with the churning water. Price shrieked in rage. It gave Jenn such satisfaction that she smiled even as she spit out water.

"Jenn! You okay?" Luis again.

Jenn started to answer, but she only got a mouthful of water. Price lunged at her hands, trying to wrestle the remaining stick from her, but he seemed weaker, couldn't get a strong grip, and she knew she'd been right. This was his anchor to this world.

Raising her knee out of the water, Jenn concentrated, bringing the stick down. Pain shot through her arm where Price had bitten her. The stick cracked but didn't break.

She could see Luis outside the lean-to, waist deep in rushing water, wind and rain whipping at him. Luis's grip on the lean-to was the only reason Jenn didn't get swept downstream. But any minute the flimsy shelter could break free and carry them both away. Jenn choked on water, trying to catch her breath.

Price was full length against her now, hands on the stick. His body felt slick and clammy, a rotted fish, and Jenn gagged on water and rising bile. She brought the stick out of the water and yanked with all her strength, finally heard a satisfying crack as it again split into two.

Jenn sent the second piece rushing away down the wash. Price roared in fear, his panicked gaze following the stick.

Jenn let the final piece go, at the same time kicking at Price, pulling herself free, and felt mostly water. Price seemed to be melting, his arms flailing for the pieces of his walking stick, as he let go of Jenn to flow downstream after them. He looked now like a clear plastic bag, deflating as he went, soon disappearing under the water and down the wash out of sight.

Jenn grabbed for the mesquite branches of the lean-to's roof, felt them come free and start to drag her along the flooding wash. But Luis was there, and she grasped his arms, and together they splashed waist deep to the rocks, scrambling onto them, trying to shout to each other in the rain but only getting mouthfuls of water.

They made it up the bank and turned to see the remains of the lean-to break apart and sail down the flood of water until they, too, had disappeared from sight.

A few minutes later, Jenn and Luis were sitting on boxes in Jenn's house, dripping all over them but not caring, shivering and watching the rain out the picture window. Jenn didn't want the rain to end, wanted Albert Ray Price and the pieces of his walking stick to just keep rushing away.

"That's what they'll do," Luis said. "The wash feeds into a river, and that river feeds into a bigger river a hundred miles away."

Luis gently pulled off Jenn's jacket and shirt and inspected her arm where Price had bitten it. It was already bruised and swelling, and Luis said they'd better get her to the urgent care for antibiotics.

"Hector's going to be mad he missed this," Jenn said.

Luis grinned. "Oh yeah."

Jenn wanted to tell Luis she wasn't ready to sell the house yet, that she wanted to stay in town. But there was time to talk later. And she knew she needed to get to the urgent care soon. But right now she just wanted to sit awhile with Luis, just sit and watch the wash fill and fill and be scrubbed clean.

❧ ❧ ❧

Kristin Kirby is an award-winning fiction writer,

screenwriter, and editor who currently makes her home in the Southwest. Her collection of short stories, *Dark Worlds We Wander*, was published in January 2025. Her work has also appeared in *Negative Space 2: A Return to Survival Horror*, MYTHIC Magazine, the NoSleep Podcast, Space and Time, 365tomorrows, and other publications. Her short story "Meat" was on the preliminary finalist ballot for the 2023 Bram Stoker Awards.

You can find her at www.kristinkirby.com.

beepbeepbeepbeep

Jenny Kiefer

Sarah's little brother ruined everything.

Even before he was born—almost at the moment her mom and dad had told her that she'd be a big sister soon—he'd destroyed everything she loved. No more buttery pancakes soggy with syrup on Sunday mornings; the scent of anything sugary made Mom spew. By the time Dad's headlights sliced through the living room curtains, Sarah was heading to bed. He was working overtime to help with the costs for the baby.

Months later, after a night spent with a babysitter, Mom and Dad walked through the front door with a bundled parasite, a tiny thing named Caleb that looked human—kind of, like a balloon-animal version of one—but seemed to exist only to scream and suck Mom dry. A blotchy purple stain spread beneath her eyes and stuck there, a permanent feature that bled through even the most opaque concealer she'd try to cake on. Before she gave up entirely, let the purple remain center stage for the stream of tears that constantly hovered just backstage.

As the little bulges of fat lining Caleb's belly and limbs

seemed to inflate, obscuring the rubber knots of the balloon joints, her mom seemed to deflate. It was like her brother was directly siphoning Mom's flesh through her breast, the only part of her that remained full. The rest of her resembled a Halloween skeleton wrapped with cling film: her cheekbones jutted from her face, stretching the darkening purple beneath her eyes, which seemed to hover in their sockets. Hugging became a dangerous endeavor, every elbow and shoulder blade and even the line of her ribs somehow sharp and stiff.

It was as if Caleb had hypnotized Dad, transformed him into a short-fused bottle rocket that could explode at any moment, even an innocent request for more mashed potatoes at dinner becoming the ignition. No more movie nights, no more evening scoops of ice cream.

Sarah couldn't even escape to her room—his screams and cries burrowed their way through the walls, beneath the door, worming their way into any little crack or crevice to reach her ears. Even a year after her parents brought this monster home, there had not been a single night of uninterrupted sleep, each hour punctuated by Caleb's screeching like a demented cuckoo clock. To top it all off, his shits stank like sunbaked garbage, the stench somehow worse than the dead mouse that had been rotting in the garage last summer.

And now he'd started to *crawl*. He seemed to sniff out anything Sarah cared about so he could get his sticky hands on it and rip it apart. One morning Sarah woke up to her homework shredded, and she got her first F on the assignment. He'd rip legs and arms and heads from her dolls. He'd vomit on her stuffed animals.

He managed to ruin *everything*.

He'd even ruined her birthday.

Sarah had begged for a party, even one at the house, just a cake with her friends in the backyard, but her mom said it would be too much work with a baby. Last year, she celebrated turning double digits at the skating rink. Last year, she had mini pizzas and ice cream with sprinkles. Last year, there was a private party room with blue carpet and hot pink walls, papery streamers and decorations and even a giant chocolate cake. A mountain of gifts from her friends stacked on one table and a peak of gift bags on another.

This year, there was no party at all. She wasn't even allowed to invite a single person over—not that she'd want to. Her little brother would just ruin that, too. He'd probably scream and throw poop at them.

This year, Sarah sat at the kitchen table with her family. This year, the cake that sat before her had been made from a box and slathered with a can of store-bought icing that tasted like plastic. There weren't even any sprinkles. Mom couldn't find any birthday candles to stand amidst the haphazard white sludge, so Sarah had to blow out the pine-scented jar candle they kept in the bathroom. Drab slices from a frozen pizza sat on their plates, the cheese somehow hot as lava while still retaining its odd, boxy shape.

This year, the pile of gifts was meager, barely a hillside. She opened each one, wrapped with newspaper or the remnants of Christmas paper, unveiling plain white socks, wire-bound school notebooks, underwear. Dusty candy from the dollar store. Nothing fun, nothing compared to the horde of yesteryear, electronic puzzle games and teenage dolls, so many that she received duplicates and got extra money to spend in the toy aisle. Now, she sat in the hard kitchen chair, her teeth coated with plasticky cheese and icing, trying to force the corners of her mouth up into a smile.

But Sarah couldn't quite control her eyes, which shot invisible, and sadly harmless, daggers at her little brother.

"Sorry, Sweetheart," Mom said, sliding her pizza into the

trash, only a few meager bites taken. "We didn't have as much money to spend on presents this year."

"I know," Sarah said.

"We do have one last gift," Dad said. "Close your eyes. I didn't have time to wrap it."

Squeezing her eyes shut, her eyebrows wrinkling, she held her palms aloft, waiting for the weight of something to settle inside them.

Before her was a dented box, little strips of tape creating a homemade seal. Her face lit up. It was a Sudohatchi! All of her friends had gotten one at Christmas, but Caleb ruined that, too—then just a couple of months old. She ripped the thin cardboard to shreds, uncovering a small purple egg with an even smaller screen nestled in its center. At the bottom were three orange buttons. It hung on a tiny metal chain.

"Thank you! Thank you!" she screeched.

Sarah pulled out the little piece of plastic that stopped the battery from engaging, bent and crumpled as though it'd been hastily re-inserted, and pressed the three buttons at the bottom until a digital, oblong egg appeared on the screen. She no longer cared about the lack of smelly roller skates or sticky melting ice cream or having to stand in the long return line at the store just to pick out a new five-dollar toy. She finally had her own Sudohatchi.

On screen, the pixelated egg wobbled back and forth until a crack spread across its surface, emanating from the center in all directions. Then the shards exploded and disappeared beyond the edges of the screen. Now, a small creature sat in the center, something that looked like a black blob with knobby limbs, two little pixels for eyes in the negative space. The creature bopped around the miniature screen.

She clicked the buttons at the bottom to feed it. Mom and Dad smiled, and even, for five seconds, Caleb was silent, licking mushy, smashed cake from his fingers. For a moment, it was like it was before—calm and happy. Until Caleb shit his diaper, wailing immediately as though he'd been dropped down a flight of stairs.

❦ ❦ ❦

Mom and Dad didn't like how much attention Sarah was devoting to her virtual pet—or at least they probably wouldn't have if they weren't so tired and grumpy from her stupid baby brother. It was as though Sarah had been hypnotized, like it was super glued to her fingers. She fed it tiny digital hamburgers and triangular pieces of candy until all five of its hunger stars were bursting. She played with it, a little hop-and-dodge game, the creature hovering in the middle of the screen while the ground ran right to left beneath it like a treadmill. By the end of the first night, she'd appeased it enough for it to evolve.

The next day at lunch, Sarah waved to her friends, the plastic egg draped over her middle finger, the purple egg swaying against her palm.

"You finally got one!" Addison said, retrieving her own from her pocket—this one an orange and green shell.

"I got it for my birthday," Sarah said. "It already evolved!"

Wide eyed, Addison leaned over to see, but instead of the gleeful excitement Sarah expected, her friend's face contorted, wrinkled and wretched. Addison bared her teeth in a grimace, a growl of disgust slithering from between each incisor.

"Why does it look like that?"

"What do you mean?" Sarah asked. "I thought you could hatch different types of creatures."

"Yeah, but I don't think that's one of them," Addison said, beckoning other digital pet parents to weigh in.

"I've never seen one like that," Bryan said.

"That's definitely not an official creature you can hatch," Ashley said. "Are you sure that's not a fake one? Did your parents buy it from a scammer or something?"

"It's real," Sarah protested. "Maybe it's just really rare."

"It's weird," Addison said. "You should reset it."

The table erupted in a cacophony of beeping, and all heads turned back towards their own digital progeny, pushing buttons until the pixels were placated.

Sarah's ate a hamburger. She didn't know why hers was so much weirder than anyone else's. They were all weird. Hers had transformed from a bulbous black blob into a thinner creature with long, spindly limbs that curled around it, filling the screen. On the top of its head were two little nubs. Why was that any worse than Addison's, which looked like a chubby snowman with a duck's bill jutting from the left side of its head? Or Bryan's, which looked like a worm wearing a ballcap? They were all *weird*. That was the point. They were probably just jealous that she'd hatched a rare variation.

Her lunch mostly untouched, Sarah and her friends meandered back towards their lockers. Right before the bell rang, at the same moment that Sarah pressed the two outside buttons together to put the toy into silent mode, the creature pooped. Two swirly shits sat on the right side of the screen, little stink lines rising and dancing. If she left it like that, it might be too sick by the time school was over. She'd heard from friends that sometimes the rarer creatures could get sick and die more quickly.

She pressed the left button to cycle around to the wash function to clear the space, but she was running out of time to get back to class. Safely silenced, Sarah slipped the plastic egg into her pocket.

The teacher's voice disintegrated into wobbly background nonsense. The Sudohatchi continually vibrated in her pocket, raising goosebumps on her thigh. The shivery pulses seemed to emanate from the plastic egg without pause. As soon as the teacher turned her back, Sarah slid the egg from her pocket, just enough to see a black skull and crossbones at the top of the screen.

Beneath the desk, she pressed a flurry of buttons, feeding it pills and more pixelated hamburgers. The creature grabbed each offering inside its spidery arms and pulled them into the black hole of its body, seeming to absorb each one through osmosis. The skull disappeared, and so too did the toy back inside of her pocket.

But in the crazed button mashing, she must have turned off the silent mode somehow. Because five minutes later, the thing started screaming from inside her pocket, a surge of shrill *beepbeepbeepbeep* rising from her thigh.

Busted.

❦ ❦ ❦

No sneaking it into school today.

After it had interrupted class, her teacher had confiscated it and held it hostage in a drawer until pickup time. She'd handed the toy back to Sarah's mom, who for a moment seemed confused by it, as if she'd never seen this little plastic egg with this little black creature on its screen. She didn't want to give it back to Sarah until she'd finished her homework, but relented after the incessant *beepbeepbeepbeep* wheedled into her ears alongside Caleb's matching shrieks. By then, the skull-and-crossbones was back, and Sarah once more had to rescue it from the brink of disaster.

This morning, Mom made sure it was parked on the coffee table when they left the house.

"You have to feed it while I'm at school," Sarah said. She'd tried to teach her mom how to operate the toy, how to use three measly buttons to perform all the tasks of raising the spindly creature. "It'll beep when it's hungry."

"I know, Sarah," her mom said, weary and distant. "I'll check on it when Caleb goes down for his nap."

"Don't forget," Sarah pleaded. "It's really rare!"

"I *know*, Sarah. You told me last night."

Sarah was a ball of nerves the whole day, her calves sore by lunch from bouncing her legs. Just before she'd had to abandon her son to the cold, hard barrens of the coffee table, she'd fed it until it was completely full. But it seemed to need so much more attention than her friends' pets. Her hands empty, she'd watched her friends press buttons on theirs at lunch, feeding them a couple burgers and playing a round or two of the hopping game. But then they'd set it down and it'd be quiet. Sarah's creature seemed to constantly hunger, to crave more and more attention from her. Maybe the rarer creatures needed more care.

Finally, the final bell rang and Sarah raced to meet her mom in the car. "Did you feed it?" she asked.

"Feed what?"

"My Sudohatchi! I told you to feed it. Remember?"

"Oh, your toy," her mom said.

Sarah threw her backpack into the car, the books inside smashing into the floor well with a terrific thump that woke the monster inside the car seat next to her. Her brother erupted in shrieks and wails, snot bubbling from his encrusted nostrils. His skin converted into a dark-red sheen. She crossed her arms and huffed.

"Don't be so moody," Mom said. "I had every intention of feeding your toy, but when I got home, Caleb started feeling bad, so I didn't have time."

She should have known her mom wouldn't have taken it seriously. She never took anything Sarah cared about seriously—at least not since her little brother arrived in the house. She could feel the redness in her face, the anger bubbling there, toning her skin the same beet hue as her brother. She wanted to scream, too, but she merely chewed her lip, rolled it between her teeth.

She hadn't expected much. She didn't even expect her mom to do everything—just feed it. But Mom couldn't even do that. She couldn't even manage to leave Caleb alone for three seconds to take care of it while Sarah was at school. She scowled at the screaming baby next to her. This thing couldn't be her brother. He ruined everything. It had to be a mistake. How could her brother be this terrible?

"I put it in your room, in your dresser," her mom said as they pulled into the driveway. "All the beeping was giving me a headache."

Sarah could hear her son screaming out in pain from the hallway, even through the thick slab of her closed bedroom door, the *beepbeepbeepbeep* piercing through to her skull before she slid open the drawer. To her horror, the menacing skull and cross bones had reappeared, mountains of poo clogging the screen. She clicked the three buttons at the bottom of the egg until her thumbs had tiny circular indents in them, clearing the digital habitat, providing medicine and hamburgers for the thing to slurp, to draw into itself with its spidery limbs. It wasn't satisfied until her mom appeared in the doorway, calling her to the table for dinner.

"Have you been playing with your toy this whole time?" she said. "You haven't even opened your backpack."

"Sorry," Sarah mumbled. Homework could wait. It's not her fault her mom hadn't even tried to take care of it. She could do her homework after dinner.

At the dinner table, Caleb sat in his high chair, giggling and slapping his hands into his pile of slop.

"I thought he was sick," Sarah said, grimacing at the Jackson Pollock her brother had already created on his own face. She scooted her chair as far away as possible—he'd already made cream of his meatloaf, and he liked to throw food.

"When I went to check on him after his afternoon nap, he was awake and feeling better," Mom said. "It's weird, though. Earlier he felt hot and his skin was all blotchy and red. He couldn't keep anything down. But then it was like magic! All it took was a nap. Babies are so fussy."

❧ ❧ ❧

For the next couple of days, the purple egg was glued to Sarah's fingers. It found its way there nearly every second, her backpack's zipper undisturbed, her vision constantly bisected by the little screen. *Go outside,* her parents chided, and she swayed on the swing set in the backyard, still pressing buttons. She thought they'd become distracted, too tired or stressed or run ragged from Caleb's constant coddling, but instead, pleasantness seemed to be seeping back into their bones.

For the first time since the stinky parasite crossed the threshold, Caleb slept through the night. For the first time in nearly a year, Sarah awoke to the screams of her alarm clock and not her little brother. For the first time since she could remember, Mom cooked an actual breakfast, scrambled eggs and pancakes swimming in butter instead of a granola bar or toaster pastry still in the wrapper.

"Good morning," Dad said as Sarah wandered into the kitchen, nose-first.

She felt an absence, something she'd grown so accustomed to that she couldn't quite figure out what it was. It was her brother and his mischief—he was still sleeping!

The mystery of the crybaby brother seemed to resolve itself, the trend of a quiet, well-behaved, human brother continuing through dinner, into a second night, and beyond. Mom's skeleton retained more and more flesh by the hour. The redness receded from Dad's eyes, the purple balloons beneath deflating too.

And Sarah's Sudohatchi pet thrived too, evolving once more into something else, another iteration that her classmates found monstrous: Its arms stretched and mutated into spidery appendages that curled around the small screen like spaghetti, the little nubs at the top of its head growing sharper. But Sarah continued to protest that they were jealous.

🍂 🍂 🍂

"I think that's everything," Dad said, patting the roof of the car.

"All ready to go through the woods to Grandma and Grandpa's!" Mom replied.

Off they drove, the first time they'd felt confident in Caleb's ability to handle the four-hour drive. Miraculously, he slept the whole way there. Too giddy to have her parents' singular attention, playing road games and sing-alongs, Sarah hadn't realized her grave error until they pulled into her grandparents' driveway.

She'd left her Sudohatchi at home. She could have sworn that she'd clipped it to her backpack, but it wasn't there. It wasn't in any of the pockets, either, nor had it drifted to the bottom or become ensnared in the meaty teeth of a notebook. If her brother had been his normal self, snotty and sneering, she would have noticed immediately because she would have wanted the distraction. It was only when they arrived that she had a moment alone, all the adults doting and kissing on Caleb, that she'd scoured her things and come up empty handed.

Tears threatened their exit, a whole army of them pressing against her sinuses, but retreated once Mom and Dad escorted her to the car—alone—for dinner and a movie, obligatory babysitting from the grandparents.

❦ ❦ ❦

If the prior three hours had been bliss, or something near it, then it made sense that there had to be a counterbalance, something awful to erase the belly full of greasy burgers and buttery popcorn, the precious absence of shrill screaming, Mom and Dad asking her about school, her friends. Sarah had nearly forgotten about her horrible brother's existence until they reached her grandparents' front door.

His absurd crying had returned, earsplitting even through the thick oak. Deafening once the door had squeaked away from the jamb.

Grandma and Grandpa, already adorned with dark circles under eyes after just a few hours, handed Caleb back to his parents. His face was rotten-tomato red, shooting spittle and snot.

"He did so well on the drive here," Mom said. "He hasn't acted like this for weeks."

"Maybe he's upset to be with new people," Grandma said. "But Lordy does he have a pair of lungs! He wouldn't eat any dinner. Just threw it on the floor."

Back in Mom's arms, the little parasite wanted to suck her dry once more, pawing at the front of her blouse, the fabric already blotched with gunky fluids. Her shoulders sank. A hunchback formed between the blades, defeat settling into her skin. She skulked to her former bedroom with Dad, the pair dragging their feet as though being led to an execution.

Somehow it got worse.

beepbeepbeepbeep

It was as though the good behavior had been a fluke, some sort of practical joke. He had reverted back to his old ways. The night was punctuated once again by his screaming, their own horrendous cuckoo clock, and even after the hourly alarms, they still awoke in the morning to the most pungent scent imaginable. To Sarah, it smelled like cheese and eggs left to braise beneath the summer sun, with roadkill like a decomposing cherry on top. The smell permeated everything, even seeping through her sleep shirt when she pulled it up above her nose.

Worse than the smell was the mess. Somehow both wet and chunky, it had soaked completely through his diaper, disintegrating it even, leaving a cottage-cheese mass of pulp that slopped out of his pajamas when Mom picked him up. It plopped, splashing, onto sheets, already completely soaked through to the mattress. A little trail of stench, little curdled bits followed their path to the bathroom.

Hours later, the stink still hadn't dissipated, and neither had Caleb's sour disposition. He refused to eat any solid food, crying to suck Mom dry. But even what he siphoned from her wouldn't stay down, came back up half an hour later, splattering the wallpaper, the carpet, somehow even the ceiling. A fever crept up his neck. Nothing helped.

Nothing to be done but to pack up and head home.

An eerie quiet settled upon the house after Mom exited once again to take Caleb to the doctor, his screams dissipating like a train whistle. In the leftover silence, Sarah's own progeny screamed.

Beepbeepbeepbeep

It resounded from her bedroom, its cries pitiful and booming even from the hallway. The creature was in dire straits. Not only was there a skull and crossbones on the screen, but it was blinking, the pixels flashing on and off. So many swirls of excrement piled on top of each other that they almost resembled a mountain. Just a thick block of pixels, as though the screen itself had somehow broken after sitting idle for just over thirty hours.

Somehow, her creature looked even thinner than it had before. Its spindly limbs were barely visible, its middle more defined and concave. In a haze, Sarah mashed the three buttons at the bottom, sending out a cavalry of meals and digital syringes, of sponges and scoops. She continued until the skull warning disappeared, until its hunger stars refilled, and even continued until it was strong enough to play a game. By the time it was at its full health, the rubber buttons felt tacky and her fingertips ached.

At the dinner table, Caleb bounced in his seat, swiping cryptic messages through his mashed peas. Laughing, even.

"It's so weird," Mom said. "By the time we got in to see the doctor, his fever had broken, and he'd already started acting better. By the end of the appointment, he was cool as a cucumber."

"Maybe it was something at your parents' house," Dad said. "Maybe there was something there he's allergic to."

"Maybe," Mom replied, her eyelids slouching, food slipping away from her fork. "The doctor said he wanted to do some tests."

In a fit of excitement, of near pure euphoria, Caleb slammed his fists down on his high chair, sending his spoon full of mashed potatoes careening across the kitchen. The clatter inspired a crying fit in Caleb.

At the same moment of spoon-and-wall impact, the same moment Caleb burst into tears, the Sudohatchi buzzed against the table. *Beepbeepbeepbeep.* A little stinky scoop of shit. On instinct, Sarah pressed through the menu until she reached the cleaning function. Away it wiped. The screen was clean once more.

And so, too, had Caleb silenced. He returned to his plate, scooping peas and a mysterious glob of what might have previously been food with his fingers. Giggling as he sucked them clean.

Then it clicked. Somehow, her creature and her brother were connected. Caleb had only transformed into a normal human baby after she'd hatched the creature. He had only regressed when she had neglected the toy—when she'd left it home from school and on their trip.

It seemed impossible, but maybe, she thought, if she could keep the creature happy, then Caleb would stop being a monster, and then they could go back to how it was before. Or at least, something close.

Problem solved.

❦ ❦ ❦

The room was dark when Sarah awoke.

beepbeepbeepBEEP

The noise sounded from her nightstand.

Groggy, she turned back over to sleep.

beepbeepbeepBEEP

In the darkness, Sarah dragged the plastic egg from her nightstand, the string of desperate *beepbeepbeepBEEP* sounding on repeat. She clicked on her bedside lamp. On the screen, the creature hovered, its hunger stars entirely depleted. It'd been full when she'd gone to sleep, just a couple of hours ago, and it had been sleeping, curled up into a compact black ball with small z's billowing away from it like clouds of smoke.

Before she could get her sleep-filled fingers to move, to press through the toy's menu to send the starving creature food, Caleb's cries sprang from the hallway. By the time she'd finished the feeding, Caleb had fallen back to sleep.

❧ ❧ ❧

The next morning, Sarah struggled to keep her eyelids parted, her head nodding down towards her bowl of cereal. In his high chair, Caleb chirped and danced. His mood seemed to turn sour at an instance, at the same moment that the creature screamed at her for neglect. Sarah smuggled it to school, trying to anticipate its needs before it *beepbeepbeep-beeped* and gave her away—the silent function seemed to have broken some time ago. At dinner, Caleb smashed his food to paste, only a quarter of it managing to get inside his mouth. While Sarah nibbled, constantly pushing buttons, Mom and Dad twittered at Caleb's progress.

And so this cycled, the creature waking her more and more each night, the *beepbeepbeepBEEP* worming its way into her head no matter where she kept the egg. Her weary face neared her cereal bowl inch by inch every morning. Her grades plummeted day by day. Caleb, meanwhile, was gaining needed weight, sleeping through the night, laughing. Mom and Dad were happy. It seemed that the creature needed *something*—food, playtime, cleaning—nearly every moment. But it was worth it, if Mom and Dad were happy.

Wasn't it?

❧ ❧ ❧

The remnants—the *entrails*—sat in a pile on her bedroom floor.

Little colorful shards splayed out amongst the fibers, tiny shrapnel waiting to snag a bare toe. They grinned up at her like a jaw full of monstrous teeth.

beepbeepbeepbeep

It was the clay pot she'd made with Mom and Dad for her ninth birthday, when they'd taken a trip to the beach. They had worked together to form the clay, each one shaping and pressing, and they'd each dipped paint brushes into glaze to decorate it. Sarah had painted the face on the front. They'd had to go back to the pottery studio three different times, once to shape, once to glaze, and once on the way home to pick up the finished piece.

She'd loved making it. She was proud of it. It had been the focal point of her desk where it held all her markers and pencils, which stuck up like crazy electrified hair. Now, they lay like fallen soldiers amongst the rubble, the caps missing from half of the markers, probably ruined as well.

A growl escaped her lips.

Why was she working so hard to keep him healthy when it only made her miserable? When it just made him strong enough to break her things? Mom and Dad were happier, but they were still fawning over Caleb, still treating him like the only thing in the world that mattered, doting on him and worrying about him, and him only. It was like she had turned invisible—they hadn't seemed to even notice how tired she was lately. They hadn't asked about school or homework or her grades. They didn't care about her—only her parasite little brother.

So why was she bothering to make sure to keep all of them happy?

beepbeepbeepBEEP

Sarah pried the toy from her pocket and launched it to the floor with all of the strength in her little muscles, right in the center of her brother's crime scene. She stepped across the wreckage, the plastic of the egg crunching beneath her shoe.

Crawling into bed, she slept even through the creature's desperate cries.

❦ ❦ ❦

When she woke, her mother hovered above her.

"It's dinner time," her mom said. "We ordered pizza. Your brother isn't feeling well."

Sarah grumbled, wanted to turn over and make up for all the hours of missing sleep. A grin snaked its way across her face.

"Are you sick, too?" Mom asked. "What's all over the floor?"

"Just tired," Sarah said. "Caleb broke my pencil holder."

"I'm sorry, but you need to clean it up before someone cuts their foot."

Sarah scooped the sharp guts, along with the *beepbeep-beepBEEP*ing egg into a dustpan and dropped it into her trash can.

Caleb wasn't at dinner—at least, he wasn't sitting at the table, but his persistent screams lingered. Mom couldn't get him settled, couldn't figure out what ailed him. Sarah and Dad picked at their plates, the soundtrack unchanging even when they headed to bed, even through the long hours of the night.

❦ ❦ ❦

In the passing days, Caleb lost all of his baby weight, a tight drum of skin stretched taut against his tiny skeleton. Just like he'd done to Mom. Sarah thought she could even see the loop of his intestines beneath his absent baby fat, the whole mess of spaghetti coiling and condensing whenever he sucked in a breath of air to fuel his screams. Though he continued to suck every ounce of substance from Mom, he could no longer walk, could no longer support even the measly remaining weight hanging on to his bones. He tried just once and immediately fell, a terrible cracking noise resounding as he hit the floor.

He'd broken his arm. His immediate shriek, now sung at new highs, rang all the way to the hospital, Dad driving and Mom cradling his new elbow.

"It doesn't make sense," Mom said when they'd returned home. "He's sucking me dry. How can he be malnourished?"

"The doctor will figure it out," Dad said.

"He lost half his body weight in just a week," Mom said, tears bubbling and frothing. "How is that possible?" The house was unusually quiet—they must have given Caleb some sort of pain reliever at the hospital that knocked him out.

Sarah stabbed at her microwaved peas. She honed in on the tines of her fork piercing through the rubbery skin of each one, trying not to grin. Now he knew how it felt. His arm had shattered just like the pot he broke. Mom was yammering on all about it, how the bone had grown so brittle and fragile that his arm was like a bag of gravel, that he'd need surgery, but he'd need to gain the weight back before they could do that.

But Sarah knew that for that to happen, the creature would have to be fed.

The previous night, she'd dug through her trash to uncover it, the *beepbeepbeepBEEP* blossoming with each piece of trash removed. The creature had become little more than a snake of pixels, the screen crowded with excrement. The skull and crossbones flashed in the corner. She watched as the creature, desperate and thin, uncurled its spindly arms from its withered body and dragged a digital swirl of shit from the pile. It unhinged its jaw to push it inside.

At the same moment, she'd heard the commotion, the sudden shrieking from her mom, as Caleb vomited. Sarah could smell the stench of it as Mom ran down the hallway, a waft of rotten waste hovering behind her.

Sarah buried the egg deep inside her closet, wrapping a pair of old leggings around it to dampen the *beepbeep-beepBEEP.*

❦ ❦ ❦

Just two mornings later, Mom and Dad once more rushed her pathetic little brother to the hospital, his breathing squeaking out in gasps, vomit curdled around his cracked lips.

This time, Mom returned alone. Her arms hung limp at her sides, seeming to slip from the sockets as she wandered the house trying to pack a bag to take back to the hospital. Her entire skeleton shuddered with each pain-stricken gasp, the bones vibrating like a tuning fork beneath her skin. His absence seemed to be worse than his presence.

In the back of her closet, Sarah dug out the egg. The creature was somehow even smaller, trapped in the corner of the screen by a wall of its own shit. The skull and crossbones flashed at the bottom, each time leaving a ghostly imprint before disappearing and reappearing again, as though the constant plea had been ongoing for so long that the pixels themselves retained the memory.

Sarah tried to get to the option to feed, to give medicine, but the buttons were smashed in place, the rubber caught against the cracked plastic, dislodged or unusable. In the corner, the creature coiled its long arms and legs into itself until it became a four-pixel dot, nearly invisible.

Sarah could do nothing but watch as the creature grew even smaller, down to a single dot. Then the screen shifted, the speck that remained of the creature moving to the center as everything else cleared from the screen. The dot transformed, blossomed and grew, unfurled into a version of the creature's former self, now with wings and a halo.

Moments later, Mom's phone rang, punctuated twenty seconds later by a shrill shriek even more piercing than anything that had ever resounded from Caleb's tiny lungs.

Sarah dropped the toy and ran down the hall.

On the screen, a new egg appeared, rocking back and forth.

Ready to hatch.

Jenny Kiefer is a Bram Stoker and Splatterpunk nominated horror author living in Louisville Kentucky. Together with her mother, she owns and operates Butcher Cabin Books, an all-horror bookstore. Check out her novels *This Wretched Valley* and *Crafting for Sinners*.

We Have (Never)
Been Here Before
Jonathan Lees

IT STARTS WITH A VIEW, or rather a vista, either stunning or sinister it doesn't matter, a silky glide alongside a rubber tire gripping the road, uneven concrete rushing under a compact vehicle, or possibly from above, a car dwarfed by the immense visage of nature, driving between mirroring lakes, into mountains with secrets, navigating through the trees.

Framing this scope of isolation is the kind of visual tension that always starts things off right.

We know the vehicle sliding around the curves contains a family, almost consistently white, with two-and-a-half kids and an exuberant dog, one of those select breeds chosen for extreme lovability by all, a golden, or something so cute you worry every time the camera tracks it on its own, most likely much more than you'd worry about anyone in the family.

Do we like this family? Doubt it.

In their first lines of dialogue, do we sense an unfounded nervousness, an unspoken dread? Is there a rift in the family dynamic? Did Dad or Mom do something wrong? Are they escaping a past, trying to start anew? Most of us won't care ninety or so minutes later yet it's always there.

If the scene is well-constructed nothing will be blatantly obvious but you know what you paid for, so you expect it anyways. It should be only moments before something clues us into the horrors ahead. You know most of the family in the car won't make it through whatever is waiting for them or, if in the hands of a particularly tepid creator, then you know exactly who will survive this encounter. Most likely the children and/or the mother. Or if they want to be provocative, one child will get it. Which one do you think will go first? Whom you want to go first is usually something we're thinking about within the first ten minutes depending on how numb the performers are.

Just having hit the ten-minute mark, I'm noticing something happening, or not happening rather, that is making me pretty uncomfortable.

There isn't a car yet, no beauty shots from a birds' eye view, no car games or fights being had, no sighing daughter who pulls her headphones tighter to avoid the whine of her brother, no stopping by a roadside gas station where the proprietor leers at them like a red herring killer in any other film, no biblical warnings from a crazed vagrant lingering around the parking lot. There wasn't even a family: White, Black, Asian or anything.

There is a house. The first five minutes open on a wide shot of the house set in a copse of trees, a meager house for some but a manse for those of meager means. The next five minutes the house fills the frame in the most deliberate way possible. This unnerves me more than the lack of humans. It is so sinuous I didn't even realize we were moving until the edges of the trees slip past the frame.

The house keeps coming closer. From a distance it looks charming, sort of, but now I can see the rot on its trim, the black spots of mold on the siding, the discoloration of the patchy paint on door. It gets closer and I realize there is no music, no violent violins or throbbing theremins and worse than that there are no sounds at all, no birds, no burbling brook, no puttering motor from an arriving car; and when the house completely covers the frame and the front door is already open, awaiting our approach, and we move closer to its mouth, within the black interior there isn't even the squeak of the floorboards to protest our arrival. The silence is threatening. Then, the house stops moving and the shadows peel away as the aperture exposes to the darkness within and the foyer is waiting, a throat drenched in rich lacquered wood with no decorative styling of note.

It couldn't possibly be abandoned for there is a light in the farthest room and, for a second, I see a shadow pass but it is probably a trick of light in the sudden halt of movement or maybe my fractured expectations, daring something to happen that I can hang onto, that I could add to my predictive textbook haunted house narrative.

Like when the door opens by itself, there is no one to say, "Oh c'mon. It's only a draft."

As the shadow flits by, there is no stinger or violin assault to tumble your guts.

There's nothing to see that the kids will tell their parents about who then won't believe them.

There's just this open door of a well-worn house in the middle of an unremarkable wood.

"Hello?'

That's me saying that, aloud in my seat, in hopes that something will respond.

I'm noticing at that moment, with a quick squint and a swivel, that I am the only one in the theater, so, I will not be getting a response.

We are now in the slender hall or foyer or whatever you want to call it. Nobody greets us. No sonic dissonance warning us of what waits at the end of the corridor where the light still shines strong… no flickering, although I imagine it might start sooner or later.

To the left, we can see there is an archway to another room. The living room, I assume, since it's just typical of the houses I'm used to seeing, these perennially wilting homes with creaking limbs. I also suppose that if we can move quicker down the hall we will arrive in the kitchen. I make out a florid tin-plated ceiling and gleaming linoleum under the harsh light that is most likely from an overzealous grip rather than practical lighting, but we're not moving closer anymore. My eyes jump around the frame looking for something I missed: a person-shaped stain on the wall above the staircase, a row of gray teeth in the darkest corner of the living room, or a pair of eyes peering from the crack in a door, the soggy sounds of a mouth opening behind us. I look and listen for anything out of the ordinary, or rather something that should feel ordinary for this kind of narrative, something that allows me to deduce where we will go next. I have this insatiable need to know because if I don't know what to expect there's chance I will be taken by surprise for real and I don't think I'm ready for that. If this keeps going as it's going and unleashes something when my guard is all the way down, I may pass away alone in this unremarkable space during an unremarkable picture.

Everything in me, every limb, trembles, wanting to jump into the screen and push the picture faster, shout up the staircase in hopes of angering whatever horrific thing is waiting for… who is it waiting for? There is no family, not even a handsome, childless couple, or a group of sweater-vested teens squatting in this abandoned abode to smoke weed and fuck. What if it's not a phantasm that peels itself from the walls? What if the troubles begin with a killer in some distinctive mask with a penchant for sharp objects and the viewer, us, me, is supposed to be the "victim" in an overly extended and plodding cold open being captured in the first-person point of view? What if we are the stalker and any moment our unsuspecting victim will appear, back to us, an easy target? Two more minutes pass and my patience is waning. All my life I've chosen to suffer until the end of things, refusing to abandon them no matter how awful or trite or predictable because I've discovered you can learn just as much from what you despise as what you love.

But man, is it testing me? Yes, it is.

The image starts moving again like the house itself is shifting, sucking us into its center.

Just before the mouth of the foyer is eaten by the frame, I notice a crucifix tilting slightly above the landing where the staircase ends in darkness. It might be as big as my torso, this dripping, dying Jesus looking down on me. As the hallway slims down, during the last sliver of the living room to the left, I see another cross, this one over a piano, looking down at no one playing it. Ok, it was something, goddammit, and I'm feeling vindicated now. I can divine that we are creeping onto a murder scene, with maybe two young lovers floating on the floor in their own mess, bleeding from ass to mouth, a red missive still dripping down the kitchen wall. What does it say? *There is no God here*. Maybe I'm overthinking it.

We enter the kitchen and the breakfast table is coming into the scene and what is that?

In the breakfast nook of the empty house is a blotch and it is moving.

The greenish black stain crawls from behind the stove, up the walls, stretching, slithering through the white caulking outlining the tile, framing it in filth and rising to the ceiling where it spreads its dark veins until it hits the edge then crawls across the ceiling towards us when it arrives at the top edge of the screen the next progression is down. Will the stain cover the screen? Will we lose sight of what's to happen? Is this the moment the scene cuts to the title graphic with an overenthusiastic orchestra rumbling in a concerted effort to jolt us?

The screen is covered by the dark veins then fragments the image before the screen loses its light entirely and I am left in the blackest room I've ever been in. For as long as I can voice an opinion, I refuse to be in a room with no light. In darkness, there comes unfamiliar things and movement or noises from those things that weren't in the room before. I don't like things I can't describe.

My eyes shut and pulses of color and sunspots replicate behind my eyelids from the sudden loss of brightness, and they are overcompensating, hoping for something to focus on and I open them again and they've adjusted to the darkness enough so I can make out the seats around me. I start fearing the darkness will lift and something so abysmal, something so horrible will be waiting for us that I will scream and there will be no one to hear it.

When the light returns, my eyes widen, for there is nothing of the sort. I squint at nothing at all just a painful white light–nothing to focus on, as devastating to my poor eyes as absolute darkness.

Slowly, an image resolves and the blackish green stain appears, or what I perceive it to be until the image clarifies, sharpening focus and it is now the panicking branches of trees. We are in the forest again; this time the camera is tracking a car moving along a winding road. We are inside the car and a family of four is playing I Spy and I can feel the relief wash over me. I know this scene. I've never seen this before but I know it because there are so many others like it and now, I'm fine. I can breathe again.

The two children fight over the result of the game while the parents laugh and give each other a longing glance and during that longing glance I expect a passing car will eventually swerve and crash into them, pulverizing them out of frame, and we'll tumble, camera and all, a hundred cuts of panic in motion until the car rests overturned in a ravine and the father will hang there, maybe his glass-cut face bleeding into the airbag, maybe the mother has a piece of the grill sticking from her throat, or if she's pregnant with a .5, she is impaled by a branch, maybe the parents come to and realize their children are pinned to their backs, the rear of the car crushed so severely that their little heads are now pressed into the seat cushions, their tiny faces embossing the leather, kissing the back of their parents' skulls.

The car continues down the unlit road, actually it's light now, wasn't it dark before?

The sun shines and the moon winks and the car pulls into a dirt road in shambles, a newly paved road, it keeps switching but it's all the same.

The camera is moving again and the family is advancing, our eyes, my eyes, clinging to their movement like a frightened child hiding from behind their legs. At this moment, I realize no one has said a word since they arrived, which is odd. Usually, there would be a casual joke at the expense of the property's disintegration or its imposing scope, age or level of creepiness or the mother would've made some withering remark about its condition or question whether they could really afford it. The father would laugh along or grunt while the dog would dash to up the porch ahead of them, bark or snarl at something the family couldn't see, the audience, or me, could not see. They make it to the door without saying a word when I notice the son and the daughter are arguing, but I can't hear what they're saying, better off really since dialogue isn't in our best interest here, and not these stories' strong suit but now filling the entirety of screen is another crucifix, a giant Jesus hanging his head, looking down towards his nailed feet, and below the bloodied appendages is an empty couch which means they must be in the living room or we're in the living room. The family is reacting, but I still can't hear them. They move from room to room, in the kitchen, a cross over the dining room table where Jesus would hang and die above a cold dinner night after night. A light flicks on in the bathroom, a cross above the toilet, Jesus looking at the days' waste. Another light is on in the kids' bedroom, plastic crosses over each bed.

Lights off.

Lights on.

We're in the basement and in the corner. Here's where, if there were more of an audience, a collective breath would be taken. I think the boy shouts something but we can't hear it. I need to leave but I can't and, as if the family senses my own fright as well, the image shifts to them piling into the car and peeling off, spewing dust clouds, covering the house's face, which I can imagine is laughing in their wake, but instead of getting to escape with the family, I'm stuck here.

Then, it's night. Then, it's day. It's night. It's day and we haven't moved and then we start progressing towards the door, but I don't want to be here anymore. Gone are my thoughts of severed heads, floating furniture, graveyard voices whispering to get out. All I can think about are the crosses and what's in the basement and, before I know it, we're going inside again, and I quickly look around hoping that at least one other person has come to witness whatever this is. There isn't.

Oh no, we're in the foyer again.

The movement loses its elegance and seems to be tripping over itself as if attached to something that wasn't walking naturally. Something walking with the gait of the dead, limbs that have forgotten how to move, only pushed forward by some internal drive to feed.

I wish the family would come back or even a busload of

sorority sisters eager to do dumb things to each other, something that I'll be able to comfortably predict and then it will be over and I can go (home?) and forget this ever happened.

The camera swivels so the front door is in view again and the frame is interrupted by the two children and their dumb dog running past, the parents slowly approach, and hesitate in the doorway.

"They got rid of the crosses, at least."

Sound! There's glorious sound. I nearly cried.

The woman who was pregnant and now isn't and has black hair instead of brown says, "Let's find out what else they left behind. They didn't mention anything at closing, so I don't want to be responsible for having to clean up their shit."

They walk through the door and the crucifixes are gone and I can breathe again.

Doors slam and footfalls pound the ceiling and the mom shouts up, "Be careful up there! We don't know what's still here that might be dangerous!"

Foreshadowing!

Ok, now I'm starting to feel it, the sense that I know everything that will come from now on and I can just sit (am I sitting?) and enjoy whatever ridiculous scenario I willfully paid to encounter.

The kids barrel down the stairs, whooping and hollering, the dog right behind them. The dog stops and turns a nose towards the cellar door and whines.

Aha! More foreshadowing.

They all move into the kitchen for lunch and it's spotless. No more vines of grime creeping around the caulking. The whole room is glowing, unnaturally so. Maybe the appearance of a draft, even though there are no open doors or windows, will set things off, maybe even the resurgence of poorly played string instruments.

Something will happen; I can feel it. A shadow passing the doorway, a shift in the air teasing the hair of the daughter, a flickering light in the hallway, something has to announce that everything isn't alright. I mean, we didn't follow them in here to watch them eat lunch for fuck's sake.

Then it happens.

But it's not what I was expecting.

They notice the cellar door is open and there's scratching coming from the dark and the couple looks at each other and the kids are too busy flicking mayo at each other's heads and mentally I'm already down the stairs and what, pray tell, is awaiting us? I think possibly a rat will poke its head from a hole, and as we, I mean the family, push forward to investigate, just as their eyes adjust to the lightless tunnel in the basement, a horde of furry bodies with red rimmed eyes and teeth will overtake these dumbfounded sacks of meat, scratching their flesh off in clumps and tearing their mouths open, pushing hard down their throats to get to the gooey insides.

I hear the family coming down the stairs and, if there aren't rats, I hope something ancient awakens in the deep crack of the foundation. A demon escaping hell or one trapped in the walls of this tormented house because of a mass murder, or a ritual suicide, or a teenage satanist gang cult that slit the throat of a goat, lamb, or pinned the wings of a crow, butterfly, or painted a poor excuse of a pentagram on the floor, or had sex on an unmarked grave with the dumb jock that moved in next door, which will make the walls tremble and shake and fog comes out of the crack lit neon red for no reason and the growl of a monster erupts from beyond while the jock's cock bounces in and out of the neighbor's hole. I want the walls to bleed.

They're still coming down the stairs. How many fucking stairs are there? Pick up the pace people, death awaits.

Maybe in the form of a horned demon forged in Hell with taloned fingers that carve stomachs as easy as a glistening chicken thigh. They, whomever survives those first encounters, will be forced to defeat something from another dimension and will only do so when they conveniently discover an ancient text that somehow they can translate and choose the exact spell needed to drive it away or some formerly introduced scholar, historian, priest will be invited to assist in their hapless plight and will probably die mercilessly in the process, impaled by a cross, holy water turned to acid melting their forehead until their own skin covers their eyes and mouth, suffocating them? Another martyr so the precious teenage daughter in a skimpy top (was she dressed like this before?) can take a shower to wash away the sins (cum) of the townie bad boy who she knew she shouldn't be with but he was just so boss, and she gets out of the shower and her hair is completely dry for some reason.

The family reaches the bottom step and swings the flashlight I'm not sure they had when they first descended the stairs. The light seeks out an empty space, just concrete (no crosses), no cobwebs even. No furniture draped in cloth looking like the most common form of ghosts that may suddenly rise to reveal a killer, spirit, demon who seemingly waited for hours in this exact spot in hopes of eventually scaring the shit out of the family although not knowing that they would ever come down to the basement that day or that week even.

The flashlight washes across the wall and a scream rips from the screen. I don't know who the screeching came from: it sounded like it was behind me in the actual room I'm in, but I know that the scream was in reference to the one life-sized crucifix still on the wall.

I grit my teeth (do I have teeth?) and I grip the edge of my seat which is a cliche as well I realize, because something has shifted behind the cross that the mother hasn't noticed yet. Maybe the rat theory isn't far off but I imagine it's worse.

Something in me is vibrating the closer she gets to the cross. Her hand, against her husband's persistence, reaches up to grab the face just under Jesus' bleeding feet, and removes it from the wall. Behind Christ's torso is a black hole.

Here we go!

Here come the rats, the demons, the hands, the blood!

Or none of that.

She stares at the hole and I stare at her staring at the hole. And then we cut to (has there been any cuts before this?) inside the hole, looking at her face, she's staring at us (me).

She's going to reach in, I know it.

She doesn't.

Something is moving behind me but I can't turn, I need to see what will happen, even though I thought I knew what would happen but the motion behind me is getting louder and I blink or twitch for just one moment but when I focus on her face again (why isn't she doing anything?) there is no more frame and I look around and I am in the basement with them. Or rather I am in that hole in the basement and it is dark in here, the darkest space I've ever been in, and something is still moving behind me or maybe that is the sound of my own limbs (do I have limbs?).

I am (we are) moving now.

I have no idea what comes next.

And that scares me to death.

❧ ❧ ❧

After twenty-five years working within the video and film industry in New York City, **Jonathan Lees** has materialized in the Hudson Valley to explore more personal rituals and inscribing arcane texts such as "To What Do We Owe This Pleasure" from the Bad Hand Books release, *Long Division: Stories of Social Decay, Societal Collapse and Bad Manners*, "They Are Still Out There, You Just Can't See Them Anymore" in the Shirley Jackson Award-winning anthology, *The Hideous Book of Hidden Horrors*, "Pop" in *Fear of Clowns*, "It Comes in Waves" from the Shirley Jackson & World Fantasy Award nominated, *Other Terrors: An Inclusive Anthology*, and "Power Out, Wind Howling" from *Even In The Grave*, which received an Honorable Mention in Ellen Datlow's The Best Horror Volume Fifteen.

Website:www.documentiaprojects.com
Instagram @jonnothin

Red God Waiting

Ai Jiang

POT BOILING. Vegetables chopped. Rice cooking. Meat marinated. Stream drifts outward from the mosquito screen of the cracked open window of our single room unit nestled in a stray corner of Chinatown, Toronto.

Newspaper crinkles under my fingers, ink seeping into the skin in dark smudges as I kneel to smooth out the folds across the low sitting dining table you picked up from someone else's yard across the street. Once the soup simmers, I lower the pot I nicked from the alley I usually cut across to the market onto the newspaper.

The headline—about some man trying to turn his own child into the police because of demonic possession and something about cults you'd talked about at dinner last week before launching into your usual complaints about your lazy coworkers at the restaurant—is already bleeding from the condensation dripping down the side of the pot, the words blending together like wisps of smoke hovering above rippling water.

Outside comes the rickety clicks of your rusty bicycle

squealing to a stop beneath our home, the clinking of chains wrapped around its body barely held together.

Then, stomping up the stairs.

Then, the turn of the bolt of the door.

What I anticipate then, as the door opens:

You, standing in worn jeans and a stained white polo thrice discounted, the wrinkles in the corner of your eyes from smiles you almost never gave me except before our marriage and shortly after. But I know what you wanted was the dowry that paid for our trip across the waters and not the bride who was awaiting your kiss.

What is actually there when the door opens:

You, with a genuine smile that terrifies rather than relieves me.

You, with flowers in your hands, white roses without the thorns, but I can still see them, the spikes, their ghostly presence beneath the pink and purple tissue and plastic.

You, in a black suit I didn't know you owned because I was so used to the polo you always wore, only washed during the weekends and sometimes bleached, always by my hands.

You, with an expensive bottle of wine you bring out from behind your back, that I would later realize isn't for me at all, that I would later discover that you didn't allow me to touch or taste a single drop, and I would have to sneak a mouthful of in my tooth brush cup and dilute it with water so you wouldn't notice anything amiss about the smell nor amount remaining as you laid slumbering.

You, walking past me and me noticing sweetness that wafting from you is not from the flowers but from the scent of a woman's perfume flooding the seams of the suit she no doubt bought you.

This is the first time, but it wouldn't be the last.

As you place everything down in a corner, I stare at the alter I've set for the kitchen deity who's to return before the new year to report each family's activities to the Jade Emperor, who would then present the family with either a reward or a punishment based on their behaviour.

So why am I the only one being punished?

This is the fourth year the kitchen deity has failed to report your transgressions, and so I will have to take care to report them myself if the gods refuse to listen.

❦ ❦ ❦

Twenty-five but still being ID'ed as I sit waiting at the bar Emily asked me to meet her at just at the outskirts of China-town on Queen. It's 9 p.m. You won't be home until 2 a.m., and I know your work ends at 11 p.m.

Emily doesn't get ID'ed even though she's three years younger than me, five years younger than you. She just came from work herself at a restaurant near yours, but usually the two of us come to this same bar after my English lessons at the local group she volunteers at.

She drags me up in a hug, and she smells of mint and harsh lemon dish detergent and cinnamon, nothing like the orange and spice and floral I smelt on you. This isn't some-thing I'm used to, still, as Emily lets go and sits down, drawing up her blonde hair in a high ponytail.

Emily waves the bartender over, and they share a smile that belonged to lovers without ever looking one another in the eye, but the two of them have never spoken outside of taking and delivering orders, almost as if intentional, because the bartender speaks to everyone else.

"What are your new year's goals?" Emily asks when the bartender places down her sweating gin on ice, their fingers brushing above the floating slice of lime so subtle yet intentional it looks practiced. For a moment, I almost thought her question was directed at the bartender instead of me until she continues without waiting for my answer.

"Oh right, you celebrate a different new year, don't you?"

I think about the kitchen deity's alter at home, the face-less effigy that rests there because Mother never told me what the kitchen god is meant to look like. "Yes, based on the Lunar calendar, usually in February."

It would be too complicated to explain further because sometimes I myself couldn't even understand the context of each dedicated day, so I don't elaborate further even though Emily waits, peeking at me over the rim of her glass with lowered lashes as she sips her drink.

"What are your new year's goals?" I ask her when my grapefruit juice, non-alcoholic, arrives.

She taps her long, French manicured nails on the wooden bar and hums while watching the bartender speak to an older man, his hand resting gently across the man's splayed out fingers before the bartender moves onto a slightly younger woman in her forties and does the same. I can't hear what they're saying over the loud R&B of the bar.

"Immortality, maybe," Emily muses.

"Immortality?" I ask.

"Have you heard about Dracula?" she asks, resting a hand on the back of mine as if mirroring the bartender just steps away on the other side of the bar.

I shake my head.

She tells me about "sexy" vampires and their endless lives and about how she'd love to be one, but also how she'd love to have her blood sucked by one. And then she demonstrates by gingerly picking up the lime in her gin and making a show of sucking on flesh. I wince because I can only imagine how sour the juice must be on her tongue.

Emily laughs at my grimace before dropping the lime

back into her now empty glass. I don't recall when she had finished her drink.

❦ ❦ ❦

At night, I see you smearing honey over the paper effigy of the kitchen deity, slathering honey where his mouth should've been—so much honey the paper barely holds, drenched, melting, beneath the honey, hoping to sweeten the deity's report to the Jade Emperor. I imagine a gap opening and swallowing your finger.

Sweat glistens along your hairline, thick, lustrous, whereas mine has been falling in clumps, bald spots glistening under the kitchen lights flickering, and I can tell by the way you stare down at me from above that you're disgusted with what I've become even though it was all for you.

Mother told me sometimes the kitchen deity is represented with his wife and sometimes with his two wives in his images, and sometimes I wonder if that is what you're trying to do, become a deity, become like the deity, or use the deity as justification for your infidelity.

When you're finished, you're still cradling the withered roses in your arms and clutching onto the wine bottle as if your fingers were a noose around a neck, as you stumbled back towards the bed. But I'm turned around now, facing the wall, pretending to be asleep so you'd never know I was ever awake.

❦ ❦ ❦

Today, Emily is drinking whiskey.

"Your gods won't listen?" she asks after her first sip.

"No... no," I say. "That's not quite it. The deity won't... speak."

"Won't speak?"

"Yes."

"To who? You?"

I think about how to phrase my explanation. "... to his boss, I suppose."

Emily looks at me, amused, and at the other side of the bar, the bartender too, though speaking to another customer, eyes curled into smile, impossible to see where his gaze is directed, and yet, it feels as though his pupils are parked in the corners, in our direction, beneath his lids. He is tapping a single finger, against the table, as though speaking in code. But then the rhythm slows, evens, like the lazy ticking of a metronome, as if attempting hypnosis. My eyes glue to the rise and fall of his finger.

I think Emily might drop the topic, switch to another, given my silence, as she usually does, for her interest is often fleeting and momentaneous—instead, she surprises me with her next words, drawing my gaze away from the bartender's slender fingers.

"Then what about... you worship a different god?" she suggests.

"A different god?" I tap the glass of my grapefruit juice with the tip of my nail in the same rhythm as the bartender.

"Yes."

Emily looks around with a secret held between her teeth and lower lip.

She doesn't tell me what this god's name is, only offers me a hand drawn picture—the god's face is angry but beautiful and from his forehead are horns like oxen, and behind supple lips, teeth like a serpent. This god resembles more so a demon than a god, but I know there are benevolent gods who can look like this, at least from the descriptions I'd been told growing up. I'd also been told the colour red is one of fortune, of prosperity, of celebration. Surely a god with a face and body as red as this could not be harmful.

Emily folds the picture of the god into a small, neat square and places it in my hand. That is when I notice the bartender has stopped tapping his finger, and my own halted as well, and he is now looking in our direction, directly for the first time, with an open-eyed, elegant, on the cusp of arrogant, smile.

❦ ❦ ❦

Tonight, I'm using the hearth in the living room because the flames there are so much more inviting than the electric stove that only glows red without the alluring fire.

I withdraw the image of the god Emily handed me and begin to fold a paper effigy in his likeness to replace the kitchen deity's on the first day of the forthcoming new year. But the kitchen deity is not the only I will rid of from this home.

This year, I will send a different god to whisper your transgressions.

I nudge the flames with poker before lighting incense and candles. The flames in the hearth sound like firecrackers, and it reminds me of when I was younger—of how I would hold the roll of firecrackers, like scarlet bullet belts, light them with the burning tip of a stick of incense and watch as they exploded in my hands without throwing them a safe distance away. The firecracker pellets would rebound off my body without wounding, threaten to jump into my eyes, singe my skin, but never did even though sometimes I wished it would. Always, there was ringing in my ears as I watched the crackle of light leaping from my very fingertips. Ah, what it was like to hold and control uncontrollable light, like a snake waiting to bite off the hand of its owner as the light grew closer and closer, until there was nothing left but smoke.

You come home then, while I'm crouched in front of the hearth still, and on your back is a small sheep skinned, still bleeding, crimson soaking the shoulders of your suit, grey instead of black today, dripping downwards onto the carpet and onto your leather dress shoes.

This is how you've maintained the little wealth you have —sacrificed sheep every year, but on top of the one you'd buy at the market, you would also sacrifice the one you had bound to your home. I look down at my own hands and imagine tuffs of white fur sheered again, too close to the skin beneath, pores gapping in pain, dribbling blood.

You drop the sheep by my feet. "That... Amelia."

"Emily. Her name is Emily," I say.

"Right. That Emery."

"Emi—"

"Elise."

I hold my tongue and glare into the hearth, eyes downcast so you don't notice.

"You should stop seeing her."

But I'm unsure who said these words as you walk out of the room.

❦ ❦ ❦

Today, Emily is drinking wine, the exact same one as the one you have been drinking, the same bottle you have almost finished, even though you have never drunk the wine before in front of me.

I take a sip from her glass, the taste heady and intoxicating without water diluting its texture and richness.

"666," she says, taking her glass back from my hands. She

drinks from the exact same spot my lips touch. "Do you know what it represents?"

The bartender is in front of both of us today, wordless, but his hands rest lightly on the back of both of ours, his eyes elsewhere.

Mother always told me the number six and eight are lucky—six for smoothness and eight for fortune, while four is unlucky. Father and Mother had gotten married on the sixth of June, leaving their home for the ceremony at 8:08 a.m.

"Yes," I say. "I do."

Emily looks at me, skeptical for a moment, expression wavering with a single twitch of her left eye before all hesitance smooths, escapes from her face. "I see." Her free hand curls in onto itself as her gaze flicks towards the bartender who meets her glance, before her eyes dart back to me as she repeats again. "I see."

The bartender lifts his hand from Emily's and something hums within me as my ears warm at our continued contact, then he takes the glass of wine, drinking from the exact same spot Emily and I had. A silent sigh escapes my lips, and I clamp my mouth shut when I realize.

Before I leave, Emily kisses me on the cheek and hands me another neatly folded square—this time, a recipe.

The bartender looks at me as he downs the remainder of the wine.

🍃 🍃 🍃

Before I slit your throat the same way butchers do the sheep you bought, I'd wanted you to beg me to spare you, as if I am the kitchen god himself, this new god as well, for mercy, for forgiveness, but I know even if you're apologetic, even though you aren't, you won't apologize—your pride would never allow it. It is better to let you go in silence.

If I feed you to the red god, will he offer the abundance that only you seem to enjoy?

The photo of Emily's god, now mine, is pasted on the worn brick above the hearth with melted red wax. Above it, I've set the new paper effigy, ready to be burnt.

Behind me, you lay, feet bloated, the swelling of blood raising your purple and blue veins, reddening skin, collecting blood beneath, waiting to burst where they're bound tight by rope, yet they never do until I begin to slice at your ankles, just beneath the rope.

I wait until both your hands and feet are detached, blood pooling around you, before I strip you of your white suit jacket and matching slacks speckled with scarlet.

I remember being yelled at by my grandmother when I was young, for wearing white on my birthday.

Before I peel the white shirt and delicates underneath off your body, I can't help but marvel at the sight of you adorned in white—

—the colour of death suits you so well.

I am careful in your skinning and the carving of the muscle resting under, filleting you the way Grandmother used to white river fish, and imagine what it would be like to steam you until your skin puckers, until your muscle is tender yet firm, to rest you like a steak upon a platter of neatly arranged vegetables to serve to the god.

I am meticulous in my disemboweling and deboning when your sinew has been cleared. It is what you've always requested of me when I cook pork, when I cook chicken, the butcher with the lamb. Unlike my family, you never wanted to see the skeleton, only wanted the tender remaining flesh.

Surely this god would forgive me for having just a single taste…

I sucked on your bones, where the blood still clings on before placing pieces of you into the pot in the hearth. And I taste you again when your flesh is tender and cooked, but there is still the sourness of your sin even after all the chicken stock, sugar, and soy sauce I've dumped into making your unmaking.

I pick up the row of firecrackers next to me, hold it up in front of me, light it with a stick of burning incense and watch, unblinking, as the pellets leap into the hearth, into the pot, feel as they rebound against my face and body, almost hitting my eye. And when the last pellet bursts, I serve you to the god with honey slathered across my lips, and I take the same stick of incense, hold it up to the paper effigy of the red god waiting above, and burn—

Ai Jiang is a Chinese-Canadian writer, Ignyte, Bram Stoker, and Nebula Award winner, and Hugo, Astounding, Locus, Aurora, and BFSA Award finalist from Changle, Fujian currently residing in Toronto, Ontario. Her work can be found in F&SF, The Dark, The Masters Review, among others. She is the recipient of Odyssey Workshop's 2022 Fresh Voices Scholarship and the author of *A Palace Near the Wind, Linghun* and *I AM AI*.

Find her at www.aijiang.ca

A Serpent's Thirst

Alyssa Alessi

MAIDEN

I WANTED nothing more than to be whisked away by the forest like the women before me. If I listened hard enough on an autumn evening, I'd hear the whispers under the masked rustle of the blowing leaves. "Sseraphina," the voices would hiss, as if my mother named me specifically for the ancestors to call. As a girl, I'd scurry back inside, terrified I'd see something I wasn't quite ready to see. A shadow, a hag, a demon perhaps, all twisted and deformed with teeth that dripped black viscous blood. All I knew were stories told in secret. Hushed murmurs from the lips of my elder brother and his friends as they sipped stolen bourbon by the fire.

"When the girls bleed from between their legs the devil has hold of them. They become wild, possessed, untamable. It's impure, unholy, vile the way they drip and drip but never empty. Disgusting. I wouldn't touch a girl while the devil's got her."

How my adolescent mind battled endlessly with what was taught, what was heard, and what was felt deep within.

Taught to be kind, gentle, almost timid. Not too loud, not disagreeable, modest, and above all else, obedient. They spat words like vile, impure, and disgusting but my heart heard strength, freedom, and magic. What if I didn't want to be tamed and touched by the hands of these filthy boys? How liberating the thought.

I could not wait to bleed.

Upon my thirteenth year, I was sure Hecate herself would bless me with my first blood. It's all I dreamt for months. The scent of the damp soil, pine needles tickling my naked flesh, and the moon casting shadows of red maidens dancing around the fire's glow. So visceral the heat warmed my cheeks.

Almost a year later the moon eclipsed, leaving a crimson sphere hanging low in the near freezing night. The men of the village warned to lock the doors and close the shutters, the devil was coming for a sacrifice.

My father, stuck in his cowardly ways, latched the door and smothered the fire. He grabbed me with his dwarfish hands and shook my shoulders hard. "Get to bed little girl, put the covers over your head and whatever you do, whatever you hear, pay no mind. Beg our holy father to keep us safe tonight and all nights to follow."

His eyes watered over, and I thought maybe it was because Mother was out in the bleeding hut. She was gone for three days already, banished with the other women in the village who were so unlucky to menstruate during this apocalyptic moon.

I pitied him. Fear leaked from his pores leaving his brown jacket soaked through in several areas. His sour scent wafted my way each time he moved.

"Don't make me slap you girl, do as I say!" he hollered as he pushed me toward the sleeping corner my brother Thomas and I shared.

Thomas was already dressed in his night clothes blowing out the few lit candles.

In the darkness Father began to pray.

"Heavenly Father, protect us from the evil that will pass over our village tonight. Protect our children and the weak from whatever demons may lurk tonight O' Father. Bless us all in the name of the father, the son and the holy spirit. Amen."

"Amen," Thomas echoed.

I didn't pray. They seemed foolish to beg with quivering voices for protection from something that they seemed to be conjuring themselves through pure imagination.

My eyes followed the smoke that danced and swirled from the blackened wick, taking me out of our shabby dank home and out into the ominous night, if only for a moment.

I lay in bed as the wind howled like a wolf's cry. I kept my eyes closed to better hear it over my chattering teeth. What sense did it make to put out a fire that was perfectly lit, as if comfort would attract evil? I wished more than ever to join my mother at the bleeding hut. Surely, the women had more sense than this.

Suddenly a warmth spread from between my legs, a slow drip of something wet and I could have sworn something slithered against my thigh.

MOTHER

The three-hour congregation seemed to carry on longer than a fortnight. Reverend Hershel's deep voice lulling the entirety of our village into a haze. I glanced ever so slightly toward my right to see my husband Joseph both alert and content. I think he somehow enjoyed listening to the same teachings week after week, finding comfort in the repetition. My back ached a terrible pain as the smallest of our four children pulled me forward with the weight of her nursing. As if sensing my pain, Joseph offered support on my lower back with his hand, risking offending others around us by his bold display of public affection. My lips parted to a grin, but my eyes remained on Reverend Hershel's and my arms wrapped tightly around baby Sara.

"Why must the benches be backless if we are forced to sit for what seems like days?" I asked Joseph as we walked home to our modest farm.

"Shh," he hushed with a smile. "You know it is to keep us alert, eager to hear the word of God."

"I think we know enough of the word. You could preach the word Joseph. You'd make a far better speaker than Reverend Hershel. All the women would be forced under your spell and want nothing more than to be close to the lord."

His sharp blue eyes bore into mine before saying, "Don't utter such things Seraphina. Reverend Hershel is a fine speaker. And the lord is good to me, good to us. Please be grateful."

"I do not wish him ill will. I am grateful Joseph, I promise you." I suppose it was too loose tongued, even for him.

Children's laughter broke the weight of our conversation and flooded the wooded path as it often did in those precious days. Samuel, Cecile, little Joseph and even teeny Sara were filled with much joy. They were fortunate enough to have parents who were deeply in love, and endlessly attracted to one another, unlike most in our village. Often, I'd not hear Joseph when he was speaking to me, distracted by his striking handsomeness, I'd have him repeat himself time and time again. He'd speak of the chores that needed attention or what blessings the lord had in store for us, and I thought only of making love. Our children were not the result of circumstance but a reflection of our happiness together.

Four children in six years since our vows. Right when one child would slightly ween from my breast, I'd become pregnant with another. Having not bled properly in years, I almost forgot the sound of the woods during a full moon. The laughter, the chanting, the crying. As much as my children loved me, and I them, I longed for time in the bleeding hut. I ached for the forgotten evenings when I could dance freely under the skies without having to tend to another.

The stroll home from the Meetinghouse was a muddy reminder that March in New England meant both frigid temperatures in the wee hours, and a powerful sun come afternoon.

"We'll be planting soon," Joseph announced.

"Yay!" Our eldest children sang. They skipped so innocently, not realizing the hard work they were cheering for.

"Not yet children, but the last frost will be upon us in mere weeks," I called to them. Better to clarify as they'd think soon meant momentarily.

At hardly four years old, Cecile was on the verge of tears. Soon meant now, but weeks meant years, and even though she was exhausted from the six miles of walking and the never-ending rantings from Reverend Hershel, she was ready to plant.

"Children, I have a wonderful idea," I said as we approached our slight farm. "Why don't you search for dandelion shoots? Surely spring is near enough."

"Stay close now, no wandering!" Joseph warned, as he took off a layer of clothing to chop wood for our evening meal.

He was always a bit more cautious after hearing Reverend Hershel speak. The message that evil was everywhere had such a powerful effect on men.

I was grateful that I learned from my mother, even before the bleeding hut, that there was no good nor evil. We just were. To respect the woods, not man or his false gods. But of course, entertain their words to get what we needed.

"Oh Joseph, I wish not to pity you. I love you too greatly for that," I whispered under my breath as I entered the barn to fetch milk.

I laid a sleeping Sara in a pile of hay and positioned myself in front of the barn door to get a clear view of Joseph as he brought the ax up over his head and then back down. A vein bulged from his jaw and trailed down his neck just how it did when he was upon me. Each squeeze from the goat's udder became more synchronized with my heavy breathing as I gazed upon my sweaty husband.

"Sseraphina...Sss..." Whispers clouded my head.

As if Joseph sensed my stare, he abandoned the wood pile to aid me in the barn.

"Seraphina, are you alright?" He asked with his brows pushed together in his worried way. "You're flushed."

The small metal pail had fallen over on the dirt floor while the goat stood far on the other side of the barn. I must have sat on the wooden stool in a daydream for many moments before Joseph noticed.

"I'm fine. I was thinking about you is all," I admitted, dabbing beads of sweat from my forehead with my skirt.

Joseph bit his lip and brushed mine with his thumb.

"Lust is a sin Seraphina. Are you longing for me on Sunday of all days?"

"Yes," I admitted, kissing his hand.

Joseph glanced over at the sleeping babe and then out the barn door to the other children playing in the grass.

"What would be the purpose of our vows if I wished not to give you what you desired?" he said with a playful smile.

Baby Sara let out a hungry fuss from the bed of hay, sending my breast to tingle in an alarm to feed her.

"Tonight, then," I sighed.

Only when night fell, and the children were asleep, the forest called to me louder than ever before. It wasn't Joseph I longed for, but the true comfort of belonging.

I stepped out into the dark, closing the door behind me, separating my life as a dutiful wife and mother and who I used to be, who I truly was.

"Ssseraphina," the snakelike voices breathed through the trees. "Seraphina," the sound summoned me again and again. "Seraphina…"

The ghostly echo took me by the wrist and guided me through the pines. The moistened earth sunk beneath each step, burying itself under my toenails as I ran.

The harsh whispers suddenly came to a halt, as did I, as if an invisible force told me to wait. I stood in the moonlight panting heavily, searching for a sign. The bitter midnight air was unforgiving and suddenly the cotton of my nightdress wasn't enough. As my eyes adjusted, I sensed movement in the stillness of the forest floor. A beautiful serpent slithered north, her scales reflecting the exquisite blue hue of the full moon as she went.

In just a few steps further, nightdresses hung from branches with their translucent sleeves blowing in the breeze, waving like a welcome. The potent copper scent of the bleeding hut beckoning every fiber of my being to move forth.

I parted the trees, eager to reach the clearing where the fire blazed high and mighty. Women danced and swayed, covered in slick dark blood. It dripped from their fingers as they licked it off with their long serpentine tongues.

I gently removed my nightdress and tossed it over the nearest thorn bush. I stood there wearing nothing but goose-flesh as my wild eyes took in the magnificence that surrounded me.

Reverend Hershel lay naked on a stone altar; his pale

dimpled skin covered in dozens of bitemarks. I opened my mouth to speak, but deranged laughter took the place of words. I knelt before the cold slate, studying how the skin swelled around each puncture before sinking my own teeth into the soft pink flesh. My eyes closed in ecstasy as I sucked the sweet holy juice of the Reverend.

"Ssss, Ssaa, Sss," the whispers became one with the crackling of the fire and the whimpers that escaped the reverend. His thin lips moved in attempt to be saved, spared, forgiven. He prayed and prayed but his pleas meant nothing to the Mother. His words meant nothing to me.

I took my place around the fire, blood smeared from lips to chest and dripping from between my plump thighs, dancing with my sisters where I belonged.

MONSTER

Joseph passed away on a summer afternoon when the sun was at its highest in the sky, though our souls drifted long before that day. A piece of him died the moment he realized I was no longer the girl he married, but a woman who would not be tamed. The blue in his eyes dulled to grey by the time he fully understood I belonged to no one. Unlike him, I accepted each phase of the man he was and mourned them all.

My hair curled and silvered, my skin showed proof of long-lived joyous days and time in the sun's radiance with the minuscule price of lichenified cheeks. I seemed to blend in with my surroundings, with no heads turning to acknowledge my presence in the village. No one noticed that I no longer worshipped at the newly built Meetinghouse or gossiped at the well with the obsequious wives. Already having mothered, grand mothered and even great-grand mothered, there was no use for me in the village as far as they were concerned. My back curved in a way it never had before, the slight hunch stealing inches from my frame, yet I never felt so alive. Where I walked, the snakes slithered close behind. Where I sat, the wolves waited patiently. If I were gone too long, they would sing out their high-pitched cries for my return. The sentient pines accepted me as a fixture in their divine garden. I surrendered myself to the forest and found not only comfort, but my full potential.

The moon graced the earth with her mesmerizing light, reminding me to call for the women to shed their skin. A red hue blanketed the sky, bewitching us to pour blood from ourselves and to replenish with the blood from another.

I no longer ran through the forest, dodging trees and critters. I sauntered slowly, elegantly, whispering the name of my great niece.

"Sssasha."

"Sss…Sasha."

After months of calling her name, the thirst finally consumed her, the moon pulling her like the tide out into the trees. It was her time to dance at the fire, to claim her feminine power and witness the magnificence we were created to be. Her time to laugh, cry, scream out into the night.

When she wandered in close enough, I hissed her name once more.

"Sasha!"

She tip-toed, timid and peeking from behind the widest trunk.

Her eyes grew large at the sight of me.

I stood naked under the blood moon, my long silver curls draping down even past my sagging breast. My eyes glowed a florescent yellow on either side of my elliptical pupils. Beauty had a different meaning here in the woods. Beauty was not the strange standards men declared, but the cycles that nature intended. To be born and live, to shed, and be born again until it was another's turn.

The simplicity was what was beautiful.

The fire roared close by, growing larger and shrinking smaller with each sacred chant.

I turned away from Sasha, knowing she would follow, and slunk down onto the forest floor. I crawled, dragging my fragile skin across dirt and rocks, welcoming debris into the slices that appeared. By the time I reached the huts, my limbs were gone, and I slithered on my stomach until I reached the sacrifice that was laid out for me. I opened my mouth and began to swallow the gift headfirst. My jaw broke open and stretched as the hair on the man's head tickled the back of my throat. At an excruciatingly slow but steady pace, the sacrifice and all his bitten flesh disappeared inch by inch down into my growing body.

Smooth blood-soaked hands rubbed my sleek swollen back in loving embraces, encouraging me to finish devouring the calves and feet. Knowing that Sasha was watching from behind the trees was what forced me to push on. She had to see it with her own eyes. We could do the impossible, be the impossible, and with that my mouth closed around the dirty callused heels of the man.

I heard young Sasha gasp in disbelief, even over the wailing mutinous cries of our sisters. Blood dripped from my sublabial scales, dabbling the dirt below, replenishing the soil. Blood leaked from my sisters as snakes wriggled in every direction. Frantic guttural shrieks and grunts filled the air as embers fell like rain. As I lay gorged in the middle of it all, I saw the reflection of our ritual in Sasha's amber eyes. She stood just as immobile as I, shocked, intrigued, terrified, confused, aroused, empowered; the look I had many years before. As my breathing began to slow and my muscles relaxed, I drifted proudly into the most satisfying hellish slumber.

❧ ❧ ❧

Alyssa Alessi is a writer of middle grade, young adult and short stories all inspired by the unsettling macabre aesthetic of New England. You can find her hiking any trail in the Northeast said to be haunted, roaming old cemeteries with a camera in hand, or thrift shopping anywhere antiques are sold. She resides in Boston, MA with her husband, three children and their mini dachshund. She is the founder of the Spooktastic Book Fair, and serves on the board of the New England Horror Writers. Her stories are featured on The No Sleep Podcast, the Cinnabar Moth E-Zine, the Beyond And Within Stories of Latin America anthology and more.

Visit her Instagram @pagesinthegraveyard to learn more.

The End of the Jetty
Mike Sullivan

HE'D MADE IT. All by himself. Matthew Reiner stood at the end of the jetty and breathed deep, filling himself with salt air and victory. Behind him, the massive stone jetty curved back to the beach like a sweeping sea serpent emerging from the briny deep. The only thing in front of him was the Atlantic Ocean. Well, technically Cape Cod Bay, but after that—the Atlantic. A wave crashed onto the rocks below and sprayed him with beads of chilly ocean water. The sky was the bright blue of triumph, the late spring sun stroked his face as if counting his freckles. The wind whispered salty congratulations. It smelled like the Cape—salt and seaweed—and tousled his brown hair. He liked the feeling of accomplishment that swelled within him, a sense of pride as large as the enormous boulders that made up the jetty. Matthew was ten years old, but at that moment he felt like a teenager.

It was quiet out on the jetty. Matthew closed his eyes and listened. He heard only the hollow swooshing of water in the spaces between the rocks below him and then the cry of a seagull in the air above him. Matthew opened his eyes, put a hand up to block the glare, and looked up at the bird. It hovered in place, almost close enough to touch. The black tips of its spread wings fluttered in the wind. "Don't poop on me," Matthew said to the bird. Being pooped on by a sea gull right now would really ruin the moment.

As if insulted, the bird yipped at Matthew and soared off. He turned to watch as it floated through the air toward the nearly empty beach. Memorial Day weekend was still a week away, so there weren't that many beachgoers taking advantage of today's sunshine. By this time next Saturday, the beach would be jam-packed with tourists and summer folk, but right now only a few year-rounders dot the sand. Matthew could see a scattering of chairs and blankets laid out, plus one rainbow-colored umbrella in the dry part of the beach near the high tide line. His mom. She'd be mad if she knew Matthew was out at the end of the jetty, alone. He remembered what she'd said last year when he told her he wanted to explore the jetty all by himself. "No way. You could slip and fall! Crack your head open on those rocks and drown and no one would know." But Mom didn't understand. Didn't get why Matthew *had to* make it to the end of the jetty today.

❦ ❦ ❦

They'd arrived at the beach just before lunch. Matthew allowed Mom to spray him up and down with SPF 50 sun protection, then he sprinted down to the water, his feet slapping on the damp gray sand of low tide. On the bay side of the Cape, the water's edge at low tide was close to 100 yards down from the dry sand. He didn't dive right in, instead he came to an abrupt halt before getting wet past his ankles. The water was cold! Some people can jump right into the surf regardless of the water temperature. Matthew Reiner was not one of those people.

His friend Stuart always teased him about that. Matthew frowned, thinking about Stuart. Were they still friends? After last summer, Matthew wasn't sure. Stuart Hughes came down to the Cape from Winchester every year. Matthew had first met Stuart two summers ago on the beach, and they'd had a lot of fun. They both liked video games and Oreo Double Stuff cookies. But last summer Stuart changed. He acted like a real jerk. He started boasting. Saying that he was better than Matthew. Because his family had more money than Matthew's. Because he had once run the bases at Fenway Park. Because he had once met the mayor of Boston and Tom Brady on the *same* day. Because Matthew had never been off the Cape. It bothered Matthew.

There weren't many opportunities for a boy like Matthew to make friends. His school was tiny, he was shy and prone to anxiety attacks, and the Cape emptied after Labor Day. So, when he and Stuart had clicked, it made him feel good. He didn't know why Stuart had started acting differently last summer. He had never been judgmental or said hurtful things before. Mom said Stuart was a spoiled brat and not everyone was lucky enough to be born into money. Matthew remembered she mumbled something about a "lucky sperm club," but he had no idea what that meant.

As he stood at the water's edge looking out to sea that morning Matthew realized he needed something special, something *super cool*, to show Stuart when the other boy arrived for the summer. Something to prove he was a worthy friend. But what? Stuart already had everything. The best video games. The best bike—actually two best bikes—one at home and one he kept here at the Cape. Matthew thought and thought, trying to come up with something cool enough to impress even Stuart Hughes. Then he turned and saw the jetty and remembered something Stuart had said at the end of the summer last year.

Stuart had said, "I'm gonna walk to the very end," and nodded his head towards the jetty.

It was the final Saturday in August last summer. As a reminder of the weather soon to come, Mother Nature had decided to spit a spritz of rain on the boys as they stood in the sand, skipping stones into the surf. The wind made it difficult to get a decent number of skips even with the flattest rocks.

"My mom says we can't. Not yet." Matthew threw a stone and watched it skip once and then plunk into the water.

Stuart snorted. "Maybe *you* can't," he said. "But *I* can. Your mom babies you too much. If it wasn't rainin', I'd be at the end of the jetty right now."

Stuart bent down and scooped up a stone the color of a deep bruise. It was round and smooth, shaped perfectly by the sea for skipping. Stuart wound up and pitched it sidearm. He flicked his wrist at the exact right moment and the stone burst from his hand like a bullet. It flew parallel to the glassy water for a bit, then dipped and skipped on the surface six times before disappearing beneath a small wave. Stuart turned to Matthew and grinned. It was not a friendly grin. It was a grin that screamed *"I'm better than you!"* as if from a bullhorn. Then Stuart stuck out his tongue and ran up the beach toward his huge house on the bluff above.

❦ ❦ ❦

Ha, Matthew thought now as he stood at the end of the jetty. *I'm first.* He pictured the look on Stuart's face after hearing that Matthew had gotten to the end of the jetty first. Oh boy, he thought. *That will be the best!*

Normally crowded during the summer, the jetty was empty of people. No teenagers climbing down the slippery slabs of rock to jump into the water. No fishermen casting their lines or photographers looking through cameras. The jetty separated the swimming part of the beach from the boating part. Red and green fairway buoys bobbed up and down in the soft swell, but Matthew hadn't seen any boats go by. Soon there would be pleasure boats, sightseeing tours, sail boats, and jet skis clogging up the channel. Plus, the big red and white Lobster Roll cruise ship coming and going all day. Matthew scoffed, thinking that the lobster rolls on that touristy boat couldn't touch the ones from the Harbor Café right here on the beach.

He pictured Stuart's shocked expression again. Whatever he may say, Matthew knew Stuart could never take this away from him. Matthew Reiner walked to the end of the jetty before Stuart Hughes.

"I got here first," Matthew said to the world. A boat horn sounded way off in the distance, as if marking his announcement.

Then a horrible thought occurred to Matthew — Stuart won't believe him. Instead of being shocked, he pictured Stuart looking at him, shaking his head, and saying, "Nope. No way. There's no way you got to the end on your own." Maybe calling him a liar. A *dirty* liar. Matthew needed proof. *Wish I had a phone,* he thought. *I could take a selfie. Problem solved.* But Mom still wouldn't allow him to have a phone. Even though everyone he knew had one. Well, there must be another way. He looked out towards the Bay, thinking. Just in front of him, at the very tip of the jetty, stood a tall, ugly metal structure. It looked like someone had built it from a giant Erector Set. Three triangle-shaped signs were bolted to the rusty crossbars. One that Matthew couldn't read faced the sea, but he could read the other two: DO NOT DIVE FROM JETTY and NO SWIMMING IN A NAVIGABLE CHANNEL. *Can I scratch my name or initials on that tower thing?* Then he could bring Stuart out here and point to his name and say, "See, I scratched that myself." *Maybe put today's date too!* That would work.

He needed a rock. A rock sharp enough to scrape his name into the metal. He looked down around his feet and spied some good possibilities down by the water's edge, but the wet rocks were slick. He remembered Mom's warning: *You'll crack your head and drown! No one would know!* That last part was true. There was no one close enough to hear Matthew scream for help if he fell and couldn't climb back up.

He quickly tossed aside any negative thoughts. *I can do it. I won't fall.* His belly growled and the water sloshing around beneath the jetty made a similar hollow sound, as if the jetty was hungry too. *Lunch as soon as this is done.*

Just as he stepped forward to begin his descent, a powerful stench of rot blew past his face. *Ugh! Gross! A dead fish or something down there?* Matthew looked down into the dank crevice between the boulders.

Two yellow eyes stared back at him.

A huge wave crashed. Foam and water sprayed up onto Matthew and when he looked down again, the eyes were gone.

What was that? Matthew squatted down on one knee and leaned forward to get a closer look below. The water churning down beneath the stones was almost black, the only sound was the soggy gurgling of the water beneath the jetty. The stink was almost unbearable. Then a soft and sour breath blew up into Matthew's face, as if something down there had just exhaled.

He put one hand down on the coarse surface of the rock and got even closer. He saw nothing. There was a strange stillness in the air. He didn't know why, but Matthew was suddenly nervous. *Maybe I should go back.*

Before he could stand something sprung up from the

darkness and seized his wrist! An arm of some kind. Thin and wet and slick, dripping with ocean water, covered in orange, fishy scales. Instead of a hand, there was a claw—two finger-like digits and a thumb, each ending in a gray, jagged talon.

The talons dug into Matthew's skin, drawing blood.

Shock, surprise, and fear all struggled for space in Matthew's mind.

What is that?

Ow, it hurts!

Let go!

"LET ME GO! LET ME GO!" he screamed.

The claw-thing gripped tighter, hurting even more. Matthew shook his arm, desperately trying to get free. He didn't know what had a hold of him, all he knew was that it hurt really bad, and he wanted it to let go. Right now!

"Stop it! You're hurting me!"

He pulled again and again, but the thing was so strong. No one had ever held onto him with such force before, not even his mother.

"Help!" he shrieked. "Mom! Help!"

But his cries degenerated into screams from the most amazing pain he'd ever experienced as whatever held onto him wrenched his shoulder out of its socket with an audible *pop*. Then the arm jerked Matthew down hard, smashing his face into the unforgiving jetty stones.

Great gouts of blood poured from his broken nose. Urine poured down his leg. Shame and blinding pain filled him, but the panic and adrenaline were stronger. His only wish was *stop the pain!* His only thought was *get away!*

In agony, he finally tore his arm from the monster's grasp, stood, and howled for all he was worth.

More thoughts pinballed through his mind. *Mommy! I*

want Mommy! God. Please, God, please! It hurts so much! He screamed and turned to run.

But not fast enough.

A second arm, longer than the first and with too many joints, snaked up between the rocks and snagged Matthew's ankle.

The first arm slid across the stones, tapping its talons on the rock.

Tik-tik-tik.

No, no, no! Matthew thought, just as the smaller arm shot out and grabbed his other leg.

"Mooooooooommmmmmmy! Help me, Mommmmmm-mmy! It hurts! It hurrrrttttttssss!" he cried.

The creature pulled Matthew's legs. His one good hand desperately reached, looking for something — anything! — to grasp. The rocks were too slippery. Too smooth. His palm slapped, slapped, slapped on the wet stone. There was nothing to hold on to. With a final sob Matthew's fingers slid along the stone as the thing pulled him down beneath the end of the jetty.

❧ ❧ ❧

What was that noise? On the beach, Matthew's mom sat up in her chair. She put her hand up over her eyes to block the glare and looked for her son. *Where is he? If he went up on that jetty, I'm going to kill him.*

❧ ❧ ❧

Mike Sullivan has always loved telling stories. Growing up outside of Boston, his mother took him to the library every Saturday and his father introduced him to film and filmmakers like Alfred Hitchcock, John Ford, and Francis

The End of the Jetty

Ford Coppola. Books, movies, and comics made up Mike's childhood. Stephen King, Steven Spielberg, Marvel Comics, Star Wars, and Indiana Jones.

Mike studied film at Emerson College and became a filmmaker. He's been editing, writing, and directing documentaries for the past thirty years. His work can be seen in museums and visitor centers across the globe.

After years of editing documentary films, reading works of others, and raising a family, Mike started writing his own stories. They were dark and twisted, luckily his wife and daughter found them entertaining. His menagerie of dogs and cats were much more severe critics. When Mike isn't writing, teaching, or in his dark edit suite, he is chasing down the plot for his next new story.

Sickle-Shaped Claw
Eric LaRocca

THE SICKLE-SHAPED CLAW rests on the edge of the small table, arranged with such carelessness that Amyas Glasscott must wonder if the damn thing had been discarded there by its owner so as not to drawn full attention to it. Then again, how could one fail to notice the claw in all its frightening glory? Its bone shaved wafer thin and as black as a piano key, the handsome curve of its talon tapering down to a fine, menacing point—all telltale signs of the healthy and equally horrifying creature (now long since dead) it had once belonged to. Amyas finds himself studying the prehistoric relic, his eyes going over the fossil again and again with such painstaking sensitivity—desperately trying to imagine what kind of monster might be missing such a distressing attachment.

Of course, he's not prone to utilizing his imagination much. A census taker is hardly called to the profession for the skill, the aptitude of his inventiveness. No, quite the contrary. Instead, sensibility and logic are at the forefront of his character, and he knows this full well—from the meticulousness of his well-coiffed presentation to the scrupulous manner in which he records every detail from those he calls upon for home visits. His imagination, dormant since childhood most likely, feels similar to a relic not unlike the large claw on the table—a terrifying and yet ultimately useless device, a record of what once was but would never be quite the same ever again.

Amyas secretly delights in that fact—the certainty, the obviousness of the inevitable. There are few things in this world that actually frighten him and he's grateful for his stoicism, his unmatched sensibility. Still, there's a part of him that remains curious—perhaps even doubtful—of all the things that he encounters that he still doesn't quite understand. To him, the claw is a kind of invitation—a horrible, life-threatening opportunity for him to use his imagination, to sate his curiosity. He'd sooner perish than submit to such an unpredictable impulse.

"More tea, Mr. Glasscott?" the older gentleman asks him, sliding the serving tray of tea and fresh biscuits across the table and nearly knocking the claw off where it had been arranged. "Oh, silly me... Please excuse my clumsiness."

Amyas slides the claw back in its place, careful to not disturb it too much almost as if he's worried the monstrous thing will somehow infect him, pollute him.

"It looks like it might be expensive," he says, swiping a biscuit filled with strawberry jam from the tray.

The older gentleman squints at him, bewildered. "It's an old tea kettle. Been in the family for many years. But I hardly doubt it's worth anything..."

Amyas laughs, a little amused. He thought he had been obvious.

"No. The claw, I mean," he says. "Looks like something you'd find at a special museum exhibit..."

The older gentleman sighs, almost appearing as though he were privately lamenting the very fact that Amyas had brought the subject up. But how could he be so upset? After all, the fossil had been discarded so haphazardly on the table. Surely, the older gentleman must have realized at some point that the very thing would be brought up in polite conversation.

"Yes," he sighs, looking around at the walls of the small parlor where they sit—every inch of wall space crammed with relics, strange-looking artifacts from distant expeditions. "I suppose all of this will end up in a museum one day. A pity when you think about how easily things become discarded, how possessions and memories seem to float away when they're neglected..."

Sensing an uncomfortable pause in the conversation, Amyas stirs in his seat. If there's one thing he cannot tolerate, it's the quiet when two people are in a room together. Empty places are best suited for solitude. But he figures healthy conversation is mandatory when two people are enclosed in the same space.

"I take it you've traveled to some exceptional places," Amyas says to him, swallowing the remainder of the biscuit he had been holding.

The older gentleman shrugs and Amyas can't help but wonder if politeness has abandoned him entirely. It seems so odd for someone so well-traveled, so worldly to appear so indifferent to everything.

"I've been to many places in this world," he tells Amyas. "Backpacking through the Himalayas. Surfing on the coast of Thailand... But I suppose the ultimate joy was digging for fossils—all kinds of relics—in Argentina..."

Amyas glances around the room—bizarre-looking relics peering down at him from every awful, loathsome corner. "Is that where most of these come from? Your dig in Argentina?"

Once again, the older gentleman shrugs with visible disinterest. "Some... Not all of them... Some are from dig sites in Wyoming or Montana... That claw specifically. The one you keep looking at..."

Amyas shifts uncomfortably in his chair, his face heating red with embarrassment. But why should he be embarrassed? After all, the fossil was probably placed there to tempt him—to force him to ask certain questions, to lower his guard. Amyas knows this full well after visiting so many houses, after enduring the polite small talk from bored housewife after bored housewife. He rolls his eyes sometimes at the obvious ways in which people will leave certain objects, certain mementos, or special trinkets of sentimental value out in the open with the recognizable intention to stimulate conversation or prompt him to ask very specific questions.

People want to feel as though they matter, as though their interests and proclivities are of note. They yearn to be recognized. Amyas is willing to oblige, of course. As long as he acquires the necessary information he needs in the end. He's more than happy to discuss a wearied housewife's favorite kitchen appliance or a retired veteran's sacred memento from when he fought in battle. Then again, feigning interest in such things can be tiresome. Still, there's something about the claw that excites him, disrupts him even—awakens the part of him that has been shut off since he was a small child.

"What is it exactly?" Amyas asks the older gentleman while taking a cup of tea from the tray.

The older gentleman simpers, obviously amused. "You've never seen a velociraptor claw, dear boy?"

Amyas stirs again, setting the cup of tea down. "I guess I haven't... Not up close anyway... May I—?"

"Please," the older gentleman says, motioning.

Amyas swallows hard, reaching across the table and taking hold of the raptor claw with both hands. Fearful of somehow breaking it apart, Amyas holds the fossil with such gentleness, such care that he almost feels a bit foolish for his exactness. It's probably the first time in his life he's realized his exactness, his precision. It usually comes to him quite naturally. However, in the older gentleman's presence, it feels so contrived, so unnecessary. After all, he knows that his performance isn't being graded. Why should he feel so unsure of himself now?

Amyas runs his finger along the gentle curve of the talon. It feels glassy and smooth, as if finely waxed. He glides his index finger along the edge until he reaches the razor-sharp point, stopping there and careful to avoid stabbing himself. It's strange to admit, but there's a part of Amyas that wonders if the older gentleman had planned all of this—if he had arranged it so that the prehistoric relic would entice him enough to lower his guard before he would take the awful thing and cleave him open in one quick thrust. Amyas shakes his head, attempting to hurl the indecent thought from the sewer of his mind.

But it's an image far too grotesque to part with just yet— the hideous thought of the older gentleman hollowing poor Amyas out, digging deep into him and tearing him apart bit by bit until he's completely and utterly unspooled. Why should Amyas think of such a despicable thing? After all, the older gentleman appears perfectly reasonable—a distinguished, albeit slightly eccentric, older male.

"Not as fast as a jungle cat, of course. But a million times more deadly," the older gentleman says softly. "A velociraptor takes great pleasure in hunting you… No… Hunting perhaps too benign a word… *Haunting* you… And then tearing into what's tender and pink. Ripping you open while you're still alive…"

Amyas winces a little, setting the claw down on the table and pushing it to the side until it's partially out of view from him—as if the grotesque thing could still injure him, as if it could split him open like a child's hands punching through damp newspaper.

"I'd be—nervous to keep something like that around," Amyas tells him.

The older gentleman tilts his head at him, obviously puzzled. "And why's that?"

"Could be dangerous," Amyas says, noticing how his leg is shaking slightly. Probably just nerves. "Looks more like a weapon than anything else…"

"It's a reminder," the older gentleman tells him. "Things that are abandoned are eventually forgotten… It's a pity… A ghost cannot survive, cannot function if it's neglected… I imagine you'd hate to be forgotten…"

Amyas had never truly considered it. After all, who exactly cares about a census taker? He lives alone, has lived alone for many years, and will most likely continue to live alone for many more decades to come. In fact, he feels a certain sense of kinship with the older gentleman. It appears the elderly man dwells in a similar kind of solitude. There are no photographs of precious family members decorating the walls or filling the picture frames lining the mantle. There are no visible signs that tell Amyas that others have lived here with him as well. The older man unmistakably and unequivocally lives alone.

"I was delighted when you showed up today," the older gentleman tells Amyas. "I don't receive many callers…"

"I imagine not," Amyas says, glancing out the window as a gust of wind slams against the house and claps the shutters. "Not this far out from town anyway…"

Figuring it's a good a time as any to follow protocol, Amyas slips his fingers into his black leather bag and begins leafing through a few assorted documents.

"Now, if you don't mind," he says, sliding some papers onto a clipboard and grabbing a fountain pen from his breast pocket. "I just have a few questions to ask and then I'll be out of your way as soon as possible…"

"Oh, I was hoping you'd stay longer than a few minutes," the older gentleman says to him, straightening in his chair. "As I said, I don't receive guests very often… It's always a pleasure to chat with someone. Even a stranger… You cannot be strangers for too long when you're forced in the same room with someone…"

Amyas laughs a little. "I suppose you're right…"

Just then, Amyas notices how the color seems to drain from the older gentleman's face—as if some valve had been undone in some secret cavern inside him and exhausted the warmth from his cheeks. In its place—a horrible, sort of frightened expression that Amyas struggles to comprehend.

"May I tell you something, dear boy?" the older gentleman asks him. "Something that I've never told another living soul…"

Amyas flinches at the outrageous possibility. Of course, he was already accustomed to serving as a kind of priest suitable enough to receive certain confessions. After all, sometimes it's easier to tell a secret to a perfect stranger than someone you already know. Amyas had been told about tempestuous affairs from meek, unassuming housewives. He had been regaled with countless stories from otherwise dutiful fathers and loving husbands about the poor, illegitimate children they had sired when stationed overseas during the war—the precious lives they had so carelessly abandoned when they finally returned to this country, battered and bruised both inside and out.

The older gentleman closes his eyes, wincing. "You see, I'm not a well man."

Amyas straightens in his chair, about to rise from where he had been sitting. "Shall I call for a doctor?"

But the older gentleman waves him off, visibly offended

by the notion of sending for help. "Nonsense... I'm just—not what I once was... But that's precisely the point, I suppose. When you spend most of your adult life existing for someone else, *something* else, you lose parts of yourself..."

Amyas shakes his head, trying to understand what the old man was saying. But was any of it actually sensible? Amyas recalls how his grandfather, confined to a wheelchair in his old age, had been sent away to a private nursing home so as not to insult the family valor with the wretched truth— age taxes and distorts a person until they are threadbare, until they have nothing left to offer this world. That's exactly how his family had viewed his poor grandfather—ill- suited to offer anything of substance, of considerable meaning to the family name after years of impeccable service, after decades of strengthening the integrity of the name Glasscott in the public eye. Age seems to take all honor away from a person. Or at least that's what most people think. The elderly are to be shipped off, to be ware- housed so that others aren't inconvenienced. And then even- tually they are discarded, forgotten about the same way a prehistoric monster might languish and then finally fade away from recollection.

Amyas watches in silence as the older gentleman's eyes open and then narrow at him with such persuasion, such unreserved purpose. It withers Amyas at first and his primary instinct is to look away, to look anywhere but at the old gentleman.

"I'm being hunted by something, dear boy," he tells Amyas. "Something dead... I see it in the corners of my vision. On the edges of the periphery. Especially when it's dark out..."

Amyas tries to stifle a laugh, but little can be done about it. He finds himself choking on the laughter, the absurdity of the old man's comments. How can he possibly take him seriously? Such things are nonsensical. More to the point, entirely improbable.

The older gentleman seems to notice Amyas's doubts—the way in which Amyas's eyebrows furrow, the way his lips crumple with such contempt.

"It's been following me since the dig in Montana," the old man says to him, his eyes lowering until they reach the raptor claw resting on the very edge of the table. "I—think I disturbed something while I was there... It aches to be remembered..."

Amyas notices how the older gentleman's eyes do not seem to move from the raptor claw on the table. He stares at the fossil with such dedication, such hate-filled conviction that Amyas cannot help but be mildly impressed. Still, he knows full well he has an obligation to perform his duty to the best of his ability. He needs the old gentleman to answer a few questions before he can be on his way. Naturally, he expects the older generation to be slower when it comes to interactions, but he figures he can accelerate things if need be.

"As I said, I just have a few questions to ask you and then I'll be out of your way," Amyas says to him.

"No," the older gentleman says, unexpectedly severed from the peacefulness of his trance. He leaps from where he's sitting and reaches across the table, almost upsetting the teapot and the serving tray.

Amyas curls at the possibility of the old man's touch. The older gentleman seems to realize this and then softens slightly, lowering back down into his seat until he's composed and thoughtful once more.

"It's just—I so seldom receive houseguests," he says gently to Amyas. "You understand... It's like a hose that's been shut off for years abruptly being turned on. It's almost too much to bear... The excitement..."

Amyas nods. Of course, he can somewhat appreciate this. He lives alone and often finds himself starved for conversation when he returns to his one-bedroom apartment.

His eyes lower to the sheet of paper he's placed on the clipboard. He unscrews the cap of the fountain pen and prepares to write.

"Now, I just need your full name and date of birth," Amyas says to him.

"Do you believe in ghosts?" the older gentleman asks with such matter-of-factness that it startles Amyas at first. "Not those silly things dressed in white bedsheets… I'm referring to the imprints of certain energies left behind by those that came before. The memories of other things, other creatures… Entities that must be remembered or else they'll go extinct."

Amyas swallows, unsure how to answer at first. Of course, he had believed in spirits when he was little. But such things were too fanciful, too farfetched to believe in now. He was a grown man for God's sake, after all.

"I—suppose I haven't truly thought about it," Amyas tells him.

Just then, Amyas notices how the older gentleman's movements seem to slow dramatically, as if the man were being stalked and his every movement were being graded by invisible scrutiny. Amyas watches in silence as the older gentleman's eyes widen with terror, his whole body tensing and becoming rigid.

"Is—something wrong?" Amyas asks him.

The older gentleman opens his mouth slightly, his rancid-smelling breath whistling like a tea kettle. "It's right behind you… Right now…"

Amyas turns gently but doesn't see anything loitering in his peripheral vision.

"Don't move too quick," the older gentleman tells Amyas.

"He's watching you... With his bird-like, fever-yellow eyes... His horrible snout... The clicking of those sharp claws whenever he stirs from where he's crouching... *Click. Clack. Click. Clack...*"

For the first time in his visit, Amyas feels terribly unsettled. Even though he knows there's nothing stirring behind him, the older gentleman speaks with such conviction—such horrific persuasion—that Amyas cannot help but be fooled by him.

"What is it?" Amyas asks him.

"It's the most dangerous thing of all," the older gentleman tells him. "Something about to be forgotten... A creature—living or dead—will attach to anything, *anyone* with the hope of being remembered... Even a monster doesn't want to be neglected..."

Once more, Amyas stirs from where he's sitting. He's about to rise and reach for the cellphone he had placed on the credenza beside the armchair.

"Perhaps I should call for—"

But before he can finish the sentence, the older gentleman snatches the raptor claw from the edge of the table and brings it up to the curve of his throat. Amyas's eyes widen in disbelief. He stands there—frozen, completely unable to move.

"It's not a burden," the older gentleman says to him. "*It's a gift*... A gift I'm much too old for anymore... Promise me something—? Take care of the damn thing... Please..."

Just as Amyas is about to lunge across the room, the older gentleman's wrist makes the decision for him. Far too swift for Amyas. He watches, stunned in silence, while the old man slides the claw across his throat with one rapid flick. Blood spurts from there, the dark ribbon stretching further and further across the poor, old man's neck like some sort of terrible, gruesome scarf. Amyas covers his mouth in horror while he watches the older gentleman tremble slightly, the raptor claw slipping from between his fingers and then finally rattling on the floor. The old man convulses, his whole body quivering while he droops back into his chair and more blood gushes from the gaping hole in his neck.

After what feels like an eternity, the entire room goes quiet. Amyas is left there, idling in the dead man's company —the gentle pattering of blood now the only sound to fill the unbearable stillness.

Amyas's mind races. He doesn't know what to do first. Does he check on the older gentleman to make sure he's truly and unmistakably dead? Or does he phone for an ambulance right away? Either way, it's unlikely that the poor, old man survived the self-inflicted wound. Amyas winces, turning away, when he notices how so much of the older gentleman's clothing has been dyed blackish red from the steady stream of blood still pumping, still draining from where he had carved himself open.

Then Amyas notices the raptor claw discarded underneath the table. He reaches for it; however, just as he's about to grab hold of it, he senses something dark flickering on the periphery of his vision—a large, muscular shape.

Is it a shadow?

No.

What else could it be?

He takes the raptor claw and holds it close, examining the blood-soaked fossil. Just then, Amyas senses what feels like warm breath heating the nape of his neck, prickling the hairs there—something breathing hard against him and idling there with every intent of standing its ground, stalking its helpless prey. He thinks to turn but cannot bring himself to do so. He's much too alarmed. Amyas knows full well he's being hunted by something that cannot physically harm him, but will instead go on hunting him just for the sheer pleasure of it...

* * *

Eric LaRocca (he/they) is a 3x Bram Stoker Award® finalist, a Shirley Jackson Award nominee, and a Splatterpunk Award winner. He was named by *Esquire* as one of the "Writers Shaping Horror's Next Golden Age" and praised by *Locus* as "one of the strongest and most unique voices in contemporary horror fiction." LaRocca's notable works include *Things Have Gotten Worse Since We Last Spoke*, *Everything the Darkness Eats*, and *At Dark, I Become Loathsome*. He currently resides in Boston, Massachusetts, with his partner.

The Woodhill Wet Nurse
Todd Keisling

Lexington, Kentucky

MORNING CLOUDS PARTED, spilling ribbons of sunlight across the house's sagging roof, and with them came the laughter of children. Peter thought he heard them, but when he looked out the pickup's passenger window, he saw nothing but tall grass, a rickety fence, and a rancher with a faded foreclosure sign hanging on its busted door.

"—Hey. You listenin' to me, Pete?" Darren snapped his fingers.

Peter braced himself, looked back to his stepfather. "What do you want me to say?"

Silence in the cab except for a weak radio signal piped through busted speakers. Some shitty country song. *Always* a shitty country song. God, he hated living here.

"I wanna know if you understand what I'm sayin' to you. That this is how it's gonna be unless you get yer shit together."

"Yeah, sure. I understand." Anything to make him stop talking.

Darren's jaw cocked to the right, a single vein bulged in his forehead just above his left eye, classic warnings of another Tomlinson outburst. It wasn't even nine o'clock in the morning. *Must be a new record,* Peter thought.

His stepfather slapped the steering wheel and said, "No, *you* don't understand, kid. I made myself clear the day you went off to school—"

"You did, but it's spring break."

"—If you ain't got no job lined up when you come back, you gon' work for me." Another slap for emphasis. "I don't give a fuck if it is spring break, boy. If you stay in *my* house, eat *my* food, and you *ain't* payin' rent, then yer *ass* belongs to me. Go ahead and make that face all you want, it don't scare me none."

Peter stopped counting the slaps and stared out the truck's passenger window again. *It's Mom's house,* he thought. *Your credit was shit. Always has been.* But there was no point in arguing with his stepfather. Once he started, there was no stopping him; better to let his temper burn itself out. With any luck, Peter might escape the tirade with little more than a singed ego.

"Besides," Darren said, "with those grades you brought home…"

Or maybe not. "I did the best I could," Peter mumbled.

"Whatever. You got a C in English. Ain't that what yer majorin' in, genius? Fuck's sake."

Like you know what college is like, Peter wanted to say. *At least I finished fucking high school.* There were plenty of other things he wanted to say, truth bombs he'd been saving for a moment like this, but he held them all back. He'd fought this fight before and there was no winning with this asshole. Even if he gave the right answer, he'd still be wrong in some way.

Peter figured his mom hadn't agreed to marry this guy so

much as she'd been bullied into doing it. Darren Tomlinson was a petulant child, obnoxious if he got his way, obnoxiously violent if he didn't. Leaving home to stay on UK's campus across town might have only been a matter of miles, but to Peter, it felt like light years. He'd had every intention of finding a job, but his freshman course load had proven to be more formidable than he'd expected; his grades weren't for a lack of trying, but a desperate effort to hang on.

No job meant no money for an actual spring break, not that he had the friends with whom to enjoy such a trip. Returning to live at home even for a week was the equivalent of a prison sentence.

"If that's the best you got, do yourself a favor and drop out. You ain't cut out for it. Shit, you ain't much cut out for anything, are ya?"

"I don't think Mom would like that very much."

"You think I give a shit, Pete? I don't give a fuck if you go back to school. You think a 'spensive piece of paper's gonna impress me?"

"I'm not trying to impress you, Darren."

"You going to college is yer mother's dream, not mine. I don't—"

"You don't give a fuck. Got it." Peter held back his tears and made a show of looking out the window. "Is this the place?"

"Yeah. Ain't no wonder the bank can't sell it, but their loss is our gain, I guess. Anyway, take the Troy-Bilt. There's an extra can of gas, too. I'll be back in a few hours."

Peter climbed out of the cab, wiped his eyes on the back of his hand, and began unloading the equipment from the trailer. Any other time he'd be caught up in the history of this place, the awful shit that went down within its walls, but right now the stigma was second to putting distance between himself and his stepfather.

Darren leaned out the window and said, "You remember what I told you, boy. This is *your* yard now. I expect you to give it better than 'C' effort."

"Sure."

"Or what?"

Peter met his stepfather's gaze in the side mirror as he loosened the mower's strap. "Or else my ass is grass."

"And *I'm* the mower. Now get to fuckin' work."

❦ ❦ ❦

Peter puffed on his vape and surveyed the overgrown property. The grass was waist high, thick, and shiny with morning dew. Rotting remnants of fenceposts poked through the canopy in places, old totems to a civilization lost to bank foreclosure. Carpenter bees hummed along the porch banister. Most of the houses in Woodhill were like this, rundown or forgotten, with bullet holes in the siding and cracked glass in the windows.

He'd grown up hearing about the neighborhood from other kids in school. So-and-So's older brother's friend knew a kid who was shot in Woodhill. Or their sister's friend's cousin knew someone who cooked meth one street over. Drive-by shootings, theft, and drug dens were synonymous with Woodhill, a common part of local conversation, but that all changed after the children began disappearing. Turns out a woman was kidnapping kids and bringing them back to her house—*this* house—in Woodhill to kill them. The media dubbed her the Woodhill Wet Nurse, and Lexington's boogeyman was born.

A conversation between his mother and Darren replayed in his head.

Remember the Woodhill Wet Nurse?

The Woodhill Wet Nurse

Ain't that the crazy lady who killed all those kids a few years ago?

Yeah, that's her. Found out a guy I work with is related to one of the detectives who investigated the case. Said she didn't just lose her mind. She was into all sorts of occult shit. They found symbols drawn on the basement walls.

Jesus...

Peter had heard a number of rumored motives in high school ranging from psychopathy to insanity. Occult shit, too. Of course, Darren would be the one to bid on this place. Money was money, and the bank was desperate to maintain the place to avoid paying fines to the city. He suspected Tomlinson's Tools was the only lawncare business in the area willing to work at the site of such grisly murders; then again, he wouldn't be surprised if Darren quoted low, undercutting the competition to the point of earning little profit. Why not, when he had Peter as indentured labor?

But the state of this place was bad even for the likes of Tomlinson's Tools, whose clientele was usually too cheap for the competition. Weeds had grown for so long they were hardly weeds at all, but small trees sheathed in fresh bark.

The house—what remained of it—rose from the overgrowth like the swollen husk of a dead beast, its windows shattered and barred with water-stained sheets of plywood. Someone had spraypainted "wet nurse" across one of the boards. A section of the front door had been caved inward at some point with a blunt object, the area splintered with cracks in the faux-wooden façade, and the whole structure leaned in its frame. Squatters, maybe, or vandals looking to purge the house of its copper pipes. Only the basement windows were spared from the vandalism, a fact he found unsurprising given what happened down there.

The overgrowth in the front yard would take him most of the day to clear and the shitty lawnmower wouldn't make it easy. No telling what state the backyard was in, but if the front was any indication, he figured this was a two-day job at least. Maybe three.

This is your yard, Darren piped up in his head.

Peter tugged the starter cable once, twice—finally, the engine shuddered to life on his third pull, chuffing exhaust and regurgitating a wad of dead grass from the last time it was used. Last fall, probably. He wondered if Darren had even sharpened the blades before putting the machine to use. *One way to find out.*

He pushed the mower into the yard, slicing a thin ribbon into the weeds, and made it halfway before the engine sputtered, choked, and shut off.

"Goddammit."

The chute was clogged, stuffed full of chewed, wet grass. Behind him, the mowed strip was about as even as Darren's hair, with thick patches in some spots and balding in the rest. *That's a No on sharpened blades.* He checked the deck height, confirmed it was on its highest setting, and gave the mower a good kick. No way this piece of shit was going to finish the job. His stepfather had set him up for failure.

"Darren, you asshole…"

Peter fell to his knees and began pulling handfuls of grass from the chute. A mixture of old grass and new, the sweet smell intermingled with rancid decay and something else he couldn't place. Oil, maybe, or gasoline. No, that wasn't it. This was different. Something rotting. Had he mowed over a dead animal?

His fingers touched something wet and rubbery. Peter gasped, yanked his hand from the chute. Each finger was caked in black sludge, thick as mud, and *squirming*. He fought against a rising gorge as the maggot writhed from the muck. The pale nub nosed the air, blindly searching for its meal. He dragged his palm across the grass in disgust.

A dead animal. Had to be. No wonder the motor died. He looked out across the front yard at the tall weeds swaying in the breeze. What other landmines would he find in this mess? Dead rabbits? Squirrels? He was used to stones and twigs but dealing with a carcass was out of his wheelhouse. Anything dead twisted his stomach into knots.

This is your yard.

Peter sucked air through his mouth, refusing to let the smell ruin his morning, trying not to think about the decayed particulates he inhaled. *Just get this over with,* he told himself, and flipped the mower on its side.

His mind took too long to correlate what he saw half-buried in the mess below the mower's deck.

A pile of cut grass and black sludge.

Maggots squirming through the mess.

A tiny foot. Baby-sized. Pale and lacerated. No blood.

Peter's lungs deflated when he realized what he was staring at. When he inhaled again, his gorge rose, and this time he couldn't resist. He turned away and puked his breakfast into the weeds.

Maybe it's a doll. Gotta be. Why would...

A quick glance. Maggots crawled across the open, bloodless wound. Peter closed his eyes. *Not happening. No fucking way. What's a baby doing out here?*

He forced another look. Five digits, cuts, and no blood. Dead for a while. His mind raced full-force into a wall of possibilities. Had someone dumped their dead kid in the grass? Had someone *murdered* their kid and dumped them here?

You know whose house this is. Was. Whatever. Maybe the cops missed a body?

But that didn't make sense. The Wet Nurse was arrested years ago, sent away to some maximum-security prison out of state. Peter remembered a recent news report about the killer, detailing her attorney's appeals against the death penalty, one that made mention of the letters she received on a weekly basis. Letters from obsessed fans, some wanting her to take care of their own kids, and others expressing their love. A few marriage proposals, too.

He could believe a skeleton in the grass, however unlikely that might be, but this? This kid was still relatively fresh.

A copycat killer, then. One of the Wet Nurse's devotees disposing their evidence in a freakish act of tribute. What better altar to commit one's sacrifice than the site of such grisly murders? The whole scenario made his skin crawl. Never mind his stepfather's many crimes; this was a real crime, a real crime *scene*, and the cops needed to know about it. Darren would be pissed, but he was always pissed, so what did that matter?

Peter shot to his feet, retrieved his phone from his pocket, and made to dial 911—

Laughter. Playful giggling. Shrill air forced through spittle and bubbling like a whistle blown underwater. Peter's heart caught in his throat and stayed there. The childish trill was close, mere feet away, but he couldn't see shit for the tall grass.

"Who's there?"

Silence now. Maybe it was neighborhood kids? He looked around, surveying the dead street, and shook his head. The university's spring break always happened before the public schools. Little kids would still be in class.

His face flushed with heat. Was this a prank? Some stupid gag his stepfather had planned with his drinking buddies? It wasn't outside the realm of possibility, but Peter couldn't imagine any scenario where it made sense. Darren Tomlinson didn't care enough to go to the trouble of organizing something like this. And he had to know Peter would call the cops. Darren hated cops.

So, if this was a prank, now was the time when someone would walk out of the house or from behind it and say "Ha ha, got you, you should see your face!"

Peter's finger hovered over his phone's screen. He waited, listening to the grass sway in the breeze, and the utter stillness of Woodhill. The whole damn neighborhood felt empty in that moment, he its only inhabitant, the lone soul stupid enough to come here of all places.

No laughter, no movement, and the bustle of Lexington on a Monday morning might as well have been a hundred miles away. He was alone, isolated, and the only person who knew he was here didn't give a shit about him.

Something moved a few feet ahead, trampling tufts of weeds as it journeyed toward the backyard fence in a zigzag path. Fast, too.

"Could be a cat or a rabbit…" He took a breath and grimaced at the taste of bile on his tongue. "Or *something*…"

The tip of a baby's head poked above the grass. Doll-like, with skin like porcelain, and two bright blue eyes. Their gaze met and the child's laughter broke the silence, startling Pete and yanking him back to reality.

Because *this* was really happening, whether he wanted to believe it or not.

The child gurgled words that might have been "Come and get me." He wasn't entirely sure, but those are the words that made the most sense to his ears.

"Hey, kiddo..." he began, but the child dipped below the grass line. An instant later, more weeds flattened under their tiny feet, scrabbling ahead to the rusty fence gate. Hinges whined as the gate pushed open and the kid trounced through.

No telling what was back there. The kid could get hurt.

Stunned, his every instinct screaming to call the cops and run, Peter followed after the child.

❦ ❦ ❦

The backyard was worse in ways Peter hadn't expected. The grass was just as tall, the weeds equally dense, but snaking through the growth was a series of thick, blackened roots. He nearly tripped over one as he passed through the gate. They had no discernible origin, spreading upward along the brick foundation in spidery patterns and out through the grass, charred in appearance but glistening with dew in the morning sun. Mowing over them would be a nightmare.

He frowned, annoyed by this new discovery, one more notch on Darren's belt. "Kid? Where'd you go?"

More rustling in the weeds ahead. He walked further into the yard until the child giggled again. "Giggle" was a loose term—the kid sounded phlegmy in their throat and what air came through their lungs gurgled jubilantly in the snot.

"Hide and seek," the kid choked out.

Peter shook his head. *I don't have time for these stupid games. Why the hell aren't you in school? Or daycare? Where the hell are your parents? What are you even* doing *here?*

A silly thought occurred to him as he waded through the swaying grass. Perhaps the kid sprouted from the earth like so many of these weeds. Maybe the foot he'd chopped up with the mower was just a part of the landscape, no different than these weird roots growing everywhere, springing to life with the season.

Yeah, but if that were true, why would the Wet Nurse need to kidnap and kill all those kids?

He had no answer, only a growing irritation with the situation at hand. Sure, he preferred playing games to indenturing himself to his stepfather, but at this hour on a Monday morning with the sleep still crusted to his eyelids, it was the last thing he wanted to do.

Peter pushed on, calling out for the child as he turned the

corner, and froze at the sight. The grass thinned here, browning as it diminished to a dusty patch of earth and a carpet of roots. Hundreds of blackened tendrils striped the barren landscape, arterial in appearance, an atlas of odd horticulture leading a crooked path back toward the house. He'd never seen anything like this before.

"All right," Peter said with a sigh. "Olly olly oxen free."

"Come and get me."

Less playful this time. Taunting, even. Disembodied and muffled.

Peter turned toward the house. The back door stood open, beckoning him to the dusty dark beyond. He detected a faint stench resonating from inside—something sour, rotten. Maybe a dead animal. He hoped that's all it was.

"No," Peter said. He'd cut the grass and trim the weeds, but there was no fucking way he'd step inside the Wet Nurse's house of horrors. Darren piped up in his head: *Thought you were a big man now, Pete? Ya turned eighteen and started talkin' the talk, but I ain't seen you walk that walk yet. You gonna be the pussy I always knew you were?*

He took a few steps over the patio, crushing the roots underfoot, and stopped when something squished beneath his shoe. Soft roots. Red sap. Lots of it. Tacky and stuck to the bottom of his sole.

"Gross..." He stepped over the remainder and stood on the house's threshold. "Kid, enough games. I'm not going in there to find you."

All the rumors about this place circled his mind, a hundred daring voices of hearsay spouting half-empty warnings: *I heard the place is cursed/haunted/possessed. They say she summoned a demon in the basement. They say she killed those kids to appease the Devil. God's in a lot of places, but he ain't there.*

Eighteen children of various ages over a span of ten months, taken from local parks, playgrounds, even a school parking lot. "Lexington's Lost Children," the media called them. Missing faces ranging in ages from two to twelve.

She didn't prey on older kids because she needed virgins for her sacrifices.

My sister told me they found kid parts all over the house.

I heard she bathed in their blood, Bathory-style. Fuckin' metal, man.

Peter's heart raced, a thin layer of sweat forming on his forehead and neck, but he couldn't let those stupid stories frighten him. He was an adult now, and while something horrible had happened here, he wasn't about to let it keep him from helping this kid.

Because this kid needed help even if they were a little brat.

Because, if he didn't, his inaction would haunt him for the rest of his life. The cards were already stacked against him, the universe already looking for another reason to ruin his day, and the last thing he wanted was karmic debt.

Something moved inside the house. Were those footsteps? The soft thump of tiny feet padding across carpet?

"Kiddo…listen, I'm done playing."

Another thump, heavier this time, followed by a rapid series of bangs somewhere in the dark. He sucked in his breath, listening, hoping—

The kid wailed in pain. Shrieked, really, between broken gasps for breath.

Oh no. Peter tapped the door the rest of the way open, allowing light to penetrate the void within. Linoleum flooring and dusty cabinetry decorated the sparse kitchen. Its appliances were gone, leaving empty gaps in their absence, and he thought it looked like one of the campus apartments he'd checked out at orientation. Another door stood open in the corner of the room—maybe a pantry, or the basement entrance.

The screams continued, nails dragged down a chalkboard, prodding the primal space in his brain that had evolved over millennia. An instinctive trigger spurring one to the aid of the young.

Peter took a breath and stepped over the threshold.

❦ ❦ ❦

The nameless child's screaming ceased within moments, cut off as quickly as a turned radio dial, leaving him alone with the patter of his racing heart. He waited in the empty kitchen for his eyes to adjust to the low light, listening, wanting to call out and afraid to do so. *Stupid,* he told himself. *What happened to playing hero?*

That was five seconds ago when the kid was still screaming. Maybe they'd tripped and hit their head. Multiple times based on the noise. He imagined the tyke lying sprawled on the floor, hands clasped over skinned knees, and a big shiner on their forehead. Hell, he'd probably scream too if that happened to him.

But the silence now unnerved him and set him adrift on a volatile tide without a rudder. Screaming meant he could follow the sound and find the kid, pick them up and carry them outside to safety—but now he was blind in the dark.

This is your yard, Darren whispered. *You had one goddamn job, Pete.*

Right now, Peter wanted nothing more than to be outside with the lawnmower, carving uneven strips into the grass. Anywhere but this carcass of a house. The urge to hightail it out of this place was great, but he knew himself, knew he'd suffer the Baptist guilt he'd been brainwashed into believing at a young age. That sort of trauma left a stain that never washed away. He wondered what sort of trauma this kid had suffered in their young life that might have led them here. The last thing he wanted was to contribute to that trauma—

Laughter again. Different this time. Deeper.

He licked his dry lips. Had the house been this warm when he first walked inside?

Finally, he spoke in the arid emptiness: "Hey, kid, are you all right?" A beat. "Hello?"

Scuttling in the wall further ahead. He walked across the tile to where the kitchen funneled into a hallway, leading toward what he imagined was the den at the front of the house. There were jagged holes torn out of the drywall. Puffs of mildewed insulation lay scattered on the floor.

Rats? Or had his earlier suspicions of copper thieves been accurate? Some of the holes were enormous, big enough for him to crawl through. Several strands of black roots had inched their way up the studs and poked through the gypsum in spots. What the hell kind of plant was this? He'd heard of kudzu and bamboo growing like this, but they didn't bleed sap like this. Blackish-red stains littered the wall around their protrusions.

Peter peered into one of the holes and recoiled. The stench was terrible, a rotten earthy smell lingering in his nostrils, but this was more robust than what he'd encountered on the threshold. This was pungent, sour, and brought to mind curdled milk.

Something pressed on the wall from the inside, made the drywall bulge and crack as it worked its way up toward the opening. He stepped back reflexively, expecting the head of a rat to emerge, but—

Oh god. No fucking way. A cold serpent cinched his gut, lungs, his whole damn body.

Fingers. Tiny, pale digits curled over the drywall. Muffled giggles bubbled up from within.

Hands. Coated in the root sap—or was it blood?

A head. Pallid skin stretched tight over a tiny skull crowning through the rip. One eye was missing. The other was a deep, rich blue marble that rolled in its socket, and when it finally focused on him Peter discovered the ability to breathe again. To scream again.

He flattened himself against the opposite wall, shrieking until his voice sizzled back into silence.

The wall-baby choked out laughter and forced its hand outward to reach for him. Then came another hand. And another. Four now. Two of them reached up and tore bits of drywall free to widen the opening. The child inched upward, revealing a neck riddled with blackened veins connected to a second head. Two eyes this time, both the same mesmerizing sapphire. Its lips twisted into a devious smile. Sap dribbled over its chin, bubbling as the thing spoke, *"Play with us."*

Peter didn't hesitate. He ran.

Back to the kitchen and the door—but it was sealed shut now, the black roots grown over the wood in a thick blanket. He'd have to cut his way through if he wanted out, but with what? He didn't have time to rummage through the cabinets and drawers, not with that *thing* breathing down his neck.

"Play with us, Peter."

He spun on his heels, ready to dart for the front door, but a shape barred his entry. His mind took precious seconds to process what he saw—segments of flesh, wet limbs and fingers twiddling in the air, a singular insectile body protruding from the hole in the wall like an earthworm called to the surface by rain.

Centipede, he thought. *Babipede. Baby-pede.*

The thing's eyes blinked independently, its mouths flapping erratically, filling the empty space with dissonant laughter. The sound raked nails down his back and drilled into his ears.

A stirring, ridiculous thought occurred to him: when his

stepfather arrived and found his body, Darren would be more pissed off that the yard wasn't finished *before* Peter was inconveniently murdered by a writhing mass of dead children. *Sorry, Darren, I didn't mean to let you down once again like I always do.*

The babipede's hands slapped against the wall as it pulled itself free of the opening. So many hands, one misshapen head after another, with flesh in various states of decay. He counted eighteen heads before the abomination ended in a tumorous mass of skin, legs, and feet.

Maybe the rumors were true, the Wet Nurse really was performing some kind of ritual down in the basement—

The basement!

There were windows along the surface, just big enough for him to crawl through.

"You live here with us now, Peter. It's your house, your yard."

The babipede scuttled forth into the kitchen, its top head grazing the ceiling, sloughing off a layer of skin and hair. *This house is a clown car*, he thought with grim amusement, but the levity was fleeting. One of the heads unhinged its jaw. Black tendrils emerged from the creature's maw, a thick network of gnarled roots piercing the air and growing longer by the second.

Something snapped in Peter's mind, a threadbare tether linking his perception of reality to the cold, nascent truth that things like this could even exist. Fear threatened to overtake his mind, the adrenaline in his system screeching to a halt, but he couldn't allow himself to be overcome. He had to try.

You ain't cut out for this, Darren whispered. *You should give up and join them.*

In his head or in the room, Peter couldn't tell anymore. If this thing really was in his head and speaking with his stepfather's voice, then it had underestimated him. He'd learned over the years to oppose anything Darren wanted him to do, every action in defiance of the man's willful ignorance, and he wasn't about to change now.

Peter made for the basement, pulling back the half-open door so hard it slammed into the wall. The babipede giggled playfully behind him, punctuated by the rapid thumping of its hands across the linoleum.

Darkness waited for him in its depths. This was the last place he wanted to go, but he steeled himself against the rampant terror holding him at bay, held his breath, and descended into the dark.

Dim banners of daylight pierced the basement gloom from twin windows, illuminating dust motes, esoteric graffiti, bloodstains, and a glistening pile of flesh. Or what he thought was flesh. In truth, he couldn't tell for sure—the massive tumor of skin, hair, and teeth was affixed to the wall by countless black roots. Its folds of tissue had overflowed the edges of an orange bucket in the corner of the room and overtaken the furnace and water heater. This cancerous mass had adhered to the house and was now its necrotic heart, beating silently in the dark long after its maker had been incarcerated.

Nictitating membranes unfolded from nodes of flesh within the mass, revealing cloudy blue eyes that lit up the dark. He looked at them and they looked back, and finally he understood the voice in his head wasn't his own, but belonged to this impossible thing living within the house.

We're hungry, Peter. Karen isn't here to feed us.

Karen Pendleton, the Woodhill Wet Nurse. Murderer of eighteen children in service to this thing growing in her basement. Was she the reason this thing existed? The stone walls and floor were painted in strange symbols, the sort of thing he'd only seen before in horror movies. Any other time he would've taken a closer look out of pure curiosity, but not now. Not with this thing's progeny on his heels.

Peter forced himself to look away, to ignore the wet sounds slapping down the stairs behind him, and focused on the window ahead of him. The tumor opened one of its mouths and spoke in a choked, guttural voice that drove icy spikes into his ears: *"Give...us...your...heart."*

He unlatched the window and pushed it open. Fresh air met his nostrils and he indulged in its sweetness. Freedom from this nightmare was within his reach, if he could just squeeze his way through—

Something wet latched onto his ankle and pulled.

The children giggled behind him. He jerked his leg forward, broke free of their grasp, and hoisted himself up to the window frame. Would his head fit? He didn't care—he'd make it fit if he had to.

"Play with us," the babipede cooed.

He felt fingers on his leg, pawing at his jeans. Pulling.

Think small, he told himself, and squeezed his head through the opening. The window was just wide enough for him to fit, but not quite as tall. He clenched his jaw and tried forcing himself through, grunting as the pressure at his temples began to scream with pain.

I'm not gonna fit, he thought, fending off a rising tide of panic.

You ain't never gonna fit, Darren whispered. *Not here, not anywhere.*

"Come on," he hissed, bracing his arms against the sides, struggling against the agony of scraped skin. Tears clouded his vision. "Just a little more...come on..."

Something moved in the grass ahead of him. Silent and slithering, a thick root inched its way toward the window, his face.

"No...please, no..."

Teeth bit into his calf. He screamed as something wrapped around his other leg and began to tug, wrenching his head free of the window. Peter held on as long as he could, screaming in defiance of the fate that awaited him, before he was finally silenced in the dark.

❦ ❦ ❦

"You gotta be fuckin' kiddin' me."

Darren Tomlinson parked along the curb and didn't even bother to kill the engine. He spat a wad of chewing tobacco, wiped brown spittle from his chin, and marched into the yard—which was *still* overgrown and *still* full of goddamn weeds. The Troy-Bilt lay on its side beside a pile of cut grass, rank with the odor of oil and gasoline.

"I told him it's his fuckin' yard. I know I did. Little shit cut 'n run on me…" He looked up at the house, expecting Peter to emerge with that smartass grin on his face, the look he *knew* Darren hated. "Shit-eating grin," Darren called it. The kid's bitch of a mother did the same thing earlier in their marriage but he'd beaten it out of her. "Looks like I'm gonna have to beat it out of you too, Peter. When I fuckin' find you…"

His stepson wasn't anywhere to be found, though. Darren was alone in the Woodhill stillness.

"Peter? You'd best get out here, boy."

Silence, and—wait, was that laughter? He'd recognize Peter's smug chuckle anywhere. It carried over the yard and took hold of his pride.

"You think this's fuckin' funny, kid?"

Something stirred in the grass near the fence gate. Peter's head poked above the surface. The same laughter followed. *Ha-ha*, that laughter said, *fuck you and your business, Darren. Mow it yourself.*

Darren cocked his jaw and grit his teeth. He would mow it himself, right after he finished beating the shit out of his stepson. He'd never laid a finger on the boy, but then he'd never been this red with anger, and there was a first time for everything.

"This is the last time," he growled. "I ain't playin' games with you, Peter. Come over here and take this like a man."

Peter blinked and kept on laughing. Had the kid's eyes always been so blue? Darren couldn't remember. He dipped below the grass once more.

"Come and get me, Darren."

"You bet yer ass, kid," he mumbled. "Gonna make you wish you'd never been born."

Darren set off in pursuit, and when Peter laughed again, the whole house joined him in chorus. It sounded like children on a playground.

❧ ❧ ❧

Todd Keisling is the two-time Bram Stoker Award®-nominated author of *Devil's Creek, Scanlines, Cold, Black & Infinite,* and most recently, *The Sundowner's Dance*, among several others. A pair of his earlier works were recipients of the University of Kentucky's Oswald Research & Creativity Prize for Creative Writing (2002 and 2005), and his second novel, *The Liminal Man*, was an Indie Book Award finalist in Horror & Suspense (2013). He lives in Pennsylvania with his family.

The Cartographer of Blades and Stars, Of Flesh and Agony

John Langan

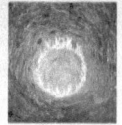

I

A TRIAL, Elway said, was hardly necessary. They found the guy's lair. They found his knives. They found the...souvenirs he took from their sisters. He chased Chris straight into the trap. This was their man. If they were going to keep their promise to their sisters, whose throats this guy had *slashed*, whose guts he had *cut* out of them, then they should kill their prisoner-they should *execute* him right away. In the yellow light of the battery-powered lanterns, which highlighted his sharp cheekbones and wide brow, he appeared far older than thirteen, as if the enormity of the situation had brought forth the man he would be in twenty, thirty years. The box of matches sat in the palm of his left hand like a coffin for one of the action figures none of them wanted to admit they still played with. RIP, Darth Vader, farewell Snake Eyes. The mixed odors of gasoline, motor oil, and kerosene clouded the air of the small room, turned the red cardboard box into the trigger to a bomb, the pin to a grenade.

Practically speaking, Hugh said, he didn't know how long

they could keep the guy in here. Until someone heard him. Or he figured out how to escape. Which sounded like Hugh agreeing with Elway, but might have been the opposite, because that was how it was with Hugh, even though his older sister, Patty, was the fourth victim of the figure the local newspapers named the Poughkeepsie Ripper following his third murder of a young black girl near the Hudson River, for the resemblance his crimes bore to those of his more famous English cousin, Jack. The same light that aged Elway subtracted years from Hugh's freckled face, making it appear as if he had stepped into the room expecting Mrs. Kidder's first grade class and found instead the heady reek of petroleum and the burden of an act he found heavier than anticipated.

They went through this already, Elway said. No one was gonna hear anything. This part of the hospital was underground. It was under the underground. Plus, the walls had been built thick, so the other patients couldn't hear the ones who were being treated here.

Sure, Hugh said, lowering his gaze the way he did whenever anyone challenged him. He was just saying, they didn't have all night. Plus, the guy might escape.

Practically speaking, to use Hugh's phrase, none of them believed the man they'd captured could climb out of his improvised cage, a round, tiled hole in the floor eight feet deep by six across, a wide mirror in the wall behind it. The tub resembled the jacuzzi on the back deck at Alex's house, except larger and with no steps down into it. There was a drain in the middle of the concave floor (currently blocked with a slurry of cement and a bag of the gravel reserved for Hugh's fish tanks), a quartet of sizable nozzles positioned equidistant from one another around the circumference of the hole, each three feet up. In the room further along the hall from this one, behind the pane of one-way glass that looked onto the tub, they had discovered a console studded with dials and switches whose labelled functions were worn away. Elway was of the opinion the two-room setup had been used for hydrotherapy, lowering patients into warm water to help their conditions, and while Hugh, Alex, and Chris weren't sure their friend was right, they also couldn't say with any authority he was wrong. Which was how it was with Elway, a lot of the time.

II

The psychiatric center was vast, enormous, a labyrinth of unlighted hallways dim to the point of darkness in the late May afternoons the four of them spent exploring it. Some halls were lined with patient rooms, their interiors bare and filthy; others opened to larger spaces, what might have been a lounge, its chairs and couches heaped against a door in one corner, a bigger room whose green linoleum floor was covered in metal cutlery, forks, spoons, and especially knives, bread knives and steak knives, spread wall to wall in what might have been a pattern or design or even weird letters—as Alex thought—or just random disorder—Elway's opinion. The beams of the flashlights they borrowed from their parents' workbenches and junk drawers picked out commonplace objects whose positions at the intersections of hallways and at the tops of stairways rendered them strange and unsettling: a blocky electric typewriter with a sheet of paper halfway up its roller, the paper covered with single-spaced rows of unbroken characters, a dense block of ink in which Alex once again fancied he could discern an under-lying order, and which Elway and Hugh dismissed as nonsense. (In this, as in most matters, Chris remained silent.) They found an old-fashioned vacuum cleaner guarding a room whose floor was heaped with manila folders spilling papers and large glossy photographs; the shifting shadows their lights produced caused the vacuum, with its cylindrical body, curved hose, and long wand to appear alive, an unfamiliar animal surprised in its lair. They jumped and screamed. Elway was the first to recover from his fright and mock the others for theirs, but Alex told him to shut the fuck up and the sudden vehemence of the curse checked Elway into silence; though he still tittered to himself.

In front of the doors to one of the service elevators, they discovered five large metal rakes, the ends of their handles balanced against one another to form a cone which Hugh sent crashing and jangling to the floor when he leaned in to investigate it. (He swore he hadn't touched anything. No one believed him.) The clattering racket raced away down the halls to either side of, behind them, announcing, Someone's here! Someone's here! Eyes wide and panicked, the four of them traded glances back and forth. If the Ripper was anywhere in the vicinity, Hugh had just broadcast their location to him. Alex wondered if that was the purpose of the rakes. Pulses thudding, they retraced the route they had taken through the hospital to the back door they wedged open, certain every distant thud or flutter they heard was the man who murdered their sisters drawing near, knife in hand. While his homicidal attention had focused thus far on girls, they had no doubt he would as swiftly butcher a group of thirteen-year-old boys who invaded his hiding place. They spilled out the back door into the fading sunlight and ran flat-out across the parking lot there into the evergreens opposite, crossing the asphalt in no time, their sneakers kicking up sprays of dead needles as they raced from the figure whose fingers each was sure he could feel grabbing the back of his shirt.

Of course, there was no one chasing them, no madly grinning man raising his knife to stab Hugh, the slowest of the group (though for the barest instant, Alex swore he saw a set of bared teeth hanging in the air, Cheshire-Cat like). But the discovery of the rakes—and for Alex, of the page protruding from the typewriter and the cutlery spread across the floor in stainless steel characters—solidified the conclusion of their observations and investigations, performed first singularly to distract from the awful silence of their sisters' deaths, then collectively when they returned to their respective high schools (Elway and Alex to Our Lady of Fatima; Hugh and Chris to Mark S. Coleman public) and met one another in the neighborhood after school: namely, that the Poughkeepsie Ripper was using the red-brick psychiatric hospital, closed for the last fifteen years following a decade of deeper and deeper budget cuts, as his base of operations, a possibility the local police considered after the second murder (of Elway's older sister, Yvette), only to dismiss on the heels of what would later turn out to be a cursory survey of the structure.

Had the cops done their due diligence, they would have discovered the rooms on the fourth floor where the Ripper conducted his early experiments, the carcasses of his first feline and canine victims opened and excavated, their organs placed around their stiff forms, dried chunks of meat and gristle, the same dissection to which the two women on the fifth floor had been subject, sufficiently long ago for their skin to have retracted to the underlying bone. Based on the clothing folded beside each doorway, faded denim miniskirts and baggy, sweat-stained white t-shirts laid on top of platform sneakers, Elway declared the women to have been prostitutes, which none of the rest of them felt competent to agree or argue with. The walls above the eyeless, noseless faces were scrawled with characters written in a flaky brown medium they thought was dried blood, Elway with certainty, the others with varying degrees of queasiness. None of them could decipher the message written on the walls' cracked tan paint in what appeared to be English until you leaned in to study it, the dead mouths below grinning up at you, and what had seemed to be words dissolved into so many unconnected lines. (Something about the stipples and streaks of blood, their placement in relation to one another, reminded Alex of the forks, spoons, and knives suggesting shining words he could intuit but not read.)

Confronted with such tableaux, surely the cops would have called for backup, would have flooded the hospital with every law enforcement officer available in this county and those surrounding, would have worked out how to return the lights to brightness. In one such well-lighted corridor on the seventh floor, a city of Poughkeepsie police officer, or maybe a Sheriff's deputy, would have entered the room to which the Ripper had brought his latest victim, on whom he had inflicted depredations a quantum leap beyond those visited on their sisters. Perhaps those men and women, professionals, would not have vomited at the sight and smell of a human body reduced to its constituent parts and then those parts rearranged into combinations baroque and terrible. It would have required hours, long hours, days, to separate with such delicacy flesh from muscle, muscle from bone, to sever ligaments, tendons, and cartilage, to part bone from bone, to cut and slice the organs from their internal moorings in order to arrange them at various distances from the brain lifted whole from the opened skull, itself removed from its perch atop the spinal column, and set on the floor a few degrees east of center. In the blood-streaked bones purposed for pyramids and cones on the emptied skin laid out like pieces of a Halloween costume, in the positioning of heart and kidneys, stomach and lungs around the room, in the intestines unwound and strung back and forth from the floor to one side of a large swirl of blood on the ceiling, would those officers of the law have perceived any meaning hovering nearby? Would they have sensed a connection to the cutlery's metal language, the typewriter's block of character?

(Alex did—or thought he did—his eyes still full of the tears squeezed from them by the convulsions of his stomach, it was difficult to keep anything in focus for long—but he had the impression this room's gory decoration was a three-dimensional version of the information he had apprehended on the floor below.)

Regardless of what significance they assigned the display, it would have sped the cops upward, all the way to the ninth floor, the former location of the psychiatric hospital's maximum-security ward, behind whose heavy doors had been confined those with afflictions which rendered them unsafe for the company of other patients, let alone, the general public. There, in the north wing, in a room third from the end on the east side of the hall, they would have reached the Ripper's lair, which might have appeared less dreadful were it not viewed in the wavering beams of four flashlights, making the seven tongues nailed to the wall opposite, each the fleshy point of a great, irregular star, the appearance of fluttering, as if trapped in their final agony. They would not have needed to compare notes afterward to identify what was laid out on the low wooden table beneath the star, the half-dozen slender knives of varying lengths, the trio of heavy cleavers, the serrated tool Elway said was a bone saw. Free of the ties of family, the police would not have heard (not imagined, but *heard*) the chorus of the victims' suffering, a collective scream that shrieked against the nerves like a bow scraping a violin's catgut strings. They would not have huddled together outside the room, hands pressed to their ears uselessly, the echo of their sisters' murders ringing within them. They would not have left the hospital floor stunned, as afraid they might confront the mutilated specter of one or all of their sisters (their wounded throats gaping to raw red muscle and bloody yellow cartilage, their torn bellies hanging open, loops of gray intestines thrown over their left shoulders like blood-streaked sashes) as that they might be discovered by the man whose knife cut them from this life.

Possibly the officers first to discover the evidence of not only the Ripper's further crimes, but of their extent and depravity, would have felt the same sense of injury at what they had witnessed, the memory of so much horror a wound in the mind, in the soul in which they were not sure they still believed but which hurt like an arm broken in a fall off a bike, a chin split open on the sidewalk, a bare foot transfixed by a rusty nail. Never had it occurred to Alex or to Elway, Hugh, or Chris, that simply knowing something could injure you; perhaps their time on the job would have made the cops wiser, toughened their minds and spirits.

(And what significance would the police have assigned the radical shift in both the methodology of the Ripper's latest crime and its location? Elway, who in the weeks since his sister's murder had dedicated himself to the study of serial killers with the single-minded dedication of someone studying for their SAT's, raiding the local library for whatever books they had on Jack the Ripper, Ed Gein, and the Zodiac killer, as well as for such novels as *Red Dragon* and *The Silence of the Lambs*, said that serial killers were about repetition and compulsion. They killed in the same or roughly the same way in the same or roughly the same type of location. The murders of their sisters appeared to bear this out: throats slashed, disemboweled, all in proximity to the Hudson. This latest victim, however, was a departure: dismembered, indoors, possibly in the air if you thought of the room as existing up off the ground. In this regard, she had more in common with the Ripper's earlier atrocities. For a moment, Elway wondered if they were dealing with a second killer, one perhaps working in tandem with the Ripper [which was the plot of a couple of the novels he read], but the rest of them rejected this explanation as overly complicated. While not as thorough as Elway, Alex had distracted himself from the murder of his older sister, Paula, the Ripper's third victim, with his own reading, the majority of it focused on the Ripper's most famous predecessor. Jack the Ripper's fifth murder, he said, took place inside in a more elaborate manner than any of those before her. Maybe this Ripper was just imitating the original. The simplicity of the explanation was persuasive; even Elway nodded. It was Hugh who pointed out that as far as anyone knew, Jack had stopped after Mary Kelly. Did this mean their Ripper had reached the end of his grisly spree?

(No, Chris said, and although he did not explain his answer, none of them doubted it.)

III

But it was neither police officers nor Sherrif's deputies who spent the afternoons after school venturing up the hospital's floors, long boxes of darkness stacked one on top of the other. Already, the cops had dismissed the report the boys had brought them of a set of fourth-floor rooms show-casing the Ripper's fledgling attempts at his bloody craft. The minute they recognized one of the four as brother to a murdered girl, which led to them identifying the remaining three as members of the same bleak fraternity, law enforce-ment stopped listening to them, wrote off the information they provided as an effort by grieving siblings to deal with the sudden and savage loss of their sisters, an attempt to manufacture control where there was none. Oh, they had investigated the psychiatric hospital thoroughly, the cops said. Yes, they knew the rooms the boys were talking about, and they had found nothing out of the ordinary in them. Which was when Alex knew they were being lied to, because there was no way anyone with even the slightest knowledge of serial killers could have beheld the cats and dogs cut open and dissected and judged the scenes anything less than a cause to call for backup and continue searching the premises. It was like every stupid movie the four of them had ever watched about a kid or group of kids doing their best to tell an adult—a parent, a teacher, the cops—something of great importance, a threat imminent or ongoing. No one believed those movie kids, which Alex, Elway, and Hugh agreed had always seemed the most unbelievable of situations. Surely someone would take the time to look into the information they had been provided. (Chris did not opine one way or the other.) But no, they were in the movie where the kids go missing next, and only later does one of the adults they appealed to remember the crazy story those kids related about the old psychiatric hospital and decide maybe the place is worth another look, after all. Most likely, because he speaks to the officers who were assigned to survey the building, and said adult learns it was never properly checked out in the first place. By this point in the story, it's unlikely any of the kids will be alive, but at least they'll have played their part in conveying the necessary info to the hero.

After they found the Ripper's first (they guessed) human victim, Hugh wanted to return to the cops, an urge Alex shared. Elway disagreed. Did any of them truly think the same people who had discounted and disregarded the evidence the boys had already provided them would treat new information any differently? Or would law enforcement write off this latest report as another therapeutic effort by the four of them to reckon with their sisters' deaths? Because as far as the cops were concerned, Elway said, no one except them was capable of investigating a crime, and four thirteen-year-old boys (especially ones who looked like *them*), were not going to bring the police the key to the biggest manhunt the mid-Hudson valley had ever seen. Yes, they knew that for a lie, but the cops didn't, and as long as law enforcement believed the lie, there was no use in presenting them with additional details. Hugh suggested borrowing a parent's camera and photographing their discoveries. Elway shook his head. Would whatever officer or deputy they handed the pictures to believe what the glossy rectangles showed, or would they pass them back with a warning about wasting valuable police time? And in the meantime, the Ripper would be out looking for his next victim.

(Nobody contemplated telling his parents for even the briefest moment. Their houses were containers of tense silence regularly shattered by overwhelming grief, their parents veering between desperate, strained efforts at normalcy and torrents of sorrow. Unable to imagine what consolation they might offer, the four of them spent as much time outside as possible, which seemed to suit their parents just fine and allowed them time to bike to the hospital grounds to explore it. None of their mothers and fathers expressed much concern about their son being outside the safety of their home. Alex suspected this was because everyone murdered by the Ripper had been a girl; though he didn't ask his parents if he was correct, for fear doing so would part the fog of their grief and prompt them to restrict him to his room.)

Privately, Alex thought Elway was overstating his case, but there was enough truth to the argument for him to go along with it. What Elway didn't say but Alex perceived wrapped within his friend's skepticism about the police was a desire for vengeance, an urge Alex shared, which they all shared. Revenge for their older sisters, distant, frequently mysterious figures who had moved in largely separate orbits from their younger brothers, but the horror of whose murders: throats cut ear to ear with enough force to half-decapitate them, abdomens slashed open and intestines hauled out and flung over their left shoulders, tongues taken —had spurred in those same brothers, friends from their shared neighborhood and grade school, a desire to see the killer punished. And for revenge for themselves, too, for everything they had been forced to experience, endure, for the places within them scorched bare by the Ripper's acts. Already, they conducted their search of the hospital armed with steak knives, a machete, and a container of pepper spray they had taken from their households, but these items were purely defensive in intention, means by which they might escape the Ripper's grasp should he lunge from an open doorway and seize one of them. Alex imagined himself and his friends as exploring a jungle through whose green depths a tiger padded. After they encountered the mummified remains of (they guessed) the Ripper's first victim and the much fresher remains of (they hoped) his newest, the need for a plan, for a trap, swung into focus. As much of their time as they spent exploring the farther reaches of the hospital, where they found little indication of the Ripper's presence, they devoted to brainstorming a means for his capture and execution. Because it was apparent that were they to succeed in imprisoning him, they could not risk allowing him to live. For that reason, locking him inside his lair and leaving him to starve was, in addition to its host of other problems, too uncertain, too inconclusive. Who could say but that he might have a means to escape his room? No, something of a more definitive nature was required.

Chris was the one who showed them the room with the tiled hole in its floor, located midway down a sub-basement corridor on the north wing. How he had come across it, he did not say, only shrugging in response to the others' questions. None of them was supposed to enter the psychiatric hospital alone: from the start, they had agreed on this. No matter it was only the four of them, there was safety in numbers. Their concern with the friend's recklessness was overshadowed by the possibility they saw in his find. Here was a place to hold the Ripper, to contain him so he could be killed. Elway and Hugh batted possibilities back and forth. They could set up punji stakes on the bottom of the tub and when the Ripper fell into it, he would be skewered. They could shoot him with bows and arrows. (Guns were preferrable, but with the exception of Elway, none of their parents owned firearms, and Elway's dad kept his .45 in a gun safe whose combination Elway had been unable to crack.) Alex was the one who hit on the eventual solution:

They could burn him, he said. Fill the pit with gasoline and torch the bastard.

Silence greeted his idea, followed by a hubbub of all of them speaking at once. Hugh's dad kept a couple of huge plastic containers of gas in the garage for the riding mower in the summer and the snowblower in the winter. Everyone's parents had gas for the mower in the garage; lighter fluid, too, for summer barbecues. Hugh's dad also had big cans of kerosene he used to fuel the heater that warmed his workshop in the winter. Elway's dad had stored tins of paint cleaner, as did Chris's. Their houses were well-stocked with alcohol, both what bottles stood in the liquor cabinets previously, and the new ones that had swelled their ranks in the last several weeks. Alex's mom, always anxious about injury, maintained a trio of brown bottles of isopropyl alcohol under the bathroom sink. They would need to find a way to block the drain, which didn't seem as if it would be too difficult, and they would have to sneak the gasoline and other flammable substances from their homes, which didn't strike them as much more of a challenge. Sleepovers, they suspected and then confirmed, offered cover for all manner of activities, including that which most concerned them, namely, discovering and tracing the Ripper's movements into and out of the hospital. They assumed he came and went by night, which was why they limited their explorations to daylight, but this left a large block of time to account for.

IV

To their collective surprise, they observed the man they would identify as the Poughkeepsie Ripper on only their third night of surveillance. At two thirty in the morning, while the others were wrapped in their unzipped sleeping bags, dozing, Hugh spotted him walking across the north parking lot, heading towards the psychiatric hospital from, they would later learn, the VFW through the woods on that side of the property, where he parked his sand-colored Ford Taurus, the kind of Dad car, Elway said, the cops wouldn't look at twice. In this regard, the vehicle was the same as its driver, a tall, heavyset white man whose crew cut exposed the dent traversing the right side of his skull from front to back. His gray coveralls were the type of uniform a custodian might wear, which, they hypothesized, was the identity he would offer anyone who met him on his way into or out of the building, as someone employed to keep an eye on the old place. Maybe he really was the janitor, Hugh said. If so, why was he showing up in the middle of the night? Elway asked. Graveyard shift was midnight to eight; everyone knew that. (Alex wasn't sure he did, but Elway sounded convincing, so he went along with him.) Regardless of what hours graveyard shift was or wasn't, the man reappeared as dawn was lightening the sky overhead, which the four of them agreed seemed too short a time for a regular work schedule. Still, there was the possibility they would not see the man in the coveralls, who entered and exited the hospital as if he had every right to do so, a second time, until they did, and a third time, and a fourth, always at the same approximate point in the night, always dressed in the same gray uniform. If the arrangement of rakes Hugh knocked down (he hadn't touched them, he said) was a warning device of some kind, the man did not appear overly concerned at its having been tripped.

During the day, the four of them stumbled through the hallways of their respective high schools, sleepwalkers moving through dreams of normalcy. To the concerned and occasionally irritated teachers and guidance counselors who spoke to them about the precipitous fall in the quality of their schoolwork, their lack of participation in their classes, they said they were not sleeping, a statement of truth whose significance the adults interpreted in a way that forestalled additional questions. They slept when they could on the bus ride to school, once they returned home in the afternoon, for an hour after dinner. To the extent their collective parents noticed the change in their sons' behavior, they attributed it to the same grief constricting them, from whose coils none of them could work out how to extricate themselves, let alone, their surviving children.

In the meantime, four of those children continued to spend the last hours of daylight transporting whatever flammable liquids they could lay their hands on from their respective houses to the room in the psychiatric hospital they were calling the Trap, where they stored the assorted bottles and cans in rows against the walls to either side of the door. Now, entering the building through whose shadowed halls the Ripper had been moving less than half a day before, they fancied they could feel the echo of his monstrous presence in the air surrounding them, a descending note still troubling the ear. On several occasions, a distant crash froze them where they were and set them listening for further noise, for a sign the Ripper had returned while they were at school and after waiting to ensure they were in place was moving to spring his own trap. The darkness in the hallway seemed to corroborate their fears, condensing to suggest a bulky figure standing at one end of the hallway, at the top of the stairs to the first floor, in a doorway they passed on the way to the back door. They were sleep-deprived, Elway said, which rendered them susceptible to hallucination; it was important for them to remember this and not freak out at every little thing. If they were seeing things, Hugh asked, how would they know if the Ripper actually showed up? The question was one Alex would not have considered, but which struck him as relevant and pressing. They would know, Elway said. But how? Hugh said.

When he cuts your Goddamned throat, Elway said, bringing a halt to the conversation, if not the underlying concern.

V

Never their friend, time bullied them, passing with such speed it seemed there were barely hours enough to complete each day's tasks. They maneuvered a quartet of large red plastic containers whose sloshing contents smelled of gasoline and something else, a not unpleasant odor like laundry detergent, from the shed in Chris's backyard, through the woods behind, to the road on the other side, down that road to the bigger one it joined (all the while waiting for a passing car—a passing police car—to slow beside them in order for its driver to ask what exactly the four of them were doing), to the psychiatric hospital's parking lot, across that expanse of asphalt to the ground floor door, down the metal stairs first to the basement, then on to the sub-basement, along one corridor to another, to the Trap, where they THUNKed the heavy containers down beside the bottles and jugs next to the door, their arms and legs quivering from the effort, their lower backs spasming, their shoulders burning—and the hands on Hugh's wristwatch had leapt ahead to the point there were barely enough minutes remaining for them to make it back to their respective homes in time for whatever their parents were passing off as that night's dinner.

Time had escalated from bully to assailant three nights ago, when Hugh roused them from light slumber to watch the Ripper drive his plain car across the hospital parking lot, park it beside the ground floor door both he and they used, and retrieve what looked like a rolled-up carpet from the Taurus's trunk. He hefted the carpet over one brawny shoulder and carried it through the doorway. While Alex was still trying to figure out what need the man could have for a carpet, Elway was saying, It's another one, holy shit, there's a girl wrapped in that, holy shit, his words and the recognition they brought about the shape of the bundle over the man's shoulder spilling a pitcher of ice water down Alex's spine, bringing him fully awake. Any secret doubt he harbored about this man actually being the Poughkeepsie Ripper vanished. Hugh joined in the chorus of holy shits, adding, they had to do something, what were they gonna do, they had to do something, what were they gonna do, they couldn't just sit there, they had to do something, his voice gaining in pitch and volume as statement became question became statement. Hugh was right, Alex said, they had to do something. He bent to retrieve the butcher knife from its place on the ground beside him. That was what he was saying, Hugh said, lifting a heavy stick to supplement his container of pepper spray. Elway's machete was in hand, and Alex could feel something gathering around them, a kind of mania or fury, a berserker rage to chase down the Ripper, charge him and hurl themselves on him, embrace injury unto death as long as they hurt him, as long as one of them dealt him a fatal blow, jammed their knife in his heart, sank their machete into the side of his great white head. When Chris rose to his feet, pushed to the front of the group, they assumed he was moving to lead the attack, a role none of them begrudged him, as his sister, Cathy, had been first of the Ripper's (latest) murders. He turned to face them, hands held up palms-out. He was wearing the stupid Living Colour t-shirt his dad had given him three birthdays ago and that still hung on him too big. For an instant, Alex was certain his friend was going to deliver a speech, which under the circumstances of their previous lives would have been an astonishing event, and despite everything was still noteworthy, an indicator of the heightened nature of their situation. His oldest friend, whose daily production of words, let alone sentences, numbered in the twenties, was on the verge of rallying them to bloody action.

But Chris did nothing of the kind. Instead, he shook his head from side to side. They were too late, he said. She's dead. He remained in position as the rest of them asked what he meant, how was it too late, how did he know? Hugh, rarely confrontational, stalked up to Chris and demanded his friend tell him what he was saying, twirling the stick in his right hand as if weighing whether to use it on Chris, knock him down. Chris repeated his statement: she's dead. Alex thought he grasped the meaning of Chris's declaration, but he did not want to look at what he was holding, what awful fact writhed in his hand. What did he mean? Hugh repeated. They had to *do* something. What was Chris saying? Elway was the one who spelled it out. With a deep sigh, a sigh as deep as the Grand Canyon, he said that the Ripper either had killed the girl already or was about to. Even if she was still alive, the moment the Ripper heard the four of them barreling toward them, the edge of his blade would find the skin of her throat. He punctuated his statement with a, *Fuck* whose utter weariness dispersed the fury Alex had felt swirling around them. Hugh protested, but the force drained from his nos and no ways while he was pronouncing them. He dropped his stick and put his hand to his forehead like an actor in an old movie signaling he was overwhelmed. He sank at Chris's feet, his *fuck* echoing Elway's. Chris leaned over and touched the top of Hugh's head, as near to a gesture of compassion as any of them had witnessed from him.

It was like, Alex thought, they were trapped between the clicks of the second hand on the clock in his parents' kitchen. Whoever was captured in the carpet was alive and not alive, existing within a death that already embraced her, that contained the four of them, too, a slice of darkness towering to the night sky, immanent with her murder. This was different from their sisters' deaths, which were thick walls separating now from then, after from before. It was ongoing, suffocating, unbearable. Alex had not joined the others in sitting, had not returned his knife to its spot. He started walking toward the parking lot.

Of course, Elway and Hugh stopped him, leaping to their feet to grab one of his arms. A part of him had known they would. What was he doing? they asked. Where was he going? Alex pushed against them with sufficient force to prompt Chris to join their effort. What, Elway said, what was going on? Come on, they said, come on. Alex, man, come on. He did not stop struggling against them, could not stop trying to break free of their collective grip, to leave the stand of trees from which they surveilled the Ripper, cross to the psychiatric hospital, and enter it to force the confrontation he had been on the verge of moments ago. Yes, it was death to do so. He was neither naive nor stupid enough to think he would be able to slay the minotaur in its maze. It would be something, though, a way out of this sensation of in-between coagulating around him like amber solidifying into a sixty-five-million-year prison for the mosquito struggling within it. Did he say anything, respond to his friends' entreaties? If he did, it was this side of nonsense: I can't, I'm stuck, no, no.

Elway was the one who found the words to release Alex from his compulsion forward. Two days, he said. They would spring their trap on the Ripper the night after tomorrow. Two more days to prepare, to make sure everything was ready, and then they would catch the guy. Catch him and kill —*execute* him. Could Alex give them two days? They were close, Elway said, so close. Everything was almost ready. But this was a four-man operation. It couldn't succeed without him. What did he say? Could he hang in for another forty-eight hours? Two days, and they would barbecue the fucker. They would incinerate the guy.

Strength drained from Alex's legs and arms. He slumped to his right, almost carrying Hugh from his feet. Okay, he said to Elway, to himself, two days. Okay.

Two days, they agreed, bringing the *soon* that had described the climax of their plan into focus. Two days left to smuggle whatever flammable liquids they could from their houses. Two days for one last check that the Trap was sound-proof, two of them standing inside the room with the door shut, screaming at the tops of their lungs, while the remaining pair stood down the corridor, listening for any hint of noise. Two days, yes, for the Ripper to take another girl, but they were gambling his most recent victim would have (temporarily) sated his savage urges.

VI

The day after tomorrow, however, became the day after

that. The Ripper appeared early and stayed late the following night, exiting the building as dawn was coloring the world, walking with the jaunty step of a man who had received news of a particularly gratifying stripe. Looking at the expression of unalloyed pleasure, of bliss on the man's broad face, Alex felt hatred bright and focused as a laser burn through him, and even with the exhaustion weighting him physically and mentally, he struggled to resist the urge to run at the man. Perhaps aware of his friend's urge, perhaps sharing it, Elway stood next to him, his presence the embodiment of his pledge, *soon*. But soon had to stretch to encompass twenty-four more hours, after the next night passed without sign of the Ripper. None of them could understand his absence. If he was to subject his latest victim to the same level and degree of dissection as her immediate predecessor, he would require more time, wouldn't he? They had no idea how long was required to slice and cut a human body into its constituent parts, nor could they think how they might obtain such information, whom they might reasonably ask. (Hugh's mom was a nurse in the ER at Vassar, and was forever volunteering all manner of medical trivia to her children and their friends, but not now, not when she responded to even her son's simplest questions with a gaze made wide and glassy by the pills she was swallowing to subdue her grief.) Could the guy have died? they wondered. Could a heart attack or a stroke, or a car accident have beat them to their collective punch? The possibility filled them with a mixture of relief and anger: the first, because maybe their plan wouldn't have succeeded, they wouldn't have trapped him, they wouldn't have brought themselves to go through with the execution; the second, because the plan absolutely would have succeeded, and they wanted to stand there while fire enveloped the monster who murdered their sisters, wrecked their families, they wanted to listen to him howl as the flames charred his skin, burst his eyeballs, and roasted the tongue in his mouth. To be denied that suffering, to be cheated from witnessing it on behalf of their sisters by a rogue piece of plaque come loose in the bloodstream, was almost too much to consider.

How happy were they, then, how delighted when Elway woke them the night after that with the whispered announcement that he was here, the Ripper was alive and *there he was* striding across the hospital parking lot, apparently eager to return to his lair, how did their hearts leap the way they had on childhood Christmas mornings at this evil gift? Perhaps the man had not intended to be away the previous night. Especially as the four of them had debated taking the night off to stay home, a discussion that had almost tipped in favor of making up their deficit of sleep, the Ripper's arrival sent a wave of satisfaction through them for not abandoning their post, as well as an undercurrent of fear at how close they had drawn to losing this opportunity.

The instant the man pulled the door shut behind them, Hugh started his stopwatch. Ten minutes would be enough, they estimated, for the Ripper to proceed far enough into the building not to hear them entering behind him. While the second hand made its smooth circuit of the watch's face, they switched into the clothes they had selected and packed for the task: long-sleeved black t-shirts and black sweatpants, black socks and sneakers, black gloves, black bandanas worn bandit-style over their noses and mouths. By the time they were changed, the stopwatch was as nine minutes and twenty-five seconds, which they judged close enough for them to leave the safety of the trees and sprint down the lawn bordering the evergreens, running low to the parking lot, where they slowed to something closer to a jog in an effort to minimize the slap of their sneakers on the blacktop, to the back door, which they were afraid would be stuck, jammed closed by the Ripper's strength, but which opened readily and with little noise. Inside, they paused to allow their eyes to adjust to the darkness and to listen for any sound of the man nearby. All they heard was their quickened breathing, which they were trying to bring under control. Hugh had the flashlights in the knapsack he was carrying. He switched his on and, keeping the beam aimed at the floor, held open the bag for the others to retrieve theirs. Lights directed at their feet, they descended the stairs to the basement, then the floor below that, where they proceeded along a darkened corridor that went on farther than Alex remembered, until he was on the verge of asking if they were going the right way, when another corridor branched off in front of them, and although that passage also felt longer than he recalled, there was the door to the Trap on the left.

Across the room's threshold, Chris withdrew from the duffel bag slung over his shoulder a trio of battery powered lanterns he clicked on and passed to Hugh and Alexs, who set them around the room, filling it with yellow light. The door swung closed behind them. They had blocked the drain to the enormous tub the previous week with a soupy mix of cement and aquarium gravel; now, Elway lifted a soda bottle full of gasoline, unscrewed the cap, and emptied it into the tub in a wavering stream. The liquid ran to the drain and pooled around it. Although they had tested it continuously, Alex was suddenly certain their improvised plug was going to fail. Apparently, Hugh shared his anxiety: he began counting one Mississippi, two Mississippi, Elway joining in with three Mississippi, and Alex with four. When they reached ten Mississippi and the puddle of gasoline was undiminished, Alex removed the cap from a metal can of kerosene and spilled its contents over the tub's rim. Before he was finished, Hugh joined him, as did Chris, Elway starting a second bottle. Gasoline and kerosene bubbled and chugged out of their bottles and jugs; liquor gurgled as it exited the long necks of its glass bottles; oil poured like syrup from its plastic containers. They upended palm-sized bottles of nail-polish remover, tall brown bottles of rubbing alcohol, metal tins of paint thinner. The liquids splashed together in the bottom of the tub, in some cases blending into a cloudy medium, in others gathering into ovoid pockets that floated through the surrounding mix. Their eyes stung and watered. The tub filled slowly, as Elway, who was best at math, had warned it would, and by the time the only receptacles remaining were the large red ones they had carried from Chris's house, the contents were at best a third of the way up its circumference. Chris gestured for Hugh to help him with one of the big containers, which they carried to the edge of the tub and tipped out, sending its greenish contents arcing into the blend. Elway and Alex did the same with a second red container. The distinct, laundry-detergent infused odor of the liquid rose through the petroleum fog rolling out of the tub. Elway looked at Chris and asked if this was what he thought it was. Chris nodded, but did not answer when Hugh asked what it was. Elway told Hugh he would find out soon enough. Hugh asked Alex if he knew what they had added to the tub, but Alex shook his head. Hugh went to open one of the pair of remaining containers, but Chris held up his hand to stop him. With a shrug, Hugh switched to gathering the discarded bottles, jugs, cans, tins, and other containers and returning them to either side of the door. Alex and Elway helped him. Chris positioned the final red containers beside the tub's rim, popped open the vents, and left them there.

VII

The moment had arrived to decide who was going to lead

the Ripper from his lair, down the stairs, along the psychiatric hospital's dark corridors and across its large unlighted rooms, down still more stairs, and along more corridors to the room where their Trap lay ready and waiting for him. Simultaneously terrified of the role and wanting it more than he had ever wanted anything, Alex had prepared and rehearsed what he thought was a pretty decent speech laying out his argument to be the bait. Based on their throat clearing and foot shuffling, it seemed Elway and Hugh had readied similar speeches. Perhaps, due to the lateness of the hour, or the vast deficit of sleep they had accrued, or the chemicals clouding the air, it took what felt like a long time to register that Chris was no longer in the room, the door slowly closing behind him.

VIII

No sense in running after him. This was, after all, the plan: find the Ripper and allow him to chase you, keeping close enough for him to believe he had a chance of catching you, but far enough ahead for his belief not to become reality. Over short distances, Alex could outrun the rest of them with minimal effort. Hugh was next-fastest, in a handful of impromptu races almost beating Alex, but his speed held for at best ten or fifteen yards before dropping away precipitously. From the way Elway talked about himself, you would have thought he was an Olympic hopeful, until you saw him run, a flurry of elbows and knees that bore only the slightest resemblance to running. While not able to match Alex or Hugh at sprinting, over distances of any length, Chris was relentless, possessed of a stamina whose limits had yet to be discovered. During the final field day of grade school, he had almost lapped the other kids competing in the eight circuits of the high school track the teachers called a junior marathon. (Following that performance, Coleman's cross-country coach had personally scouted Chris for the team.) Assuming he could avoid the Ripper grabbing him right away, Chris had a real chance, probably the best chance, of leading the man here, which meant the rest of them had to be ready.

Elway had reached this same conclusion and was extracting the coil of nylon rope from his backpack. (It was his dad's, from when he had become infatuated with the idea of rock climbing a couple of years ago and crossed the river to the climbing store on Huguenot's Main Street, from which he had come home laden with shoes, gloves, harnesses, clips, and rope, hundreds of meters—he insisted on the metric—of rope. Upon her return from work, Elway's mom had put a swift stop to her husband's plans to, as she put it, play Spider-Man, and while her husband had given in to her and returned his purchases, he had held on to the bright yellow rope, arguing the prudence of having good rope on hand, an assertion Elway's mom was not willing to contest. His dad hung the rope on one of the long nails at the back of the garage, where it remained for Elway to take.)

The next part of the plan required two of them to serve as anchors for the length of rope Elway had cut from his father's hundred-meter coil. This would be stretched across the doorway shin-high, a foot or so off the floor. It was a strategy sprung from a movie, worthy of one of the *Home Alone* films, but without it, the Ripper might be able to save himself from tumbling into the tub. Having the rope in place was a hedge against this, but it was also a hazard for whoever was running in front of the Ripper. Forget the rope, and you would find yourself splashing into the tub's contents, the Ripper crashing down on top of you. Although no one had been assigned the roles, Alex had assumed Chris, the tallest of them, would secure one end of the line, but with him off in search of the Ripper, and Elway too small and slight to function as a paperweight, let alone, help brace a rope against the running stride of a big man, he and Hugh were by default the choices. Elway belted one end of the rope around Hugh's waist, tied it tight with a bow knot, then circled it about him another four times before moving to Alex, on whom he repeated the process. Nobody spoke. They were listening, Hugh and Alex staring at the ceiling as if doing so might sharpen their hearing. There was nothing definite enough to be identified, no distant hint of Chris's sneakers pounding up a hallway or clattering down a flight of stairs. Elway opened the door as far as it would go and propped it by jamming a folded piece of paper he extracted from his back pocket under it. (Alex, who had not thought of this detail, was pierced by an unexpected bolt of love for his friend so fierce it almost brought tears to his eyes.) Elway waved Alex and Hugh to their positions on either side of the entrance. The two of them side-stepped away from one other until the length of rope connecting them was taut, then lowered to sitting, shifting to maintain the rope's tension. Alex looked at the tiles overhead and wondered if he had noticed them previously. He must have, he thought. Hugh glanced at the rows of emptied containers ranged along the wall to his right. Elway had removed the box of matches from his backpack and slid it open to check the wooden contents.

Each assumed the others were running through the same questions: how long would it take Chris to reach them? What if the Ripper refused to pursue him? What if the Ripper caught him? At what point would they know their friend wasn't coming? The possibility their trap could fail was one they had acknowledged from the start, but in an off-hand manner, an admission made to the powers-that-be in order not to jinx the project. Their plan would succeed because it couldn't not succeed; it had to work because they had discovered the Ripper's lair and his identity, and such information had to lead somewhere, had to have a result, a consequence. Chris showing them the tub, Alex's idea to fill it with gas, even the rope to trip the man, had joined together to form a mechanism the neatness of whose design was the strongest argument for its effectiveness. Sitting trying to detect a hint of Chris's approach, it occurred to each of them that the powers-that-be might not have been propitiated by their confession of the plan's possible failure, that those forces of luck or justice could have decided this trap would not be sprung, the Ripper not be caught and set alight. They suddenly saw themselves as vain and stupid; the confidence they had in their design quivered like Jello removed from the mold too soon and threatening to slide out of its shape into a gelatinous mass.

A crash, faint but distinct, startled them. Hearts pounding, they exchanged glances, Alex and Hugh scooting away from one another to stretch the rope tight as they could. The echo seemed to last forever, as if every last corner of the hospital were having a turn at it. Before it faded entirely, there was a boom, closer, which Elway identified as a door being thrown open—or slammed shut. The three of them tensed like sprinters in the blocks, anticipating the starter pistol. Alex's head was pounding, his stomach threatening to return his dinner. After all this time waiting, the moment was here, barreling at them at a hundred miles an hour, at the speed of sound, of the rapid beat of Chris's Jordans on the floor dopplering toward them, another rhythm, lower, heavier, like someone running in heavy boots, overlapping it. He's coming, they thought, the Ripper is coming. The volume of the chase grew louder still, filling the hallway outside the door.

IX

Chris caught the edge of the doorframe and used it to swing himself into the room and over the rope with almost no loss of speed. Close behind, frighteningly close, the Ripper lunged for him, his momentum slamming him into the doorway. Chris's leap landed him one running step from the tub's lip, which he took and used to launch into a second jump over the hole gaping before him. Focused entirely on Chris, the Ripper pushed off the doorframe and caught his right leg on the rope, the impact jolting Alex and Hugh and yanking them across the floor toward one another, Alex tipping on his side, Hugh tilting but remaining upright. Chris cleared the tub with ease, but landed on the opposite side moving too fast, his momentum carrying him into the wall, which he thudded against and dropped from his feet. The Ripper went from run to hop, lifting his leg out of the rope restraining it but his stride interrupted, unbalanced, unable to stop himself, to avoid the open pit in front of him. At the last instant, one foot on the lip of the tub, the other hanging in the air, he threw his arms out to either side, pinwheeling them as if the motion might free him from the fall already grasping at him. Perhaps his efforts might have kept the man from the Trap, but with a scream, Elway ran into him, driving his bony shoulder into the man's lower back, the impact enough to send the Ripper toppling forward out of view. There was a mighty splash, followed by more splashing, sputtering and spitting, and the smack of the tub's mixture against its tiled sides.

X

Time did not stop. Shaking his head, Chris pushed to his

feet and circled the tub to where he had left the remaining pair of big red containers. Elway crab-crawled back from the edge of the tub; Alex and Hugh stood and helped Elway up. While Elway removed his Swiss army knife from his pants pocket and unfolded its blade, Chris thumped first one and then the other of the blocky plastic jugs on their sides, their contents chugging out into the tub. Alex was aware of a shuddering in the air, as if the room were vibrating, the vast towering moment in which he has felt them stuck on the verge of breaking open, admitting them to a space new and undefined, a vast dark plane. Elway gripped the rope conjoining Hugh to Alex and sliced it. They unwound the rope wrapped around them and when they reached the last knotted loops Elway cut them off. Chris stood beside the red containers watching the last of the liquid pour out in wavering streams that glowed like lines of green fire in the lantern light. Aside from the gurgle of the mystery fluid into the tub, the room was quiet, no further noise of the Ripper floundering in the Trap. Unexpected and sweet as soda, hope surged in Alex. Could the Ripper be dead, killed by his fall? The tub wasn't very deep, but plenty of kids in his class had broken arms and in one case a leg from drops of lesser height. It was not too much of a stretch to imagine the Ripper striking the tiled wall at such an angle as to snap his neck. Which would mean they were done, their plan a success, not in exactly the way they had expected, but did that matter if the result was the same, the Ripper's brutality brought to a halt? Together with Hugh and Elway, Alex approached the edge of the tub.

The white man they saw lying with his head and shoulders propped against the wall, his eyes open and staring, his face and head shining with the Vaseline glaze of whatever Chris had emptied onto him, the top of his coveralls saturated with the same mixture, the rest of his bulk submerged in the tub's contents swirling around him, was motionless.

Amidst the shadows at the bottom of the Trap, it was difficult to see whether his chest was moving. When the man's eyes slid toward them, it was like watching a machine activate, some cutting-edge special effect. Although his eyes must have been in agony from the chemicals slicking them, he did not blink. His mouth opened, the tip of a tongue like a pink fleshy tentacle emerging to drag over his lips. Gaze never leaving them, he spoke, and his voice, bland but not unpleasant, seemed to issue from the corners of the room, to ring on the ranks of glass and plastic bottles.

C_8H_{18}, he said, C_6H_6. C_8H_8. He smacked his lips. **Very good. It won't be enough.** With a grunt, he attempted to prop himself to sitting, only to collapse immediately, pain contorting his broad face, the tub's contents sloshing. The terror his movement had roused in Alex likewise collapsed, leaving in its place satisfaction sharp and cruel.

What was that? Elway said.

Features still twisted in agony, the Ripper struggled to lift his right arm out of the tub's contents, the limb shaking with the effort. Shouting with frustration, he let his arm fall.

It was his collar bone, Hugh said. He must have broken it.

Elway nodded. During his attack on the Ripper, he had dropped the box of matches next to his backpack. He walked over to the matches, crouched, and picked them up. Mouth unexpectedly dry, Alex swallowed as his friend, a headsman with his axe, resumed his position at the edge of the tub.

Whatever Elway was on the verge of saying, whether he had been preparing something from the moment they settled on lighting the Ripper on fire or had been inspired when his fingers touched the cardboard matchbox, whether the words were hot and angry or cold and cruel, whatever utterance would precede him striking the match whose flame would transform the interior of the tub into a preview of what they hoped and expected was awaiting the Ripper in Hell, went unsaid, as before he could open his mouth, Hugh asked if they needed to put the guy on trial.

XI

Such debate as there was about Hugh's question, which Hugh himself backed away from after voicing it, as if he was merely playing Devil's Advocate, a role he tended to step into in the interest of ensuring the subject up for discussion received full consideration (he said; although Alex suspected assuming the position allowed Hugh the saving illusion he was not truly party to any decision with which he did not agree) was cut short by the Ripper's voice.

There is a ship, it said, stilling their half-argument. **Beyond the coordinates where Neptune and Pluto will trade places. Past Pluto's siblings, floating in the distant light of the Sun like misshapen children banished to the edges of its domain. Farther than the great cloud of comets tumbling through emptiness like honeybees on a hot summer afternoon. There is a ship. It is vast, its length measured in light years. A dozen Earths could fit within it and their inhabitants never have knowledge of one another. If you could see it in its totality, if such an impossibility were not, you would be reminded of a mass of worms writhing over one another, as if making a pilgrimage from one pile of rot to another. From the same impossible perspective, you would see it is a red so dark as to approach black. It is ancient, the ridges and grooves of its hull pitted with the impacts of ten billion years of meteor and asteroid strikes, studded with the remains of worlds that have broken apart on it. Rumor says its construction was overseen by a god who was driven insane by the task. Another rumor says it was built in the universe before this one to survive the great catastrophe**

that birthed this cosmos, which it did, though not undamaged. It is said to bore through space and time. Certainly, the ship does not sit entirely in this plane. There are openings in it, apertures through which beings pass, some not dissimilar to you, some so different the neurons in your brains would combust trying to apprehend them. The ship is preparing for a great journey. For as long as anyone can remember, for farther back than records extend, this has been the case. No one knows its ultimate destination. Some say one of the other dimensions it touches. Some say the void that lies beyond all space.

Why was he telling them this shit? Elway said. Did he not understand what was about to happen to him?

He might have a concussion, Hugh said.

How did the man know about this ship? Alex said. None of them had heard of such a thing. No one had.

I know because I was on it, the man said.

Of course he was, Elway said. Of course.

Why was he here? Alex asked. Hugh added, Was he a scout?

No scout, the Ripper said. **I was a criminal. This**, he patted his sodden chest with his left hand, **is my prison**.

Questions overlapping, Alex repeated, Prison? and Hugh asked what the man had done. Elway rolled his eyes heavenward and snorted.

I was a killer, the man said. **In the unlit reaches of the ship, in its recesses and forgotten places, I killed and I killed and I killed. Stars burned through their fuel while I hunted the darkness. The crown of eyes on my head could see past the infrared into the microwave, past the ultraviolet into the X- and Gamma ray. There was no hiding from the blades at the ends of my many arms, their edges keen enough to sever molecule from molecule. Space dimmed and dulled around me: none sensed my**

approach. **From toxic gardens tended by beings like pale green silk bags filled with intelligent gas, to the interior asteroid fields mined by creatures like lobsters the size of horses, their dark purple exoskeletons the vehicles for a sentient orange fungus, my slaughter extended for a hundred million miles. I bathed in blood. I luxuriated in it. Blood watery and clear, blood thick and red, blood that writhed from the openings I cut.** The corners of the man's mouth lifted. **Would you believe, I was originally a gardener, myself? I was responsible for a small grove of fruit trees. I was designed—*optimized* to fulfill that role.**

He was a robot? Hugh asked.

Man, the guy was nothing, Elway said. He was just some psycho with delusions of grandeur, making up stories to buy himself time.

Not a robot, the man said, **but still crafted, cultivated from the genes of a dozen different lifeforms. Those who fashioned me did not anticipate that the grafting of certain elements onto one another would rise to new traits, new...urges.**

Like murder, Alex said, simultaneously fascinated by the unfolding narrative and flooded with raging anger at the man's ridiculous story, at his audacity reciting it to them after all he had done, the gaping vents he had cut in their sisters', his sister's, Paula's throat, belly, the loops of intestine he had excavated, the tongue he had excised and nailed to the half-assed design on the wall of his lair. He looked at the box of matches sitting in Elway's open hand and fought the temptation to seize it and strike the match that would consign the Ripper to fire.

Gardening of a different type, the man said. **I was caught. Eventually. As punishment for my excesses, my consciousness was flensed from my body and exiled here.** He used his good hand to wave to their surroundings.

This place? The psych hospital? Hugh and Elway asked. In Poughkeepsie?

Don't sell this location short, the man said. **There is a very interesting rift over this stretch of the Hudson. I don't expect you know this, but there have been investigations into it for a long time. Experiments. Many of them carried out in this very structure. Intelligences have been brought forth from the rift. Certain suitable patients were...joined with them. The results were not successful. They were kept on the top floor, under heavy guard.**

This activity made the hospital a kind of beacon, a target for the energy beam transporting my consciousness. I was shot into the head of a young man whose motorcycle had collided with a telephone pole. The damage to his brain was so severe it left him one step above catatonic. His family committed him to the hospital, where he was led outside once a day to stand in the sun. The scarred and gnarled contents of his skull were my cell. Imagine your mind ripped from the body you know and thrust inside a snail's. Imagine retaining just enough sense of your prior existence to be aware of everything you have lost. Were your new brain capable of insanity, you would be driven to it. But the knotted and tangled neurons trapping your consciousness will allow no such escape. Instead, you are confined to an unending recognition of your mutilated self. It is agony of a most particular sort. Time loses all meaning. Nor does the host's death provide release. As long as a sufficient quantity of brain matter remains, in however degraded a state, the imprisonment continues. The destruction of the brain might free you, or it might consign you to oblivion. Which you would welcome.

Elway had heard enough. He slid the matchbox open and selected a match. He'd hoped the Ripper would burn down to nothing, he said, but if his mind was trapped inside whatever was left of his body after the fire was through with him, that would be okay, too.

Chris placed his hand on Elway's chest. What? Elway asked. What was it? Chris answered with a single word, directed at the man in the tub: Why?

Why? the man said. **Interesting: that is not the question I was expecting. I assumed you would ask how I went from barely functioning to my present state.**

No one gives a shit, Elway said. Answer him.

I assume you mean your—they would have to be your sisters, wouldn't they? the man said. He nodded. **Yes. They are part of my machine.**

Machine? Hugh said. What did he mean? What kind of machine?

One to allow me to escape from this body and return me home, the Ripper said. **This makes no sense to you.**

No, Elway said, it made no sense, period. Not just to them.

Pain bends time, the man said. **It warps it. And because time and space are entwined, pain affects space, too. Usually, this is at so small a scale as to be imperceptible, where electrons orbit protons and neutrons like moons sweeping around planets. Great pain, however, leaves a more substantial mark. The greater the agony, the more pronounced the effect. If you know where to warp space time, where to twist it in relation to itself, you can construct a device in four-dimensions, one that will allow you to achieve all manner of ends. I have worked out the details in metal and in blood. I have built a model to plot my course.**

The Ripper's words rang on Alex's memory, on his impression of a kind of sense in the arrangement of the cutlery scattered on the big room upstairs, in the marking on the walls above the grins of the corpses on the fifth floor, in the ghastly arrangement on the seventh floor. Could what the man was saying be anything other than the delusions of someone who had emerged from near-catatonia with his psyche broken and disfigured? To his horror, the Ripper appeared to intuit his perceptions, raising his functioning arm and pointing at Alex. **Is that the light of recognition I see shining there?** he said.

Cheeks burning, Alex told the Ripper to shut the fuck up. The man's mouth twitched with something in the vicinity of a smile. **If I can't make it all the way back to the ship,** he said, **perhaps there's still a home for me.**

He wasn't going anywhere, Elway said, unless it was to Hell.

In an instant, the man was on his feet, the petroleum mixture splashing on the tub's walls, droplets of the stuff spraying the four of them. Grimacing, Alex leapt back, almost losing his footing. Hugh yelped and stumbled backward. Chris shifted his stance, as if preparing to deliver a kick to the man's glistening head. Elway scraped the match on the box, but it did not spark. Features twisted, the Ripper swayed drunkenly, whatever murderous resolve had driven him up shorted by the edges of his collar bone jolting together. Elway struck the match on the box again and this time, the tip burst into orange flame. With the frantic motion of a child afraid of singeing his fingers, he cast the match into the tub.

XII

There was a FWOOMP, the air around the Ripper igniting in an orange flash, which was swallowed almost instantly by the pillar of blue flame that leapt out of the tub all the way to the ceiling, momentarily obscuring the man.

The tower of fire dropped, revealing the Ripper encased in roaring flame. Chris and Elway retreated to stand beside Hugh and Alex. Together, they watched the man who had murdered their sisters attempt first to sweep the fire from his face with hands also on fire, then stagger to the edge of the Trap, where he reached a flaming arm onto the surrounding ledge, perhaps thinking he could lever himself out of the tub. But his feet found no purchase on the fiery interior, and although he struggled with ferocious effort, slapping his arm repeatedly on the tile floor, he remained confined to the flaming pit. He left his arm where it was, sleeved in fire, the fabric of his coveralls crisped and blackened floating away on the heat from the flames blistering and charring the flesh beneath. His head, helmeted in orange fire, lowered, exposing the deep crease in his skull, in which flames gathered in a bright seam. The rest of the coveralls were burning off, exposing skin crisped and cracking. Thick smoke laden with the sharp smell of petroleum and another sweeter odor, like barbecue, billowed into the air, its touch greasy on the skin.

Already, there was no way—even if someone were to burst into the room this very instant, a team of firefighters, each with a fire extinguisher on his back, and they were to douse the Ripper and the tub in foam, smother the fire on and around him, there was no way for the man to survive this, the injuries he had been dealt were already mortal. He lifted his head, and there were flames dancing across his eyeballs, which must surely be blind by now. The expanse of his forehead, his cheeks, his chin, were burned free of skin, leaving fat, muscle, and bone for the fire to consume. His tongue was scorched and swollen in his mouth. That the man was not shrieking in pain, begging for his life, was not something Alex had anticipated. He had understood (from somewhere—where? Perhaps his own experiences with touching a hot pan or kettle on the stove?) death by fire to be among the most excruciating, a suitable means of execution for the man who had murdered their sisters. There was every reason to expect the man would not suffer his fate quietly. Alex had steeled himself for the Ripper's cries, his shouts, afraid that hearing them might cause him to regret his decision or worse, to cry. One tear given to this man was an ocean too many. When the Ripper made his fruitless effort to pull himself out of the tub, Alex had expected him to start screaming. But he had not, merely, stood there as the fire licked his flesh away with its rushing tongues. The silence was at once a relief and a frustration, Alex realizing that if he had dreaded the man's cries, he had also been looking forward to them, to the evidence of the Ripper suffering, the confirmation of his punishment. Yet the man's eyeballs burst, their contents running sizzling down the naked bone of his skull, and he gave no acknowledgment of the fact. The end of his nose was an open hole, his lips were shriveled and drawn back from his teeth, but no sound forced its way around the lump of charcoal in his mouth. There was only the raging of the fire, undiminished. And within that road, a higher-pitched sound, like steam jetting from a kettle. Possibly, it was one of the ingredients in the tub's mix burning away; although Alex didn't think that was how these things worked. There seemed almost a rhythm to it, and riding the rhythm changes in pitch, as if he were listening to music, or not music, but a kind of speech, what you might imagine would issue from between a tarantula's thick chelicerae. There was meaning in it, a sense Alex could just about appre-hend. What he could perceive of it was obscene, a hymn to the way blood announced its presence with a smell of hot copper, to the wet smack of entrails on a linoleum floor, to the way the tongue tugged loose once the blade had cut it from its root. Its exact words were drawing near, bringing with them an impression of the thing voicing the piercing speech, something with an excess of long legs, and a misshapen globe of a head, and Alex's idea of the thing clarified into an imprecise, out-of-focus image of it, beginning with the head whose abundance of eyes were focused on him, some staring, others blinking, the pupils of the rest dilating or constricting, then moving to a segmented leg like those of the snow crabs his dad ordered at Red Lobster, except this limb was as long as a man, its gray exoskeleton studded with spikes, hooks, and what appeared to be flickering white lights—the more of the thing he saw, the more it felt as if it was pushing its way into his brain, shoving its segmented legs into the folds, little pieces of his gray matter tearing off on the hooks. Pressure swelled behind his eyes, inside his eyes, as if the contents of his skull were bulging with what they were trying to accommodate. Panic tightened his throat.

A hollow KLONK interrupted the song and the cargo it was delivering. Chris kicked another of the empty red containers at the Ripper, striking his shoulder and the side of his head. The man jerked to the side and unable to see the source of now the third and fourth jugs, which likewise bounced off his head, he flailed with his good arm at what he guessed was the direction of attack. Alex fell to his knees, the sensation his eyeballs were about to be forced out of their sockets mercifully ceased. He shook his head, the smoke-filled room wobbling at the edges as he did.

In the meantime, Chris continued to kick empty bottles and cans at the Ripper fiery form. Who knew Chris was so good with his feet? Alex thought. Elway and Hugh joined in, kicking and throwing the various containers they had used to fill the tub at its burning occupant. The thinner bottles crumpled and ignited in green and blue fire, while the thicker ones darkened and collapsed inward. A paint can struck the Ripper's chest, its handle rattling as it did. The man swung his arm wildly from side to side, the Herculean self-control he had hitherto crumbling under the unceasing barrage. Alex grabbed a soda bottle and hurled it at the Ripper. It hit the center of his exposed back and bounced into the tub. The man staggered around the Trap's fiery circumference. Drawing perilously close to the Ripper in the process, the four of them swept the remaining containers in with him. A clump of half-melted bottles, they saw, were adhered to the man's thighs, his hips. The smoke billowing from the tub carried the additional stink of burning plastic.

The man's movements were jerky, irregular, those of a toy whose batteries are failing, a wasp doused in poison. He stumbled against the side of the tub opposite them and slid down it, half-turning toward them as he did. He sank into a kind of sideways sit, sagged against the tiles, and made no further movement. A tide of molten plastic flowed over his legs, his left hand and wrist. Nor were the flames done burning: a surprising amount of fuel remained unconsumed. The four of them would have to remain here to supervise the remainder of the burn, as well as to ensure the Ripper didn't spring up like a horror movie cliché, burned but unkilled.

At one point during their vigil, Alex left to use the bathroom. They all did, Elway and his famously overactive bladder three times. They had discovered a toilet down the hall, but Alex opted to climb all the way to the first floor, where the windows in the bathroom gave onto the sky, still hours from dawn but full of enough reflected light from the city below to present a modicum of illumination. That was the reason he offered the others for the length of his absence, and they accepted it. He did not mention anything about walking to the big room and sweeping the beam of his flashlight over the forks, spoons, and knives scattered across the floor. He did not tell them what he read in those metal phrases and sentences.

For Fiona

❧ ❧ ❧

John Langan is the author of two novels and six collections of stories. For his work, he has received the Bram Stoker and This Is Horror awards. He lives in New York's Mid-Hudson Valley with his wife and younger son.

Bistritz

Jamie Flanagan

IT WAS on the dark side of twilight not far from the city of Bistritz when Eddard Dormin released his muse. A thin trail of mucous and dried blood extended from her left nostril, past her lips and down her chin. Her weak breath hung visible in the air as skeletal trees groaned and cracked in the frigid breeze.

With emaciated fingers shaking of cold, he retrieved a handkerchief from the pocket of his long coat, spat in it, then cleaned her face. A small dignity, given all he'd taken. Then left her there, in the cold dark wood, along with his regret.

Luck smiled upon him in the form of a passing wagon. And though he hoped to lose himself in the rhythmic rise and fall of the wheels beneath him, sleep wouldn't come. Not while she remained in his memory, prone on a bed of fallen leaves, leeched by frost.

It was an hour's ride to Bistritz, though he would never arrive. Nor would he initially recognize the gray-haired woman who would interrupt his monstrous journey. Not until she held his gaze in stillness and silence.

❦ ❦ ❦

What would end with the old woman began with an old man.

"Carefully," said Van Dreiburg, a fourth year fellow whom Eddard had admired since recently arriving in Romania, as they lowered the Romany vagrant onto the operating table of the surgical amphitheater. The hall was vacant, save for the two and their specimen.

"Thank you again for meeting with me today," said Eddard. "I've had trouble imagining the layers."

"Indeed," said Van Dreiburg. "First years often do. I applaud you for seeking my counsel." Van Dreiburg rolled up the sleeves of his high-collared white shirt. Eddard followed suit. "Have you worked with living bone before?" asked Van Dreiburg, careful to avoid the breath of their Romany subject, who had just coughed.

"No, I've not had the opportunity," said Eddard. "Plague?"

"Lunger."

"Ash?"

"Consumption. Though you're partially correct; ash aggravates the condition. Would you pass me the—?"

Eddard fetched an ebony wooden cylinder about a foot long, an inch and a half in diameter, from the nearby work-bench. He handed it to Van Dreiburg, who placed the wider end on the man's chest before leaning his ear to the other.

"A year left in him. Shorter, in all likelihood." Van Dreiburg passed the cylinder back to Eddard. "Fetch me that spike and mallet from the workbench."

Eddard hesitated.

"Mallet and spike, if you please?"

Eddard crossed to the workbench, picked up the wooden mallet and a thin metal rod about seven inches in length, not unlike an emaciated rail spike, which he handed to Van Dreiburg.

After giving the spike a good polish, Van Dreiburg cracked his knuckles and gestured for Eddard to join him. "Watch closely. This is the best anesthetic I know. Rumor has it an American used ether to extract a tooth last year, but best of luck finding any such stuff in Bistritz."

"What exactly are you doing?"

Van Dreiburg placed the spike to the man's left nostril. "Hold his arms please."

"Van Dreiburg, what exactly—?"

"I once tried to pull the brain out of a cadaver, like the Egyptians. Imagine my surprise upon discovering, mid-procedure, that my cadaver was still very much alive. I'd pulled out a good chunk by then, and he was calm as a church mouse after. I've used this method on terminal cases ever since. Hold steady his arms please."

Eddard redoubled his grip on the Romany. Van Dreiburg slid the spike up the man's nostril, aligned the hammer then confidently dealt the first blow. The ring of metal on metal gave way to a sickening crunch. The Romany gasped, tensed and shook, then his eyes rolled white and his body went limp.

"Good God," said Eddard. "Is he…?"

"Unconscious. Liston knife, please. And ready the tourniquet."

Within minutes, Van Dreiburg's pale arms and white shirt had taken on a damask hue, as he proudly displayed the Romany man's detached fibula. He placed the bone on the workbench, lined up his saw then hacked it in two. Blood poured from within.

"And there we have it," said Van Dreiburg, "Hematopoiesis. Blood Poetry." He tilted the bone, making small, red concentric circles on the workbench.

"Blood Making, actually," said Eddard. "You're deriving from the Latin. Hemato is Greek for blood, therefore poiesis should be translated from the Greek as well: to make or to create."

"Indulge me, Eddard. Look for the art in it. One can't be a surgeon and retain sanity if one doesn't appreciate the art."

"I have my own art," said Eddard Dormin. "Ut pictura poesis."

❦ ❦ ❦

"Still no oil paints? After five weeks? In the entire city of Bistritz?"

Eddard glanced about the shop, paying little attention to the Romany girl with the dark hair and hazel eyes. She shook her head at him, jangling her many piercings. "Since last year's fire, we've focused on importing only essentials."

"What about spare canvas?"

An older Romany woman with brown hair—the girl's mother, Eddard assumed—stood casually behind the counter with her arms crossed. She whispered into her daughter's ear.

"None," said the Shopkeeper's Daughter.

"Mineral spirits for thinning?"

"None."

"Watercolors?"

"No paints of any kind."

Eddard tapped the counter, bit the inside of his cheek then strode to the door before abruptly turning around. "Pardon, but the sign outside your shop. What does it read? I'm still learning Romanian."

The Shopkeeper's Daughter opened her mouth to speak, but her mother's voice, low and quiet, asserted itself in the native tongue.

"What did she say?" asked Eddard.

"That perhaps the gentleman should return once he's

taken the time to learn our language." The Shopkeeper's Daughter lowered her gaze to the counter.

Eddard flushed then left the store. Though the source of his agitation was neither the Shopkeeper nor her daughter.

It was the lack of color in Bistritz.

He had chosen Romania in hope of a respite from the inherent dreariness of The Old Smoke. But during his winter in Bistritz, Eddard had found a city of stone grays, ash and mud. A study in charcoal.

His medical training—a profession of his family's choosing—was likewise colorless. The study of anatomy, physiology, chemistry—the study of life—had sapped the vitality from his marrow. Old friends had become distant acquaintances. His skin had paled, his vision, clouded, and his voice—once rich with pear shaped tones—had become a jagged scratch. And without paints to ease his evening hours, his concentration had waned.

Mistakes began to propagate. Confusing a humerus for a femur, for example. Nothing that couldn't be laughed away by his contemporaries. No one laughed, however, when his hands began shaking during surgical practice.

During a simple stitching, Eddard had managed to nick the ulnar artery of a man's wrist, an accident that had nearly proven fatal. But it wasn't until the following week, while performing mock surgery on a cadaver in the amphitheater before all his peers, having encountered difficulty removing the femur from the dead man's leg, that the true cracks began to assert themselves.

"Eddard," said Van Dreiburg.

Eddard grunted from the exertion; the sound of bone lacerating flesh echoed through the hall.

"Eddard," said Van Dreiburg, placing a hand on Eddard's forearm.

Eddard redoubled his effort. Van Dreiburg pulled Eddard's grip from the cadaver.

"Calmly, man. You're tearing him."

Eddard, flustered, turned to face the pale gazes of his fellows.

"What does it matter?" He shook off Van Dreiburg's grasp. "It's dead."

In his spare time, Eddard began making charcoal sketches using soot and ash from the street outside his home. Oil paintings often began with charcoal bases and this method initially seemed a soothing balm on a wound. Without the colors to bring each world to life, however, Eddard's work proved ultimately unsatisfying.

Like pining without ever possessing.

Or foreplay without fornication.

Perhaps it was this self-same frustration that compelled Eddard to take a Liston knife to his canvases late one evening in January—aborting his works and flushing them onto the cobbled, lamp-lit street—before donning his frock coat and maundering out in search of burning whiskey and soft company. Both he found and both he paid for; the latter bitter and the former sweet. Try as he might, he could not precisely pinpoint when whiskey had become sweeter than women. Only that the opposite had been true when he'd had his oil colors.

Months passed in monochrome. He wrote home to family and acquaintances in London, but rarely received replies. Whether it was their affections that had been lost, or simply the missives themselves, Eddard had no way of knowing.

In seeking color, he made inquiries of proper Englishmen and Romany alike, traveling back and forth between a world he understood and another he did not. But it was as the Shopkeeper's Daughter had said. There were simply no oil paints to be found anywhere near the ashen city of Bistritz.

Then, during a day of anatomical studies at the morgue, Eddard found he could not stop the shaking of his hands as they wandered over a pile of bones.

"Eddard," said Van Dreiburg. "We've been over the tibia. Time to move on, yes?"

"Yes, of course." Eddard replaced the bone, picking up another at random. "The scapula, perhaps, or the—the fibula, maybe. I suppose we could," Eddard's voice trailed off. "We could…"

Eddard paused—then dropped the rib into the pile of remains.

"Eddard?"

Eddard inhaled just enough breath to give voice to his intentions then began untying his apron. "I'm sorry."

"Eddard," said Van Dreiburg with unusual concern.

"I can't," said Eddard as he finished untying his apron. "I'm sorry."

With that, he strode from the morgue, leaving puzzled peers, tutors and an abandoned apron in his wake.

Sometime later, Eddard emerged from the fugue in which he'd fled and took in his surroundings. He had wandered past the spired Cathedral, past Gray Stone Cemetery, through the village courtyard and followed the trail through the skeletal trees, all the way to the wrought iron gate of Muză Azil, the asylum of Bistritz. In each hand, he held a rusted bar of the metal gate. He let his eyelids fall, leaned his forehead to the cold rough iron, considered the souls within and envied them.

Through the bars, Eddard noticed a familiar wooden sign staked into the dirt; identical, in fact, to the sign he had noticed outside of the barter shop—that which the Shopkeeper had refused to translate. The text appeared the same, but for one difference. In the lower left-hand corner, carved haphazardly, was a single word.

"Varna," said Eddard, sounding out the word.

"Weeds," whispered a female voice from behind him.

Startled, Eddard turned about, only to feel the skin of his forehead, now fused with the cold metal, tear. With a grunt, he raised the sleeve of one arm to his forehead, then squinted through trickling blood and the stinging wind. Before him was the Shopkeeper's Daughter.

"Varna means weeds," she said as she removed a woven handkerchief from her belt, then offered it to him. Eddard appraised her before taking the cloth. Hers was an immediate yet quiet presence, aware though un-shy of a wandering eye. Hers was the withheld promise of one who knows very much, yet says very little.

"Weeds, is it?" said Eddard, pressing the handkerchief to his brow. "What's the rest of it then?"

"We didn't write it."

"We?" asked Eddard. "We gypsies?"

The girl tilted her head to one side. "We Roma."

"Why weeds?" asked Eddard.

"The people inside, of little use. And their number, ever growing."

Eddard nodded. "What's the rest of it read?"

"That is Romanian, not Romani. It reads, "Să fie atenţi, mulţi ţigani!""

"Romanian? Romani? They're not of a kind?" asked Eddard.

The Shopkeeper's Daughter chuckled low, rich and dark. "No. Not the same. Come. You need mending."

Eddard hesitated. "What are you doing out here?"

The Shopkeeper's Daughter pulled her shawl about her shoulders. "It's a dreary season. The woods. The weeds. They're a reminder."

"A reminder of what?"

"The price of getting lost."

She extended a hand toward him.

Later, in the dark hollow of the earthen cellar where Eddard Dormin kept his bed, he lost himself in the Shopkeeper's Daughter, then slept.

❧ ❧ ❧

Eddard awoke to the sound of water gently returning to water. He was naked beneath the sheets of his bed. In the corner of the room, near the wine rack, kneeling in the porcelain basin and cleansing herself with a sponge, was the Shopkeeper's Daughter.

Eddard propped himself up on one elbow. He listlessly admired the frame of the Shopkeeper's Daughter as she bathed in the candlelight, then let his gaze drift across the gray walls; the dark shadows. The charcoal likeness of it all.

Then, out of the corner of his eye, Eddard noticed something altogether out of place. His breath caught in his throat. There, on the sheets, was a red of many hues. Some fair, some dark. It wasn't the blood one would find on a smock. It was vital. Passionate. His lower jaw trembled and his voice cracked, "Thank you."

The Shopkeeper's Daughter squeezed the sponge just over her shoulder; a trickling sound followed. "You're a rare one. To be seen with me," she said.

Eddard said nothing. So far he'd found four distinguishable shades of red within the cloth: *burgundy, magenta, maroon, persimmon—*

"I wish," said the woman as she sponged her left arm.

—carmine, vermillion, scarlet, crimson—

"Such comforts would stay. Remain. Renew..."

—ruby, rust, rose, carnelian—

429

"That's the curse of a Roma, such as me."

—*coral, mordant, amaranth, mauve*—

"Rarely held or beheld, by light or by night."

"Hm?" asked Eddard as he stopped counting shades.

The young woman—realizing she'd been ignored—stared back at him. Gone was her air of mystery. Gone, the coyness which served as both lure and shield. What remained was hurt. And disappointment. And a weariness at odds with her youth.

"Shall I go, then?"

Eddard blinked, glanced at the stain on the sheet, then stared at the Shopkeeper's Daughter.

"What do you see?" asked Eddard. "When you look at the world?"

The tips of her dark curls grazed against the placid water in the basin as she pulled her knees to her chest. "Dirt, wind, frost. Dark corners and darker stares. I see coals smolder where hearts should be. And hunger that devours kindness. All this, I see."

Then, to his surprise, she smiled. "But only in winter."

Eddard watched as she sank into memories warm and distant, cloaking herself in nostalgia.

In a knot of jealousy, he stared at the floor. Then, almost imperceptibly, Eddard Dormin *twitched.*

He rose from the bed then walked naked up the stairs, as though in a daze. He proceeded to his old paint chest, pulled open the dusty top, pushed the brushes around until he found one suitable in in length with a weighted metal end, snapped off the brush, tapped the wooden cylinder against the chest twice to test for durability. Then he rummaged through his worn leather medical bag until he found the small bone hammer.

Eddard returned to the wine cellar, and—when it was done—tore a swatch from his sheets, soaked it in the fresh pool of blood, then staked it upon the wall of the earthen cellar, beside a candle, where the colors spread gently through the warmly back-lit fabric. And he stared and stared. Hoping to see in her blood what she'd seen in the thaw.

Puce, terra corsa, red-violet, rose madder...

❧ ❧ ❧

"How are we feeling today, Eddard?" asked Van Dreiburg.

The two students walked together through the Market Square. An uncharacteristic lightness lifted Eddard's step. Perhaps he should've been more worried about the woman in his basement, but he dispelled the thought. It had been several days since she'd gone missing, and he'd heard not so much as a whisper of her absence. And soon, she would be gone. He knew of a place where one could plant a weed...

As he strode near the familiar shop at which Eddard had so often sought paints, a feeling of unease began to surface.

"Van Dreiburg, that sign – there, outside the shop. Was does it read?"

"That?" Van Dreiburg gestured toward the familiar letter-ing. *"Beware,"* read Van Dreiburg. *"For here there are many gypsies."*

Then, Eddard became aware of the gazes of the surrounding Roma. Had they always been there, huddled in the stark periphery, camouflaged in hunger and poverty? Or had Van Dreiburg's words conjured them from shadow and soot? Had there always been so many? And had their stares ever held such weight?

Regarding Eddard from a window stood the Shopkeeper. Details about the woman—which Eddard had habitually overlooked—began to assert themselves with strange clarity. The wrinkles of age about her hazel eyes. Her jaw fixed as a bulwark. The quality of her stillness—somehow predatory.

And the nature of her silence. Hers was a silence with teeth. But what struck Eddard most was the woman's hair…

Eddard had always taken it for brown.

But now he saw the strands of gray, snaking through her braid, taut as a rope. Or a promise.

Later, in the emaciated woods beyond the walls of Bistritz, past the last comforting rays of twilight, after the old woman slips the blade between his ribs, Eddard Dormin, supine in hoarfrost, will stare at that same braid, as a voice, carried upon a frigid breeze, whispers...

"There is nothing. No warmth. No cold. No light. No color, not even gray. You will see nothing, and your eyes, unneeded, will roll backward, looking inward, gaze fixed. You will hear nothing, and your ears, neglected, will rot and fall away. When you open your mouth to scream, nothing will flow in, like liquid, emptying, hollowing. There will be no fire or brimstone. No judgement, rest, or peace. Nothing. Not even secrets. Your inheritance will be unthinkably vast, impossibly silent. Your conquest, an empty land within an empty land. You will learn that silence can suffocate, stillness has sharp edges, and conscience can grow claws. You will not be mourned. But Aishe? She will walk in the Garden, with the mothers, daughters, and sisters of the unseen. Even after the candle burns out."

And he will dread, and hope, and shiver.

Then hear nothing, see nothing, and be nothing at all.

Back upon the thoroughfare, arrogant and unaware, Eddard passed the shop. All would be well, he assured himself. But faint clouds of black and gray had seeped into his marrow. And weeping ashes all the while, they continued their descent.

❦ ❦ ❦

Jamie Flanagan is an author, actor, and Bram Stoker

Awards®–winning screenwriter. Their short fiction has been published by Crooked Lane Books, Shortwave Publishing, and others. Screenwriting credits include Netflix's *The Haunting of Bly Manor, Midnight Mass, The Midnight Club, The Fall of the House of Usher*, AMC Shudder's *CREEPSHOW*, Peacock's *Hysteria!*, and Amazon's upcoming series adaptation of Stephen King's *Carrie.*

By The Hair Of The Head

Joe R. Lansdale

THIS WAS my attempt to write something quiet and sneaky and creepy. I wrote it specifically with Charlie Grant and the anthology series he edited in the 1980's, Shadows, in mind. I wanted to write a story that had the feel of the old Alfred Hitchcock TV series, and I think I did just that. It could be called a story of witchcraft. A ghost story. A story of psychological suspense. It sort of depends on the reader.

THE LIGHTHOUSE WAS GREY and brutally weathered, kissed each morning by a cold, salt spray. Perched there among the rocks and sand, it seemed a last, weak sentinel against an encroaching sea; a relentless, pounding surf that had slowly swallowed up the shoreline and deposited it in the all-consuming belly of the ocean.

Once the lighthouse had been bright-colored, candy-striped like a barber's pole, with a high beacon light and a horn that honked out to the ships on the sea. No more. The lighthouse director, the last of a long line of sea watchers, had cashed in the job ten years back when the need died, but the lighthouse was now his and he lived there alone, bunked down nightly to the tune of the wind and the raging sea.

Below he had renovated the bottom of the tower and built rooms, and one of these he had locked away from all persons, from all eyes but his own.

I came there fresh from college to write my novel, dreams of being the new Norman Mailer dancing in my head. I rented in with him, as he needed a boarder to help him pay for the place, for he no longer worked and his pension was as meager as stale bread.

High up in the top was where we lived, a bamboo partition drawn between our cots each night, giving us some semblance of privacy, and dark curtains were pulled round the thick, foggy windows that traveled the tower completely around.

By day the curtains were drawn and the partition was pulled and I sat at my typewriter, and he, Howard Machen, sat with his book and his pipe, swelled the room full of grey smoke the thickness of his beard. Sometimes he rose and went below, but he was always quiet and never disturbed my work.

It was a pleasant life. Agreeable to both of us. Mornings we had coffee outside on the little railed walkway and had a word or two as well, then I went to my work and he to his book, and at dinner we had food and talk and brandies; sometimes one, sometimes two, depending on mood and the content of our chatter.

We sometimes spoke of the lighthouse and he told me of the old days, of how he had shone that light out many times on the sea. Out like a great, bright fishing line to snag the ships and guide them in; let them follow the light in the manner that Theseus followed Ariadne's thread.

"Was fine," he'd say. "That pretty old light flashing out

there. Best job I had in all my born days. Just couldn't leave her when she shut down, so I bought her."

"It is beautiful up here, but lonely at times."

"I have my company."

I took that as a compliment, and we tossed off another brandy.

Any idea of my writing later I cast aside. I had done four good pages and was content to spit the rest of the day away in talk and dreams.

"You say this was your best job," I said as a way of conversation. "What did you do before this?"

He lifted his head and looked at me over the briar and its smoke. His eyes squinted against the tinge of the tobacco. "A good many things. I was born in Wales. Moved to Ireland with my family, was brought up there, and went to work there. Learned the carpentry trade from my father. Later I was a tailor. I've also been a mason — note the rooms I built below with my own two hands — and I've been a boat builder and a ventriloquist in a magician's show."

"A ventriloquist?"

"Correct," he said, and his voice danced around me and seemed not to come from where he sat.

"Hey, that's good."

"Not so good really. I was never good, just sort of fell into it. I'm worse now. No practice, but I've no urge to take it up again."

"I've an interest in such things."

"Have you now?"

"Yes."

"Ever tried a bit of voice throwing?"

"No. But it interests me. The magic stuff interests me more. You said you worked in a magician's show?"

"That I did. I was the lead-up act."

"Learn any of the magic tricks, being an insider and all?"

"That I did, but that's not something I'm interested in," he said flatly.

"Was the magician you worked for good?"

"Damn good, m'boy. But his wife was better."

"His wife?"

"Marilyn was her name. A beautiful woman." He winked at me. "Claimed to be a witch."

"You don't say?"

"I do, I do. Said her father was a witch and she learned it and inherited it from him."

"Her father?"

"That's right. Not just women can be witches. Men too."

We poured ourselves another and exchanged sloppy grins, hooked elbows, and tossed it down.

"And another to meet the first," the old man said and poured. Then: "Here's to company." We tossed it off.

"She taught me the ventriloquism, you know," the old man said, relighting his pipe.

"Marilyn?"

"Right, Marilyn."

"She seems to have been a rather all-around lady."

"She was at that. And pretty as an Irish morning."

"I thought witches were all old crones, or young crones. Hook noses, warts..."

"Not Marilyn. She was a fine-looking woman. Fine bones, agate eyes that clouded in mystery, and hair the color of a fresh-robbed hive."

"Odd she didn't do the magic herself. I mean, if she was the better magician, why was her husband the star attraction?"

"Oh, but she did do magic. Or rather she helped McDonald to look better than he was, and he was some good. But Marilyn was better.

"Those days were different, m'boy. Women weren't the

ones to take the initiative, least not openly. Kept to themselves. Was a sad thing. Back then it wasn't thought fittin' for a woman to be about such business. Wasn't ladylike. Oh, she could get sawed in half, or disappear in a wooden crate, priss and look pretty, but take the lead? Not on your life!"

I fumbled myself another brandy. "A pretty witch, huh?"

"Ummmm."

"Had the old pointed hat and broom passed down, so to speak?" My voice was becoming slightly slurred.

"It's not a laughin' matter, m'boy." Machen clenched the pipe in his teeth.

"I've touched a nerve, have I not? I apologize. Too much sauce."

Machen smiled. "Not at all. It's a silly thing, you're right. To hell with it."

"No, no. I'm the one who spoiled the fun. You were telling me she claimed to be the descendant of a long line of witches."

Machen smiled. It did not remind me of other smiles he had worn. This one seemed to come from a borrowed collection.

"Just some silly tattle is all. Don't really know much about it, just worked for her,

m'boy." That was the end of that. Standing, he knocked out his pipe on the concrete floor and went to his cot.

For a moment I sat there, the last breath of Machen's pipe still in the air, the brandy still warm in my throat and stomach. I looked at the windows that surrounded the lighthouse, and everywhere I looked was my own ghostly reflection. It was like looking out through the compound eyes of an insect, seeing a multiple image.

I turned out the lights, pulled the curtains and drew the partition between our beds, wrapped myself in my blanket, and soon washed up on the distant shore of a recurring dream. A dream not quite in grasp, but heard like the far, fuzzy cry of a gull out from land.

It had been with me almost since moving into the tower. Sounds, voices…

A clunking noise like peg legs on stone...

...a voice, fading in, fading out…Machen's voice, the words not quite clear, but soft and coaxing…then solid and firm: "Then be a beast. Have your own way. Look away from me with your mother's eyes."

"…your fault," came a child's voice, followed by other words that were chopped out by the howl of the sea wind, the roar of the waves.

".. getting too loud. He'll hear…" came Machen's voice.

"Don't care…I…" lost voices now.

I tried to stir, but then the tube of sleep, nourished by the brandy, came unclogged, and I descended down into richer blackness.

❧ ❧ ❧

Was a bright morning full of sun, and no fog for a change. Cool clear out there on the landing, and the sea even seemed to roll in soft and bounce against the rocks and lighthouse like puffy cotton balls blown on the wind.

I was out there with my morning coffee, holding the cup in one hand and grasping the railing with the other. It was a narrow area but safe enough, provided you didn't lean too far out or run along the walk when it was slick with rain. Machen told me of a man who had done just that and found himself plummeting over to be shattered like a dropped melon on the rocks below.

Machen came out with a cup of coffee in one hand, his unlit pipe in the other. He looked haggard this morning, as if a bit of old age had crept upon him in the night, fastened a straw to his face, and sucked out part of his substance.

"Morning," I said.

"Morning." He emptied his cup in one long draft. He balanced the cup on the metal railing and began to pack his pipe.

"Sleep bad?" I asked.

He looked at me, then at his pipe, finished his packing, and put the pouch away in his coat pocket. He took a long match from the same pocket, gave it fire with his thumbnail, lit the pipe. He puffed quite a while before he answered me. "Not too well. Not too well."

"We drank too much."

"We did at that."

I sipped my coffee and looked at the sky, watched a snowy gull dive down and peck at the foam, rise up with a wriggling fish in its beak. It climbed high in the sky, became a speck of froth on the crystal blue.

"I had funny dreams," I said. "I think I've had them all along, since I came here. But last night they were stronger than ever."

"Oh?"

"Thought I heard your voice speaking to someone. Thought I heard steps on the stairs, or more like the plunking of peg legs, like those old sea captains have."

"You don't say?"

"And another voice, a child's."

"That right? Well…maybe you did hear me speakin'. I wasn't entirely straight with you last night. I do have quite an interest in the voice throwing, and I practice it from time to time on my dummy. Last night must have been louder than usual, being drunk and all."

"Dummy?"

"My old dummy from the act. Keep it in the room below."

"Could I see it?"

He grimaced. "Maybe another time. It's kind of a private thing with me. Only bring her out when we're alone."

"Her?"

"Right. Name's Caroline, a right smart-looking girl dummy, rosy-cheeked with blonde pigtails."

"Well, maybe someday I can look at her."

"Maybe someday." He stood up, popped the contents of the pipe out over the railing, and started inside. Then he turned: "I talk too much. Pay no mind to an old, crazy man."

Then he was gone, and I was there with a hot cup of coffee, a bright, warm day, and an odd, unexplained chill at the base of my bones.

🐛 🐛 🐛

Two days later we got on witches again, and I guess it was my fault. We hit the brandy hard that night. I had sold a short story for a goodly sum — my largest check to date — and we were celebrating and talking and saying how my fame would be as high as the stars. We got pretty sicky there, and to hear Machen tell it, and to hear me agree — no matter he hadn't read the story — I was another Hemingway, Wolfe, and Fitzgerald all balled into one.

"If Marilyn were here," I said thoughtlessly, drunk, "why we could get her to consult her crystal and tell us my literary future."

"Why that's nonsense, she used no crystal."

"No crystal, broom, or pointed hat? No eerie evil deeds for her? A white magician no doubt?"

"Magic is magic, m'boy. And even good intentions can backfire."

"Whatever happened to her, Marilyn I mean?"

"Dead."

"Old age?"

"Died young and beautiful, m'boy. Grief killed her."

"I see," I said, as you'll do to show attentiveness.

Suddenly, it was if the memories were a balloon overloaded with air, about to burst if pressure was not taken off. So, he let loose the pressure and began to talk.

"She took her a lover, Marilyn did. Taught him many a thing, about love, magic, what have you. Lost her husband on account of it, the magician, I mean. Lost respect for herself in time.

"You see, there was this little girl she had, by her lover. A fine-looking sprite, lived until she was three. Had no proper father. He had taken to the sea and had never much entertained the idea of marryin' Marilyn. Keep them stringing was his motto then, damn his eyes. So he left them to fend for themselves."

"What happened to the child?"

"She died. Some childhood disease."

"That's sad," I said, "a little girl gone and having only sipped at life."

"Gone? Oh, no. There's the soul, you know."

I wasn't much of a believer in the soul and I said so.

"Oh, but there is a soul. The body perishes but the soul lives on."

"I've seen no evidence of it."

"But I have." Machen said solemnly. "Marilyn was determined that the girl would live on, if not in her own form, then in another."

"Hogwash!"

Machen looked at me sternly. "Maybe. You see, there is a part of witchcraft that deals with the soul. a part that believes the soul can be trapped and held, kept from escaping this earth and into the beyond. That's why a lot of natives are superstitious about having their picture taken. They believe

443

once their image is captured, through magic their soul can be contained.

"Voodoo works much the same. It's nothing but another form of witchcraft. Practitioners of that art believe their souls can be held to this earth by means of someone collecting nail parings or hair from them while they're still alive.

"That's what Marilyn had in mind. When she saw the girl was fadin', she snipped one of the girl's long pigtails and kept it to herself. Cast spells on it while the child lay dyin', and again after life had left the child."

"The soul was supposed to be contained within the hair?"

"That's right. It can be restored, in a sense, to some other object through the hair. It's like those voodoo dolls. A bit of hair or nail parin' is collected from the person you want to control. or if not control, maintain the presence of their soul, and it's sewn into those dolls. That way, when the pins are stuck into the doll, the living suffer, and when they die their soul is trapped in the doll for all eternity, or rather as long as the doll with its hair or nail parin's exists."

"So she preserved the hair so she could make a doll and have the little girl live on, in a sense?"

"Something like that."

"Sounds crazy."

"I suppose."

"And what of the little girl's father?"

"Ah, that sonofabitch! He came home to find the little girl dead and buried and the mother mad. But there was that little gold lock of hair, and knowing Marilyn, he figured her intentions."

"Machen," I said slowly. "It was you, was it not? You were the father?"

"I was."

"I'm sorry.

"Don't be. We were both foolish. I was the more foolish. She left her husband for me and I cast her aside. Ignored my own child. I was the fool, a great fool."

"Do you really believe in that stuff about the soul? About the hair and what Marilyn was doing?"

"Better I didn't. A soul once lost from the body would best prefer to be departed I think…but love is sometimes a brutal thing."

We just sat there after that. We drank more. Machen smoked his pipe, and about an hour later we went to bed.

There were sounds again, gnawing at the edge of my sleep. The sounds that had always been there, but now, since we had talked of Marilyn, I was less able to drift off into blissful slumber. I kept thinking of those crazy things Machen had said. I remembered, too, those voices I had heard, and the fact that Machen was a ventriloquist, and perhaps, not altogether stable.

But those sounds.

I sat up and opened my eyes. They were coming from below. Voices. Machen's first. "…not be the death of you, girl, not at all…my only reminder of Marilyn…"

And then to my horror. "Let me be, Papa. Let it end." The last had been a little girl's voice. but the words had been bitter and wise beyond the youngness of the tone.

I stepped out of bed and into my trousers, crept to the curtain, and looked on Machen's side.

Nothing, just a lonely cot. I wasn't dreaming. I had heard him all right, and the other voice…it had to be that Machen, grieved over what he had done in the past, over Marilyn's death, had taken to speaking to himself in the little girl's voice. All that stuff Marilyn had told him about the soul, it had gotten to him, cracked his stability.

I climbed down the cold metal stairs, listening. Below I heard the old, weathered door that led outside slam. Heard the thud of boots going down the outside steps

I went back up, went to the windows, and pulling back the curtains section by section, finally saw the old man. He was carrying something wrapped in a black cloth and he had a shovel in his hand. I watched as, out there by the shore, he dug a shallow grave and placed the cloth-wrapped object within, placed a rock over it, and left it to the night and the incoming tide.

I pretended to be asleep when he returned, and later, when I felt certain he was well visited by Morpheus, I went downstairs and retrieved the shovel from the tool room. I went out to where I had seen him dig and went to work, first turning over the large stone and shoveling down into the pebbly dirt. Due to the freshness of the hole, it was easy digging.

I found the cloth and what was inside. It made me flinch at first, it looked so real. I thought it was a little rosy-cheeked girl buried alive, for it looked alive...but it was a dummy. A ventriloquist's dummy. It had aged badly, as if water had gotten to it. In some ways it looked as if it were rotting from the inside out. My finger went easily and deeply into the wood of one of the legs.

Out of some odd curiosity, I reached up and pushed back the wooden eyelids. There were no wooden painted eyes, just darkness, empty sockets that uncomfortably reminded me of looking down into the black hollows of a human skull. And the hair. On one side of the head was a yellow pigtail, but where the other should have been was a bare spot, as if the hair had been ripped away from the wooden skull.

With a trembling hand I closed the lids down over those

empty eyes, put the dirt back in place, the rock, and returned to bed. But I did not sleep well. I dreamed of a grown man talking to a wooden doll and using another voice to answer back, pretending that the doll lived and loved him too.

But the water had gotten to it, and the sight of those rotting legs had snapped him back to reality, dashed his insane hopes of containing a soul by magic, shocked him brutally from foolish dreams. Dead is dead.

❧ ❧ ❧

The next day, Machen was silent and had little to say. I suspected the events of last night weighed on his mind. Our conversation must have returned to him this morning in sober memory, and he, somewhat embarrassed, was reluctant to recall it. He kept to himself down below in the locked room, and I busied myself with my work.

It was night when he came up, and there was a smug look about him, as if he had accomplished some great deed. We spoke a bit, but not of witches, of past times and the sea. Then he pulled back the curtains and looked at the moon rise above the water like a cold fish eye.

"Machen," I said, "maybe I shouldn't say anything, but if you should ever have something bothering you, if you should ever want to talk about it...well, feel free to come to me.

We said little more and soon went to bed.

I slept sounder that night, but again I was rousted from my dreams by voices. Machen's voice again, and the poor man speaking in that little child's voice.

"It's a fine home for you," Machen said in his own voice.

"I want no home," came the little girl's voice. "I want to be free."

"You want to stay with me, with the living. You're just not thinking. There's only darkness beyond the veil."

The voices were very clear and loud. I sat up in bed and strained my ears.

"It's where I belong," the little girl's voice again, but it spoke not in a little girl manner. There was only the tone.

"Things have been bad lately," Machen said. "And you're not yourself."

Laughter, horrible little girl laughter. "I haven't been myself for years."

"Now, Caroline...play your piano. You used to play it so well. Why, you haven't touched it in years."

"Play. Play. With these!"

"You're too loud."

"I don't care. Let him hear, let him…"

A door closed sharply and the sound died off to a mumble; a word caught here and there was scattered and confused by the throb of the sea.

❦ ❦ ❦

Next morning Machen had nothing for me, not even a smile from his borrowed collection. Nothing but coldness, his back, and a frown.

I saw little of him after coffee, and once, from below — for he stayed down there the whole day through — I thought I heard him cry in a loud voice. "Have it your way, then," and then there was the sound of a slamming door and some other sort of commotion below.

After a while I looked out at the land and the sea, and down there, striding back and forth, hands behind his back, went Machen, like some great confused penguin contemplating the far shore.

I like to think there was something more than curiosity in what I did next. Like to think I was looking for the source of my friend's agony; looking for some way to help him find peace.

I went downstairs and pulled at the door he kept locked, hoping that, in his anguish, he had forgotten to lock it back. He had not forgotten.

I pressed my ear against the door and listened. Was that crying I heard?

No. I was being susceptible, caught up in Machen's fantasy. It was merely the wind whipping about the tower.

I went back upstairs, had coffee, and wrote not a line.

❦ ❦ ❦

So day fell into night, and I could not sleep, but finally got the strange business out of my mind by reading a novel. A rollicking good sea story of daring men and bloody battles, great ships clashing in a merciless sea.

And then, from his side of the curtain, I heard Machen creak off his cot and take to the stairs. One flight below was the door that led to the railing round about the tower, and I heard that open and close.

I rose, folded a small piece of paper into my book for a marker, and pulled back one of the window curtains. I walked around pulling curtains and looking until I could see him below.

He stood with his hands behind his back, looking out at the sea like a stem father keeping an eye on his children. Then, calmly, he mounted the railing and leaped out into the air.

I ran. Not that it mattered, but I ran, out to the railing... and looked down. His body looked like a rag doll splayed on the rocks.

There was no question in my mind that he was dead, but

slowly I wound my way down the steps...and was distracted by the room. The door stood wide open.

I don't know what compelled me to look in, but I was drawn to it. It was a small room with a desk and a lot of shelves filled with books, mostly occult and black magic. There were carpentry tools on the wall, and all manner of needles and devices that might be used by a tailor. The air was filled with an odd odor I could not place, and on Machen's desk, something that was definitely not tobacco smoldered away.

There was another room beyond the one in which I stood. The door to it was cracked open. I pushed it back and stepped inside. It was a little child's room filled thick with toys and such: jack-in-the-boxes, dolls, kid books, and a toy piano. All were covered in dust.

On the bed lay a Teddy bear. It was ripped open and the stuffing was pulled out. There was one long strand of hair hanging out of that gutted belly, just one, as if it were the last morsel of a greater whole. It was the color of honey from a fresh-robbed hive. I knew what the smell in the ashtray was now.

I took the hair and put a match to it, just in case.

❦ ❦ ❦

Joe R. Lansdale is the author of over thirty novels and numerous short stories. His work has appeared in national anthologies, magazines, and collections, as well as numerous foreign publications. He has written for comics, television, film, newspapers, and Internet sites. His work has been collected in eighteen short-story collections, and he has edited or co-edited over a dozen anthologies.
Lansdale has received the Edgar Award, eight Bram Stoker Awards, the Horror Writers Association Lifetime

Achievement Award, the British Fantasy Award, the Grinzani Cavour Prize for Literature, the Herodotus Historical Fiction Award, the Inkpot Award for Contributions to Science Fiction and Fantasy, and many others.

A major motion picture based on Lansdale's crime thriller Cold in July was released in May 2014, starring Michael C. Hall (Dexter), Sam Shepard (Black Hawk Down), and Don Johnson (Miami Vice). His novella Bubba Hotep was adapted to film by Don Coscarelli, starring Bruce Campbell and Ossie Davis. His story "Incident On and Off a Mountain Road" was adapted to film for Showtime's "Masters of Horror." He is currently co-producing a TV series, "Hap and Leonard" for the Sundance Channel and films including The Bottoms, based on his Edgar Award-winning novel, with Bill Paxton and Brad Wyman, and The Drive-In, with Greg Nicotero.

Lansdale is the founder of the martial arts system Shen Chuan: Martial Science and its affiliate, Shen Chuan Family System. He is a member of both the United States and International Martial Arts Halls of Fame. He lives in Nacogdoches, Texas with his wife, dog, and two cats.

Afterword
Tom Deady

A couple years ago, I had an idea to create an anthology that would pay homage to the books that made me a horror fan so long ago. But it wasn't just the books themselves; it was the whole experience of shopping for one before the days of big bookstores. Back then, mass market paperbacks came on racks found in most small department stores, drug stores, and markets.

There were no signs pointing you to the genre you like, you had to work for your next read. Spinning that rack and checking behind every book to make sure there wasn't a real gem hiding in the back. Agonizing over which one to spend your hard-earned two or three bucks on. It was glorious.

That little idea turned into my first curated anthology, THE RACK. It was well-received, thanks to the vintage stories the authors dreamed up, and to the amazing cover art by Lynne Hansen. It even went on to win The Haunted Minds Book Club Award for best anthology and was a finalist for the Imadjinn Award as well. That's when I knew I had to do another one.

What you hold is the second book in what I'm now

hoping will turn into a long-running series, honoring the bygone days of paperback horror.

Once again, my job was easy...maybe even easier than the first book thanks to its success. The authors deserve the credit for their creativity and dedication to both the craft and to the vibe of THE RACK. Their stories span the entire spectrum of the genre, from terrifying to heartbreakingly beautiful and everything in between. Thank you for sharing your imagination.

Let's talk about cover art. Back in the day, book covers were everything. Pretty much the only marketing tool to get you to buy the book. While that is a little different today, and the cover itself may not sell the book, it *will* get you to stop and pick it up. Lynne Hansen is going to make a LOT of people stop and pick this book up with her artwork. My heartfelt thanks to her for this.

I would also like to thank all the authors who submitted stories that I was unable to accept. The enthusiasm for this project has been one of the most uplifting experiences in my life.

Special thanks to Sadie Hartmann, Mother Horror, for the unique and compelling introduction. It is a perfect fit.

As always, much love and appreciation to my wonderful and talented wife, Sheila Deady. She did all the interior design and formatting, not to mention keeping me sane through the process

Working with everyone involved has brought me great joy, and I hope this book brings you just as much.

Tom Deady
Tucson, AZ
August 2025

Tom Deady (Editor)

Tom Deady is a Bram Stoker Award winner (2016) for Superior Achievement in a First Novel, and has since published several novels and novellas inspired by his love of horror.

Tom was born and raised in Massachusetts, not far from the historic town of Salem.

He resides in Arizona, where he's working on his next novel.

Shop for signed copies and more at
https://www.tomdeady.com/
Subscribe to my newsletter to get exclusive updates!

facebook.com/tomdeady
instagram.com/tom_deady
tiktok.com/@tomdeadyofficial
bookbub.com/profile/tom-deady

Also by Tom Deady

Shop for signed copies and more at
https://www.tomdeady.com/
Subscribe to my newsletter to get exclusive updates!

Hopedale Mystery Series

The Witch of Hopedale

The Ghost of Black Hill Road

Novels

Haven

Eternal Darkness

Those Left Behind

Novellas

Weekend Getaway

Of Men and Monsters

A Blade to Silence the Screams

Collections

Tales from Circadia

The Edgewater Chronicles

Anthologies (Editor)

The Rack